OPERATION REUNION

BY
JUSTINE DAVIS

First published in Great Britain 2013
by Mills & Boon, an imprint of Harlequin (UK) Limited,
Eton House, 18-24 Paradise Road, Richmond, Surrey TW9 1SR

© Janice Davis Smith 2013

ISBN: 978 0 263 90357 7
ebook ISBN: 978 1 472 00715 5

46-0513

Justine Davis lives on Puget Sound in Washington State, watching big ships and the occasional submarine go by, and sharing the neighborhood with assorted wildlife, including a pair of bald eagles, deer, a bear or two and a tail-less raccoon. In the few hours when she's not planning, plotting or writing her next book, her favorite things are photography, knitting her way through a huge yarn stash and driving her restored 1967 Corvette roadster—top down, of course.

Connect with Justine at her website, justinedavis.com, at Twitter.com/Justine_D_Davis, or on Facebook at Facebook.com/JustineDareDavis.

For Miz Cedar Dogge
February 25, 2001–April 24, 2012

Cedar was intelligent, inquisitive, willful, demanding, bratty, expectant, a dragon in a golden retriever's body. She never met a stranger and fully expected everyone she met to love—and pet!—her, and they generally did. She was the perfect travel companion, the consummate hostess, an intuitive and compassionate friend. She always had a twinkle in her eye and a smile on her face. She always got the last bite of everything I ate and took her duties as pre-wash cycle for the dishwasher very seriously. She loved when I bought a Kindle because it gave me one more hand available to pet her with while I read. She loved to go to the dog beach—not for the dogs, or the beach—but for the pets she received from all the dog-friendly people there; a roll in a dead crab and some seaweed was always a bonus. Her favorite thing in the world was a good roll in some scratchy grass, even better if some wild creature had left something good and stinky there first. She was a force of nature who has left very big paw prints on our hearts and a huge hole in our lives. I miss her every day.

Sharyn Cerniglia
Cedarzmom

This is the first in a series of dedications from readers who have shared the pain of the loss of a beloved dog. For more information visit my website at www.justinedavis.com.

Chapter 1

Kayla Tucker stared at the note in her hand. She was barely aware of the woman opening the post office box next to her, stepped out of the way of the man emptying trash, ignored the girl chattering loudly into her cell phone, all without looking up from the page obviously torn out of a spiral notebook.

The note wasn't signed. If it had been printed, she could have pretended it was a mistake. That he hadn't written it. But there was no mistaking the handwriting; the slightly crooked hand, falling off the lines in her brother's typical way, was definitely Chad's.

Of course it was, just like all the others.

The writing blurred suddenly. She blinked, once, twice, then a third time. The last line swam, then cleared.

I'm sorry. I love you, sis.

She swore inwardly. "Then why did you leave, damn it? We could have fought this!"

Furious, mostly at herself for letting this latest in the long line of notes get to her, she wadded the ragged-edged piece of paper and the envelope into a tight ball. Dane would be unhappy yet again, she thought.

No, she thought as the memory stabbed at her. Dane Burdette would not be unhappy. Because he wasn't around anymore. He'd given up on her at last.

His image shot through her mind, vivid and painful. Tall, lean, dark, silky hair that kicked forward over his brow, golden eyes alight as he looked at her, flashing his killer smile. The smile that had grown rarer and rarer as the time passed.

Smothering the usual ache at the thought of the man she'd once expected to spend her life with, she slammed the small metal door of the post office box closed, turned the key and yanked it out. She turned on her heel and walked toward the door. She tossed the wadded up note into the trash can just outside.

"Kayla!"

The last thing she wanted to do just now was talk to someone. But she thought she recognized the voice, so she stopped, turned. And was enveloped in a huge hug.

"I'm so glad to run into you this morning. I was going to call and tell you—Leah and I actually went out to dinner last night."

Kayla managed a smile for the older man who several weeks ago had brought his reluctant wife to the counseling group she ran. "I'm glad to hear that, John. How did it go?"

"Not perfect, but better than I expected. And she's encouraged enough to try something else now."

"That's good to hear. Very good."

She meant it. She'd started the group for victims of violent crime as a means to help herself after the brutal murder of her parents, but in the process she had found a calling. She'd even gone back to school so she could be certified. And moments like this were why. Leah Crandall had been mentally immobilized after her son had been killed by an armed robber at a convenience store, and this was the first time she'd done anything socially normal in more than a year.

Kayla hoped they would make it, she thought as John promised he and his wife would continue with the group and would see her at the next meeting. So many marriages didn't survive the death of a child; the murder of that child only made it worse.

The overcast morning matched her mood as she headed for the parking lot. She glanced down the row of parked vehicles toward her own, the little blue coupe Dane had always kept in perfect shape for her. She spotted a familiar motorcycle parked across from it and slowed her steps. Rod Warren truly was the last person she wanted to see now. Or ever. She'd had an aversion to him ever since she'd found him trying to burn holes in the wings of a living butterfly with a magnifying glass when they were kids. She'd tried to stop him, even though he was older and bigger, and had in return been pinned against a wall and groped in a way she was too young to completely understand.

But Dane had, and when she'd told him about it, Rod had later shown up with a split lip and a black eye, and he'd kept a wide berth from then on. Still, she'd never forgotten the repugnance she'd felt. But the rider of the motorcycle with the picture of a nude female arranged in a particularly obscene way on the tank was thankfully nowhere in sight, so she kept going.

She was almost to her car when she changed her mind.

She should keep the note. The envelope with the postmark at least; this might be the one time when it helped. She turned around and began to walk quickly back. She felt the breeze of her own movement edging her tears sideways across her cheeks.

A loud clank echoed against the block wall of the post office. And the trash can she'd tossed the crumpled note into rolled into her path. She stopped, staring. There was no wind to catch the now-empty metal container, nor anyone to knock it over. The janitor had worked his way around to the other side of the building, and nobody else was even close.

No human anyway.

But there was a dog.

Sitting beside the toppled trash can was a dog, a striking

animal with a thick, longish coat colored black from the tip of his nose past his upright, alert ears all the way down past his shoulders, where the color of his fur changed to a rich, reddish brown.

He was looking at her rather intently.

And he had what she would swear was her note between his front paws. It had to be, she thought. The can had just been emptied before she'd tossed it. The wadded paper and envelope lay on the cement in front of him as if carefully placed. He must think it was some sort of ball to play with.

For a moment she pondered the dangers of approaching a strange dog. He wasn't huge, but he was far from small. Big enough to be intimidating, to make her wary.

And then he grinned at her.

She knew it was silly, but she couldn't think of any other way to describe it. His mouth opened, revealing some formidable teeth, but it was impossible to be frightened when his tongue lolled out on one side and the corners of that mouth seemed to curl upward.

Just when she had decided it might be safe to pet him, at the same time reaching for her note, he moved. He grabbed up the note and she froze. But he was holding it in a way that seemed oddly gentle. Like Dane's sweet Labrador, Lilah, used to hold her pups long ago, so gently there was barely a dent in the fur. The memory made her ache even more for the man who had left her.

And then the dog got up and started to go toward the parking lot.

Angry at herself for tossing the note in the first place, Kayla didn't know what to do. She wanted it back, desperately now, but she didn't want to provoke a strange dog into biting her.

The dog stopped. He looked over his shoulder at her. And waited.

Images from countless movies and television shows flashed through her mind. Was she supposed to follow him? Did dogs really do that? He took a couple of steps, still looking at her, the note still held almost delicately in his mouth.

She followed tentatively. He started off again. Not running, not teasing her as some dogs did, playing a canine version of keep away; he just trotted off. He headed into the half-full parking lot, past the obscene motorcycle and toward the second row of vehicles. When he looked back yet again, as if to be certain she was following, she could have sworn his dark eyes were urging her, compelling her somehow.

Kayla shook her head sharply.

"It's a *dog*," she muttered under her breath.

She picked up her pace, determined now to retrieve the note. She'd only thrown it away in the first place because she was so upset over Dane.

She passed her own car, then the big pickup parked next to it and the tiny electric car next to that. With her mind distracted for an instant by the absurd contrast between those two vehicles, she was late to realize the dog had come to a halt beside the driver's door of the next car in the row, a dark blue SUV that was a few years old but looked in perfectly maintained condition and had the glass hatch in the back raised up.

Her breath caught as the driver's door swung open and a man slid out. She stopped sharply, momentarily unable to move. He was tall, lean, hair as dark as midnight, with a forbiddingly strong jaw. But that jaw was unshaven, and his tousled hair spoke of a hurried morning rather than trendy style. Still, she took a step back instinctively.

He hadn't seen her yet. He crouched down beside the dog, who was fairly wiggling with pleasure yet holding gently on to that ball of paper. Kayla felt her anxiety fade as the man smiled and reached out to scratch below the dog's right ear.

"That'll teach me to leave the back window open. What'd you find, boy?"

The man's voice was low, steady, strong. He took the paper wad from the dog, who surrendered it easily and looked almost humanly satisfied, as if at a job well done. And then the dog looked back at her, staring in a way she'd never seen from any animal. She felt pinned in place, for a moment helpless and unable to move.

Meanwhile, the man had taken the note out of the crumpled envelope. *Her* note.

The spell broke. "That's mine," she said, afraid after she'd spoken that she'd sounded like a spoiled child who'd had a toy taken from her.

"I gathered," he said, and she realized she'd been wrong; he'd known she was there all the time.

And then he straightened. And she realized just how tall he was.

Most men seemed tall to her, at five-three. But this one had to be at least six feet, and something about the way he held himself made him seem even bigger. That he was obviously fit and strong only added to the impression.

She sucked in a breath, trying not to be intimidated. Nothing would happen here, in such a public place as the post office parking lot.

Then his face changed, softened, and his icy blue eyes warmed.

"Hayley," the man said, his voice raised just slightly.

Kayla frowned, puzzled. Then had her answer as a woman stepped past her, a post office receipt in one hand.

The dog greeted the woman effusively, on his feet, tail wagging madly. The woman reached to scratch the same spot the man had as she glanced from dog to man to Kayla. Mirth was in her voice and echoed in vivid green eyes as she spoke to the animal.

"And now what have you done, Cutter, my lad? And why are you running around loose anyway?"

The dog yipped, short and sharp.

"He jumped out the back and took off like…a dog with a mission," the man said as he lifted one arm toward the woman. She stepped into the shelter of it so naturally that Kayla knew these two were together in a way few people were. She could feel it, coming off of them in waves, could see it in their faces—love, respect, comfort and, in the glance they exchanged, passion.

She smothered a sigh. She'd known all that once. She'd had a place like that at Dane Burdette's side, a warm, safe, welcoming place. And she'd thrown it away. Dane was a man of near-infinite patience, he'd proven that for years, but she'd pushed and pushed until she'd finally found his limit.

The pain of losing him wasn't just emotional; it was a harsh, physical hurt, an aching for him with heart, mind and body. Oh, yes, body, she thought with an inward moan. Sometimes at night she would curl up into a ball and weep for missing him beside her, loving her. She gave herself an inward shake; if she let herself slide back into that morass of pain and loss, she'd break down sobbing right here in public, in front of these total strangers.

Belatedly she realized she'd seen the woman inside the post office, that she'd walked past her on her way to her post office box. She'd been comparing the woman's warm, auburn hair to her own shorter, dark-brown bob, wondering if a change would help her outlook.

Not that anything could help because Dane had walked out of her life.

"I was just about to go round him up when he came back," the man said, gesturing with the note. "It seems he stole this."

"Stole?" the woman named Hayley asked as she looked at

the balled-up paper. "Can you steal something someone obviously didn't want?"

Kayla tried to explain. "I…"

The man looked at her, and she hated the way her voice faded into nothing. But it was too big, too complicated to explain. Still, there was something oddly calming in this man's eyes, as if he'd reached out a hand to steady her.

Kayla tried to get a grip; whoever these two were, they clearly weren't a threat. Stick to the simple facts, she told herself.

"I didn't mean to throw it away." She sighed, corrected herself. "I mean, I did throw it away, but I shouldn't have. I'd like it back."

"Of course."

He handed it back without hesitation, reassuring her further. She smoothed out the note, realizing after a moment that the paper wasn't even damp from the dog's mouth. She glanced at the animal, who was looking up at her intently. She'd never had a dog, and suddenly she wondered if this one would have the same effect on her if she was more familiar with them. Or if it was just this dog who could look at her in that piercing way that made her feel as if she shouldn't move.

"He's…a beautiful dog."

"He is," Hayley said. "And clever enough to be amazing and annoying by turns."

Kayla smiled at that. She thanked the man, nodded at the woman and turned to head back to her car.

The dog stopped her.

Not aggressively—in fact, he was looking up at her with the same tongue-lolling grin she'd seen before. She tried to walk around him, but he moved to block her again.

"I'm sorry," Hayley said quickly. "He's a herding dog by breed, and it's his nature."

She reached for the dog's collar. Before she could grasp

it, the dog dodged slightly, the bright blue, boat-shaped tag Kayla had caught a glimpse of rattling. Cutter, she thought. Hayley had called the dog Cutter. As in coast guard cutter? Was that why the man looked so imposing, some military background?

The dog yipped again, now looking from her to his owners and back. He clearly wanted something, but—

He snatched the note again, right out of her hands.

Kayla let out a startled yelp that probably sounded like the dog's yip. This time the animal didn't run off. Instead, he turned and with a startling sort of delicacy, presented the note to the woman, who glanced at it, then up at the man beside her.

"Uh-oh," the man said.

"So it seems," Hayley agreed.

Kayla had no idea what they were talking about, what was going on, but it was all starting to make her nervous again. And no amount of telling herself she was perfectly safe here, out in the open in a public parking lot with people coming and going around them, seemed to help. Without Dane solidly by her side, she felt vulnerable.

She summoned up all the old coping tricks she'd been taught in the days after her world had been shattered. It was only normal she be nervous around strangers, even after all this time, she told herself. And she knew how to deal, really she did.

"Please," she said, trying to sound merely polite instead of pleading, "that's personal."

"Someone's in trouble," the woman said. It wasn't really a question. But her voice was so soft, so gentle, it eased Kayla's rising anxiety.

"Yes," she admitted. That much was clear in the note now open for all to see, so there didn't seem much point in denying it.

The man spoke. "Time for names, I think. I'm Quinn Fox-worth. This is my fiancée, Hayley Cole."

"Congratulations," Kayla said, not sure what else to say in this odd situation.

"And this rascal," Hayley said, scratching the dog's ear again, "is Cutter."

"Nice to meet you."

It was automatic and sounded utterly inane. She needed to get out of here, collect her thoughts. But first she had to get that note back.

On the thought the dog moved once more, this time closer to her. And then he was leaning against her leg, looking up at her with what for all the world looked like reassurance.

"What an…unusual dog," she murmured, half to herself.

"You have no idea," Hayley said, her tone wry.

"He has a nose for trouble," Quinn agreed. "In this case, apparently, yours."

She looked up at the man then. And read the same kind of reassurance in his eyes that she'd fancied she'd seen in the dog's.

"It's my brother's trouble, really."

Now why had she said that? She didn't make a habit of discussing her ugly family history with strangers.

"And now ours," Hayley said quietly.

Kayla blinked. "What?"

The woman gestured at the dog. "This wasn't coincidence. But we'll explain all that later. In the meantime, let's go somewhere where we can talk and figure out what to do about your problem."

Kayla took a step back. Or tried to. The dog, once again, was there. He seemed uncannily able to sense her every move before she made it.

"Who are you?" she asked, something dark and unsettling churning in her stomach.

"Friendlies," Quinn said, as if he'd sensed her fear.

"We just want to help," Hayley said. She glanced at Quinn, such pride in her face that it went a long way toward soothing Kayla's nerves. "It's what we do."

"You can't help. Nobody can."

Bitterness spiked through Kayla. She'd accepted the lost years, the thrown-away money, but Dane.... Losing Dane was—

She cut her own thoughts off.

"This is beyond anyone's help," she said. "It's a lost cause."

"Well, now," Hayley said, "isn't that convenient? Lost causes are our specialty."

Chapter 2

Dane Burdette paced the width of his home office, turned, made the return journey, then turned again. Although the apartment was large enough, this den was a small space, one that overflowed with equipment that now also filled the adjoining dining area.

A sound from outside brought him out of the reverie he'd slipped into and back to reality. A reality that, for the first time in more than a decade, didn't have Kayla in it.

His jaw tightened. He rubbed at the back of his neck, trying not to think about Kayla doing the same, as she so often did when he'd been working too many hours. And he barely managed not to look for the hundredth time this morning at the photograph on his desk, the picture he'd taken at the Washington coast last year, catching her at her most beautiful, happy, smiling, looking almost carefree. It was clear to even the most casual observer that the love and warmth in her eyes was aimed at the person behind the camera.

It nearly ripped his heart out every time he looked at it. He'd done the right thing. Finally. He'd meant what he'd said—he couldn't go on like this. Ten years was enough.

Too bad knowing that didn't stop the urge to give in, to go to her and patch things up. Again.

But he'd meant it this time. He'd spent too long living with her obsession. She'd idolized her big brother, believed completely in his innocence and had never given up trying to find him. She'd traveled thousands of miles, going every time one of those damn notes arrived, chasing postmarks. And every time it came to nothing. She'd spent time, money and much of her energy on the quest, and there was no end in sight.

He glanced at the heavy dive watch Kayla had given him for his twenty-fifth birthday. She'd be at the post office even now; she went every Friday to pick up the mail for her counseling group, but in truth she was both hoping for and dreading the arrival of another communication from her brother. Dane himself was long past hoping; he was firmly in the dread category.

He needed to quit wearing the watch, he thought. Even though he liked the solid weight of it on his wrist, that Kayla had chosen it and given it to him—and the passionate night that had followed—was not something he wanted to be reminded of at every move.

"I had to do it," he muttered under his breath, as if actually saying the words would be more convincing to a heart and mind that felt as if something vital had been torn away.

At this point, Chad Tucker's guilt or innocence didn't matter much to him. What mattered was that Kayla couldn't seem to move on. It wasn't that he didn't understand—he did. He'd been there that night, in the bloody, awful aftermath. He'd been the one to hear her scream, the one to run to her, to pull her out of the room that held the nightmare. To this day he couldn't imagine what it must have been like for the teenage girl to walk into that hell.

That it was a girl he cared about made even thinking about it difficult. And he had cared about Kayla since the first day he'd seen her, a slight, fragile-looking fourteen, sitting on a limb high up in the old tree between their houses. She had been staring downward, turning her head this way and that, and he'd realized after a moment what was going on.

"Stuck?" he'd called to her.

"Not yet," she'd answered, making him laugh.

She'd been in his life one way or another ever since that day. Until now. Until he'd had to leave her, had to walk away. Even though it was like leaving a part of himself behind. But he knew—

"Dane?"

He spun around, a little embarrassed that he hadn't realized his roommate and business partner Sergei was standing there. He needed to get his head back in the game.

"I need to go if I'm going to make it on time. Don't want to speed out of here because our downstairs neighbor the cop is out washing his car. Is what you sent last night the final cut?"

"Yes."

"I'll be on my way then," his partner said.

But he stopped in the doorway and looked back. He and Sergei Kesic had built their small, digital video promotion company from nothing to a going concern, thanks to Dane's knack for tailoring the product to individual customer needs and Sergei's no-nonsense, bottom-line sales approach that appealed to companies in a belt-tightening era.

"You sent it at 3:00 a.m.," Sergei said.

"Did I?"

"You're keeping some pretty long hours, buddy."

"Don't be late," Dane said. The last thing he wanted was to get dragged into discussing the reasons behind his late nights and lack of sleep. Sergei hadn't asked why he'd suddenly taken to sleeping here instead of at Kayla's, and he didn't want that conversation to start now.

He had to put it out of his mind, he told himself as Sergei shrugged and left. There were decisions to make, plans to go over.

A sour laugh escaped him. Plans. Yes, indeed, plans. He'd had a lot of those.

He yanked the watch off his wrist, opened a desk drawer, shoved it in the back and slammed the drawer shut. One more step, he thought. And he should do it now, when he knew where she'd be, at the post office checking for another one of those damned notes. He would go over to Kayla's and pick up the last of his stuff.

And leave his key.

He winced at the thought but shored up his determination and grabbed his key ring from the desk. He pried the ring open and worked the gold key off, fighting memories of the night she'd given it to him.

He shoved the key in the watch pocket of his jeans.

With a final glance at the photograph, he headed for the door. That picture was going, he told himself firmly. As soon as he got back.

This was crazy.

Kayla stared at the business card in her hand. It looked official enough, but anybody could churn out a good-looking business card. And there was no indication on the card of exactly what the "Foxworth Foundation" did.

They had walked across the street to the small city park and were seated on the stone wall that surrounded the kid's play area, deserted now at this morning hour. The dog that had started all this was sprawled in the grass, basking in the morning sun and looking decidedly smug.

"Does he do this often?" she asked.

"Cutter?" Hayley said.

"Yes. Does he drag total strangers with a problem to you?"

"As a matter of fact, yes."

Kayla blinked. Hayley smiled.

"He has a knack," she said. "I don't know how he does it, but he seems to know when people are troubled."

"And he brings them to you?"

"It's not usually as…neatly as today," Quinn said with a wry smile. "But yes, he does."

Kayla glanced at the dog, who seemed blithely unconcerned about the entire situation. As if his job was done, she thought, even as she realized she was going a bit overboard with the anthropomorphism.

"And he makes it pretty obvious," Hayley said, "that he expects us to fix whatever's wrong."

Whatever's wrong, Kayla thought. And lost causes are their specialty?

I love you, but I won't—I can't—*stay and watch you throw the rest of your life away on a lost cause.*

Dane's final words as he had walked out her door echoed in her mind, drowning out every other thought. He'd been upset with her before but always seemed to find a reserve of patience she marveled at even as she used it up. But this time had been different. She'd heard the finality in his voice, seen the sadness in his eyes. The man she'd loved since she was fourteen had finally had enough. His departure had left her bereft and a little stunned at how completely off balance her already damaged world now felt.

"Whatever it is," Hayley said softly, "let us help. It's what we do."

Kayla looked up. "Lost causes?"

"Yes."

"Who are you?" She glanced at Quinn, gestured with the card, remembering his introduction. "You're the Foxworth."

"One of them," he said.

"What's this foundation do?"

"What should be done but isn't," Quinn said, with a warm glance at Hayley that made Kayla miss Dane all the more.

"They—" Hayley caught herself, smiled and went on, showing Kayla she wasn't used to saying it yet, "*we* work for people in the right who don't have anyone else to help them."

Curious now, she looked at them both. "Who decides who's in the right?"

Quinn grinned suddenly. Kayla could have sworn she heard Hayley's breath catch; she didn't blame her, it was a killer grin. Nothing on Dane's, of course, but still....

"That's the joy of being privately funded. We decide. We have a crack research team to help in that."

"Research team?"

"You'd be amazed," he said, his voice taking on a wry note, "how many people sound like they're in the right until you look into the other side."

Kayla sighed. "Then you won't want to help me," she said.

"Why do you say that?"

"Because the other side is the police, and when you look into it you'll probably find some notes saying I'm delusional, disturbed or maybe just crazy."

"Are you?" Hayley asked, sounding merely curious and not at all bothered by the mention of the police.

"No!" Kayla stopped, sighed. "I'm...determined. Dane thinks I'm obsessed. But he and Chad never got along anyway."

She realized she was starting to sound a little mental, talking to total strangers about people they didn't know. She should get out of here. Whoever these people were, they couldn't really do what they said they did. People didn't just help strangers like that. Did they?

And even if they did, what she'd said was true. If they looked into this they'd find all the evidence the police had pointing to Chad and probably some mentions of his sister. Not nasty ones, she didn't think; they had been kind, if unbelieving. They'd probably just gently suggested, in some police jargon, that the suspect's little sister was a bit nuts, driven to the edge of insanity by what had happened.

She needed to get out of here. Getting one of these notes always revved her up, and she needed to calm down, to think. How she was going to do that when she no longer had the option to go to the one person who had always helped her with that, she wasn't sure.

Oddly, the moment she decided to get up and leave the dog awoke from his snooze and scrambled to his feet. Before she could rise he was there, as if he'd somehow read her mind and was once more preventing her from leaving. The animal leaned into her, resting his chin on her leg as he stared up at her. And suddenly it was impossible to move.

"Why don't you start at the beginning?" Quinn suggested.

"And pet Cutter," Hayley added. "It's remarkably soothing."

Kayla nearly smiled at that; people got so silly about their animals. But maybe if she did pet the dog, he'd be satisfied and get out of her way. She lifted a hand and ran it over the dog's head, then, remembering what Quinn and Hayley had done, added a scratch below his right ear. The dark eyes never wavered, but he let out a sound that was amazingly like a happy sigh.

It was soothing, she thought, startled. She felt calmer, steadier. And when Quinn again suggested she start at the beginning, to her surprise, she did.

"Chad is my big brother. We moved here when I was fourteen. He was sixteen. Two years later, ten years ago, our parents were murdered in a home invasion robbery. The police suspected Chad. He ran. I haven't seen him since."

"Well," Quinn said to Hayley without any of the horrified reaction Kayla was used to whenever she told the tale, "that could give Rafe a run for his money for succinctness."

"I'm sure she's had to tell it a few times," Hayley said.

Although there was a world of sympathy in her voice, the auburn-haired woman didn't gush. Nor did she recoil from the blunt, grim story. Kayla was a little amazed at how comforting that was. Like petting this darn dog, a motion she only now realized she'd continued the entire time she'd been speaking. And it really did soothe her at a time when she needed it.

"That," Quinn said, gesturing at the note that began it all, "is from him?"

She nodded. "I get one every few months. He never says where he is, or has been, just that he's sorry he had to leave, he didn't do it and he loves me."

"Where do they come from?" he asked.

"Oregon. Northern California. Idaho. Montana once."

"So he stays in the northwest, generally."

She nodded.

"And what do you do when you get one?" Hayley asked.

Kayla shrugged. "The only thing I can do. I go there, wherever he sent it from."

"Have you ever found anything?"

She sighed. "Nothing useful. I don't have a current photo, obviously. I tried an agency that aged up an old one for me, but it didn't help. A few times in the beginning someone thought they remembered seeing him, but most times it's like he was never there."

"He's gotten better at it," Quinn said, sounding thoughtful.

They both seemed so open, so willing to listen, unlike the police, or even Dane, who had grown so weary of it all.

"I set up a page on a couple of social media sites," she said, "but it's the same problem. And I got more junk than genuinely helpful stuff. Even got some real creeps, pretending to want to help."

She shivered at the memory; if Dane hadn't insisted on going with her every time who knows what would have happened. Twice, guys who looked nothing like their own profile photos, had shown up obviously with something other than help in mind. They'd taken one look at Dane and departed hastily.

"It's definitely a cold case after all this time," Quinn said.

"That's what the police say, too. So why would you help me?"

"I know something about worrying about a brother," Hayley said. "I have one I haven't heard from in months. Walker's not on the run, or in trouble that I know of, but I don't know where he is or how he is."

So the empathy in the woman's voice had been real, Kayla thought. It helped her decide.

"I believe Chad. He didn't do it. I don't care what the police think they know—I know he didn't. He couldn't."

"If it's true, then we'll prove that," Hayley said. "You're not alone any longer, Kayla. You have—"

She broke off as Cutter's head came up suddenly. His eyes had been closed as Kayla petted him—in fact, he'd seemed to be snoozing as she stroked her fingers over his soft fur—but something had clearly brought him to alert. She'd heard nothing, but her ears weren't as keen as a dog's. As Kayla glanced around, she saw nothing different than it had been moments ago. There had been a few people coming and going while they'd been here, and the dog hadn't reacted at all.

She would have written it off to unfamiliar dog behavior if not for two things; Hayley never finished her sentence, and Quinn immediately stood up. And suddenly he was no longer the friendly man with the nice smile, but someone altogether different, alert, ready and capable. He glanced around much as she had, but then he looked at the dog, watching, waiting, as if for some signal.

Cutter's head moved sharply in what looked, impossibly, like a nod.

"What have you got, boy?" Quinn's voice was low, and Kayla heard something in it that hadn't been there before, some edge that made her think Quinn could be a very dangerous man. The dog made an answering sound she couldn't quite describe. Hayley stayed silent, her gaze flicking from man to dog and back, waiting.

The only thing Kayla was sure of was that this, or something like it, had happened often enough that none of the three found it unusual.

She shifted to look around again, wondering what had set the dog off. He seemed to have settled on a direction now, looking out toward the street. And then, unexpectedly, his tail began to wag just slightly. She looked that way and saw nothing amiss—an older couple walking arm in arm, a kid on a skateboard, a man crossing the street from the post office parking lot, a car—

Her gaze shot back to the man. A man heading quickly toward them. The way he moved, with that easy grace and long stride, the way he held his head, the gleam of the morning sun on dark hair....

Dane.

Her pulse kicked up, as it always did at the sight of him. But how had the dog known, of all the people around this morning, that this was the one? And what was he doing here anyway?

Hope leaped in her, but she quashed it; Dane hadn't been angry when they'd parted, or she would have nurtured that hope that he would, as he always had before, get over it. He'd been quietly weary in a way that told her as nothing else could that he was done.

"It's not that I don't admire your loyalty," he'd said. "I do. I just could have used a little more of it myself."

She shivered at the memory of the words and of her own freezing reaction when she'd realized, for the first time, he'd used the past tense.

"You know him?" Quinn's voice broke through the awful memory, and that edge in it shook her back to the present.

"Yes," she whispered. She couldn't think of another thing

to say that would explain who this man was to her. There were no words that were adequate. But as she looked at Quinn, then Hayley, she realized she didn't have to.

They knew.

Chapter 3

"**W**ho the hell are you?"

Dane stared at the man standing between him and Kayla. The guy looked tough, solid and ready for anything. Just about matched his own mood, Dane thought. Which made no sense; who Kayla hung out with wasn't his business anymore. Not that that had stopped him from bolting over here when he'd spotted her with two strangers.

"He's my fiancé." Dane's gaze snapped to the woman who had been sitting beside Kayla. It was further evidence of his mood that he hadn't really focused on her before; she was lovely, and if her words hadn't completely disarmed him, her smile might have. "I'm Hayley Cole, and this is Quinn Foxworth. Behave, both of you."

Dane wasn't sure if she meant him and Quinn or Quinn and the dog. The dog who was looking at him in the oddest way. Not in the love-filled, melt-your-heart kind of way Lilah always had, but with an intensity that spoke of a clever brain behind those amber-flecked dark eyes.

"And you, I gather, are Dane."

The man's voice was steady, with no particular inflection, but Dane couldn't help thinking this was a man who would react quickly and effectively if necessary.

It hit him somewhat belatedly that this stranger had known who he was. And the only way that could be was that Kayla had told him.

His gaze shifted quickly to the woman who had been part

of his life for so long. Had she really told these strangers about him? Maybe even how he'd walked out on her, telling her wrenching story, making anybody who hadn't lived it with her over the past ten years wonder what kind of heartless bastard left a woman whose life had been torn apart like that?

A sense of betrayal filled him, and he took a step back. But it turned out to be only a half-step; somehow the dog had gotten in his way and he had to stop.

"I thought you were through with me," Kayla said. Her voice was quiet, unemotional. And that sparked a new feeling in him, one that was almost anger. She didn't even think they were worth fighting for?

That he didn't want to fight with her, that he never had, was something he cast aside just now. He focused on the fact that she sounded so calm. As if she'd processed that it really was over. And instead of crying over it, or getting angry at him, she was…accepting?

"So that's it?" he said sharply, ignoring the three unknown onlookers. "You just quit on us?"

"You're the one who left." She gestured with the note. "And he's still out there, Dane."

"Yeah. And I'm here. I've done nothing but support you and love you and help you for ten years, while that spoiled, manipulative brother of yours plays with you, taunts you, but is too big of a coward to come back and deal with the mess he left you with."

"Dane! He's not—"

He held up his hands; he really had had enough.

"He always skated by on his looks. He used you, took for granted that you'd always worship your big brother." Dane grimaced. "And I guess he was right about that."

His anger faded as once more the reality hit him in the face. This time she was silent when he took a breath. And he realized he had no right to stay upset at her for talking about them—and him—to strangers when he'd just dumped a pile of dirty laundry in front of them. To their credit, they'd said nothing, but they hadn't left them alone either.

"I tried, Kayla. I really tried." He heard his own voice, realized he sounded as tired as he felt after that last burst of pained rage and resentment. "But I can't play second fiddle to your fixation any longer. I won't. The woman I…loved is buried beneath this obsession and I can't find her anymore. You're on your own."

"That's just it," Kayla said, showing a spark of spirit now. "I'm not on my own anymore."

She waved toward the couple standing a couple of feet away in a gesture that seemed to include the dog.

"They're going to help find Chad."

Suspicion bit as hard and deep as that dog probably could if motivated. Ignoring the jab of pain at the reminder that, although she'd given up on them, she obviously wasn't about to give up on her obsession, Dane spun on his heel to stare at the trio. On the surface they looked harmless enough—handsome guy, beautiful woman, nice-looking dog. Quite the picture they presented.

He didn't believe it for a minute. And he hadn't forgotten his first impression of the man as someone not to take lightly.

"Are they?" he said, focusing on the man introduced as Quinn. "And just how much do they want you to pay for this 'help'?"

One corner of Quinn's mouth quirked, and Dane saw something flicker in the man's eyes, something that looked strangely like approval.

"Nothing," Kayla said.

Dane turned his head to look at her. "Haven't you learned? Didn't that phony P.I. and that guy who took you for five grand in California teach you anything?"

Kayla flushed. He hated doing it, but somebody had to

protect her from herself, and right now he was the only one around.

The dog moved and, oddly, came to sit between him and Kayla. The animal looked from him to her and back, with an expression that looked for all the world like impatience. Dane shook his head; he loved dogs, but he didn't usually impart human qualities to them.

"Quinn?"

It was the other woman who'd spoken, drawing his gaze. She looked the picture of innocence, which made him even more suspicious.

"Yes," the man said. "I think so."

Another stab of pain shot through him. He and Kayla had been like that once, able to communicate without words. But lately he'd quit trying, or even asking what she was thinking, because his gut knew one more admission that she was worrying about her brother would send him over the edge.

And it had.

"Walk with me," Quinn said. Dane eyed him warily. "You have questions," the man said in answer to his look. "I'll give you all the answers you want."

"And I'm supposed to just believe you?"

"No," Quinn said. "I expect you to do your homework and then decide if you believe us."

That surprised him enough to make him follow the man's lead. And if he wanted to be out of earshot of Kayla, it could mean he wanted to hear the other side of the story.

"That note she got today…" Quinn began as they neared a stand of cedar trees along one edge of the park.

"Don't bother. I know exactly what it said. 'I didn't do it. I love you. I'm sorry. Forget about me.' Even as he keeps sending them so there's no hope she ever could."

Quinn stopped walking and turned to look at him.

"I know that sounds harsh," Dane said, "given what she's been through."

"Crimes like that have a far-reaching ripple effect," Quinn said. "They touch many more lives than just the immediate family."

The rather detached yet undeniably true observation made Dane take a second look at the man. He was as tall as he himself, and while Dane biked and ran to keep in shape, he doubted he was as strong as this guy looked. He'd been thinking of adding some weights to his regimen, and just looking at the arms on this guy was enough to convince him.

"Look, I know she loved Chad, but he was…"

"Spoiled and manipulative?"

Dane's mouth tightened. "Yes. Chad never once had to suffer the consequences of his actions in his entire life."

"His parents protected him?"

Dane nodded. "He was the firstborn, and he was spoiled rotten. Until Kayla came along. He was jealous at first, but she adored him so much he finally decided he liked it. She would do anything for him, and he wasn't above using that."

"You didn't know them back then."

He didn't sound particularly accusatory, but Dane was raw enough that he answered a bit sharply.

"Their father told me the first part. The last part I saw for myself. Chad used Kayla from the day he realized she was smarter than he was. I don't know how many school papers he conned her into writing for him, even though she was two years younger. Or how many times he convinced her to lie for him, cover for him, with their parents. A couple of times she even took the blame for something he did when he was skating too close to the edge with their father."

"How long did that go on?"

"Until I was able to convince her she wasn't doing him any favors."

Again Quinn studied him for a moment. "You've always had her best interests at heart."

It didn't seem to be a question, but it reminded Dane he should be worrying about those best interests now. "Who are you? And what's all this crap about helping Kayla find Chad?"

"It's what we do."

"Find missing persons? You some kind of private investigator? Because she's been there, and she got taken. I proved that and convinced her to give up on them," he ended with a pointed glare at Quinn.

He didn't mention the large insurance policy their parents had had, with Kayla and Chad as sole beneficiaries. It wasn't a huge fortune, but it was enough to tempt unscrupulous types. Hayley Cole seemed innocent enough, but there was an edge about this man that made him wonder. He just hoped Kayla hadn't been foolish enough to say anything about the money. He didn't think she would; she might be foolishly obsessed, but she was far from a fool, and she'd learned her lesson after that P.I. ripped her off.

Of course, he also didn't know how much of that money was left after ten years of pouring it into her endless search.

"No, we're not private investigators," Quinn said. "We don't work for just anybody. Only people we believe in."

"And you do it for free? Right." He'd slipped from skepticism into outright sarcasm, but Dane didn't care. He might be through with Kayla, but that didn't mean he didn't care at all; he couldn't turn it off like a faucet.

"That's why we're very particular about what we take on." The man's mouth quirked wryly. "Unless it's somebody Cutter brings to us."

Dane blinked. "The dog?"

Quinn sighed. "It's a long story. But the bottom line is, he's better than a lie detector."

The whimsy of that, coming from a man like Quinn Foxworth, almost made Dane smile. But his own reaction made him even more wary; he knew predators often used animals to lull their targets into trusting them. They didn't seem the type, but did the type ever really seem like the type? He shook his head before his thoughts got even more muddled.

"I think your canine lie detector misfired on this one," he said.

"Kayla mentioned you and Chad didn't get along. Were there other reasons?"

Dane's jaw tightened. "Nothing that has anything to do with this. Why should I believe anything you say?"

Quinn looked at him thoughtfully. He pulled out a business card and handed it to him. "I'm not going to give you answers you'll question. Find your own answers. Do that homework."

"You can count on it," Dane said, letting more than a hint of warning into his voice. "And you stay away from Kayla until I do."

Chapter 4

Dane leaned back in his chair, staring at the computer monitor, tapping his pen on the note pad at his side. The top page
was full of scribbled notes; his search had been easier than
he'd expected. And quicker. It had only taken him a couple
of hours to become convinced.

He'd ignored most of the stuff on the website for the Foxworth Foundation. Anybody, as he knew better than most,
could put together a website and put anything they wanted
on it. It was a sad fact that if it looked genuine enough, far
too many people took it at face value. The Foxworth site gave
away very little information, however, as if anybody who went
looking for it had to already know what they did.

But he'd noted the areas across the country that had contact numbers for them and then called local authorities in
those places. Many had never heard of the foundation and
some had heard of them but not had any contact with them,
but a few had dealt with them directly, and it was those he
concentrated on.

The results were impressive, to say the least. More than
one cop or D.A. he spoke to admitted they'd been wary at
first, or even irritated that Foxworth was treading their turf,
but because most of the cases were cold anyway, they'd decided to let it play out, figuring the amateurs wouldn't be able
to do much anyway.

"Boy, were we wrong," one detective told him. "They
wrapped up a rape and murder case we'd had to move on

from years ago. And they didn't care about taking credit for it either, which smoothed some ruffled feathers around here."

And that seemed to be the theme from the official side. And there were enough stories like that to make him begin to believe the Foxworth Foundation might be for real. So he'd gone on to track down stories about those cases and then find some of the people involved, the people who had turned to Foxworth for help.

The stories there were even more impressive, and the praise imparted was heartfelt and moving. Not only for the success rate, but for the kind of things they took on. From reuniting long separated family members to helping a troubled teenager find the right path, from giving a lost soul a new lease on life to giving a grieving family a reason they could bear for someone's suicide.

And then there was the stolen locket. It was the only memento an adopted child had had of her real mother, and it seemed Foxworth had set upon finding that as wholeheartedly as they had what some would consider more important cases.

He shook his head and sat upright. What he should be focusing on, he told himself, was the fact that on more than one occasion, Foxworth had been instrumental in proving the innocence of people suspected of crimes. Nothing quite as grim as Kayla's parents' murders, but still….

Maybe they could. They seemed to be very good at what they did, and he couldn't deny he liked the idea of what they did.

He picked up the business card and looked at it for a moment. He thought of the stories he'd heard, how many people had said simply, "Someone gave me their card and told me they could help."

He picked up the phone again. This time he dialed the number on the card. To his surprise, Quinn Foxworth himself answered.

"It's a policy we have," the man explained. "Each card has our own number on it. We like to maintain consistency of contact."

"Don't you get a lot of spam calls that way?"

"Some. Better that than make somebody who's feeling helpless jump through the hoops of a big phone menu system."

He heard sounds in the background, some equipment running and the familiar harsh honk of a heron passing overhead; Quinn was obviously outside.

"What if you can't answer right then?" he asked.

"Then it rolls over to our head office. But a live person will always answer."

"That's in St. Louis?"

"Been doing that homework, I see."

"Yes. Detective Saunders in Phoenix says hello, by the way, and Mrs. Louis sends her love."

Quinn laughed. "I thought you might be thorough."

"Yes."

He heard the sound of a door and the background noises ended. Dane wondered where Quinn was, where he'd stepped inside.

"So have you decided we're who we say we are and do what we say we do?" Quinn asked.

"Let's just say I'm open to the idea."

"Fair enough. And I'm ready to believe that you had nothing to do with Kayla's murders."

Dane went still. "What?"

"Your alibi was solid."

"Yes, it was." He'd been with five other kids and a teacher at a college prep study session at the time of death, and he'd never left or been out of sight. He had been home barely fifteen minutes when Kayla's horrific screams from next door had sent him racing over there. "What the hell are you doing investigating me?"

"We're working for Kayla. We'll do whatever it takes to get her the answers she wants."

"Even if it means wasting time on innocent people?"

"If Kayla's right, that means the real guilty person is still out there."

Dane couldn't argue with that. It was something he thought about often, even if Kayla didn't seem to.

And it was the size of that "if" that always threw him.

"Ready to tell me why you and Chad Tucker didn't get along?"

"Hasn't Kayla already told you?"

"I'd like your version."

"Why?"

"We don't build the kind of success rate we have by only listening to one side."

"Fair enough," Dane said. "I didn't like him. Part of it was that in school I was one of the nerdier kids, and Chad was one of the cool guys."

"You don't look like much of a nerd."

"That's because Kayla challenged me to change that."

"Challenged you?"

"She said we couldn't change the fact that people judged on appearance and bought into stereotypes—except by breaking that stereotype. So I started running, lifting weights to get into shape. Found I liked it, and it cleared my head for the tech stuff. And she was right. People looked at me differently, tolerated the…geek in me because that wasn't all I was."

"So she's as wise as she seems."

"Wiser. She was fourteen at the time. Still just the girl next door, who felt like the little sister I never had."

"But she already had a big brother."

"Yeah," Dane said, his tone sour. "And Chad didn't like me either."

"Not surprising, if you saw through him."

Quinn really was open to the idea that Chad might not be the good guy Kayla insisted he was, Dane thought. So he'd meant it when he'd said they weren't taking her viewpoint as the only one. Encouraged by that, he went on.

"When Kayla turned sixteen and her folks let her date, Chad kept trying to set Kayla up with his best friend, Troy Reid. I'd started to look at her differently then, and he wanted to get her away from me. Her folks went along with him—they adored Troy, he was the catch of the whole town, and they thought I was too...something. Her mom, especially."

"But it didn't work. Kayla stayed with you."

"She's incredibly...loyal."

He stumbled over the word, remembering how he'd thrown the word at her the day he'd finally walked away.

"Were there other reasons Chad didn't like you?"

Dane had the uncomfortable feeling Quinn already knew. What was that they told lawyers, about never asking a question you don't already know the answer to? Hell, maybe this Quinn was a lawyer, for all he knew.

"He got into some trouble, a couple of times, right after they moved here."

"Stole a bike, joyriding in a senior citizen's car, breaking into a convenience store for cigarettes?"

So he did know. Dane filed that away to remember when dealing with this man.

"The bike was mine."

"And you reported it."

"My folks did. I didn't care all that much by then—I'd started to drive, but it was a really good bike. And I remembered Chad asking how much it was worth."

"And you told the police that?"

"Yes. And they tracked it down, found who he'd sold it to." Dane jammed his fingers through his hair. "Even then he blamed somebody else. Said Rod Warren, a local punk, had put him up to it. But Chad was no angel, no matter what Kayla thinks."

"Do you think he could have killed them?"

Dane sighed. How long had he been wrestling with that thought? How many times had be been on the verge of telling Kayla just that, only stopping himself because he couldn't bear to see her face if he turned on her. Because that's how she'd see it, he was sure.

In the end, he gave Quinn the answer that had always been his bottom line, even as he realized it stemmed more from his love for his own parents and an inability to relate to the idea of parental murder, than a real belief in Chad's innocence.

"He had no reason to. They were good people. They loved him."

"The police seem pretty certain. He was their only real suspect."

"I know. After he ran, I don't think they ever really focused on anyone else."

"They're a small department, overloaded, and they labeled the case cold fairly quickly. Not their fault—they just don't have the manpower."

"Kayla keeps pushing them, but..."

"They're down to wanted posters and flyers and the occasional search of criminal databases, probably spurred by her pushing."

"And everything is still focused on Chad."

"Yes."

"But Kayla's right about the fact that there's an innocent explanation for all the evidence," Dane said, feeling the need to be fair despite it all. "They found cigarette butts with his DNA outside, but he always snuck out there to smoke. His fingerprints were on the den window, but that's how he always snuck out."

"All true."

"But he ran," Dane said, coming down to the final, damning fact.

"Never a good sign." Quinn sounded completely neutral, like a man who truly hadn't made up his mind. "If it wasn't Chad, who do you think it could have been?"

He had spent literally years batting that one around in his mind. "The only one who ever seemed likely to me was Rod. He tried to hang with Chad, but Troy was too straight-arrow to like him, so that got in the way. For that matter, I always wondered why Troy hung with Chad—they were so different."

"Why did Rod seem likely?"

"He scared Kayla once when she tried to stop him from some kind of twisted experiment with setting butterflies on fire. He…touched her."

Quinn was silent for a moment. "And did he ever again?"

"No. He did not even go near her. Ever."

"I see," Quinn said with what sounded like amusement and understanding. "So, is this Rod still around?"

"Yeah. And he's been in trouble a few times. Breaking into houses and stealing cash."

"Sounds promising. Did the police look at him?"

"They did," he admitted. "But he gave them an alibi they believed."

Quinn didn't miss the inference. "But you didn't?"

"The alibi was that he was with another kid. One he used to harass. Unmercifully. Really harsh stuff. But the kid swore Rod was with him. The cops bought it, figured the kid had no reason not to but every reason to finger Rod if he could."

"But?"

"After that, the harassment stopped."

"So you think he made a deal with the kid?"

Dane shrugged. "Couldn't prove it, but it seemed…coincidental, to say the least."

"We'll check him out," Quinn said.

"What the hell can you do that the cops can't?"

"We have resources. And sources. Time. The manpower. And we have an open mind about Chad's guilt."

"What if you come to believe he's guilty?"

"Then we'll tell Kayla just that. Gently but honestly. Hayley's good at that."

A memory of the couple as they'd stood together this morning in the park shot through his mind. Quinn had constantly been touching Hayley, and vice versa. Little brushes, a touch on the arm, brushing back an errant strand of hair. Even when they were clearly focused on something else, they were still touching, even if it was as simple as standing so close their arms touched. Not quite joined at the hip, but close.

Dane recognized it because he and Kayla were the same way.

Pain jabbed through him, knotting his gut. He and Kayla had been the same way.

"Can you really do this? Can you put an end to this one way or another?"

He didn't care that he sounded angry. And he knew quite well he wasn't asking the real question. Asking that would sound more pitiful than he was willing to sound before a man like Quinn Foxworth.

"We can. And we have people who will help Kayla deal with whatever we find."

His confidence was bracing. Dane had spent so long being unable to do anything, about Kayla or her obsession, that he'd slid into unfamiliar territory—hopelessness.

If what he'd learned today was true, these people were the best and brightest at what they did. If they couldn't find Chad, maybe Kayla would finally admit it was over, maybe she would finally move on.

Maybe he'd moved his things a bit too soon. He tried not to let hope rise too far. But it was one last shot, the last chance for them, and he couldn't say no.

Chapter 5

Kayla tried to tamp down her excitement as she hurriedly made her bank deposit. She wouldn't have stopped at all if her mortgage payment wasn't set to go out in three days. But Hayley was gracious about the errand, waiting in her car, and as soon as Kayla was done here, they'd be on their way to what Hayley called the Foxworth building.

After a friendly goodbye to the teller, who happened to be her neighbor's niece, Kayla stuffed her deposit receipt into her purse as she groped for her keys and the fob that would unlock her car door. At the same time, she tried to shoulder the heavy glass door of the bank open.

The door suddenly swung open. "Hey, pretty lady," a familiar voice said, "let me get that for you."

She looked up into the face of Chad's best friend.

"Hi, Troy." Troy Reid gave her a wide smile as he held the door for her. "How are you?" she asked.

Troy had been part of the fabric of her life ever since they'd moved here and he and Chad had become fast friends. Her parents had both liked him, and she suspected they'd secretly hoped some of his charm and friendly manner—and his politeness with adults—would rub off on her brother.

He shrugged. "Things are pretty grim here. I'm thinking of leaving soon."

Kayla felt a surge of empathy. "I understand."

"I admire you, Kayla. It takes courage to stay in the place that has so many ugly memories."

"I'm in a different house, different neighborhood. That helps. But this is home for me. You always wanted to get out of here."

"And I did, for a while," he said with a wry smile.

"Did I ever tell you how wonderful I thought it was that you came back to take care of your mom after your dad died?"

"Yes," he said, then with a smile added, "but you could tell me again."

"It was."

She meant it. It wasn't just guilt that made her say it; she hadn't made it to Troy's dad's funeral. It had been less than a month after the murders, and she just hadn't been able to face it. Troy understood, had been more than kind about it— something she'd always appreciated.

"But not wonderful enough to pry you away from Dane."

She was sure, after all this time, the irritation in his voice was feigned. His laugh a split-second later proved it. And Dane was not a subject she wanted to discuss just now.

"So, you'll be leaving again now?" she asked hurriedly. "Nothing really holding you, if you want to leave, I mean, with both your folks gone."

Well, that was tactful, she thought. Teach her to dodge without thinking.

"And my best friend," Troy said. "Don't forget that."

Kayla blinked. As if she could forget. But until it had come together like this, she hadn't quite realized just how many losses Troy had suffered. As many, in fact, as she had, albeit not in such an ugly way.

"You know, I still don't believe it," he said. "I know what the police think, and he ran and all, but I still can't believe Chad really did it."

The words, from someone who knew Chad almost as well as she did, were balm to her battered spirit.

"Thank you," she said fervently.

He studied her for a moment. Then, gently, he asked, "You still don't believe it either, do you?"

"No. No, I don't. Chad couldn't. Wouldn't."

"I agree." He sighed. "I'd have been trying to prove it myself, if it hadn't been for my dad, then my mom getting sick."

"I know you would," she said.

"Are you still looking for him?"

She nodded. "And I have some help this time. Some people from the Foxworth Foundation."

He blinked. "Who are they?"

"They specialize in helping people when no one else will. Especially with what they call lost causes."

"Never heard of them. Are you sure they're legit? I wouldn't want you getting taken."

You and Dane, she thought. "Thanks for worrying," she said.

Troy reached out and touched her shoulder comfortingly. "If there's anything I can do," he said.

"They may want to talk to you, since you were Chad's best friend."

"Send them around. I'll be happy to talk to them."

"Thank you, Troy."

She felt much better now, she thought when Troy had gotten into his car and gone. He had that knack. And knowing she wasn't the only believer in Chad's innocence helped.

If only Dane felt the same way.

"You really don't know where your brother is?"

Kayla looked at the woman across the table from her. Hayley shook her head. "No. But Walker is just a born wanderer, I'm afraid. I know he loves me, and I love him, but he just has this need to see what's over the next mountain. And eventually, he always calls." She smiled then. "But now it feels like I have a ton of siblings. Everybody at Foxworth seems to think I need looking out for."

Kayla couldn't help smiling at her tone of mock grievance. "Is that good or bad?"

"Mostly good."

"You don't seem like you'd need a lot of protecting."

"I don't," Hayley said. "But they love Quinn, and he loves me, therefore…"

She ended the simple yet moving statement with a wave of her hand.

"Nice," Kayla said, trying to quash the now familiar ache that was always threatening to crush her, making it hard to breathe.

"Very. And unexpected."

Hayley's cell phone chirped the arrival of a text message. She excused herself to glance at it. Kayla guessed, from the way her mouth curved into a soft smile, that it was from Quinn.

Kayla glanced around, looking for distraction from the pain that was so close to the surface. She'd been surprised when Hayley had directed her so far out; in fact, she had begun to feel a little leery the farther they'd gone. She supposed that was why it was Hayley, because if she'd been riding with Quinn, she would have been a lot more nervous; for all his offering to help he was still a stranger.

At just the time she really began wondering if she'd made an awful mistake, they'd arrived here. They'd left the city limits of Redwood Cove and entered a more rural county area. The three-story green building was somewhat isolated in a clearing hidden by a thick stand of tall evergreens. The color blended with the trees, making it even harder to spot. There were no markings, not even a street number or name.

"Sometimes we make people unhappy with us," Hayley had explained. "So the less obvious we are, the better."

Off to one side was what looked to be a large warehouse, and on the far side of that, a flat concrete pad with markings painted on it, and an orange wind sock that had been barely stirring in the minimal breeze. A landing site for a helicopter.

"I would have thought you'd have an office in Seattle," she had said.

"Quinn picked this one, and he's not a city boy at heart," Hayley had answered.

No trace of the city here, Kayla thought now as she sat at the large table. The windows here in the top-floor meeting room were large, giving a full view of the rest of the clearing, the trees that ringed it and the sky above. Which was blue today, a clear early-summer day that made the long gray days of winter seem worth it.

Something moved in one of the trees, a large maple amid the firs. Kayla leaned forward, curious, and her breath caught when she realized it was a bald eagle. No, two of them, she thought, a pair, looking as if they were snuggling together on the sturdy branch.

"And that," Hayley said, "is one of the reasons Quinn set up on the third floor even though we're only using half of the first and the second not at all. They come here often."

That bit of information reassured her in a way nothing else could have; the idea of a man like Quinn choosing to situate his office up two flights of stairs just to watch birds—albeit glorious, magnificent birds—was somehow very comforting.

"Tell me about Dane."

Kayla stopped breathing altogether for a moment as the pain she'd quelled for a moment rushed back. Was she that easy to read? Or was Hayley just that perceptive? Probably both, she thought.

"He's obviously crazy about you," Hayley said.

"He was." Even Kayla could hear the ineffable sadness in her voice. Just the sound of it made her sadder still.

"And you?"

"I've loved him in one way or another since I was fourteen."

Hayley simply waited. Kayla sighed.

"That's when we moved here. I met Dane the next day. I climbed the tree between our houses and couldn't get down."

"So he is literally the boy next door?"

"He was then, yes. And he was…wonderful."

She hesitated. She didn't want to say anything that made them think badly of Chad, not when she was asking them to believe her and help prove him innocent, but she also couldn't not give Dane his due. He might have given up on her, on them, but she couldn't deny he'd stuck with her longer than anyone else would have, that he'd been there for her every step of the way until even his considerable patience ran out.

"He was like a brother at first," she said. "Only nicer." The subtext "compared to Chad" was there, and she guessed Hayley knew it, but she couldn't bring herself to say it aloud. Besides, didn't all siblings abuse each other in that familial sort of way? "Dane laughed with me, not at me, for being a skinny, bookish girl with braces. He knew how it felt to be the odd one. You wouldn't believe it now, but he was kind of a geeky-looking guy back then. People teased him, so he understood how I felt."

"He certainly grew up nicely."

She smiled. "Yes, he did. We kind of made a pact. To work on ourselves, but not to let them change who we were inside. We couldn't change other people, but we could change ourselves, challenge the stereotypes."

"That's pretty deep."

"That's the kind of thing we talked about. We used to have long, esoteric conversations about the state of the world and how to fix it, what era of time we'd like to go back to and why, that kind of thing. Even though he was a couple of years older, Dane never treated me like a dumb kid who didn't know anything."

She missed those days, she thought. And wondered if Dane did, too—missed those long talks about everything but themselves because they were fine and destined for a long, happy life together.

"So, you set out to what, change what people assumed?"

Kayla nodded. "Dane started working out and found he actually liked it. Pretty soon he was so fit and strong nobody bullied him to his face anymore. He could throw a football better than any guy in school, but no matter how much they recruited him he wasn't interested. That caught people's attention. He never changed who he was. He was still into computers, but he was making *that* cool."

"And you?"

"I swore I'd never be ashamed of being smart. Never try to hide it. I'd kind of started to do that because I thought the cool kids might like me better."

"It's been my experience," Hayley said with a wry smile, "that most of the 'cool kids' are in fact anything but."

Kayla laughed. "That's what Dane said."

"When did he stop being your surrogate brother?"

Kayla blushed. "I always had a crush on him. But he… well, I was just a kid. The difference between fourteen and sixteen is a lot bigger than sixteen and eighteen."

"Is that when it changed?"

"Sort of. At least, it started to, and then…my parents were killed."

"And Dane was there for you."

Kayla nodded. "Every minute. He never left my side. He took care of things I couldn't, did things I didn't have the presence of mind to even think of."

She fought off the memories, trying not to let them swamp

her. It didn't happen often anymore, but when it did, it was as fresh and vivid and horrible as if it had been yesterday.

She felt the warmth of a touch and realized Hayley had reached across the table to put her hand over hers.

"I can't imagine." Those vivid green eyes were fastened on her and full of warmth and concern. "That you're even upright is a testament to your strength."

"Dane used to think that," Kayla said with a sad smile. "Now I'm afraid he just thinks I'm crazy."

"Ten years is a long time." Hayley's voice was very even, and Kayla wondered how hard she was having to try to keep it that way.

"So I should give up on my brother?"

"I didn't say that. You are between the proverbial rock and a hard place."

"Chad has his flaws—I'm not blind—but he's no killer. I can't just quit on him. People say I should forget about it, but—"

"You can't."

"No."

"That's always irritated me," Hayley said, as casually as if they were discussing the weather, "when people say forget about it, put it out of your mind. Like the memory is a physical thing you could grab and shove in a box and hide. You can't. But you can reduce the time you spend on it, and the only thing that can do that is time."

"Dane says quit feeding it."

"Good way to put it. But it still takes time. You can not dwell on it, you can have other things ready to supplant it for when it pops into your mind, you can keep busy to distract yourself, but you have to do all that long enough that it recedes from the front of your mind. And you can't when these notes keep coming."

Kayla was so grateful Hayley seemed to understand that she felt her eyes begin to tear up.

"Thank you for understanding." Something occurred to her, and as she looked at Hayley's gentle smile—no wonder her Quinn adored her, she was wonderful—she decided to ask.

"You've been there, haven't you?"

"Yes. My mom died last year, of cancer. And my father was a cop. He was killed in the line of duty when I was twelve."

Kayla's breath caught. "How awful."

"That's how I know forgetting's not possible. Just like Quinn does."

"He…lost someone, too?"

"He was younger than you were. Just a little guy. His parents were both on that airliner a terrorist brought down—bombed—over Scotland in 1988."

Kayla gasped. "I remember my parents talking about that, on the anniversary of it, when I was little. They were horrified, all those innocent people. They thought it was one of the worst things that would ever happen."

"I wish they'd been right," Hayley said quietly.

The unmentioned memory, of the even more hideous attack that had happened thirteen years later hung between them for a moment.

"That was, in essence, the reason our foundation exists. When they turned the man who did it loose, the injustice of it, when those men in back rooms who had never suffered the loss made that decision, Quinn made one of his own."

"And started the Foxworth Foundation?"

Hayley nodded. Kayla understood.

"September 11 was one of the reasons we moved here," Kayla said. "My parents wanted to be out of the city. My mother couldn't even bear to look at a skyscraper, and my dad would stare at every jet that flew overhead until it was out of sight."

She stopped abruptly, the old, sad irony battering at her. She heard a bark from outside and wondered vaguely if it was Cutter.

"And two years later, they were dead anyway."

Hayley's words would have seemed cold, harsh even, had they not been spoken in such a gentle voice. And if they hadn't been exactly the words Kayla had been thinking herself.

She tried to pull herself together. Everything seemed so much closer to the surface than it had been for a while. It was like that whenever a note came, but she had to admit this was more. Because this time she was dealing with it without Dane's help, without his steadying presence, without his unwavering strength bolstering her.

"Yes. They were."

"What happened to you? At sixteen, you were too young to be on your own," Hayley said.

"My dad's sister happened, bless her. She took me in until I went off to college. Aunt Fay never had kids of her own, couldn't, but she loved me. She did her best, we got along great, she was fun and smart and the best thing that could have happened to me, under the circumstances."

"Dane," Hayley said.

"He was already in college by then. I—"

"No. I meant…" She gestured toward the door to the meeting room. Kayla turned.

He was here.

Chapter 6

Quinn, who had come into the room right behind Dane, signaled to Hayley and they left them alone to talk. It was, oddly, Cutter who seemed most reluctant to go. The dog, who had arrived with Quinn, lingered in the doorway, looking from Kayla to Dane as if he didn't want to leave them alone.

Maybe he thinks we'll start fighting, Kayla thought with a sigh.

But when Dane crossed the room and sat in the chair Hayley had vacated, she realized that, although he seemed tense, he wasn't angry. She could read his mood almost as well as her own, sometimes better, and he wasn't angry. Because he'd given up? Had he let all the anger go when he'd walked away?

"I checked them out," he said abruptly. "From what I could find, they seem to be who they say they are."

Kayla went still. If he no longer cared at all, surely he wouldn't have bothered, right? She didn't ask, mainly because she wasn't sure she wanted to hear the answer. She didn't know why he was here, and she didn't want to ask that either. Instead, she explained what Hayley had told her about the founding of Foxworth.

"So Quinn was a victim," Dane said.

She heard the musing note in his voice and understood; it was hard to picture today's strong, tough Quinn as any kind of victim.

"He was only ten," Kayla said. "And Hayley's father was a police officer who was killed when she was twelve."

He drew back slightly. "Is that why you trusted them both so quickly? You felt connected because of all that?"

"I didn't know all that then. But I knew they understood."

"And I don't."

"I didn't say that. I've never said that."

"But I'm lucky, right?" He was starting to sound confrontational. "I'm not a member of the club. I'm the only one here not damaged by tragedy."

She winced at the oblique reference to her counseling group. She'd called it Collateral Damage because that's what they were. Just as wounded as the actual victims, yet still up and walking around. She'd thought of Walking Wounded, but that didn't make the point she so strongly believed in— that the perpetrators didn't care who else they hurt. In war, it was an expected part of the grim business. But for civilians, it was the ugliest of side effects.

"Believe me, it's a club you don't want any part of." She took in a quick breath. "Besides, I always thought you'd been damaged by mine. Because you loved me."

As quickly as that, his demeanor changed. He let out a long, compressed breath.

"All right," he said. "If these people are as good as they say, maybe they can do something."

Her heart leaped in her chest, and hope sparked to renewed life.

"Dane!"

He reached across the table and took her hands in his. The touch, the contact, made joy well up inside her, as if some vital part of her had been restored.

"Listen to me, Kayla. I'm willing to give them a chance. Everything I've found indicates they are really good at what they do."

"Yes," she answered, tightening her fingers around his, feeling an elemental fear that if she didn't hang on, he would somehow vanish again. "Yes, I think they are. Maybe even the best. Hayley showed me some of their case records. No names, but—"

"Then if they can't find Chad, it's likely nobody can."

She saw suddenly where he was going. And knew his next words would require a decision from her. A difficult one. But nothing could be more difficult than his absence from her life the past two weeks.

"Yes," she finally said.

"Then if they can't, if this comes to nothing, will you quit making this the sole purpose of your life?"

She drew in a deep breath. She'd had a brief taste of life without him, and it had been immediately clear that it was worse, much worse, than life without knowing how and where Chad was. And she knew Dane, knew she'd pushed him to the edge, and that he was here now at all was a testament to the power of what they'd built together from the day he'd climbed up that tree to sit beside her. He'd understood her even then, that what she'd wanted, needed, wasn't someone to come along and rescue her, but someone to help her figure out how to rescue herself.

She knew what she would be promising if she said yes.

"I won't ever stop wondering, or worrying," she said, wanting it to be perfectly clear.

"I wouldn't expect you to. I just want to know that you won't obsess over it anymore, that you'll take back your own life. Our life, together."

He didn't say, "Or it's over," but the words hung in the air between them as clearly as if he had.

"Will you give them a real chance and enough time?"

"I'll give them a full, honest chance, if you'll agree to accept whatever they find."

Still feeling torn, she nevertheless gave the only answer she felt possible.

"All right," she said.

Dane let out an audible breath. And then he was on his feet, pulling her up and into his arms. Kayla nearly wept at the rightness of it. She clung to him, trembling at how close she'd come to losing this, losing him, forever.

She didn't know how long had passed before she heard a slight jingle from the doorway. She looked up and saw Cutter trotting into the room, tail up and waving slightly. The dog came to a stop before them and sat down. He looked at them both, with an expression Kayla would have sworn was satisfaction.

Quinn and Hayley followed the dog into the room.

"Why Cutter?" Kayla asked.

"He came with the name," Hayley said, reaching to scratch the dog's ear. "He turned up on my doorstep with only that tag. I tried but never could find out where he'd come from."

The dog tilted his head way back to look at Hayley without changing position, looking so comical as he did it that Kayla couldn't help but laugh. She heard Dane chuckle beside her and savored the sound of it; she'd missed his easy laugh, not just in the past two weeks but, she had to admit, for much longer. She'd caused that, she realized regretfully.

"I spent some time with a friend of mine this afternoon," Quinn said in a back-to-business tone as Hayley gestured everyone back into the chairs around the table. "Sam works for the local sheriff's office."

Kayla sank down into the chair Dane held for her, feeling suddenly wobbly. This all seemed to be happening quickly now that it had begun. She'd only met them this morning, yet Quinn was already on the move.

"The sheriff's office? But the Redwood Cove police handled the case."

"Yes, but the sheriff's office did most of the forensics. Redwood Cove doesn't have its own lab."

"Oh. Yes."

"Sam was able to pull up the reports for me, at least the basics. The locals trust this guy. He can get answers that others can't because of that."

"Meaning distraught, crazy family members?" Kayla knew she sounded bitter but couldn't help it.

"They never thought you were crazy. And if you were distraught, they knew you had good reason."

She sighed. "To be fair, they never said so. In fact, except for a couple who got sharp about it, told me they had their suspect and to give up, they were unfailingly kind. Even though I knew they hated to see me coming."

"Cops get that way when they can't help any more than they already have."

"But they could have. They could have looked for other suspects, they—"

She stopped herself before the whole, long, painfully familiar spiel unwound.

"You know what the evidence was," Quinn said gently. "It's pretty conclusive that Chad was in that room either during or shortly after the murders."

"The bloody fingerprint," Dane said.

Quinn nodded. "He's certain it was left while the blood was…"

Quinn's voice trailed off as he looked at Kayla.

"Still wet," she finished for him. "Fresh. I know. I've heard it a hundred times. I'm used to it."

"It's still awful," Hayley said. Her tone was comforting, but nothing made Kayla feel better than Dane's arm tightening around her.

"Yes. But I'm not going to fall apart talking about it. I really don't wallow it in every day."

She managed not to glance at Dane, although that wasn't

really fair; he'd never accused her of wallowing, only of letting this overwhelm her own life.

"I never disputed that Chad was there," she said. "He still came to the house often, even though he'd moved out. He'd sneak in through the den window and then head to the kitchen to get food."

"So you think that's what he intended that night? To raid the fridge?" Quinn asked.

She nodded. "And he found them lying there in the den, panicked and ran."

"Leaving you to deal alone, as usual," Dane said.

Kayla stiffened. Dane let out a compressed breath. "Sorry," he muttered. "I'll stop. I promised you one last shot, and I meant it."

Neither Quinn nor Hayley commented on the moment of tension, although Cutter let out a low whine as if he'd sensed it and didn't like it. After a moment, Quinn nodded.

"I'll need some things from you," he said. "Names of Chad's friends, his interests. Then the same about your parents."

Kayla frowned slightly. "That was all in the reports."

Quinn smiled. "Sam bends the rules occasionally, but letting those reports leave the building without me jumping through all the hoops would be outright breakage. That we'll have to do through regular channels."

"Sorry," Kayla said. "Of course."

"Plus, I'd like to save bugging the local LEOs for things we can't get anywhere else. They're a bit understaffed."

"Back at the time, they were thinking about dissolving the department and going back to contracting with the sheriff because they were so strapped and short-handed," Dane said. "Maybe that's partly why they didn't pour a lot of energy into this after Chad ran."

Kayla wanted to hug him for that; it was the most support-ive thing he'd said lately.

"I know once they verified where I'd been at the time of the murders," Dane went on, "they didn't have time to talk to me much."

"Except when you'd push them, for me."

He deserved that acknowledgment, Kayla thought. For a long time, longer than most would, Dane had been right there with her, at the forefront, pushing, nagging, pressing the po-lice. Dane gave her a smile that further warmed a heart that had been nearly frozen by his departure two weeks ago. He'd really asked so little of her, she thought. And she'd abused that.

"It got so they hated to see us coming," Dane said.

"Can't blame them," Quinn said. "It's a small department, they've got a huge case on their hands and they have no re-sources or experience dealing with that kind of thing. Sam said Detective Adams was a good guy, but he was out of his depth on this. And by the time he asked for help, what trail there was had gone cold."

"He knows that," Kayla said quietly. "He admitted that to me last year, when he retired. He feels guilty about it."

Dane gave her a sideways look. "You never told me that."

"You didn't want to hear anything about it by then," Kayla said, carefully keeping any sort of accusation out of her voice; Dane was back at her side, and she simply had to keep him there. She knew that now, that nothing mattered more.

"I'll need the same info from you, too," Quinn said to Dane. "Anything and everything you can remember."

Dane nodded.

"And no comparing lists," Hayley said. "You each have your own memories and viewpoint, and we need them as pure as possible."

Kayla nodded, although the words made her a little nervous. Dane and Chad's mutual dislike was going to color Dane's recollections. But he was doing it, cooperating, which was more than she'd had this morning. She didn't ever want to feel that alone again.

She would keep her promise as Dane was keeping his, she vowed. She would pour all she had into this last-ditch effort, she would do whatever Quinn and Hayley said was necessary and, in the end, she would accept the results.

And then, she swore silently, she would do what Dane had wanted her to do for a very long time now.

She would move on.

Chapter 7

All the way back to her house, Kayla fought the memories
stirred up by spending two hours writing down everything
she could think of—the name of every one of Chad's friends,
descriptions of those she couldn't remember the names of,
every place he used to hang out and putting a star on the most
frequent, even listing the times he'd gotten in trouble and with
whom. She didn't want to sugarcoat anything.

Dane had commented on that, when he'd seen her list after
finishing his own, shorter one and going over it with Quinn;
Hayley had taken Cutter outside for a run while they worked.
Kayla had been grateful for that; the dog was almost spooky
in the way he looked at them, the way he seemed to sense
every change, every shift in mood, and understand it in a way
that had to be impossible for a dog.

"You told them about when he got arrested twice," Dane
had said.

"Yes." She'd stood up to face him. "Once, all I wanted was
to prove Chad innocent. Now I just want the truth."

Dane had blinked, clearly startled. "When did that happen?"

"About two weeks ago," she had said, knowing he'd understand. "Everything changed two weeks ago."

They'd agreed at the Foxworth facility that they'd spend
some time searching their memories for anything they might
have forgotten, any additional details that might help.

She pulled into her driveway now and for a moment just sat there.

She had considered, seriously, that she might have to sell her beloved little house. She'd bought it with the cash from the sale of her parents' home, a place she had known she could never set foot in again. She didn't want to move again, but she didn't think she could bear to live here without Dane. They weren't living together in the usual sense—he still had his place, but he also ran his business out of the den, and the work tended to spill over into the rest of the house. So he spent most nights here unless he was on a major project and working eighteen-hour days.

That boy'll go far. He's not afraid of hard work.

Her father's words echoed in her head. As did his tone, touched with a sadness it had taken her a few years to figure out was over not being able to say that about his own son.

Her father had liked Dane, although that hadn't stopped him from keeping a close watch when Kayla had been younger. But he'd soon been convinced Dane looked at her like a little sister, and sadly, he was a much better protector than Chad was, standing up for her more than once when those who thought her too studious and odd started harassing her.

And then Dane was there, pulling his compact SUV in beside her, and her world snapped back into balance. For a moment the relief that he was back swamped her, making it impossible for her to move.

He waved at her next-door neighbor, Mr. Reyes, who was out working in his yard as usual. The man called out a cheerful hello and went back to trimming his hedge. It was a measure of how distracted she was, Kayla supposed, that she hadn't even noticed him there.

Dane came over and opened her driver's door.

"You okay?"

"I will be," she said, meaning it.

But when they got inside, it didn't take long for her improved outlook to be shaken. She noticed first one thing, then another, ran to the bedroom then the bathroom and finally turned on him.

"Your things are gone."

He didn't deny the obvious. "Yes."

"They weren't this morning."

"I knew you'd be gone this morning so I came over and got them. I didn't want to fight."

The same sort of creeping chill that had overtaken her when she'd realized he was serious this time began to envelop her again. He really had left her. He'd packed up all of the things that had gradually made their way over here—toothbrush, clothes, books, razor, the laptop he kept here in case something came up that was too much to handle on his tablet, all of it was gone. The reality pounded at her in a way it hadn't when his familiar things were still there, and she realized she hadn't really accepted it, investing hope in those inanimate objects, hope that he didn't really mean it.

Now she knew he had. And was thankful he hadn't done it before.

"Then why," she said when she thought she could speak without her voice wobbling, "did you show up at the post office?"

He didn't dodge that either. But then, this was Dane, who was utterly honest, forthright and occasionally blunt. As he was now.

"This," he said, reaching into the watch pocket of his jeans and pulling out the square gold key that had been on his key ring since the day she'd given it to him five years ago.

A shiver went through her. "Dane—"

He waved a hand. "Let's not. We're going to deal with this, give it our best shot, and then…then we'll see where we are."

Slowly, reluctantly, she nodded. She wanted to know now, wanted to hear him say he was back, that things would be fine, that they would pick up their old, familiar life.

He didn't say any of it.

He's an honest one. Doesn't just tell you want you want to hear. I admire that.

Again her father's voice echoed in her head, as clearly as if he were standing beside her.

And she wondered if she'd really gotten Dane back at all.

Dane watched as she turned the pages of the old scrapbook she'd dug out of a box in the back closet. It seemed a good idea, to help stir any memories that might help.

He'd seen it before, had gone through it himself, because he wanted to know everything about her and loved seeing the early pictures of a wide-eyed, dark-haired pixie who had seemingly faced the world with an endless wonder.

There were several of her and her brother together, with Kayla generally staring up at him adoringly while Chad looked annoyed and sullen. They were eighteen months apart, Dane knew, and he'd often wondered if things would have been different, if Chad would have acted differently toward her, if it had been more.

She turned another page and there was the photograph he'd been waiting to see. Kayla, now a brand-new junior, off to her first school dance. A worldly high school graduate himself now, about to leave for college, he'd come by to return a borrowed book that evening and found her father chuckling over the fact that she and her mother had been holed up all afternoon, preparing.

But when Kayla, barely sixteen, had come down the stairs, Dane wasn't chuckling at all. His odd, shy, bookish, tree-sitting buddy was nowhere in sight. Instead he saw a young, slender woman with graceful curves highlighted by the fitted, strapless, shimmery dress she wore. Her hair was smoothed into a sleek sweep, her eyes seemed huge and luminous, her mouth touched with a color that made him wonder what it would be like to kiss it off.

And that had taken his breath away.

She'd come to a halt at the bottom of the stairs and given him an impish smile.

"Did it work?" she asked.

"I— What?"

He knew he sounded like he felt—gobsmacked.

"I promised you I was going to play the game, do all the girly stuff, just to show them I could if I wanted to."

"Kayla." It was all he could get out, even though she was suddenly looking anxious.

"It's like we talked about," she said, the anxiety echoing in her voice. "Show them I can, then when I don't, they know it's because I don't *want* to. My choice. Just like you did, making the football team, getting everybody fired up about how good you are, then walking away because it was your choice not to play their game."

"And that had its down side, if you recall." He'd proved his point, but he hadn't realized some would take it as dissing the whole school by not wanting to play for the team that represented them.

"But they respected you," Kayla had said. "That's all I want."

He didn't remember now what he'd finally said to ease her nerves. But he'd made her smile, reassured, so it had worked. And he spent the remainder of his own evening reminding himself she was still his young, very smart, annoyingly honest and perceptive sounding board. And he was still the boy next door to her, her sounding board in turn, sometimes her protector, but always her listener.

"Dane?"

He snapped out of his reverie.

"I remember that night," he said, unable to help or care that his voice was a little husky. "Two years seemed so little separation and yet so long."

"I didn't ask you to wait until I was eighteen."

"Anything else seemed a little too…predatory to me."

For a moment she just looked at him, and then she smiled, that slow, dawning Kayla smile that always reminded him that there was warmth in the world, no matter how cold it might seem at any given moment.

"You were—and are—a gallant man, Dane Burdette."

Her use of the old-fashioned term made him smile in turn, even though he hadn't felt in the least gallant at the time. Only his vow to wait until she was eighteen had made his new-found appreciation of her as a woman acceptable. Where his eighteen-year-old self had found the will to wait he wasn't sure, although he was ruefully aware that the stigma of dating a high school girl when you'd graduated had played a bigger part than he'd like to admit. With Kayla's support he had flouted the expected norms with some success, but he had found himself unable to get past that bit of peer pressure. And he'd harbored the notion that maybe, if he put her off-limits, he'd just get over her in that two years.

He hadn't.

And then three months after that dance her parents were dead, changing both their lives forever, and self-control was no longer an issue. He would no more risk further damage to her already shattered soul than he would cut off his own arm. He'd shoved his newly awakened awareness of her into a cage and locked it, setting out to be what she needed and only what she needed—a strong shoulder, a comforting ear and a safe place to be.

He'd succeeded, he thought.

He'd just never expected to be in essentially the same place ten years later.

Chapter 8

Kayla woke up screaming. And alone.

The nightmares had, thankfully, become rare. But when they came, they were as vivid and terrifying as ever. And real, all of it—walking into the dark den, hearing the odd squish of the carpet, reaching for the light switch, then wishing she hadn't as the scene flashed into being before her stunned eyes.

Normally Dane was there to hold her, easing her out of the remembered horror gently, not pushing her, not giving her meaningless platitudes, not telling her it would be all right when it never could be, but simply holding her, his strength and understanding flowing to her as if there were a direct connection between them.

But Dane was not here.

He had left early last evening, refusing to settle right back into the routine they had developed over the years. She supposed she should feel hurt, but she was more scared than anything. This further evidence that things weren't the same had rattled her. He was back, and yet he wasn't. It pounded home to her anew that their relationship had been damaged.

Shaking, she reached for her phone. She knew it was late, after midnight, but she couldn't help it—she had to hear his voice. If he was angry that she'd woken him up, so be it.

He answered on the first ring and sounded anything but asleep.

A possibility hit her, biting deep. It was Friday night. And until today, until the Foxworth Foundation had been brought into things, Dane had been through with her.

A date. Had he been out on a date? Was that why he'd insisted on leaving early? Had he already started seeing someone else? He would never have cheated on her; she knew that as surely as she knew his eyes were golden. It just wasn't in him. But he'd told her he was done two weeks ago. Enough time to ask someone else out. More than enough time if he'd already known her, whoever she was.

And whoever she was, she likely had a much simpler life, free of trauma and tragedy. Dane would probably find that wonderfully refreshing, and—

"Kayla?"

Stop it, she ordered herself. Get a grip. "I'm sorry," she said into the phone. "I know it's late."

"Did you think of something?"

It took her a moment to realize what he meant, and the only thing that stopped her from letting out the sound that rose in her throat was the fear it would sound like some crazed woman's maniacal laughter.

"No, but I learned that there's something worse than my old nightmare."

His voice changed then. Went softer, gentler. "You had it again?"

"Yes."

"Not surprising. A lot of old memories were stirred up today."

"Are you one of them?"

"What?" He sounded puzzled now.

"An old memory."

"I know that nightmare shakes you up, but what are you talking about?"

"Did you have a date tonight?"

"What?"

"You insisted on leaving. It's Friday night. It's after midnight and you're wide awake."

She heard him let out a long breath. "So you decided I was out on a date? That's three facts and an awful lot of supposition."

"Not decided. Wondered."

He answered her in typical Dane fashion: honestly and a bit bluntly. "That it's Friday has nothing to do with anything. I'm not there because I'm not sure you can really leave this behind if the results they get aren't what you want, and I'm not going to lay myself out for that kind of pain again. And I'm awake because, damn it, I miss you and can't stop thinking about you."

And in those few words, spoken with an edge in his voice, he blasted Kayla's silly panic to bits.

"Oh."

Her voice sounded tiny even to her. For a long moment, silence hung in the air between them.

"I promised you I would move on after they find…whatever they find."

"I know you did."

"You think I didn't mean it?"

"You've spent ten years on this quest. It's been a huge part of your life—it's sunk into your bones. So I think promising now, and really letting go when it's over, are two different things."

She couldn't deny a single word he said. Nor could she think of a single thing to say that would convince him she'd meant what she'd said.

Maybe he was right. Maybe when the time came, she wouldn't be able to just let it go.

"I'm sorry about the nightmare." He sounded cooler now, less on edge.

"It's all right. Like I said, I found out there's something worse—waking up to the reality that you're gone."

There was a pause before he said quietly, "I just can't slide right back into life as before, Kayla."

"I'm going to start now," she said. Her voice still seemed a little shaky, so she added some emphasis. "Right now."

"Start what?"

"Wrapping my mind around the idea—the fact—that when this is over, if they don't find him, I'm done. I'll always wonder and worry, but I won't lose you over him. Chad's my brother, but you're my life."

Her voice had gotten stronger as she went. As had her resolve.

"I love you," Dane said after a moment.

"I know," she said. "Or you would have walked away long ago."

It was an admission she'd never made to him before, although she'd often thought it, often wondered why he hadn't left her to find somebody without all her baggage. She'd never dared speak it, for fear it might make it really happen. But now that it had, she felt compelled to speak the words.

Now she had to live up to them.

Dane leaned back against the pillow he'd tossed on the end of the sofa in his living room. He'd given up on the bed around eleven, laughing ruefully at himself.

"Can't live with her, can't sleep without her," he'd muttered just before his phone had rung. He'd grabbed it, needing to hear her voice, answering before he remembered he'd sworn not to jump right back into the life he wasn't sure yet had changed at all.

Amazing how one phone call could make everything feel so different. She'd been different, sounded different. And in a good way for him.

...there is something worse than my old nightmare.

He couldn't even begin to describe the feeling that gave him. When he'd walked away he'd been afraid that she would simply go on, filling in whatever empty place he left behind with her quest, perhaps even welcoming his absence so she could focus on it completely.

When it came right down to it, he'd never been sure how big a place he had in her mind and heart. If it was bigger than Chad. Selfish, maybe. But true. He knew she loved him; the question that had always nagged at him was how much.

At the same time, he'd felt he was being unfair. What was she supposed to do—just go on with her life as if her brother had never existed?

He rolled over, punching the pillow with more force than was necessary. He wished now he'd stayed. But the part of him that had been ripped open when he'd finally walked away was still raw, and his fear was real.

He only realized he'd finally fallen asleep when his cell rang and woke him. His pulse jumped, but when he looked at the screen before answering it wasn't Kayla's number.

"Dane? Quinn Foxworth."

"Oh."

He sat up. The crazy thought hit him that they'd already found Chad. He glanced at the time on his phone. Nine-fifteen. The realization that they'd been on the ten-year-old case barely twenty-four hours steadied him.

"I woke you?"

"Sorry. Rough night."

"I can call back—"

"No, no. It's okay. What did you want?"

"I needed to ask you about something. On your list, you said Chad used to hang out with a chop shop guy."

Dane rubbed at his eyes. "Yeah. That's where he met Rod. Rumor was the guy had a place over on Raccoon Bay, an old barn he used. Can't remember his name, but when Chad got nailed for joyriding, I thought maybe it was more than just that."

"You thought maybe he was stealing the car?"

"I wondered."

"Did you tell the police?"

"Not that I suspected Rod. I told them Chad was friends with the guy. They went from there. But they said later they couldn't find any proof Chad had meant to actually steal the car." He felt compelled to be fair and added, "And he was heading back toward where the car had been when they stopped him."

"Did Kayla know?"

"I don't know if she knew Chad hung with the guy sometimes. I never said anything to her about it—she was already touchy enough."

"She truly loves her brother."

"Yeah." Dane hesitated, then asked, "You have any brothers or sisters?"

"One."

"I don't. I figure maybe that's why I don't get it. Maybe I really don't understand."

"It's like any family thing," Quinn said. "Different depending on the people. I've come across some siblings who hate each other fiercely. And some who merely coexist without much interest in each other."

"What about you?"

"I'd die for Charlie," Quinn said simply.

No, Dane thought after he disconnected the call, maybe he just didn't get it. He tried to picture what he'd do if Kayla was accused of something he was certain she hadn't done, but it was a different kind of thing. He thought of Sergei, who had been his friend for years, and helped him start Sound Digital Video. What if he was accused of hacking a bank or something even worse? The idea was laughable. Serge might sneak his way into the hottest gaming company around, but nothing more.

But he tried to imagine the scenario. If Serge vanished after the crime, how would he feel? What would he do? To what lengths would he go to find him and help him?

A long way, he thought. But ten years of unrelenting searching?

It was, Dane thought as he wearily headed for the shower, a lousy comparison. Serge was a good friend but not a brother. And the crime wasn't some computer hacking but a literal hacking, the slaughter of two people.

He thought of his own parents then, all they'd done for him, given him, how they'd supported him, believed in him, even given him a loan to keep SDV going until it started gaining some traction in a crowded field. The day he'd paid them back was one of the best of his life. They were proud of him—he knew that. And he loved them both. It was one of the reasons he'd lasted as long as he had with Kayla's quest. He couldn't imagine losing them both and in such a horrible way. If he'd had a brother, maybe he couldn't believe he could kill two loving people like that either.

He knew not all parents were as good as his—his were living proof of the old joke about how the older you got, the smarter your parents seemed to get—but Kayla's, from what he remembered, hadn't been bad, although he'd thought they favored their son a bit too much.

Which made what Chad was accused of doing make even less sense.

Hot water streamed over him, and he felt a bit more awake. He finished quickly; he had an online meeting today with an app developer in Nevada who wanted a video for an upcoming trade show.

He was just pulling on his socks when his phone rang

again. His pulse kicked up, but a quick glance showed the smiling picture of his mother, one he'd taken a couple of years ago at their thirtieth wedding anniversary. Odd how that happened sometimes—he'd think about them and then they'd call, or he'd call and his mom or dad would say they'd just been thinking about him.

He reached for the phone, thankful he hadn't told his folks about his decision to leave Kayla so now he didn't have to explain why he was back. His mother had been telling him, gently and with love, that perhaps he should find someone more willing to focus on him than the past. She cared for Kayla, but she loved her son and wanted him to find the kind of happiness she had with his father.

His answer had always been that he was happy. He loved Kayla and admired her loyalty to her brother. But in some part of his mind he was agreeing. He wanted someone who wasn't caught up by the past, who was focused on a future with him.

Problem was, he wanted that person to be Kayla, and he hadn't been ready to give up on that.

Until two weeks ago.

And now?

What happened now, he thought as he prepped himself to sound cheerful to his mother, depended on Kayla.

And Quinn Foxworth and his crew.

Chapter 9

Dane tapped his fingers idly on the restaurant table as he waited for Kayla.

She was trying. Truly making an effort. Dane could see that. Whenever she wasn't working, she was pushing for them to be together. She called him regularly, texted him and told him she loved him so often that the ache inside started to ease up. This was the way he'd always wanted it to be. He should be happy. He was happy. He'd be delirious if it wasn't for the nagging question of how long this would last.

She rarely mentioned Chad or even the Foxworth Foundation. He knew she was likely in regular contact with Quinn and Hayley, but she said nothing. Had there been no developments, or was she just not telling him?

He nearly laughed aloud at himself.

You can't have it both ways, he told himself. You either want her to talk about it, or you don't want to hear it. That's a conflict you can't resolve by updating drivers or getting new hardware.

That sort of humming awareness he had whenever she was around suddenly kicked into high gear. Oddly, he thought of Cutter and how the dog not only knew someone was coming, but also who. Maybe the dog really was more human than canine.

Or maybe you're more dog, he thought wryly.

Whichever, his instincts were right because a moment

later he saw her coming down the aisle of the restaurant toward him.

There wasn't a trace of the gawky, skinny girl from the tree branch in the lovely, graceful woman approaching. Her hair, cut in that way that made it sweep forward in a smooth curve just at her jawline, made him want to see it tousled from his hands and a night of passion again. The gray silk blouse tucked into black slacks emphasized the curves he knew so well. Need cramped his body, and he had to consciously suck in a breath to get any air at all. He barely managed to stand as she came to a stop beside the table.

"I'm not late, am I?"

She sounded anxious, and he shook his head, still unable to speak for a moment. She slid her bag—he'd always thought that huge thing she carried too large to be called merely a purse—off her shoulder and settled into the chair he held for her.

He was breathing again, albeit a bit deeply.

"How was work?" he asked, taking refuge in small talk.

"Sad."

He barely managed not to say, "Isn't it always?"

Kayla's grief counseling service for crime victims and their friends and families was thorough, coordinating and running group meetings of survivors, arranging appointments with therapists and often personally contacting people she thought could benefit from their services. It was the brainchild of Kayla herself and a wealthy private benefactor who had been in need years ago but there had been nothing of the kind available, nothing with this kind of specific focus. So the woman had channeled the money left to her by her murdered husband into this idea and hired Kayla to run it.

And Kayla was great at it—he knew that, just as he knew it was work that was much needed.

He was also convinced that it was part of the reason she

had never been able to move on from her own tragedy. He didn't doubt that, as she told him, it helped her to help others who lived with the same kind of grief, but it also meant she was immersed in it every day. He would never ask her to quit—and if he did she'd probably have been the one to walk away—but he wished she could find a little more balance. But it didn't appear she saw the irony of someone who'd never quite gotten over her own grief counseling others.

"A new arrival?"

"No. I didn't mean sad like that. Sad because Mr. Egland is leaving."

He quickly placed the name. "That's the older guy whose wife died in the arson fire?"

She nodded. "He's going back home to Texas."

"I thought you talked him out of that."

"We talked him out of making the decision when he was so torn up with grief he wasn't thinking straight. Now he's calmer, more rational, and we all agreed it was the best thing for him to be close to the rest of his family."

He caught the undertone in her voice. "But you'll miss him."

"Yes. He's a very sweet man."

"You get so involved with them, Kayla." They'd had this discussion before, but he couldn't seem to help himself. "And then it hurts you when they move on."

"But it makes me proud, too. Proud of what we do."

"You should be," he agreed. "I just wish it wasn't so consuming."

"Actually," she said, her voice a tad too casual, "I've been thinking of cutting back a little."

"What, to ten-hour days instead of twelve?"

"Look who's talking, mister I'll-just-work-a-little-more-on-that-project-tonight-even-though-it's-midnight."

Dane lowered his gaze. She knew him too well. One of the

reasons they had ended up living at her place was because he had this habit of coming up with the perfect solution to a problem right around that midnight hour. At his place, all he needed to do to go back to work was walk down the hall to the den. And then he would be sucked in for hours.

It was a habit he'd slipped back into in the two weeks they'd been apart, if for no other reason than it was the only way he could avoid the pain for a little while.

"What if we both cut back?" he suggested, figuring because she was trying so hard not to make everything about this new search for Chad, he could at least make an effort, too.

"And give the time to us? I like that idea," she said, so heartfelt his doubts receded. And when she reached across the table to take his hand, he felt as if all the pain and sadness of the past two weeks—hell, of the past two years—fell away.

"We're so damn good together, Kayla," he said softly.

"Yes. We always have been. And I took that for granted. I'm sorry."

And with that quiet, heartfelt apology, Dane felt a flood of renewed love and hope. They would make it, he thought. Foxworth would find what they found, or they would not find anything, but it didn't matter.

They would make it.

"Tonight was wonderful," Kayla said, meaning it with all her heart.

"It was. The salmon was great."

"I didn't mean the food."

"I know."

She realized then that he felt as awkward as she did, standing on her doorstep—what had been *their* doorstep—and feeling unsure about what would happen next.

She knew what she wanted to happen. She just didn't know how to go about getting it. She was afraid to assume he was ready to pick up where they'd left off, no matter how much she wanted exactly that.

She looked up at him, and he met her gaze steadily. With that knowledge borne of years of loving this man, she knew that although the decision was his, the asking must come from her. For a moment she wrestled with how to say it, then finally remembered this was Dane, and with Dane the best way was always upfront and honest.

"Will you stay?"

The simple question hung in the air for a moment, and Kayla would have sworn her heart had stopped beating in the silence. Was it that hard a decision for him? Had she lost him after all?

Then he let out a long breath.

And smiled. That lovely Dane smile she so loved.

They were going to be all right.

It wasn't like nothing had changed because things had. The bedroom was the same, but they weren't. She was a little thinner—eating had been the last thing on her mind when he was gone. The fact that he was too heartened her somehow; she'd had a vision in her mind of him going on happily, glad to be relieved of the burden of her baggage.

But it was more than that. It was the way he carefully, slowly undressed her, caressing each inch of skin revealed as if he'd never seen it before. She understood because every bit of him, broad shoulders, powerful arms, the cords of his neck, was newly precious to her. He'd even stopped her after she'd pulled off his shirt, when her fingers would have gone to the top button of his jeans.

He was handling her as if they'd never been together. As if it was that first night, when she'd turned twenty-one.

She had thought she would want to hurry. She'd been aching for him every moment since he'd walked out. She'd imagined, if this ever happened again, that they would be wildly hungry from the time apart. But now—

As she put her hands on his shoulders to try to pull him closer, he released her bra and gently, almost reverently cupped her breasts. Her breath caught. For a moment that seem liked forever he simply held her, as if he were savoring the feel of soft flesh rounding into his hands.

That halted breath escaped in a low moan as, at last, he brushed his thumbs over her nipples. Her hands slid help-lessly downward, gripping the solid muscle of his upper arms as she swayed. Still he moved slowly, so slowly, and finally she understood.

He was seducing her all over again, not because she was unwilling, but in case she had forgotten how unutterably good they were together.

His presence, she realized as at last he let her work down his zipper as he did the same with hers, wasn't the only thing she'd taken for granted. She'd taken this for granted, this hot, physical connection. It had been this way since the beginning and hadn't faded at all in five years. He could still make her shiver from across a room, and she knew, with a quiet, femi-nine sort of pride, that she did the same to him.

"This is forever, Kayla," he'd said that first night. "No turning back. Are you sure?"

"Is that why you made us wait?" she'd asked.

"You needed to be old enough to know for sure what you want."

"I've known since I was fourteen," she'd told him.

It had been nothing less than the truth. She'd loved him since the day, instead of insisting on helping her out of that tree, he'd climbed up to join her. And instead of helping her get down, he'd inspected possible routes, told her which one he himself would use, and then let her do it herself.

Now, she owed him this, she thought as they at last went

down to the bed in a tangle. No more protests or pleas for him to move faster, to satiate the hunger that had been building. She gave herself up to his hands, his mouth. This would be at his pace, but all the while she knew his goal was to drive her mad with need, and in the end her pleasure would be as great if not greater than his. Because this was Dane, and he knew her, knew how to touch her, to kiss her, to take her exactly as she wanted to be taken.

And the next time, because now she was sure there would be one, she would return the favor, calling up everything she'd learned of him, of what he liked, to make sure he would be the one driven mad. She would show him she understood, that she knew what they'd nearly lost, how rare and special it was.

And then he was easing into her, hot and hard, slow and taunting, and rational thought fled. Her body arched in eager anticipation as he slid home bit by bit, and the low groan that broke from him, the first sign he wasn't as completely in control as he'd seemed, made her every muscle clench.

He lifted his head, looked straight into her eyes. "Don't throw this away, Kayla."

She tightened her arms around him. "No more taking for granted," she said.

Her words were apparently what he'd needed to hear because he abandoned all efforts at teasing slowness and began to move with an urgency that was no less compelling. Kayla gave herself up to the driving stroke of his body, let slip all restraint and reveled in the sweet, delicious fact that he was hers again.

For now.

Chapter 10

This time Kayla smiled when she saw the dog racing out to greet them. He seemed delighted to see his new friends. In fact, when he skidded to a stop in front of them and looked from her to Dane and back again, he seemed delighted not just to see them, but to see them together.

"Cutter, you are a very different dog," Dane said, reaching down to scratch his ear.

"Isn't he?" Kayla said, glad she wasn't the only one who saw it. "Hayley says sometimes she thinks he's more human than dog. But smarter."

Dane laughed. It was a good sound, one that gave her hope.

They headed toward the building. Quinn had called Kayla and asked her to meet him here. She had called Dane, who insisted on coming with her, as she knew he would. He'd made a promise that he would see this through with her, and Dane always kept his promises.

They started to turn on the gravel path that led to the main door of the building, but the dog cut them off. Then he trotted a few steps to their right, away from the door and along the path that led to the warehouse. He stopped and looked over his shoulder at them.

"I've been here before," Kayla said. "That's what started this."

"What?"

She realized she hadn't really told Dane what had happened that morning. It had sounded so silly, the idea that the dog had purposely snatched Chad's note and carried it off to the very people who were helping her now. She'd been afraid he'd dismiss the whole thing out of hand; Dane was a very practical and sometimes literally minded guy. And in retrospect, it sounded silly even to her.

"He...sort of led me to them," she said. "I thought he was just playing, but now I'm not so sure."

Cutter gave a short bark, walked a few more steps, stopped and looked back at them once more.

"Led you like this, you mean?" Dane asked.

"Yes." She sighed. If she couldn't tell him the truth, what hope was there for them anyway? "I'd thrown away Chad's note. He took it right out of the trash can and did this until I followed him to Quinn."

She expected him to say something about her being silly or fantasizing, expected him maybe even to tease her for thinking the dog had humanlike intelligence. He did neither.

"You threw it away?"

She knew him well enough to understand. And after last night, she knew he needed, deserved, to hear it. "I did. I wadded it up and tossed it. It wasn't worth what it had cost me."

He let out a long, compressed sigh.

At that moment, Cutter apparently lost patience with their lack of attention. Or their stupidity, Kayla thought. The dog trotted back and circled behind them. He didn't quite nip at their heels, but he nudged them both pointedly.

"I guess we'd better cooperate," Dane said.

His voice sounded strange, and she couldn't tell if he was sorry the conversation had been interrupted or if he was relieved. He wasn't like other guys she knew of from her friends, often dodging anything that could be described as serious discussion of the relationship. Those friends envied her the way she and Dane were always able to talk. But despite last night, things weren't usual between them now and hadn't been for a long time.

"I love you."

It burst from her as her mind seized on the declaration as the one most important thing to say right now.

"I love you, too," he said. "Enough to give us this one last chance."

The finality in his voice told her he meant what he said. Last night had been a reminder of what she was risking. For all his easygoing nature and his tremendous patience, there was a line Dane would not be pushed past, and she had reached it. She had made promises she intended to keep, but she'd be the first to admit that if they found Chad—

Dane stopped dead in the open doorway of the warehouse, where Cutter had led them.

"Whoa."

The man who had been tinkering with something on the sleek, black helicopter inside spun around, his right hand whipping to his side. For an instant Kayla's breath caught; he'd moved like he was used to having a gun there. But then he noticed Cutter and went from alert and primed to relaxed and smiling.

"A little warning would be good, buddy," he said to the dog who trotted toward him. The dog made a strange noise that sounded oddly like a snort of disgust. "Yeah, yeah, they're friendlies. I get it."

He walked toward them then. "Hi. You must be Kayla and Dane. I'm Teague Johnson."

He held out a hand. Kayla took it, noticing that while he didn't have a crushing grip, he didn't treat her like she was some delicate flower who would crumple at a solid clasp, either. Still, she noticed when he then shook Dane's hand, it was firmer. A guy thing, she thought.

And he was definitely a guy. From his buzz-cut sandy-brown hair to his battered leather jacket to his jeans with a hole in one knee, he was a guy. There was something about him, in the way he stood, the way he carried himself, that made her wonder, as she had with Quinn, if he'd been in the military. If so, it had to have been recently; he looked young.

"Nice," Dane said, gesturing at the helicopter. There was an undertone of awed appreciation in his voice.

"That it is," Teague agreed with a crooked grin that made Kayla smile in turn. "Quinn's newest toy. He got tired of trying to arrange transport when we needed to move in a hurry."

"And he can afford that?" Dane asked.

Teague laughed, apparently not hearing, or at least not reacting to, the faintly suspicious note in Dane's voice. But Kayla wasn't sure anyone who didn't know him as she did would notice.

"Thanks to Charlie, our resident financial genius, the Foxworth Foundation can afford a lot. What we do isn't always cheap."

"So you work for Quinn?"

"I'm part of his team, yes," Teague said. "Lately he's been letting me fly this baby."

"That's nice," Kayla said as she looked at the aircraft. She supposed it was nice, to him. "They make me a little nervous. I've never flown in one, and I hope to keep it that way."

"Well, if you don't like this, we have a pretty little blue and white airplane out at the airstrip," Teague said.

"Charlie must be really good," Dane said dryly.

Cutter gave a low sound and darted away, drawing their attention for a moment.

"Quinn," Teague said.

"What?"

"That was his Quinn sound. He must be back."

"You're saying he has different sounds for different people?"

"For Quinn and Hayley he does. Hayley's is a happy bark. Quinn's is that rumble. Me and the guys, we have to share one. Except Rafe. For some reason he gets his own." The crooked grin flashed again. "I swear, that dog isn't really a dog. I'm not sure what he is, except he's part of the team."

Kayla liked that. Liked that the dog was apparently accepted and welcomed by all. It made her feel better about them somehow.

"What happened there?" she asked, pointing to what looked like a patch of some kind that marred the sleek black surface.

"Same thing that happened there," Teague said cheerfully, indicating an odd, ragged hole farther back that she hadn't noticed yet.

"That looks like a bullet hole," Dane said.

"It is. That one doesn't affect anything, so Quinn wanted to keep it. Sort of a souvenir."

Kayla stared incredulously. "A souvenir? A bullet hole as a souvenir?"

"It's from the mission where he met Hayley," Teague explained.

That bit of information startled her and, oddly, warmed her a little. It was a strange feeling.

"Did she shoot at you?" Kayla asked.

Teague laughed. "She would have if she'd been armed, I think. We did sort of kidnap her."

Kayla gasped. Dane, perversely, laughed. "Now that's a story I'd like to hear."

"Some other time."

Quinn's voice came from behind them, and they turned to see him entering the warehouse, Cutter trotting at his side.

"Right now," he went on as he and the dog came to a halt beside them, "we need to talk about a possible lead."

Kayla's breath caught. "To Chad?" she said, then felt silly; what else?

"It may amount to nothing, and I warn you, it's not fresh, but it's the first thing we've turned up."

Kayla felt the old, eternal hope rise within her. And as they walked back toward the main building, she reached down to scratch behind Cutter's right ear in silent thanks. The dog made a soft, yowling little noise that sounded for all the world like encouragement.

Kayla shook her head in wonder. Maybe Teague was right, and he wasn't really just a dog.

She didn't know how or why this had happened, but she felt heartened about her brother for the first time in a long time, and for that she had to thank this furry conspirator.

Chapter 11

Dane stared down at the image on the paper on the table before him.

"Wow."

Kayla seemed beyond words, and looking at the computer-generated picture of Chad at his current age, he understood why.

"We tried doing this a couple of years ago for the social network pages she set up," Dane said, "but it didn't come out anywhere near this good."

"It's a special talent. Our tech guru, Tyler Hewitt, is a genius," Quinn said. "We do a lot of missing person cases. He took some standard image-aging software and tweaked it a bit, and the results have been amazing."

"He looks different," Dane said, "yet I'd recognize him in a minute."

"Is this what you wanted me to see?" Kayla asked. "Is this for flyers or posting or—"

"Someone thinks they saw him."

Kayla jumped. "Easy," Dane said. "He said it's not fresh."

"But it's more than I've had in so long," she said almost breathlessly. "Where?"

"A small town in Northern California. Not impossibly far from the note you got from Redding."

"That was three months ago." Kayla said it evenly, but Dane suspected she was trying to keep disappointment out of her voice, remembering she'd been warned the lead wasn't fresh.

"Yes. But it's a starting place."

"Who recognized him?"

Quinn shook his head. "It wasn't that definite. Just that the picture looked like somebody they'd seen. In a video game store."

Kayla's head came up sharply. "A video game store? That was one of Chad's passions."

Quinn nodded. "That's why we took this one seriously."

"How'd you manage this?" Dane asked. He didn't want to burst Kayla's bubble, but this seemed a bit much after only a few days. "This is hundreds of miles away and a little town, but you just happen to come across the one person who thinks he saw him?"

"We didn't. Not in the sense you mean."

Quinn leaned back in his chair. To Dane's surprise, the look he gave him seemed almost approving.

"You know we don't charge money for what we do," he said.

Dane instantly registered the key word in that statement. "Money," he said.

"What we've done instead," Quinn said, "is build a network. Of ordinary people across the country, people who don't stand out, who don't make people clam up like the police sometimes do, people who can watch, notice, without being noticed much themselves."

Dane's gaze narrowed. "You're saying…that's what you charge for your help?"

Quinn nodded. "Help in turn, at some later date. Most of our people are happy to do it. They never forget what it was like to be the one backed into a corner, the one at the end of their rope, the victim of injustice."

"Like you were," Kayla said softly.

Quinn's gaze shifted to her, but he said nothing.

"Your parents." If Quinn was upset, it didn't show, except maybe in a slight lowering of his brows. "Hayley told me. I think she thought I needed to know you really did understand," Kayla continued, apparently feeling the need to explain or to defend Hayley.

"Then I trust her judgment," Quinn said. Briskly, he went on. "We'll be leaving for California first thing in the morning."

"Taking that little toy in the warehouse?" Dane asked.

Quinn grinned suddenly, like a guy with the coolest car in town. "It is sweet, isn't it? But no. We'll take the plane. The Siskiyous are mountains I take seriously, and I'd rather be way above them."

"Okay," Kayla said.

There was undeniable excitement in her voice, and Dane supposed he couldn't blame her. And he realized that if this turned out to be just another disappointment for her, he wasn't going to be very happy with Quinn and company.

"I'll let you know as soon as we speak to our person there if it seems there's anything to this."

Kayla shook her head. "You won't have to. I'm going with you."

Dane went still. Quinn's gaze narrowed. "I don't think that would be the best idea," Quinn said. "And it's not necessary. We'll check it out, and if there's anything to it then you can—"

"No. I want to go now. I need to. I need to *do* something. Something besides sit at home and wonder."

"You've already logged more frequent flyer miles than any pilot, searching for Chad," Dane pointed out.

"Don't you see? This is the first chance in months, the first real possibility somebody may have seen him!"

Dane thought she was building this up too much, and obviously so did Quinn. But Dane knew that when Kayla focused on something, there was no stopping her. It took a considerable effort for him to quash the reaction that had become nearly automatic over the past couple of years. He'd promised her he would give this a full, honest shot. One last time.

Then it would be over, one way or another.

"All right," he said. "We'll both go." He glanced at Quinn. "Assuming there's room in this plane of yours."

"There's room," Quinn said. "But it's still not a good idea. It could well be a wasted trip."

"Won't be the first," Dane said. He saw Kayla wince, and he sighed. "Sorry. I meant what I said. This gets every chance to work."

So if I have to walk away, I can walk away clean, knowing I gave it as much as I could.

He hated that those were the words that formed in his mind, but he couldn't deny them. It was the truth. For all the sweetness rediscovered last night, it hadn't really changed anything. If Kayla couldn't or wouldn't give this up, or at least relegate it to second place in her life, then he would have to walk away again. No matter that it would nearly kill him to do it.

He was tired of being that second place holder himself.

It simmered in him as they headed back to her place to pack a small bag in case what needed to be done couldn't be done in a single day. He'd brought his own things back inside; they'd never made it out of his car anyway.

By the time they got there he was at a near boil. He wanted her to be crystal clear on what she was risking, what she was on the verge of throwing away. Last night's slow, sweet reunion had been one thing, but he was in no mood for slow and sweet now. He was fighting for his life, for their life together, and the kid gloves were off.

He grabbed her the moment they stepped inside. He kissed her fiercely, demanding her full attention. After a moment of startled surprise she gave in, kissing him back as if she understood.

But then this was Kayla, and she always understood.

As if that kiss had been the spark to tinder, the fire they'd always shared leaped to life. But he wasn't satisfied with that; he threw fuel on the flames, tearing at her clothes, needing, demanding, until she was with him, yanking at his shirt, his jeans.

They went down to the floor right there, no niceties this time. In seconds he was inside her. He felt her nails dig into his back at the sudden invasion, but it wasn't enough. He wanted her clawing at him, wanted her as mad, as desperate as he was, wanted to stamp himself on her so completely she would never, ever be able to forget this moment. He wanted her tied to him forever, and he used his body to tell her in the only way he could express it right now.

He clenched his jaw and held back, even as she began to go wild beneath him. She locked herself around him, as if she knew exactly what he wanted and that made it what she wanted, too. He rolled to his back, taking her with him, giving control over to her now, wanting her to show him she was as hot as he was. He needed to see it, to feel it, and somehow all the fear and frustration that had been growing in him for so long seemed wrapped up in that need.

As if she knew, she rode him with an eager ferocity that nearly drove him out of his mind, and in the last seconds, when he knew he couldn't wait any longer, he rolled them back and drove deep, heard her cry out, felt the first clenching of her body around him, then let himself go as her name ripped from his throat.

Inside the small airplane, Kayla sensed Dane's tension, knew the effort he was making to keep his promise to her. It made her feel better and worse at the same time; better because he was keeping to his word, and worse because it was clearly an effort. She realized with a sinking feeling that he thought this was going to be as fruitless as every other trip she'd made and that he was only coming with her because he'd promised her this one last chance.

She looked around the interior of the plane again, hoping for distraction. She and Dane had once taken a flight to Victoria, B.C., on a seaplane that had been even smaller than this, and she'd loved it. Much better than the helicopter that Dane had seemed so enamored of.

The young man who had been working on that helicopter was at the controls of the plane now, with Quinn in the copilot's seat. Somewhat to her surprise, Hayley had come with them.

"I'm the unofficial flight attendant," she said with a grin, handing out sodas.

There was no separate cockpit, so she was able to turn and hand a can to Quinn and offer one to Teague, who declined. Hayley's seat and the empty one next to her backed up to the pilot's, whereas Kayla's and Dane's faced forward. The cabin was finished nicely, with leather seating and large, rectangular windows, and there was plenty of room for Dane's long legs to stretch out.

"Nice," Dane said.

"Quinn's other toy," Hayley said with a smile. "He wanted a small jet, but Charlie slapped the purse strings shut on that."

Dane had been looking back at the cabin, but now he leaned forward to study what he could see of the instrument panels. It looked horrifyingly complicated to Kayla, although not much different than the big-screen gaming system his friend and partner Serge had. Dane had such an affinity for things electronic she wouldn't be surprised if he could figure most of them out simply by watching them long enough.

"It's pressurized?" Dane asked after a minute or two studying one section of the controls.

Hayley nodded. "Quinn was able to justify to Charlie the need for a pressurized cabin with all the mountains around us."

"I thought only jets were pressurized."

"This is the single exception in small planes. And that," Hayley said with a laugh, "is the sum total of my knowledge, I'm afraid." She gestured toward the front. "You want more, you'll have to ask them."

Dane smiled. "I will."

"Maybe on the way back you can sit up front."

"That," Dane said, his eyes alight, "would be exceptionally cool."

His excitement made Kayla smile. For a moment she wondered if he'd come along as much for the plane ride as for the search for Chad. And why not? she asked herself. She was glad he was enjoying the flight—it made her feel less guilty.

"Who takes care of Cutter when you have to leave?" Kayla asked.

"Usually our neighbor, who adores him. Or he stays with Rafe, another of our team, when he insists."

"The guy or the dog?" Dane joked.

"The dog," Hayley answered, sounding dead serious. "I think he knows Rafe's in a rough patch right now because he's been spending more time with him. Plus, the man has never had a dog, so Cutter's determined to introduce him to the joys."

Both Dane and Kayla blinked.

"I know, I know," Hayley said with a laugh. "But believe me, hang around Cutter long enough, and you'll start thinking that way, too."

The plane bounced slightly, as Quinn had warned them it might as they went over the mountains. Kayla shifted in her seat to look out the window. The movement, and a physical awareness that stopped just short of soreness, reminded her in a very personal way of what had happened between her and Dane the moment they'd set foot in her house last night. It wasn't that they hadn't had wild, hungry sex before, but nothing quite like that. From the beginning Dane's intent had been clear, he'd wanted to drive her crazy and he'd succeeded.

Admirably.

She felt her cheeks heat at the memory and was glad her face was turned away at the moment. Only the sure knowledge that, in the end, he'd been as wild as he'd made her let her regain some composure.

When they reached the small airport, the plane set down with a gentle thump that Kayla barely felt. She glanced toward Teague.

"He's good," Hayley said. "And almost as good with the helicopter. Quinn's been teaching him."

"I always wanted to learn to fly," Dane said, startling Kayla.

"You never told me that," she said.

He glanced at her. "I have. You just weren't hearing much at the time."

His tone was gentle, not accusing, but she felt stung nevertheless. Not by him, but inwardly; if he had indeed told her that, and she had completely missed it, what else had she missed? What else had been lost in the fog of grief and confusion?

She'd always thought she remembered everything about him, that she knew him better than anyone, that if someone asked her what his hopes, his dreams, his innermost thoughts were, she could tell them.

Now that confidence was shaken, and she didn't know how to feel about that.

It was still nagging at her as the five of them piled into the rental car Hayley had arranged the day before. Teague, as the shortest of the three men at a mere five-eleven, was relegated to the back seat while Quinn drove and Dane took the passenger seat. Hayley teased him gently about it, but Teague's crooked grin never faltered.

"Hey, I'm back here with two beautiful ladies—seems like I'm the lucky one," he said.

"Just remember who signs your paycheck," Quinn said in clearly mock warning.

"Yep," the irrepressible Teague retorted, "Charlie."

Hayley laughed, and the easy camaraderie lightened even Kayla's mood.

The town was close by, and it only took a few minutes to reach their destination. Kayla felt her pulse begin to pick up the moment she saw the sign for the game store. It looked like just the sort of place Chad would hang out. And when they stepped into the interior, with rows of the latest in games and equipment, and even a section for fan gear, it felt even more so.

The man behind the counter glanced at them, then put down the game controller he'd been inspecting. Light gleamed on a smooth, bald scalp fringed by silver hair. So much for the stereotype of gamers all being geeky fan boys, Kayla thought.

"Help you?"

"I'm Quinn Foxworth," Quinn said, holding out a hand. Somewhat to Kayla's surprise, the man reached out and grasped it without hesitation, and the handshake was welcoming and hearty.

"I'm Colin Brown. You're the folks who helped Henry Shigeta," the man said. "He told me you'd be coming."

"Yes."

"What you did, that did my heart good," the man said. "They'd been fighting that bastard Inskip for a long time. Always thought he was crooked as the day is long."

"And you were right," Quinn said.

"Damn straight. Taking bribes, letting his 'friends' build whatever they wanted wherever, but keeping good people like Henry and his wife from building the home they'd planned their whole lives on their own property. Not sure three years in jail is enough, though."

"I was more concerned that he never have power over people again," Quinn said. "And I think we took care of that."

The man smiled widely. "That you did. Now," he said briskly, "you're here about that picture Henry showed me?"

"Yes."

"I've been studying it, and the more I looked the more familiar he looked. So I went around and talked to Dustin." He glanced at their little group. "He's a kid who's always hanging out here. He knows all the regulars, so when a stranger comes in, he notices. So I showed him the picture."

"Did he know him?" Hayley asked.

Colin nodded. "He recognized him right off. 'That's that Chad guy,' he said."

Kayla's heart took a little jump in her chest and her knees went a little wobbly. In the same instant she felt Dane's arm around her, supporting her.

That's that Chad guy.

If Dane hadn't been holding her, she might well have sunk to her knees on the floor.

Chad.

At last.

Chapter 12

"It was still three months ago," Hayley said.

Dane watched as Kayla nodded. She hadn't said much since they'd left the game store. They were sitting now in a booth in the town's only restaurant, a small place built to resemble a railroad dining car. It looked old, but Dane noticed a small alcove at one end that appeared to be an internet setup with a single computer, and he'd seen a sign in the window indicating free Wi-Fi. They were the only people here now, and he wondered if the place got busier later on or in the evenings.

Quinn and Teague had left them here while they went on what Teague called a recon. They would get the lay of the land, Quinn had said, then they'd all decide what to do.

"But it fits," Hayley was saying now. "The time frame is about right, given when he mailed the note from Redding, which is only thirty miles from here."

Dane realized then that Hayley was probably here to babysit them while Quinn went and did...whatever it was he did in cases like this. If Kayla had taken Quinn's advice and stayed home, it probably would have been just Quinn and Teague making this trip, or maybe even just Quinn himself. In this small town where everybody seemed to know everyone and everyone's business, Dane was guessing Quinn would have little trouble getting people to cooperate. After what they'd done for the Shigetas, he wasn't surprised that the Foxworth reputation obviously preceded the man with the name.

Dane had been a little surprised that Foxworth had become involved in such a small, relatively insignificant local case as the Shigeta's fight with the county government. That they had only improved his opinion of them.

They were, he thought, genuine champions of lost causes, just as they said. He liked that.

He just wasn't sure he liked what had just happened. If Mr. Brown and the kid he'd spoken to were right, and Dane had no reason to think they weren't, the lead was still three months old. Yet Kayla was as wound up and excited as if they'd walked into the game shop five minutes after Chad had walked out.

"It's just the closest I've been," Kayla said, fiddling with the salt shaker on the table, spinning it with restless fingers. He'd never seen her completely still for long while awake—it just wasn't her nature.

"I understand," Hayley said. "I just don't want you to get your hopes up too high, when we don't know if this will really lead to anything. It could—"

She broke off, and Dane knew before she looked that Quinn must be approaching; he could see it in the look in Hayley's eyes. Did he look like that when he saw Kayla after even a short time apart? He was willing to bet he did.

And then Quinn was there, sliding onto the booth bench beside Hayley, kissing her cheek before he turned to face them.

"He was hitchhiking," Quinn said without preamble.

Dane heard Kayla's breath catch.

"How'd you find that out?" Dane asked.

"Guy at the hardware store said I should catch up with the postal carrier. Said she'd been on this route for fifteen years and knew damn near everything about everyone. And that if there'd been a stranger around, chances are she'd know more about him than anyone."

"I gather you found her?" Dane asked.

"Yeah." Quinn's gaze shifted to Kayla. "She recognized Chad."

Dane felt her tense beside him. But she said only "And?"

"He was out on the highway. She said it was raining, and he looked pretty wet and miserable, but she's prohibited from picking up hitchhikers."

"But he was all right?"

Kayla's voice was so full of worry that Dane felt a jab of guilt. She loved her brother and he was the only immediate family she had left, and if he really was innocent as she believed, then he was a victim second only to their parents. He shouldn't have made it so hard on her.

"She thought so. He wasn't hurt or anything."

Kayla let out a relieved sigh as the waitress, a young, bored-looking woman who refilled their coffee, added a mug for Quinn, then vanished anew into the back, probably thinking they weren't worth her time because they weren't ordering lunch.

After she left, Quinn continued.

"She said he was only a few blocks from the senior center, so she sent him there. Said she knew they'd take him in, dry him off and feed him."

"We should go there," Kayla said, making as if to rise immediately.

"Teague's already there. He was on that side of town, so I called him and gave him the info. He should be here soon with whatever he finds."

"Oh." She sank back down. "Thank you."

"We'll find what's here to be found," Quinn assured her, then, in an almost warning tone, added, "But as I said from the beginning, I can't promise you'll like it."

"I have to know," Kayla said. "But I hate just sitting here. I feel like I should be doing something. Anything."

"You have been," Dane said quietly. "For ten years you have been."

She turned to look at him. "But I've never been this close," she said, eagerness building in her voice. "Surely you see that now. This is real, this is a chance finally to really find my brother and bring him home!"

Several things hit Dane at once. First was the fact that, until now, he'd never really thought she'd find him, so he'd never considered what would happen if she did. Bring him home? He could only imagine what that would be like. And he didn't like the feel of it at all.

Kayla's expression changed as she watched him. "Aren't you even a little happy about it?"

No. No, I'm not.

He didn't speak it because he was afraid if he did he'd sound like a spoiled child who'd just been told another baby was on the way. It didn't matter; she read him anyway.

"Fine," she snapped. "Why did you even come if that's how you feel?"

That the usually private Kayla was dragging this out in front of Quinn and Hayley told Dane volumes. He looked at her, at the set of her mouth, the rekindled resolve in her expression.

She was as determined as ever. And he felt a slow, creeping chill overtake him as he finally admitted to himself she would keep this up to the ends of the Earth if she had to.

She was lost to him.

Even as he thought it she turned away. "What do we do next?" she asked eagerly.

"We wait and see what Teague found out," Quinn said with a nod toward the window. Dane looked and saw the pilot headed for them at a brisk pace. He looked like a man who had something to say.

He could feel the renewed energy fairly radiating from Kayla as Teague joined them.

"What did you find?" she asked before he'd even sat down.

Teague glanced at Quinn. Something seemed to be communicated between the two men in the moment before Quinn nodded.

"She wants to know it all," he said.

Teague nodded, but his usual friendly smile was missing when he spoke. "They remember him, all right."

Kayla leaned forward eagerly. "They do? Did he say where he was going?"

Teague hesitated for about three seconds, and Dane got the sense he was trying to find a better way to say what he had to say. And he found himself, despite it all, waiting uneasily for what was coming.

"They remember him," Teague said at last, "because he cleaned them out when he left."

Quinn leaned back. Hayley sighed. Kayla frowned. "What?" she asked, clearly puzzled.

"He emptied the Bingo box." Teague's tone was remarkably level, but his sentiments on the action were still obvious. "Two hundred and fifty dollars. Stole every last penny."

Chapter 13

"Are they sure it was him?"

Kayla sounded doubtful, and it dug at the raw spot inside Dane that knew they were over for good. The knowledge hadn't reached his heart and gut yet, but his intellect knew in that cold, dispassionate way that was the beginning of the human mind learning to accept the unacceptable.

"Oh, please," Dane said, unable to hold back. "Don't defend him. Why would a guy who stole the money his eight-year-old sister saved up for a bike feel a qualm about stealing from senior citizens?"

Color flared in Kayla's cheeks. "I wasn't defending him. I was just asking if they were sure."

"They were," Teague said, his voice more sympathetic now, as if, although he despised what her brother had done, he felt sorry for Kayla. Whether it was for having to deal with this news, or for just having a jerk of a brother, Dane wasn't sure.

Hell, he wasn't sure of anything anymore. The brief interlude when it had seemed they might make it, when she'd been ready and willing to put all this on the shelf where it belonged and go on with their lives, had apparently been only that, an interlude. A precious, beautiful, intimate interlude, destined to end.

Chad Tucker had stolen something much more valuable than the contents of that money box from him and left him with only the sad remnants, memories of the life he'd thought was going to be forever. He'd always assumed they'd get married, had even figured her twenty-fifth birthday would be the day he'd formally ask her. He wanted her to have a chance to live enough to be sure, although he'd been sure for years. But by the time that birthday had rolled around, he'd been so tired of all things Chad, he hadn't proposed after all.

"There was a witness who saw him take it and run for the back door," Teague was saying. "By the time the local sheriff got there, he was long gone."

"Did you talk to the sheriff's office?"

"Yes. They looked up the report for me. Nothing much there except the usual conflicting eyewitness descriptions. But I talked to several people who were there that day. They all agreed the guy in our image was him, but there was nothing that helps figure out where he is now."

"Anything else?" Quinn asked.

Teague's mouth quirked. "I felt kind of bad, bringing it up again. Apparently there's an ongoing disagreement between the folks who wanted him hunted down and arrested before he spent it all on drugs, and the ones who thought if he needed the money that badly they should have just given it to him. It was getting kind of heated when I left."

Dane winced inwardly. That sounded a little too close to the arguments he and Kayla had had over her brother. Maybe there really was no middle ground, anywhere.

To her credit, Kayla didn't try to defend Chad once she'd heard Teague's story. She sat silently, looking troubled. His instinct was to comfort, as it always had been with her, but he quashed the urge. It was going to be a long, hard battle to kill the habits of more than a decade, and he wasn't looking forward to it.

But he was starting to accept that it was going to be necessary.

"It's your call, Kayla," Quinn said. "Do we keep going?"

"I…" She hesitated, flicked a glance at Dane. He said nothing. He already knew what she was going to say.

It's not your business anymore, he told himself. And that alone jabbed at him sharply. Disengaging was going to be a painful process.

"I can't quit now, not this close."

And there it was, Dane thought.

"Kayla," Hayley began.

"I know," Kayla said. "It could come to nothing, but it's still the most definite information I've had in all this time. Every other time, nobody remembered him, not even at the post office where he mailed the notes."

"This all would have been easier if he'd used email to contact you," Quinn said. "We could have tracked that, found an IP, and Tyler would have had it nailed down in a hurry."

"He could have. He obviously looked at her support group's website to get the P.O. Box, and the email address is right there. But he didn't," Dane said, beyond caring now that he sounded as bleak as he felt. "Because he doesn't want to be found. Not even by Kayla. Maybe especially not by her."

"What's that supposed to mean?" she asked, clearly stung.

He told himself it didn't matter. That he didn't care anymore. And while even as he thought it he knew the latter wasn't true, he was afraid the former was.

"He's been toying with you for ten years," he said, letting out some of his frustration. "Just when you start to get past it, another one of those damn notes comes. Never enough for you to find him, just enough to remind you he's out there. To make sure you never forget."

"I don't want to forget!"

"You think he doesn't know that?"

Dane was aware that Hayley was staring out the window, clearly trying to ignore them. Quinn, however, was listening to every word, not in the manner of someone who enjoyed hearing other people's disputes but more like someone who wanted every tiny bit of data in case it might help.

Dane wondered what Quinn would get out of this exchange. And it was a measure of the devastation he was feeling inside that he didn't really care.

"What do you want me to do?" Kayla demanded. "Just pretend he's not out there? Maybe stay home, spend his half of the insurance money? Maybe you'd like that, is that it?"

Under normal circumstances, Dane would have laughed that ridiculous accusation off, but nothing was normal about how he was feeling right now.

"What if you did find him?" he asked. Now that it had occurred to him, he wondered if she had ever thought beyond the immediate goal herself. "You talked about bringing him home. Did you ever think what that would mean? That the first people waiting to welcome him would be the police?"

Kayla's eyes widened, and the color drained from her cheeks. She was too smart for it not to have occurred to her, but her expression told him she'd put this in the "deal with it when it happens" category.

"Did you think that because they didn't have the manpower and resources to go on an out-of-state manhunt that they'd just forget about him?"

Kayla turned to look at Quinn. "But…you'll help me prove he didn't do it, right?"

"We'll help you find the truth," Quinn said gently but firmly. "I warned you from the beginning you might not like what we find."

Kayla lowered her eyes to her coffee mug, as if the last bit of dark liquid held the answers she wanted to hear.

"And you agreed to accept what they found," Dane reminded her.

"I know that." There was a snap in her voice.

"But you won't, will you?" Dane said wearily. "You'll just

go on and on, throwing your life away, throwing our lives away."

Her head came up sharply. "That's not true."

"How long are you going to live in complete denial, Kayla?"

"I'm not in denial. You think I don't know we may never find him, may never be able to prove he's innocent?"

"No. I think you'll never face the real truth." Dane knew he was headed into no-return territory, that if he continued he'd be looking at nothing but ashes. But wasn't he anyway?

"And what truth might that be?" Quinn's voice came from across the table, sounding calm and merely interested. Dane never took his eyes off Kayla. She was glaring at him, and in that moment he let go of the last, tiny shred of hope.

"That Chad did it," he said flatly.

Chapter 14

Kayla was still shaking. She tried to tell herself it was anger that was causing the tremors that gripped her, but deep down she knew better. Oh, there was anger, but it was dwarfed by a rush of other emotions she couldn't even begin to sort out, not yet.

Dane thought Chad was guilty.

Had he always? If so, how had she not known that?

She'd known he had never believed in the hunt for Chad the way she did, but he'd supported her, at least until recently. She'd even admitted he had a right to feel the way he did; when the tenth anniversary of her parents' murders and Chad's disappearance had rolled around, she'd been a little stunned herself to realize how long it had been and how relatively little she'd accomplished in those years.

And she had meant everything she'd said. She'd meant her promise that she would accept whatever Foxworth found or didn't find and move on. She'd been so relieved when Dane had agreed to give them another chance and had spent the past few days beyond grateful that he had come back. Nothing meant more to her than Dane and what they'd built between them.

Except that it had apparently all been built on a lie.

She hadn't said a word since Dane's flat declaration. Nor had he. At least not to her.

He had spoken to Quinn privately. The man had taken Dane aside, no doubt to quiz him on his accusation. She'd watched, still a little in shock. She could only imagine what Dane was telling him.

Meanwhile Hayley had gently reassured her that this changed nothing, that Foxworth would continue as long as she wanted them to, while Teague made an awkward escape as soon as he could, looking uncomfortable with the sudden flare of emotion. She couldn't blame him. She'd like to escape herself.

When the little town was dry of information, including the tiny clue Teague had gleaned from one of the seniors that Chad had talked about Seattle before he'd absconded with the money, they headed back to the small airstrip.

It was no less awkward there when Dane jumped at the chance to sit up front with Teague. She reminded herself that the suggestion he do so had come on the flight down here, before any of this had happened, but somehow that didn't make it seem any less a pointed display of the new, seemingly unbridgeable distance between them.

They'd been in the air for half an hour when Hayley, who had been talking quietly with Quinn in the back-facing seats, got up and crossed the small cabin to sit beside her.

"He's just tired of it," she said. "It's been ten years."

"He promised," Kayla said, aware she sounded a bit like a thwarted child but unable to help it at the moment. "He said he'd see this through with me."

"Apparently he thinks he has. And he does have a point."

She didn't want to hear any defense just now, but she didn't want to antagonize the only people left on her side either.

"This lead may be more detailed than you've ever had before, but it's still three months cold. We know more, and that will help, but I'm not sure how much closer we really are."

Kayla winced. Maybe they weren't on her side either. Maybe she really was alone in this.

"Quinn said we'd keep going as long as you wanted us

to. He meant it. It's only been a week, so we've really only just begun."

Soothed slightly, Kayla tried to pull herself out of the emotional murk. "What's the longest you've spent looking for someone?"

"Well, I don't know all the Foxworth history yet. I do know there are some cases that have gone for more than a year. And two that are still open after longer than that."

She glanced over at Quinn, who was reading through his own notes taken during the hours spent canvassing the small town.

"Those are the ones that eat at him. He hates not being able to at least give people the kind of closure he never got."

"He's a remarkable man," Kayla said, meaning it.

"Yes, he is," Hayley agreed, her voice soft, full of love and admiration and respect. All the things she herself had always felt for Dane.

Until now.

"I won't say he didn't mean it," Hayley said, obviously seeing Kayla's gaze flick up front to Dane and then quickly away. "I can't read his mind. But I'm guessing he feels like he's been putting his life—your lives—on hold for ten years, and now he's thinking it's never going to end."

"I think he pretty much ended it today."

"Doesn't have to be that way," Hayley said. "You can get past this."

"Get past him believing my brother is guilty?"

Hayley gave a half shrug. "I got past Quinn kidnapping me."

Kayla seized on the diversion. "Teague said something about that. It was really true?"

Hayley nodded. "In the middle of the night, Cutter and I both, in that blessed black helicopter of his."

"And those were really bullet holes?"

"Yes." Hayley's expression changed; whatever memory had just struck her, she didn't like it much. "And I'd be happy to tell you the whole, annoyingly heroic, self-sacrificing story, but right now I think you need to focus on one thing."

"Finding Chad," Kayla said with a nod.

"I was thinking more along the lines of deciding how high a price you're willing to pay."

This time it was Hayley who glanced forward to the copilot's seat where Dane sat, giving every appearance of being engrossed in Teague's explanations of what was going on, and no doubt asking very intelligent questions about the "slick, new avionics" Teague had been so eager to show off.

"He's a good man, Kayla. They don't come along every day."

Don't lose a good man chasing after a bad one.

Someone had told her that once. Crystal's mother, she thought. Although she obviously hadn't meant it to refer to Chad. Or maybe she had; Crystal had always had a bit of a crush on him.

Kayla felt the old ache and tried to quash it. Crystal had been her best friend. Or at least she'd thought she was her best friend; the girl, and the friendship, had vanished after that bloody night. In adult retrospect she was sure Crystal just hadn't known how to deal with such trauma, hadn't wanted to be around it. It was a dose of harsh, grim reality delivered years before a young mind knew how to cope. Kayla didn't blame her, not anymore, but it still hurt to have been abandoned that way.

Only one person had stayed, only one person had been there through it all, supporting her, helping her on every step of the awful path she'd had to walk.

And he was sitting a few feet away, yet at the moment as far away as the moon.

Don't lose a good man chasing after a bad one.

Dane was definitely a good man. She could never deny that, no matter what happened between them.

She just couldn't accept that her brother was a bad one.

Chapter 15

Teague had gone into such detail that by the time they landed, Dane felt as if he should be able to fly the darn plane himself. But he'd given all the information less than his full attention. Because it was hard to concentrate when your whole life had just fallen apart.

He wished he hadn't said it, but at the same time he was glad it was out. He'd been thinking it for a long time.

Do you really think he did it, or are you convicting him in your mind because he's ruining your life without even being here?

Quinn Foxworth's words echoed in his head. And Dane wasn't really sure of the answer.

"I've been where she is," Quinn had said. "And I wanted the person who murdered my parents dead as much as she wants to find Chad."

"And you got that, eventually." Even as he'd said it, Dane knew it wasn't a good analogy; Quinn, he suspected, was the kind of man who would want to do the job himself.

"After he got to spend three years at home with his family, three years that we and the families of the other victims never got, I'll never get over that."

"But look how you channeled that," Dane had countered. "Into something really good."

"Kayla's work is something good."

He was still chewing on it as they piled into the car they'd come to the airstrip in early that morning. Funny how different things had been then. If he could have imagined how it would go, he never would have gotten on that plane.

He couldn't deny Quinn's words. She was doing good work, and she had credibility with grief-stricken fellow travelers that couldn't be denied. It made her very effective.

It also drained her. In fact, he thought now as they went about the business of deplaning, the real problems had started about then. At first he'd been glad, no, delighted that she'd found something to do other than search for her brother. But the work did take a lot out of her, and he suspected there simply wasn't enough energy for all three: the work, her obsession with Chad, and him.

He'd just never thought it would be him who would lose. He'd always thought she'd get past it, get over it, that it would gradually fade.

He told himself to snap out of it as they reached the Foxworth buildings. It hadn't faded, and it was time to accept it never would.

He and Kayla had come in his car, so there would be an uncomfortable trip back to her place. And then he would, once more, gather up what things he had there—only this time they wouldn't be going back.

They got out of the big SUV. Dane heard a bark, and Cutter came dashing toward them, he wasn't sure from where. The dog greeted Hayley and Quinn joyously and gave Teague a nudge that seemed almost teasing. Then he turned to Dane and stopped. The animal looked from him to Kayla, who was standing a careful three feet away. Cutter came forward, stood between them for a moment, then sat.

A sound escaped from the dog, something so much like an exasperated, weary, human sigh that Dane blinked.

"Did I mention," Hayley said casually, "that Cutter has very good instincts about people who belong together?"

Kayla let out a harsh, compressed breath. Dane made himself not look at her.

"How is he with insurmountable obstacles?" he asked sourly.

"I don't think the word insurmountable is in his vocabulary," Quinn said dryly. "Which is, by the way, huge. For a dog."

"Not so huge for whatever he really is," Hayley quipped.

The awkward moment passed, although Cutter was still looking at them both as if he were contemplating drastic action.

"—stolen money would have bought him a ticket if he was really headed back north." Dane tuned into Quinn as he spoke to Kayla. "We'll start working that angle."

Dane tuned back out again, telling himself it no longer concerned him. He separated himself, walked over toward his car, hitting the button on the fob to unlock it.

To his surprise, Cutter followed him. And positioned himself between Dane and the driver's door.

"What? I didn't pet you hello, so I can't leave?"

He reached down and scratched behind the dog's ears, but it had no effect. Cutter never even reacted, and his steady, intense gaze was unnerving.

"What do you want me to do?" Dane asked; clearly the dog wanted something.

For the first time Cutter's gaze shifted, to Kayla, now twenty feet away. Then the dog's eyes were back on him, steady, intense, commanding.

Dane gave a sharp shake of his head. He was giving this animal far too much credit. He was, after all, just a dog.

When Kayla finally came over to the car, she came nowhere near him, nor did she say a word as she opened the passenger door. Cutter didn't pull the same stunt with her, so apparently in the dog's view, he was the one who was supposed to bend. Again.

"Sorry, buddy," he said to the dog, "I can't. Not this time."

For an instant something flickered in the animal's eyes, something oddly like understanding. Acknowledgment. Something.

And he was losing his mind, giving human attributes and intelligence to a dog, however remarkable he might be.

He got into the driver's seat. Cutter trotted around the car to the passenger side, where Kayla had now slid into the seat. He poked his nose at her, then rested his chin on her knee. She bent over the dog, petting him, crooning something he couldn't hear into those alert ears. Maybe that's what she needed, Dane thought. A dog. A companion who would never question what she was doing, never begrudge her her obsession, who would go along with her every desperate effort unconditionally.

The light was fading as he started the car and headed back to the little house he'd thought of as home for nearly four years now. They didn't speak, and the atmosphere between them grew stiffer, chillier, with every mile.

When they got there, he pulled into the driveway but not the garage. Kayla glanced at him, and he knew she had seen this simple action—or lack of action—for the sign it was. He wasn't staying.

He got out, slamming the car door shut with more force than was necessary. He regretted it when he realized her neighbor, Mr. Reyes, was outside working on his pickup, and the noise had made him look their way. But after a friendly wave he stuck his head back under the hood. At least it wasn't the man's wife, who would have come over to say hello and put them through ten minutes of agony as she chattered on.

Kayla just sat for a moment, then got out of the car, moving gingerly, as if every motion hurt. He had to stop himself from going to her.

"Let me grab my stuff, and you'll be rid of me," he said, hating the way he sounded but not able to stop the bitterness that was welling up in him from seeping into his voice.

"Fine."

Short, sharp, to the point. Not a word of protest, not a single request to reconsider.

"Kayla—"

"Just hurry and get out," she snapped. "Get it over with."

It was done. The rupture was complete and final. She'd made her choice, and it wasn't him.

He was so focused on that choice that he was unprepared for the flood of memories that hit him the moment they walked into the house. The past few days, when they'd made love hungrily, everywhere, whenever the need took them, every sweet touch flavored with gratitude that they hadn't lost this singular passion.

He couldn't deal with this. He grabbed up things and threw them in the duffel bag he'd stuffed into a corner of the closet. Clothes, shoes, razor, toothbrush, books, his tablet, they all went haphazardly into the bag and he zipped it hastily shut; he'd sort it all out later.

He intended to just leave. To walk out the door without a word because there was nothing left to say. But as he passed the bookshelf in the living room, something stopped him. He looked at the row of framed photographs she had there. Her parents, them all as a family, and at the other end one of him she'd taken last year, and Chad's high school portrait.

He reached out and moved Chad's picture in front of his own. It was childish, he knew it, but he did it anyway. Then he turned around to look at her.

"You've made your choice, Kayla. I hope you're happy with it when you're a lonely old woman still chasing a phantom."

"What makes you think I'll be lonely?" she retorted. "Do you think you're the only man in the world?"

He knew it had been a mistake; he should have just walked out as he'd intended. "No," he said quietly. "But no other man will love you like I do."

It wasn't until he was back in his car, sitting in the darkness, trying to will himself to turn the key, that he realized he'd used the present tense.

With a realization of just what was ahead of him, just how long and hard learning to live without her was going to be, he started the car and drove into the night.

Chapter 16

Kayla awoke from the dream with a gasp. For a moment everything seemed strange. Nothing looked right. Disoriented, she jerked upright. Once she had, the familiar outlines reassured her; she wasn't in the bedroom, but the living room.

But nothing could reassure her after that dream.

The peaceful quiet of the night surrounded her; this had always been a quiet neighborhood. It was one of the reasons she'd chosen it. Deciding to move had been instantaneous; she knew there was no way she could stay in the house that her parents had died in. She'd sold it to the first person who'd been willing to buy, taking a loss and not caring.

Dane had tried to slow her down to no avail. Hayley understood, she thought. Her mother had died of natural causes, she'd told her, otherwise she never would have been able to stay in her home—which wasn't far from Kayla's—either.

But whether or not he agreed with the move, Dane had helped. As usual. In fact, he'd been the one who'd found this house in the first place, although she'd fallen in love with it the moment she'd seen it.

As usual, he'd known exactly what she'd needed, just how much space, the big trees providing a sense of privacy and the small garden that was glorious in the spring and summer, tempting her outside. The little house had nestled in that setting like a fairy tale cottage, and she'd nearly giggled in appreciation.

Dane had helped her change the inside slightly, opening

up the kitchen to the living room so it didn't seem so small and closed in and then adding the big windows to look out on that garden, which in turn inspired her to keep working on it.

She'd been happier here than she'd thought she could ever be again. And yet now it seemed like a hollow, echoing place she wanted to escape.

She'd given up on sleep after two restless hours in her empty bed. Dane's absence hammered at her, no matter how she tried to pretend, going about her routine as if nothing had changed, hoping the ritual of washing her face, brushing her teeth, checking her alarm, would soothe her troubled mind and allow her to sleep. She had to work tomorrow, and there was no way she could miss the scheduled sessions—there were new people just starting on the long, sad path, and she needed to be there to help.

None of it worked.

Finally conceding there was no way she was going to sleep, she'd gotten up and moved to the living room. Curled up on her couch, she'd turned on the television, then turned it back off, picked up a book then put it down, finally grabbed her phone and played a mindless game until her eyes couldn't bear it anymore.

Just before two she'd finally dozed off, only to have her weary brain take Dane's words and tweak them into a too-real scenario; she'd been putting the photographs he'd moved back the way they'd been when she'd caught a glimpse of her own reflection in the glass of the framed portrait of Chad. A reflection of a wrinkled, gray-haired woman who looked a bit mad.

Needing to move, she uncurled her legs and stood up. She didn't turn on the lamp on the table beside her, didn't want the light to emphasize the emptiness of what had once been her beloved little home. In the dark, she could pretend it wasn't empty, pretend Dane was just in the other room, as always.

She could be in denial.

How long are you going to live in complete denial, Kayla?

"I'm not," she said aloud to the quiet room.

Denying she was living in denial.

She let out a disgusted sigh, angry at herself, at Dane, at the world in a way she hadn't been for a long time.

Defiantly, she walked over to the shelf of photos. She picked up the one of Chad Dane had moved and put it back, telling herself she wasn't glad she couldn't see any reflections in the dark.

She admitted she was glad she couldn't see Dane's, the pain was too raw, too fresh. But then, she didn't have to look to see the images in her mind. She knew them as well as she knew her own image. The picture of her whole family, the last taken while it had still existed, the shot of her parents at their twentieth—and last—anniversary. Then Chad with Troy, working on the motorcycle they had later crashed into the sound, which had then resulted in the joyriding incident; a guy couldn't be without wheels, Chad had said, laughing it off.

And then Dane. She had many more of him, some in other places in the house, but the one here was her favorite. It captured the essence of him, quiet yet energetic, thoughtful yet not brooding, serious but with a grin just about to break loose and light up his eyes.

And everything else within a hundred miles, she thought.

The ache welled up inside her until she nearly cried out at the pain of it. And there in the dark, she moved the pictures once more. Held Chad's for a moment, thinking the words that had kept her going for so long; she had to do this. She had to care about Chad because no one else did. She was all he had. But the old mantra wasn't working tonight.

She put the photos back exactly as Dane had moved them, with Chad's portrait blocking him.

Because he'd been right.

She did cry then, unable to stop it. She felt the despair building, knew she was on the verge of a meltdown the likes of which she hadn't had in a long time. Before she'd always had the mysterious, unknown killer to blame for the destruction of life as she'd known it.

Now she was very afraid she had no one to blame but herself. She—

An explosion of sound so loud she felt it as much as heard it was followed instantly by a simultaneous flare of yellow light and a shock wave that knocked her into the bookshelves.

She staggered, too stunned to even grab at anything for support. She went to her knees. She heard an odd, crackling sound. Struggled to her feet. And then she smelled smoke. Only a little, then suddenly it billowed out of the back of the house, harsh and thick. She coughed.

Fire. The house was on fire. Smoke was filling the room, making her cough harder and harder, and she realized flames could soon follow. But it was the smoke, wasn't it? Wasn't that the real danger? Didn't more people die of smoke inhalation than actually burned?

Stop thinking, start doing, she ordered herself, while you can still breathe at all.

She dropped to her knees and found some clearer air. She began to crawl, not really thinking of anything except getting away, getting outside. She headed for the front door, or at least where she thought it was; had she gotten turned around in the chaos?

It was getting harder and harder to focus, to breathe; her body was slipping out of her control as it coughed forcefully, trying to rid itself of the smothering smoke.

She heard a yell from outside, over the sound of the fire licking away at her home.

Dane?

No, Dane was gone. He'd left her; she'd thrown him away.

Dizzy with fear now, she tried to reach for the doorknob. She couldn't find it as the smoke spread, lowered.

Was it gone?

Everything else was.

Dane was gone.

Chad was gone.

Her parents were gone.

Why not join the parade?

The last thing she remembered was a rush of cool, night air, and the fleeting thought that maybe death wasn't so bad after all.

Chapter 17

Sirens.

Quinn came awake sharply. Immediately alert, he was assessing before Hayley even stirred beside him. He raised up on one elbow. The noise continued, and he turned his head slightly. North to south, he thought. And far enough away that he began to relax a little. A few blocks over and pulling away, he thought. And out here a block was a significant distance.

The sirens stopped. The only sound was the drip of rain from the eaves; the summer shower had started just after one. He knew that because Hayley, who loved the sound, had gotten up to open the window. Naked. Which had inspired him to welcome her back to bed in a way that had made him think very fondly of the Northwest's ever possible rain.

"Quinn?"

Hayley's soft voice came out of the dark. Just the sound of her saying his name was enough to tangle him up inside; sometimes he still had trouble believing this incredible woman was his.

"Can you tell where it was?"

"It's all right. It's not too close. Go back to sleep."

He dropped back down, rolling to his side to pull her into the curve of his body. She was soft and warm and sleek and smooth and he wanted her all over again despite the fact that they'd made love well into the night last night, as if they'd needed to reassure themselves that they were fine after seeing Dane and Kayla's love start to crumble before their eyes.

He heard another sound that distracted him from the decision of whether to let her sleep or pursue the urge that was building in him. This one was from inside, the sound of a dog's quiet footfalls. Cutter.

The sirens must have unsettled him, Quinn thought. Probably even hurt those super-sensitive ears of his that seemed to hear at incredible distances even for a dog.

And then Cutter was there, his head up to see into the bed, looking at them. Even in the dark Quinn knew it because he could see the faint gleam of the dog's eyes reflecting what light there was. He had a vague memory of reading that dogs could see better than people at night. It had been in the spate of dog research he'd done after the drug cartel case. The case that had brought Hayley—and the uncanny, sometimes too clever Cutter—into his life, changing it forever, in ways he would have never dared hope for.

"Hey, furry one," Hayley said to the dog, reaching out a slender arm to stroke the dog's head. "We're okay."

As if that had been all he needed—to know his people were okay—the dog gave Hayley's fingers a quick swipe with his tongue and turned away.

"That dog is…." Words failed him.

"Yes, he is," Hayley said, and he could hear the smile in her voice. "Lucky me, I have two of the most amazing males on the planet right here with me."

Well, if that was how she was feeling, that made his decision easier. He leaned over her and nibbled lightly on her ear and felt with satisfaction the tiny shiver that went through her. He pulled her closer, ready to—

Cutter was back.

This time he nudged Hayley slightly with his nose. His cold nose, Hayley indicated.

"Settle down, Cutter," she told him. "It was just sirens,

and they weren't that close. Somebody's having trouble, but not us."

But the dog began to pace, then pace and whine, from the bed to the bedroom door and back again.

"Is he usually like that?" Quinn asked. He'd seen a lot of unique behavior from Cutter in the past few months, but not this. "After he hears sirens, I mean?"

"No," Hayley said. "They're rare out here, and they wake him, of course, but he settles back down quickly. And he never whines like that. This is…odd."

Odd. Used in conjunction with Cutter, that was never something to ignore. Quinn sighed. Shelving his erotic plans, he sat up. Hayley sat up beside him. Quinn reached for the lamp on his side of the bed.

Light flooded the room. The room that, thanks to Hayley's gentle understanding, was as much his as hers. She'd told him she wanted to make changes anyway, once she'd decided to stay here after her mother's death, but she'd been putting it off. So she'd insisted they move everything out of the house, put back only what he liked, and make mutual decisions on adding new things. "That way it's new for both of us," she had said. "I don't want you to feel like a guest in someone else's house."

Because he'd practically been living in the Foxworth office, in a room at the back downstairs that he'd converted to a functional bedroom, he wasn't about to complain, but he appreciated the gesture more than he'd ever expected he would. In return he decided not to rebuild on the property Foxworth owned next door, although he'd had the ruins of the house there removed. Now Cutter had lots of room to run and explore without ever leaving home turf.

The dog had stopped his pacing when the light came on and had spun around to look toward them. After a moment, when they didn't move, he sat in the middle of the floor and began to howl. Loudly.

"What the…?" Quinn exclaimed.

"I don't know," Hayley said. "He's never done that."

She got up and went to the obviously distressed dog, kneeling beside him. "Cutter, sweetie, it's all right."

Quinn watched as she hugged the dog reassuringly. Cutter accepted the gesture with another swipe of his tongue, this time over her chin, but the ear-splitting howling resumed.

Only now, in between howls, the dog seemed to be focusing on Quinn. And when Cutter was focused on you, Quinn had quickly learned, it was good to pay attention.

Feeling a bit like the sheep these Belgian breeds were known to herd, he got out of bed himself.

"Okay, dog," he muttered as he joined Hayley crouching beside the animal, "you got us both up, now what?"

The howling stopped. Cutter darted away, disappearing for a moment into the small walk-in closet off the master bathroom.

He came back with a shoe.

Hayley drew back, startled, as the dog dropped one of her lug-soled slip-ons in front of her, then raced back to the closet.

He came back again, this time with one of Quinn's battered, lace-up military boots, which he dropped very nearly on Quinn's bare foot.

Then Cutter spun on his hindquarters and darted to the bedroom door, where he sat, looking over his shoulder at them with every evidence of impatience, as if he were waiting for his not-too-bright humans to get the message.

Quinn looked at Hayley, whose expression told him she was as bewildered as he was.

But if there was anything he'd come to know since these two had made his life something full of joy and wonder instead of the steady slog of determination it had once been, it was that you ignored this dog at your peril.

Hayley sighed.

Quinn echoed it.

"I guess we're going…somewhere," he said. "In the middle of the night. In the rain," he added with a wry grimace at the dog.

"Yes. And given this started with the sirens," Hayley began.

"We start by finding where they went," Quinn finished.

Dane hadn't been asleep—in fact, he had just made himself stop pacing the floor again when the knock on the door startled him. Considering the hour, it had been more of a pounding than a knock. His brows furrowed. Probably woke the neighbors in both apartments beside him. He picked up his phone and tapped it to see that it was after 2:00 a.m.

"Dane Burdette, Redwood Cove police, open up."

For a moment he thought it was Jarrod, the cop from downstairs, making a lousy joke. But the guy didn't seem the type. A million scenarios cascaded through his mind as he crossed the living room. Maybe they'd finally found Chad. But why would they be here? Wouldn't they go to Kayla?

Fear spiked through him. If his long suppressed suspicion was true, if Chad really had murdered their parents, then what would stop him from coming back for his sister? It sounded crazy; she'd been his sole defender for so long, but then, Dane didn't get how somebody could kill their parents in the first place.

His brain raced through all those chaotic thoughts in the time it took him to get to the front door. He shifted his phone to his left hand and grabbed the doorknob just as another hammering came.

"Okay, okay," he was saying as he pulled it open.

Two uniformed officers stood there. One about his own age, one older. They both looked stern. No, beyond that. They looked grim. And wary. Watchful. It was a small department, and he wondered what was so important they sent this percentage of it to his door and at this hour.

"What's wrong?" he asked.

"We need to talk to you, Mr. Burdette."

Puzzled, and still fighting the chaos of his thoughts, he stood aside to let them in. The older man's name tag said R. Carpenter, the younger D. Harvey.

"Is this about Chad? Did he come back?"

The two men exchanged glances. "Chad?"

"Chad Tucker. He— Never mind. If this was about him, you'd know the name, right?"

"Tucker. Related to Kayla Tucker?"

A stab of foreboding shot through him, and Dane's stomach knotted. "Her brother. Is she all right?"

"Interesting that you're worried about that."

It took everything he had not to let his rapidly building panic show. "Her brother," he said slowly, "likely murdered their parents ten years ago. Then vanished. If he's back—"

"I remember a little about that case," the older officer said. "It was pretty ugly."

"Then you should know why I'm worried. Is Kayla all right?"

"How do you know about that case?"

"I lived next door at the time. I was the first one there, when Kayla started screaming."

"Were you?" the older man said, in an odd tone.

"She was just a kid. Sixteen. If you'd heard what she sounded like, you would have come running, too."

"And you were how old?" It seemed the older officer was taking charge of things, and the younger one was staying silent. Dane wondered if he was a trainee or something. He looked young enough.

"Eighteen," he answered.

"The same age as the primary suspect," Carpenter said.

Apparently he remembered more than just a little about the case, Dane thought.

"I think you'd better come with us, Mr. Burdette."

"I'm not moving a step until you tell me if this has to do with Kayla, if she's all right."

"From what a witness tells us, you had a fight with Ms. Tucker earlier tonight."

"A fight? What the…."

Mr. Reyes. He supposed the little scene in the driveway could be interpreted that way.

"We've been…disagreeing. About her brother. She insists he's innocent, I think he's not."

"Where have you been since that time?"

"Here. I came straight here."

The younger officer looked him up and down. The older officer walked around him, looking at him even more intently. Looking for what? Dane wondered.

"You're still dressed."

"I knew I wasn't going to sleep so I didn't bother trying."

"Hmm. Convenient."

Dane didn't like the way this was going. And he still didn't have an answer about Kayla.

"What the hell is going on?"

"What have you been doing all night?"

"I had an online chat session with a company in Dublin we're prepping a video for." He added, "It was 1:00 a.m. here, but nine in the morning there."

"They can verify that?"

"Sure."

"I'd like to take a look around your apartment, Mr. Burdette. Do I have your permission?"

"You tell me if Kayla's all right, you can look all you want." He was starting to feel desperate now.

The older officer moved to face him head-on. Dane got the distinct feeling he was being studied, assessed. Why? He was just forming some vague idea that the man wanted to see how he'd react to what he was about to say when the words came and blasted any further thoughts out of his mind.

"Ms. Tucker's home was firebombed tonight."

A sensation Dane hadn't felt since the night he'd heard Kayla's screams from next door flooded him. He staggered slightly as an enervating chill sapped strength from his muscles and put his brain in a fog. He heard a sound and vaguely realized he'd dropped his cell phone.

Kayla.

"Is she…?"

He couldn't say it. He just couldn't. The officer just looked at him, waiting, for what Dane didn't know.

The phone he'd dropped rang. Feeling as if he were moving underwater he looked at it. Hoping against hope Kayla's familiar photo would be showing.

There was no photo at all. Just a name, the most recent one he'd added to his contact list.

Foxworth.

Slowly, still feeling that numbing paralysis, he bent to pick up the phone.

The officer beat him to it. He glanced at the screen. "Foxworth again," he muttered.

"I need to answer it," Dane said, a little amazed he could still talk at all. But Foxworth, either Quinn or Hayley, might know something, and at least they'd tell him. Unlike these guys, who seemed to be playing some kind of game he didn't know the rules to.

"Put it on speaker," the officer said.

"Speaker?" Didn't they have to have a warrant to listen to somebody's calls? he wondered.

"You were the last one to see Ms. Tucker. And we haven't had a chance to check out these Foxworth people yet. If you've got nothing to hide, put it on speaker."

Nothing to hide. And it wasn't a suggestion or even a request. It was an order. And Dane suddenly, belatedly realized that these deputies weren't here to deliver bad news.

They weren't here to tell him the woman he'd loved for years was dead.

They were here because he was a suspect.

Chapter 18

"You won't believe this, but Cutter sent us."

Kayla wiggled her nose in irritation at the oxygen cannula the E.R. staff insisted she keep on. She felt much better now, and she wished they'd take it off. But when she spoke, or tried to, her voice was just raspy enough that she thought maybe they were right about it.

"He did?"

Hayley nodded. "We heard the sirens—you're not that far from us—but when it quieted down we didn't think much more about it. But Cutter wouldn't let us go back to sleep. He started pacing the bedroom, whining, coming over to us, then walking to the door, back and forth."

Kayla thought of her initial encounter with the dog and then the way he'd led them to Teague in the warehouse. That part wasn't surprising.

"Finally he sat in the middle of the room and started howling, like a wolf looking at a full moon. We had to get up before he'd shut up."

"But then he did?"

Hayley laughed. "Yes. He was too busy dragging our shoes over to us. We got the clue at that point."

"Are you sure he's just a dog?"

"Sometimes, I'm not sure at all."

Kayla shifted, winced as the three stitches in the back of her left shoulder pulled slightly. She knew she'd gotten off lucky with some cuts and what would be a colorful array of bruises. The smoke had been the worst, but Mr. Reyes, bless him, had gotten there and broken the window in the front door to open it in time.

"Where is Quinn?" she asked.

"He's talking to the investigators." Hayley smiled. "There's always a bit of lag time while they check us out."

"Like Dane did," Kayla said, that stubborn inner ache rising, making her outward injuries pale in comparison.

"He was pretty thorough," Hayley agreed. "He was worried about you."

"He's not anymore," Kayla muttered.

"Don't be so sure. I've seen you two together. You don't turn feelings like that off so quickly."

"It wasn't quick. It took ten years." She sounded as bleak as she felt. She knew she had driven him to this.

"Don't give up yet," Hayley said gently. Then, "The investigators will be here momentarily, I'm sure. Is there anything you want to tell me before they arrive?"

"I don't know who it was," she said. "I didn't hear anything. I couldn't sleep so I was in the living room."

"That probably saved your life," Hayley said.

"The house," Kayla began.

Hayley shook her head. "I don't know. The fire department was still all over it when the paramedics loaded you up. I wanted to stay with you, so I didn't really see how bad it was."

"Thank you," Kayla said. "I would have felt...really alone if you hadn't."

Hayley smiled. "You're not alone. But think, Kayla. Was there anyone around? Did you hear any cars, any noises in the yard?"

Kayla tried, replaying the awful night in her mind, but nothing surfaced. "I don't remember anything, but I was pretty upset, so I'm not sure I would have noticed."

But the process of trying to remember if she'd heard or

seen anything unusual kick-started Kayla's brain. Things tumbled into place, and with a little shock she realized that someone had tried to kill her tonight.

And that made her realize she'd been so focused on finding Chad and proving he hadn't killed their parents that she hadn't spent a whole lot of time thinking about who actually had.

"Do you think this is connected? To my parents, I mean?"

"It does seem odd that shortly after we start looking into things you get attacked."

Kayla didn't know whether to hope this was all connected or hope it wasn't.

"Maybe my work, maybe somebody from the counseling group? One of them had a son murdered a month ago."

"We're looking into it," Hayley agreed.

"Definitely." Quinn's voice came from over Hayley's shoulder as he parted the curtains and stepped into the E.R. alcove. "How are you?"

"Okay. I think."

Quinn nodded. "A detective and the arson investigator are right on my heels. Anything I need to know?"

"She doesn't remember anything out of the ordinary," Hayley said.

"Not surprising. Maybe later. How bad was your fight with Dane?"

"Fight?"

"In the driveway."

Kayla frowned, then remembered Mr. Reyes had been in his own driveway at the time. Given the man had saved her life, she found it hard to be upset with him.

"It wasn't a fight. We were a little tense, snapped at each other, but that's all."

"Any threats?"

Kayla blinked. "What?"

"Did he make any threats. 'You'll be sorry,' 'I'll make you pay,' anything like that?"

Bewildered, Kayla stared at him. "Dane?" She sounded as incredulous as she felt. "Of course not. Dane would never say—"

She broke off, suddenly realizing the import behind his question.

"No! No, no, no. Not Dane. Never in a million years."

"You sound awfully sure about a guy who just walked out on you," Quinn said, his gaze never leaving her.

"He had every right to do that," Kayla said miserably. "But it doesn't change who he is inside."

"You're interfering in an investigation, Mr. Foxworth."

The warning came from behind them in a voice that held the ring of command.

"Ms. Tucker is a client, Detective Dunbar," Quinn said without missing a beat. A dark-haired man in civilian clothes, but with an air about him that matched the voice, pushed aside the curtains. Even Kayla could have guessed he was a cop. He was tall and rangy and looked fit and tough. A touch of grey at his temples suggested he might be older than Quinn, although he didn't really look it otherwise.

"Is Dane Burdette a client, too?"

Quinn hesitated, which already Kayla knew was unlike him. She took advantage even as she wondered if he'd done it purposefully, to give her this chance.

"Yes," she said quickly. "And he did *not* do this. He would never, ever do anything remotely like this."

"I've heard the same from the family and friends of everything from terrorists to serial killers."

He didn't say it coldly or cruelly; in fact, if anything his tone was sad as he looked at her.

"He didn't do it," Kayla insisted. And it struck her suddenly that she was once more in the position of protesting the innocence of someone the police seemed to have already decided was guilty.

"He has no alibi. He can't prove he wasn't there," Dunbar said.

"But that's not the question, is it?" Quinn said. "The question is can you prove he was?"

"Where is he now?" Kayla demanded.

"You seem very concerned," Detective Dunbar said. "Didn't you two just break up yesterday?"

"I've loved him since I was fourteen," Kayla said, "and I still do. You're not listening." She shook her head, then wished she hadn't as the room spun a little. She closed her eyes. "God, do the police never listen?" she whispered.

"I'm listening," Dunbar said, sounding different now, but Kayla felt too drained at the moment to answer. As if he sensed that, although Kayla wasn't yet ready to cede that much sensitivity to him, he changed tack and began to question her instead on what exactly had happened.

She opened her eyes and went through it all again but remembered nothing new to add to the account.

"So you say you heard nothing, saw nothing, until the actual explosion itself," the detective said. He didn't say it in an accusing tone, but to Kayla it sounded that way anyway.

"I wasn't even in that room," she explained again. "I was in the front of the house."

"Still, a broken window makes a lot of noise."

"Is that how it was done?" Hayley asked.

The detective didn't look at her as he nodded; he kept his gaze on Kayla's face.

"I'm not the arson people, but it looked to me like there was a small explosion in addition to a pretty standard Molotov cocktail, with the ignition point at the foot of the bed, although it spread fast enough and was hot enough that I'm thinking there might have been more than just gasoline involved. Probably trying to destroy any evidence."

Kayla smothered a shiver. She hadn't realized until this moment just how narrow her escape had been. If she had stayed in bed, she might well be dead.

As if he thought he'd put her off guard, Dunbar went back to his questioning.

"And you were upset," the detective said. "Distracted, by the fight you had earlier."

"It was not a fight," she insisted, pushing back another shiver of reaction. Right now it was more important to convince this man. "And I was upset by Dane's absence, not a couple of sharp words."

She closed her eyes again, feeling battered now.

"It was Dane's choice," she heard Hayley say.

Kayla's eyes snapped open. It didn't seem like Hayley to rub it in.

"Exactly," Quinn agreed, looking at the detective. "He's the one who walked away—she didn't leave him—so why would he turn around and try to kill her?"

"Maybe he's angry over why he had to walk away," Dunbar said. Kayla thought she heard doubt in his voice, as if he'd wondered that himself. Then again, maybe it was wishful thinking.

"When Dane gets angry, which isn't often, he goes out and rides his bike twenty miles," Kayla said. "If he's really mad, he does half of it uphill. *That's* how he deals with anger. Not blowing things up or…"

Her voice trailed off. The very idea of Dane trying to kill anyone, let alone her, was beyond absurd, too absurd to deserve being put into words.

The detective's cell phone rang. Kayla supposed the no phone rule in emergency rooms didn't apply to police. He walked a few feet away and answered quietly.

Moments later he was back. His gaze was fastened on Quinn.

"You're that Foxworth? The one who helped take down that cop-killer over in Seattle?"

"We played a small part, yes," Quinn said.

"Word I got was it was more than a small part. He shot you."

Kayla's eyes widened, and she saw Hayley's gaze snap to Quinn.

"Not well," Quinn answered dryly. "He left me standing."

"So that scar's from some 'stupid accident'?" Hayley said, her voice tight.

A glance at the woman's face confirmed this information was news to Hayley, too. Hayley's expression told Kayla there would be a discussion about this later. She didn't envy Quinn; the woman did not look pleased.

"It was stupid. But the bullet ended up being the final nail in his incarceration coffin," Quinn added.

The detective smiled then. Which made his next words as he turned back to her even more ominous.

"Burdette's in custody."

Chapter 19

"He wouldn't. He didn't," Kayla said fiercely, staring at Quinn and Hayley as if she could will them to believe.

"You must feel like you've spent half your life saying that," Hayley said, reaching out to take Kayla's hand.

"But with Chad it's just faith. With Dane it's rock-solid fact. He simply would never do such a thing. To anyone."

Quinn studied her silently. Detective Dunbar had left them, with an admonition to Kayla that he'd want to speak to her again later. It wasn't quite "Don't leave town," but it was close enough.

And now, she thought, he was off to grill Dane. Already assuming he was guilty, just as the police then had assumed Chad was guilty. History repeating itself. She stifled a moan, barely.

"We'll get it straightened out," Quinn promised.

"You believe me? That he wouldn't do this?" Kayla pleaded.

"He doesn't seem the type," Quinn said. "Not a sneak attack like this."

Kayla felt a little less pressure in her chest. "He's not. At all."

"Who is?"

"What?"

"Who would be the type? If it's not Dane, it's somebody else. Who?"

Kayla blinked. "I have no idea." Her earlier thought ran

through her mind, that she'd been so focused on proving Chad hadn't killed their parents that she hadn't thought enough about who had. Now she was looking at that same kind of question again, with the intended victim clearly she herself.

Belatedly, something about his question occurred to her.

"Wait, you think this is someone I know?"

"It's someone who obviously knows you. Or at least enough about you and your home to place that bomb in the most likely place. So it's a possibility."

That made it all even worse.

Kayla shook her head, wishing she could think more clearly. This time, at least, the room didn't spin.

"So now you think this isn't connected to my parents' murders?"

"I think it's far too early to take any options off the table," Quinn said.

"I wish the police had thought that way ten years ago," Kayla said, not caring about the bitter note that had come into her voice.

"I think," Quinn said, "you might find Detective Dunbar a different type."

"Type?"

"He's ex-LAPD. I get the feeling he takes things a bit personally. It may be why he left. That kind of cop takes a real beating in places with frequent serious crimes."

"Personally?" Hayley asked.

Quinn nodded. "The kind who takes the work home with him. Good for victims, not so good on the cop."

"He didn't seem to be on my side," Kayla said.

Quinn smiled. "Don't mistake me. He's still a good, thorough cop, I think. What he did here was pretty standard. He has to ask those questions, look for holes in your story. It's his job."

"What kind of holes?"

Quinn shrugged. "They have to consider all the possibilities. Insurance on the house, for instance."

With her fuzzy head, it took her a moment to get there. "You mean…I might have done this myself to get the insurance money?"

"It's been done. And you were safely out of the room."

"She needed stitches and oxygen. Your interpretation of the word 'safely' and mine obviously don't match," Hayley said, and there was such a "We're going to talk about this later" tone in her voice that Kayla nearly smiled despite her turmoil. Quinn had some explaining to do about that getting shot business, obviously.

"I love…loved my house. I would never—"

She broke off. It all seemed like too much; she wanted nothing more than to lie down and sleep for a week. Tears brimmed and she dashed them away angrily. She would not be one of those weepy women who fell apart. She'd done that once, gone completely to pieces, and while Chad's fate was apparently being sealed she'd done little to head it off. She'd only made it through at all because of Dane's unwavering support.

And now he was in trouble.

With an effort she sat up.

"I want out of here."

"Whoa," Hayley said. "Take it easy."

"I've been x-rayed and hooked up to machines for hours. I'm fine, and I want out of here." She yanked the oxygen tube over her head and pulled the clip-like monitor off her finger.

"You're fine now," Quinn said. "Smoke inhalation can be tricky. Sometimes you seem fine at first, but a day later your lungs—"

"I'll deal with that a day later then," she said.

Quinn grimaced slightly, then said, "I'll find the doctor."

After he'd gone, Kayla looked at Hayley. "I have to help Dane. He didn't do this."

"I know."

For a moment Kayla just looked at her. Was she merely placating her? Trying to keep her calm?

"He wouldn't do this. He felt he had to make a choice and he did, but he would never try to hurt you."

Just hearing those words from someone else was a salve to Kayla's battered emotions. Tears escaped this time, and before she could wipe them away Hayley was handing her a tissue.

"We'll help him," Hayley assured her. "Whether this is connected to Chad or not."

After a study of the improving trend of her oxygen saturation levels since she'd been here and securing a promise she would return for a follow-up comparison chest X-ray, and after Hayley had assured her Kayla wouldn't be left alone for the next couple of days, the doctor agreed to release her.

"The coughing resumes, or she starts sounding more hoarse, I want her back here."

"If I have to carry her," Quinn said, and Kayla wasn't quite sure if that was a promise or a threat.

"I want to see Dane. Even if he doesn't want to see me."

"He's still being questioned, I'm sure," Quinn said. "For now let's get you cleaned up and some clothes that don't smell of smoke."

"Clothes," Kayla said, almost numbly. "I probably don't have any, do I?"

"We'll deal with all that," Hayley said as they got into Quinn's SUV.

Kayla paused before sliding into the backseat. "My car."

It wasn't a question, but Quinn answered as if it had been. "The garage looked fine from what I could see. The fire fighters did a good job keeping it from spreading. The fire itself was confined mostly to the bedroom. The rest of the house seemed okay, except for smoke damage. Definitely reparable."

She didn't answer, although she appreciated the information. It was too much to think about just now.

"If you ever wanted a bigger bedroom, now's your chance," Quinn said.

"Is that your version of looking on the bright side?" Hayley asked.

"My version of the bright side is that she's not dead," Quinn said.

A moment passed before Hayley said, "Point taken," with a smile.

They were, Kayla realized, talking to each other so she wouldn't feel pressured to join in. And not for the first time tonight—well, it was nearly morning now—she was thankful for this remarkable couple who had come into her life.

Or been dragged into it, she thought, remembering the determined dog who had brought all this about.

Hayley turned in her seat to look at Kayla. "I'm a bit taller than you, but we're close enough in size I think we can find you something to wear. Then you need to get some sleep."

"But—"

"I'll check on Dane's status," Quinn said, correctly interpreting her protest.

It occurred to her finally to wonder where they were going. Had the smoke affected her brain, her thought process? The doctor had said it could but that she didn't think she'd breathed enough to do damage, and surely if that were the case she wouldn't have released her. She must just be tired. She had, after all, been up all night.

"Where are we going?" she asked.

"You're coming home with us," Hayley said.

That sounded surprisingly comforting. The only pang it gave her was the realization that if things were as they should be, it would be Dane taking care of her and they'd be headed to his apartment.

What turned out, oddly, to be most comforting about it all was the greeting she got when they arrived at the house tucked into the trees. She heard the bark first, looked up and in the growing light of dawn saw Cutter racing toward them. The moment she opened the car door, the dog was there, bypassing his own people, as if he could see they were fine but he wasn't so sure about her. He nudged her with his inquisitive nose and licked at her hands and then her face when she bent to greet him.

"Hello, Cutter," she said formally. "I guess I have you to thank for sending the cavalry."

The dog whined, his tail wagging madly. As if satisfied now she was truly all right, he danced over to greet Hayley, who had exited the car also. The dog then looked into the vehicle at Quinn.

"I'll go do another round with Detective Dunbar," he said, and Kayla had the oddest feeling he was explaining to the dog as much as anyone.

Somehow, it wouldn't surprise her.

Chapter 20

Dane paced the small, windowless interview room. Two and a half strides one way, three the other. Definitely small.

He'd been here for hours now, and every minute of it had been spent worrying about Kayla more than himself. He'd managed to find out she was alive, but they would not tell him her condition. She might yet die, as far as he knew. It was killing him not to be able to go to her, and he tried to focus on something else.

A firebomb.

It seemed too bizarre, too impossible to be real. Who the hell would toss an incendiary device into Kayla's house? Why? She'd never done anything to hurt anyone—only tried to help people who were dealing with a grief she knew all too much about.

His logical mind warned him against making assumptions based on too little information, but he couldn't help thinking this somehow had to be connected to her parents' murders. And maybe that was logical; what were the odds that an average citizen would twice in their lives be a direct casualty of violent crime?

But after ten years?

His mind tried to spiral toward grim images of a smoking, burning ruin of what had been Kayla's—and his—home once more, and he yanked it back.

The door opened. The same detective who had questioned him before stepped in. Dunbar. In another life, he might have liked the guy, Dane thought. He kind of reminded him of his father—not now, he wasn't old enough, but back when his father had been the same age, mid-thirties, maybe forty.

"Did you see Kayla?" he asked as the man shut the door behind him; he'd heard him tell one of the officers he was heading to the hospital when he'd left a couple of hours ago.

The man didn't answer. He crossed the room and tossed a folder on the small table in the center of the room.

"Sit down."

"Did you see her? Is she all right? Tell me, damn it, and I'll sit all you want."

Dunbar studied him for a moment. "You're not in the strongest bargaining position here."

"I want one simple answer to one simple question. You want answers to many. Sounds like you'd be getting the best of the deal."

Dane thought he saw the man's mouth twitch at one corner. "Can't say I don't admire your logic," he said. Then, coldly, "You should be thankful she's alive. Murder by arson is a death penalty special circumstance."

"Yeah, I heard," Dane said. The officer now standing outside the door had almost gleefully pointed that out.

"That'll land you in Walla Walla waiting for the needle or the noose." He'd said it as if it were the chorus of a song, Dane had thought. Not that it mattered. He wouldn't care, not if Kayla was dead.

But she wasn't. He clung to that.

"Sit down," Dunbar said, "and I promise you before I leave, you'll have your answer."

"Is this your carrot on a stick approach? Forget it. I want to know how Kayla is. Now."

"You don't trust me?"

Dane had to think about that one. "I was raised to trust the police," he finally said. "To believe you're the good guys.

And I do. If it was anything else, if it was anyone but Kayla, I'd be in that chair telling you whatever you want to know."

"But you broke up with her."

"You don't turn off a decade of loving somebody overnight."

Something flickered in the detective's eyes, something dark and shadowy. As if a vision from a nightmare of his own had just shot through his mind.

"No," he agreed softly, "you don't."

"Please," Dane said, just as softly, "just tell me if she's all right."

Dunbar studied him for a long, silent moment. And at last, as if he'd reached some sort of inner conclusion, he spoke.

"She's all right. Minor smoke inhalation, a couple of stitches was the worst of it."

A wave of relief swamped Dane. He sat, not in response to the answer and the agreement so much as because he wasn't sure he could keep standing.

Kayla was all right.

"She reacted pretty quickly, considering," Dunbar was saying. "She got down on the floor and I'm guessing got to the door before the smoke did much damage. And her neighbor got her outside right away."

"Bless Mr. Reyes," Dane said, still feeling a bit wobbly.

Dunbar pulled out the chair across the table and sat down himself. "Lucky for her he was still up and awake, and he ran over."

"He's a night owl. Thank God."

"He said you were a…good kid, I think is how he put it. Said you helped him fix his garage door once."

Dane blinked. "Yeah. Couple of years ago. He had the old style, with the big springs, and one of them broke."

"And the lady on the other side said you saved her cat."

Dane was completely puzzled now. What the hell was all

this about? "I… No. The cat could have gotten down from the roof by himself, and would have, but I was afraid Mrs. Kramer would have a heart attack over it first."

"If you didn't do this, who do you think did?"

The abrupt change back to the grim business of the night threw him. As, he thought, it was probably intended to.

"I've been trying to figure that out," he said. "It just makes no sense to me that it's not…connected to what happened ten years ago. Nobody could want to hurt Kayla. She spends her life trying to help people who are going through what she went through."

"But she deals mostly with crime victims. Which puts her on the radar of criminals."

Dane frowned; he'd not thought of it quite like that. "You mean you think this is related to her work?"

"I'm leaving all options on the table at this point."

Dane had the sudden thought that if this man had been the one investigating Kayla's parents' murders, perhaps things might have turned out differently.

"I can't help you with that. What happens in those sessions is confidential, and Kayla never talks about it."

"Never?"

"I mean, she'll tell me someone new joined and why they're there, but what they say in those sessions is sacred to her. She'd never reveal it, so I don't know anything. Not even names."

"Sounds like an AA meeting."

"It is like one in that people have to trust her to open up. She'd never betray that trust."

"Then who else would want her dead?"

Dane winced at the bald statement. Maybe it was the shock, but he was still having trouble wrapping his mind around the idea that anyone would want to kill Kayla.

"My first thought was Chad," he admitted. "That maybe he was back."

"And you think he'd try to kill her? His own sister?"

"If he killed their parents, why would that be a stretch?"

"According to Ms. Tucker, that's a very big if."

"I know. She's never believed he did it."

"But you did?"

"Not in the beginning. I stood by her and helped her search for him, thinking he had just panicked and run. But the more time passed and he didn't come back but kept sending those notes…"

Dane's voice trailed off, and he shrugged.

"You changed your view."

"He just wasn't acting like somebody who was innocent."

"So you think he's back? And tried to kill his sister?"

Dane sighed. "I don't know. None of this makes any sense. If Chad's back, why would he try to kill her? Wouldn't he at least talk to her first, find out if she was still insisting on his innocence? Why would he kill the one person who'd stood by him the whole time?"

"You're assuming he knows that."

Dane's brows furrowed. "I… Yes, I guess I am." Another thought hit him. "Are you thinking maybe Chad feels she's a threat?"

"There's never been any direct contact, right? If I were a guy who murdered my own parents, I might be thinking my stubborn little sister would never give up looking for the killer."

"You mean he thinks she's looking for the killer, which would be him, rather than what she's really been doing, which is trying to find him to prove him innocent?"

Dane turned the idea over in his mind. It made sense.

"But then why would he keep sending those notes?" he asked. "Why wouldn't he just cut off all contact?"

"That's the kink in that theory," Dunbar admitted. "Which brings us back to the other big question. If it isn't connected to the murder of her parents and it isn't her brother, who else would want her dead?"

Something in the way the man was looking at him told Dane what he was thinking.

"Look, I know you have to look at me, I know there's some hideous statistic about how often murders are committed by someone the victim knows. Hell, I've even used those stats, trying to get Kayla to admit the possibility Chad killed their folks. But I didn't do this, and the more time you waste with me, the less time you're spending looking for the guy who did."

"Funny thing about my job," Dunbar said, leaning back in his chair. "I get to decide what's a waste of time and what's not."

Dane sighed. "What do you want from me? I've told you where I was, everything that happened. What else is there?"

"Let's say, just for the sake of this discussion, I believe you."

Hope surged in him, and Dane was almost taken in by Dunbar's casual tone. He had to remind himself this was no normal discussion—this was an interrogation.

And I'll bet he's good at it, Dane thought.

"Give me some alternatives," Dunbar said. "Her brother, I got that, but as far as we know he's not around."

Dane shook his head in frustration. "I told you, there's nobody. This is Kayla, for God's sake. She's…she's…"

He stopped. None of the words that came to mind were going to help him. Because they all stemmed from the pain of having to walk away from her and the life he'd always thought they'd have.

"No angry clients, ex-boyfriends?"

"She's been mine since we were kids," Dane said. "Everybody knew that. Chad used to rag on her about us—'two nerds in love,' he used to say. When she turned sixteen she… blossomed, I guess. People noticed."

"Guys noticed."

Dane nodded. "Guys who never noticed her before. I mean, Chad's friend Troy always used to ask her to leave me for him, but she thought he was just teasing his best friend's little sister. But then other guys started asking her out."

"And?"

"She always said no. In case you hadn't noticed, Kayla's loyal to the core." His mouth twisted wryly. "Which is why we're in this mess."

"So you're sure she never cheated on you?"

Dane laughed, short and sharp. "She doesn't have it in her. That's just not who she is."

"Thought you had her under control, did you?" Again Dunbar's voice seemed a hair too mild.

Dane laughed again at the very thought. "Nobody 'controls' a woman as smart as Kayla. I'm saying if she wanted out she'd say so."

"Hmm."

Nice and noncommittal, Dane thought. And the silence that spun out afterward invited him to fill it with anything to relieve the tension. Yes, Dunbar was good, he thought. He said nothing more.

A rap on the door disrupted the silence. Dunbar rose and went to talk with the officer outside. The door closed, leaving Dane to wonder what was going on now.

There was no clock in the room, he supposed intentionally; you couldn't complain about how long you'd been in here if you didn't know how long it had been. He couldn't even look at his phone for the time because they'd taken it when they'd brought him here and were probably going through it call by call, contact by contact.

At first he hadn't been worried, other than that they might screw something up, settings or something. There was nothing in that phone that shouldn't be—no incriminating pictures or texts or mysterious phone numbers. Nothing in the least suspicious, unless you found a game of Drone Hunt suspicious.

But now he was wondering. Who knows what might seem suspicious to the police?

Sitting there, alone after Dunbar's interrogation and with the immediate dread about Kayla relieved, the reality of his situation finally began to sink in. And no amount of knowing that that was probably exactly how they wanted him to feel helped alleviate it.

And perversely, ironically, he found himself wondering if he'd been wrong, if maybe Chad was innocent after all.

It could happen. He was sitting here a prime suspect, wasn't he?

And for the first time, it occurred to him to wonder if he was a prime suspect to Kayla, too.

Chapter 21

When the interview room door opened again, Dane was surprised to see Quinn Foxworth come in alone.

Dane glanced at the door, then back to Quinn.

"Aren't they afraid I'll try to strangle you or something?" he asked wearily.

"I think they're assuming I could defend myself," Quinn said.

Dane didn't doubt that. Quinn Foxworth was a tough guy in a very literal sense.

"And I told them they could wait until your lawyer arrived, or let me talk to you now and avoid the burden of attorney-client privilege," Quinn said.

"I don't have a lawyer," Dane said, puzzled.

"You will if it turns out you need one. We have a couple on call. Frankly, I don't think it will come to that."

"You're more confident than I am."

Quinn smiled easily. "That's part of the game. They keep you worried and off balance so you'll make a mistake, say something you shouldn't, to give yourself away."

"But there's nothing to give away."

"So I've been told. Rather vehemently, I might add."

Quinn's expression told him by who. "Kayla," he said, relief softening his voice. "She's really all right?"

"Yes. Cuts and bruises mostly."

Dane finally let himself believe it. Quinn saw his reaction. "They told you that, didn't they?"

"Eventually," Dane said, remembering the battle of wills with Dunbar. "But I wasn't sure they weren't just saying she was okay to get me to talk."

"Good thinking. And if Dunbar had really thought you were guilty, a good tactic."

"You think he doesn't? I mean, I practically lived in that house. It's not like there's not evidence of that."

"I think if he really thought you were guilty, he wouldn't have let me in here no matter what I said."

Dane looked around the room. "Are they listening?"

"Probably," Quinn said cheerfully. "Not a problem."

"Kayla believes I didn't do this?"

"Her defense of you was what they call 'spirited.'"

Dane felt the pressure that had been building in him since he'd wondered if she, too, suspected him, ease a little.

Apparently Quinn found his expression easy to read. "After ten years of her believing in her brother, why would you think she'd abandon you so quickly?"

"Because I said I thought he was guilty. It's the only part of her life where she's not...reasonable."

"Do you really think he did it?"

"I did," Dane admitted. He glanced around at his surroundings and added, "Then."

"Easier to see how the wheels of the system grind when you're in the middle of it, isn't it?"

"I've always believed the cops were the good guys."

"They are," Quinn said. "And I get the feeling Dunbar is a particularly good one. But they're human, contrary to what some think. And when you're fighting a constant, never-ending battle like they do, there are going to be mistakes made."

"Like arresting the wrong guy?"

"They haven't arrested you yet," Quinn pointed out. "There are cases, yes. But remarkably few, considering. More often the courts—or politicians—have a tendency to let the wrong guy walk."

Because Kayla had told him Quinn's history, of how and why the Foxworth Foundation had come to be, Dane was amazed he could speak so calmly about it.

"I didn't do this," Dane said, already weary of protesting his innocence and feeling again that perverse twinge of empathy for Chad.

"I believe you. You didn't do this."

He hesitated. This man had no reason, no long history with him to draw on to reach that conclusion. "You do?"

Quinn nodded. "And I promised Kayla you'd get all the help you need to prove it."

Relief swamped him. And he realized what he felt had to be somewhat like what Kayla had felt when she'd realized she had effective, resourceful help in her search for her brother.

"I'm beginning to realize I've been…not as understanding as I thought I was," Dane said with a grimace.

"A dose of walking in another's shoes does tend to promote understanding," Quinn said.

Quinn's cell chirped the arrival of a text message. He pulled it out and read what appeared to be rather lengthy text.

"I'll be right back," he said and left the room. Dane didn't start pacing again; he wasn't sure he could even get up. He was suddenly tired, almost shaky, as if the adrenaline that had been coursing through him from the moment he'd heard about what had happened had finally ebbed, leaving him enervated.

The door opened again, and Dunbar was back. This time he had Dane's cell phone and handed it over to him. It was turned on with a familiar screen glowing.

"I like the game," the detective said. "You do that?"

"My partner," Dane said. "He does a little designing on the side."

"Cute. He should market it."

"He may," Dane answered, puzzled by the change in attitude.

"Let me know. You'll be able to because you won't be leaving town."

"I hadn't planned to," Dane said, but the last word was spoken to the detective's back as he walked away.

And then Quinn was back.

"Let's get you out of here."

"Out?" Dane was almost afraid to believe it. "I can go?"

"Yes." Quinn nodded his head toward the door.

"What—"

"Let's go," Quinn said, leading him out.

Dane took the hint and stayed quiet. Unlike his arrival, his exit was through the front door. He followed Quinn out the double glass doors into a brilliantly sunny morning.

"It cleared out," he said, blinking at the brightness. The sun rose early this time of year, and even now, at 5:30 a.m., it was well clear of the Cascade Mountains.

"Good thing it rained last night," Quinn said.

"Because of the fire."

Quinn shook his head. "Because that's probably the main reason you're walking out of here."

Dane's brows lowered. "What do you mean?"

Quinn unlocked the doors of the blue SUV and they got in.

"So be thankful for the rain," Quinn went on, "and the cop that lives downstairs from you."

"Jarrod? What's he got to do with it?"

"His parking space is next to yours."

"I know, but—"

"He worked a split shift on DUI patrol last night. Got home about 3:00 a.m. His car was wet. Yours was dry. He noticed."

"Damn," Dane said, half to himself. "Thank you, Jarrod. I'll wash your car for you next time."

"It's not enough to clear you completely—you could have used another method to get there—but it got you out for now."

"I'll quit complaining when he parks crooked."

Quinn grinned as he started the engine. "He wasn't real happy when Teague woke him up two hours after he got to bed, but he cooperated. Called Detective Dunbar right away."

They pulled out of the parking lot. Dane wondered where they'd be going but was more curious about what had just happened.

"That was the text?"

"Part of it." Quinn shrugged. "The officers talked to most of your neighbors, but they knew your neighbor had worked that late shift, that he'd been on the street at the time of the explosion, so they let him slide, figuring they'd check with him later. We weren't so considerate, I'm afraid."

"Thanks for that," Dane said fervently. "What was the other part of the text?"

"It was word from our tech-head, that he'd pulled your on-line messaging session with the company in Dublin from your system. Under the circumstances, I didn't think you'd mind."

Dane drew back. "He hacked me? How'd he do that? I've got some pretty tight security in place."

"So he told me. But he's good," Quinn said.

"He must be really, really good."

"He is."

"Now they might say anybody could have been pretending to be you," Quinn said.

Dane shook his head. "I've got a log of that discussion. It's pretty detailed, with stuff only I would know."

"Good."

Quinn made a right turn, away from Kayla's place and his apartment building.

"We're not going to Kayla's?"

"No. I think you'd best stay away for a while. Later maybe."

"Afraid I'll get upset? It was practically my home, too."

"No. It's the returning to the scene of the crime thing. Arsonists have a tendency to do that. Don't want to make Dunbar change his mind."

Dane sighed. "Not sure I want to see it anyway."

"Actually, from the front, it doesn't look like anything happened. It was just the back. The bedroom."

Dane suppressed a shudder. "God. She could have been killed."

"If she'd been in there, yes."

"Why wasn't she?"

Quinn glanced at him. "Same reason you weren't sleeping at two in the morning, I imagine."

He couldn't deny that so Dane fell silent, wrestling with the one question that now seemed paramount. He hadn't bombed Kayla's house, so who had?

"Who the hell would have done it?" he muttered.

"That's the real question, isn't it?" Quinn said. "If we take you out of the picture, then the most likely possibilities are it's connected to what happened ten years ago or to Kayla's work now."

"But why would anybody try to hurt somebody who's just helping people? And if it's connected to her folks, why now, after all this time?"

"If we knew those answers we'd have the answer," Quinn said as he made another turn that told Dane they were headed out to Foxworth.

"Dunbar said all options were still on the table."

"I said he's a good cop."

"So you think he's considering the other possibilities?"

"I know he is. I'm guessing the speculation is that somebody in her counseling group is a threat. They're all the victims of crimes, which means there are perpetrators. Maybe one that's still on the loose is afraid Kayla will discover something from one of them."

"But then why not go after the person? Why go after her?"

"Exactly the problem with that theory."

"Then it has to be related to her folks, even if it was ten years ago."

"That's a long time to stay dormant," Quinn said.

"But something's changed," Dane said. "She has you looking into it now. It's not just her trying on her own anymore."

"Yes."

"Foxworth has a high level of success. If the killer found out you were involved…"

"It could be that our presence has stirred up something," Quinn said, "whoever the killer is. And the bottom line is always that there's no statute of limitations on murder."

Dane absorbed all the implications. "That means…he's back."

"Assuming he ever really left, yes."

Quinn's calm tone told Dane the man had already realized that. He was beginning to doubt Quinn was ever really surprised by anything.

"What now?"

"Now? We turn up the heat."

Chapter 22

Dane heard the trumpeting bark and saw Cutter already racing through the open warehouse door the moment the SUV cleared the trees.

"He doesn't miss much, does he?"

Quinn laughed. "I don't think he misses anything."

There was a bright red smaller SUV Dane hadn't seen before parked near the office building door.

"That's Hayley's," Quinn said. "They're here."

They. "You don't mean just Hayley and Cutter, do you?"

"I doubt Hayley—or Cutter for that matter—would let Kayla out of their sight just now."

The dog was at the passenger door of the car, waiting with ill-concealed impatience for Dane to exit. Puzzled, Dane glanced at Quinn.

"Why isn't he over there waiting for you?"

"He knows I'm all right. You, not so much. He always knows who needs checking on."

Dane opened the door and stepped out. Cutter moved to him, sniffing, looking, nudging. Finally he sat, apparently satisfied that Dane had come to no harm while out of his care.

"You," Dane said, rubbing a hand over the dog's dark head, "are something else, dog."

Cutter made a sound that Dane could only call satisfied. Whether it was that he was all right, or that he had finally realized the uniqueness of this animal, Dane wasn't sure.

Cutter's head turned just slightly, back toward the warehouse. Seconds later a man came out, someone Dane hadn't seen before. Tall and rangy, he walked with a barely perceptible limp on his left side. He was wiping his hands on a shop rag; he'd clearly been working on something mechanical.

"Rafe Crawford, Dane Burdette," Quinn said.

Rafe nodded, indicating with the greasy rag why he wasn't offering a hand to shake. "Checking out the backup generator."

Dane nodded at the man. Without the distraction of a handshake, it was the man's eyes he noticed; they reminded him of Kayla's, not in color but in a certain quality of having seen too much, of reflecting too much pain lived through.

Opposites, he thought, the two Foxworth men they'd met. Teague, with his easy, crooked grin and jokes, and now this man, unsmiling in face or eyes. That interested him—as much as anything outside his own current dilemma did just now.

"Is it working all right?" Quinn asked the newcomer.

Rafe nodded. "Not that it's as crucial, now that you're living…elsewhere."

Quinn's smile, quick and contented, was the only answer he gave to that.

"You got things settled in Boise?" he asked.

Rafe nodded again. "Everybody arrived. Happy reunion."

"Good. Why don't you take some time? That was a tough one."

"I'm good."

"Didn't say you weren't."

Rafe glanced at Dane. "Thought you might need another body on this one."

"Interested?"

"Cold case," Rafe said with a shrug.

"All right then," Quinn said. "Meet us inside."

"I'll go clean up."

"What was that all about?" Dane asked. It was obvious

the two men were old friends; they'd spoken in the kind of shorthand that showed long familiarity.

"Rafe's got a thing for cold cases," Quinn said. "And he never gives up on them."

"He and Kayla should relate then," Dane said. There was none of the recent sourness at the thought in his voice or his mind; nearly losing her had wiped all that away, at least for now.

But it hadn't really changed anything. It hadn't caused some great revelation about how much he loved her—he'd already known that. He'd always known that.

Just like he knew he always would love her.

Even if he had to go on without her.

Hayley met them at the door.

"You're here early," Quinn said.

"She just couldn't bear to stay still any longer, so we came here."

"How is Kayla?" Dane asked, unable to hold back the question long enough to offer a hello.

Hayley didn't seem offended by the lack of a greeting. "She's steadier now. She'll be sore tomorrow, I'm guessing, but for now she's all right. As soon as we're done going over everything, I'm going to run over to her place and see what I can salvage in the way of immediate needs."

"They'll let you in?" Dane asked.

She smiled. "I checked just now, and the arson investigator has pulled all his evidence. Besides, the fire chief was a friend of my father's. I'll get in."

"Do they know what it was yet?"

"They're still reconstructing. But I'll pester them until we know."

Quinn snorted. "You, a pest? Nah."

She smiled sweetly at him. "If I wasn't, we probably wouldn't be here now."

Quinn's voice went soft. "And I wouldn't trade that for anything."

"Nor would I."

Dane shifted as pain jabbed through him. He and Kayla had once sounded like that. Teasing in the most loving way possible. Hayley flicked a glance at Dane, and he knew something must have shown in his face because she went on briskly.

"Kayla wanted to come, too, but I don't think that's wise. And she doesn't need to see the damage yet."

"Agreed," Quinn said. "I think they should both stay away until we find out who was really behind this."

"Teague's working on that, by the way. He called while you were at the police station, said he had an idea he was going to check out."

"That's why I hired the boy," Quinn said with a grin. "Let's get started."

The moment she heard footsteps on the stairs Kayla knew, with that sort of sixth sense that always told her when Dane was nearby, before they even got close to the door. Hayley had been in and out a couple of times, and the tall, lean, intimidating man she'd introduced as Rafe Crawford had come through that door once, but this time it was Dane. She could feel it.

She drew in a deep breath and tried to steady herself. She'd rehearsed it all in her mind from the moment Hayley had told her Quinn had gotten Dane out and they were on their way. She would greet him like a normal person. It would be awkward, sure, as it always was between former lovers, she supposed. She didn't actually know; Dane was the only lover she'd ever had.

The only lover she'd ever wanted.

She would greet him no differently than, say, she would

greet Quinn when he came in. Pleasantly but as a man who didn't belong to her.

It hit her again, as it had so many times last night before her world had exploded. He didn't belong to her anymore.

Which meant he was free to belong to someone else.

Images shot through her mind, of Dane with some unknown, carefree, unhaunted woman who could give him the kind of love he deserved, free of baggage. She could see him smiling with her, laughing with her, making love to her. It hurt so badly she would swear she was bleeding inside.

Quinn and Hayley had been there for her last night, she couldn't deny that. But it wasn't the same, not by a long shot. Nothing could replace the comfort and knowledge of a shared history. She'd always had Dane to turn to for comfort. Had always counted on him to be there. And then he was gone, and she felt more lost than she had since the night she'd come home to find her parents lying dead in their blood-spattered den.

Was it worth it? Was this endless pursuit really worth it? Trying to find someone who clearly didn't want to be found even, or as Dane had said, maybe especially not by her?

She'd thought before about quitting, but she hadn't. She'd even sort of prided herself on not giving up. But was it truly all worth it if it cost her the one person who had always been her rock?

She felt the sudden urge to call it all off, to finally give it up, except that now it had gotten even more complicated.

Now someone had tried to kill her.

The door opened. Quinn came through first.

And then there was Dane, looking tired and almost as haggard as she felt.

All her good intentions vanished and she ran to him. She couldn't help herself—he looked so weary. She may have had the worst of it physically, but to see Dane, strong, steady Dane, look like this was more than she could bear.

She threw her arms around him. After a split-second delay perhaps only she would notice, his arms came up and wrapped around her. For a long moment they simply stood there, as if either of them would fall without the support of the other.

Don't talk, she ordered herself. Don't say anything because then you'll have to face reality, that this is only temporary, that it's only because of what happened, that he's holding you because you were hurt, that he would do it for anyone who needed it because he was the kind of man who helped.

He spoke first.

"You're really all right?"

She nodded against his chest.

"Stitches?"

She nodded again, this time hunching her left shoulder to indicate where.

"Your hair smells different."

She sighed at the simple yet intimate statement. And gave in.

"Yes. I borrowed some of Hayley's shampoo."

She felt him move then, lifting his head to look at Hayley and Quinn, who were quietly ignoring them.

"Thank you for taking care of her," he said.

"Of course," Hayley said. "Do you want some more time? We could go—"

"No."

The flat statement dug into that painful place inside Kayla. She heard Dane draw in a deep breath.

"I'll take care of her now. I'm not leaving her alone again until this is over."

Hope, battered, bloody, yet ever-ready to rise again, stirred from that painful place. As if he'd sensed it—of course he did, Dane always knew—he quickly smashed it into oblivion.

"Nothing's changed," he said to her. "I just want to walk away by my choice—not have that choice made by someone else, leaving me to grieve your death."

Kayla shuddered, then straightened and stopped leaning on him. Just as she was going to have to learn to do the rest of her life.

Chapter 23

"Thanks, Chief Byers," Hayley said into her cell phone, then pushed the button to disconnect.

They had all fallen silent when the call from the fire chief had come in. They were seated around the same table where they'd begun this barely a week ago. So much had happened in that short time, Kayla thought as Hayley listened carefully.

"He got the reports just now," Hayley said as she set the phone down.

"Good of him to call so quickly," Quinn said.

"He and my dad were close. When I was little he was like my uncle. And he helped when my mother was ill and was there for me when she died."

"That puts him on the 'come running if he calls' list for me then," Quinn said.

To Kayla's surprise, Hayley blushed. It reminded her that, relatively speaking, their relationship was fairly new. Of course, relative to her and Dane, and at their ages, most were.

She glanced at him surreptitiously. He'd taken a seat across the table from her this time, making an obvious, physical point about the new distance between them. She should have expected this, she'd thought when he'd done it. Dane was not a man to make a decision and then crumble at the first difficulty. The strength that had always been hers to borrow when needed was now arrayed against her, and he was as distant as if that table was miles wide.

She was distracted slightly when Cutter showed his displeasure with the new arrangement. He walked from Dane to her and back again, nudging them and whining quietly.

"Not now, sweetie," Hayley said softly to the dog, who sighed audibly and plopped down on the floor. Kayla felt the weight on her right foot and looked down to see his head resting on her toe. Coincidentally—or perhaps not because this was Cutter—his tail appeared to be wrapped around Dane's left ankle, as if the dog would maintain contact between them even if they wouldn't.

She scratched the dog's ear, straightened and looked at Dane. He didn't react. His expression was stony, emotionless. If he'd noticed the flash of warmth, of tenderness between Hayley and Quinn, or the oddly touching action of their dog, he wasn't reacting.

She had put that expression on his face, she thought sadly. She had never meant to do that.

Kayla tuned back into what Hayley was saying about the device used to start the fire.

"—the explosion was apparently some type of homemade grenade. The fire starter was a rather amateurish Molotov cocktail, he said. The bottle he used was too heavy to shatter, so it only broke into a couple of big pieces, which contained things a little."

"That doesn't help narrow it down much," Quinn said. "It could still go either way unless Chad had a fascination with fire. Did he?"

This was clearly directed at her, Kayla realized. "No," she said. "Never."

"Never interested in blowing up toy buildings or cherry bombs in mailboxes or the like?"

"No," she said again. "Firecrackers as a kid, but we all did that. I don't think he'd even know how to build something like this, even it if was simple."

"Too much like chemistry," Dane said. "Which is too much like work."

"That's—"

"True," Dane said, cutting her off. "Did you think I really believed that chem homework you asked for help with was your friend Crystal's?"

"A moot point," Quinn said rather quickly, as if he thought another kind of explosion was imminent. "He's obviously had enough time to have learned."

"And he didn't have to learn well. Good thing he never did, isn't it?" Dane asked.

Kayla opened her mouth to protest, a reaction she hadn't realized until now had become so automatic. She stopped herself and remained silent. Something about Dane's tone was...different.

"But it was effective enough," Hayley said. "If Kayla had been in that room, the outcome would probably have been very different. If there's a next time—"

"If there is she won't be alone," Dane said.

The words should have heartened her, and they would have if Kayla hadn't just realized why he sounded so odd, why his voice was so different. Gone was the trace of irritation, impatience. He was speaking in a dispassionate voice. Like a man not personally involved.

He was speaking as if he were some kind of bodyguard who had never met her before, as if he were simply doing a job he felt obligated to do.

This is what it would be like, she thought, if Dane really didn't care. Fear grew in her until she could hardly breathe. With an effort almost as great as it had taken to get to the front door last night, she reined in her rampaging thoughts and made herself pay attention.

"—he thinks Foxworth would quit and go away, even if

he'd been successful, he's very, very wrong," Quinn was saying. "We don't give up."

Kayla remembered Hayley telling her something about a leak, possibly a mole, who had threatened the operation that had thrown her and Quinn together. And that Quinn would never, ever stop until he found who it was. It eased Kayla's mind a little, that idea, that even if something happened to her, there were people now who would carry on.

"What about Rod Warren?" Dane asked. "If he was into burning small creatures...."

"Good point," Quinn said.

"And torturing animals is frequently a warning sign of sociopathic behavior," Hayley said.

"Why don't you call Detective Dunbar and plant that idea," Quinn said. "He liked you."

Hayley let out a muffled, embarrassed sound. "Please."

"Trust me on this. I know when a man's looking at my fiancée that way." Hayley blushed then. "Fortunately, I also know he's the kind of man who'd never poach."

Hayley glanced at Kayla as if for female support. "Don't you just love it when they go all guy on you?"

"Yes." With an effort, Kayla didn't look at Dane. "As a matter of fact I do."

Dane said nothing, and Kayla wished she'd kept her mouth shut.

"Do we have that list of the crime victim group members?" Quinn asked quickly, as if he'd sensed the tension.

"I have it," Hayley said, pulling a sheet out of the file. Then she turned to the laptop computer that sat on the table beside her. "And here's the background we've turned up on them. I finished entering it all from Teague's notes while we were waiting for you to get here."

Quinn smiled at her. Kayla remembered Hayley telling her about how she'd begun actually working with Foxworth, after meeting—and falling for—Quinn. How she'd been rather rudderless after her mother's death, and finding this work that so appealed to her had been the second-best thing, after finding Quinn, that had ever happened to her.

Obviously she'd gotten into it wholeheartedly and efficiently. She envied them the obvious solidity of their lives together. She was sure they would make it. While she and Dane might not.

She clung to that "might" with a fierceness that she knew was foolish even as she did it. One look across at Dane's face told her that.

"Here's the one that had caught my eye," Hayley said as the screen went live and an image flashed up on the screen.

"Art Solis?" Kayla asked, startled.

"He's working for a building contractor now, but he used to work for the Department of Transportation. Road construction. Assigned to a mountain district."

"They occasionally use explosives," Dane said, as if he were contemplating a merely interesting puzzle.

"No!" Kayla shook her head. "Art would never hurt anyone. He's a sweet, nice man. He was devastated by his daughter's death. In fact, he's still in the processing stage, practically nonfunctional."

Hayley patted Kayla's hand. "I said he *had* caught my eye. But the call from Chief Byers changes that."

Quinn nodded. "Not dealing with a pro here. And if he's in the state Kayla describes, not likely. But then again, if he's in that state, he might have been sloppier than he would have if he were thinking straight."

"But why would he?" Kayla asked. "Samantha was killed when her car was broadsided by an escaping bank robber. Why would that make me a target? In fact, why would I become a target to any of them?"

"Maybe none of them are thinking straight," Dane said.

"He's right," Hayley said gently when Kayla tightened her jaw to keep from reacting. "You know better than most that grief can deeply affect your thinking."

"Reasons are something we may have to figure out later," Quinn said. "Right now we just need to know if there are any others with the potential."

They began to go through the list. Kayla watched uncomfortably as the familiar names flashed by on the screen. She knew the painful stories behind every name, and she didn't like that they were being paraded like this. She hadn't betrayed any confidences, had only given names that weren't confidential anyway, but Foxworth clearly had an efficient and far-reaching research capability.

She simply couldn't believe that any of them would be involved. Why would a victim who knew the pain they had experienced do something that could cause someone else the same kind of pain? She knew there were people out there who were simply wired wrong, sociopaths, even psychopaths, but none of her people fit that description. She just couldn't wrap her mind around the idea—

Quinn's cell phone rang, and Kayla was thankful for the interruption.

"They wouldn't," she insisted quietly as Quinn turned slightly away to listen to whoever had called. "They've been through too much pain themselves to want to cause it for others."

"Sometimes grief can send people over the edge," Dane said. It was in that same, uninvolved tone, yet Kayla couldn't help wondering if it had been aimed at her. She heard Quinn speaking to whoever had called but so quietly she couldn't understand what he was saying. She focused on Dane's assertion.

"Those are the people who don't come looking for help

in the first place," she said, keeping her voice even with an effort.

Dane didn't look at her when she spoke, but he did look thoughtful. "Fair point," he said.

Fair. Oh, yes, Dane was fair. He always had been. Sometimes it had annoyed her, when she was running hot over something and he insisted on pointing out the validity of some aspect on the other side. But now it just hurt. Because when it had come down to something that hurt her, personally, he'd ever and always tossed that out and stood with her. He'd always had her back, whether he agreed completely or not.

Until now.

Quinn stood up, and all three still seated at the table looked at him. He slipped his phone back into his pocket. For a moment he said nothing, and Kayla felt apprehension building inside her. When his gaze shifted, and settled on her, it spiked into fear.

"That was Teague," he finally said. "He's been out covering old ground to see if anyone saw or heard anything that might tie into the firebombing."

"And?" Dane asked when Kayla didn't, couldn't speak.

"He didn't find anything new there. But he did learn something else."

When Quinn didn't go on immediately, Kayla found her voice. "What?" she demanded because it was clear that whatever it was, Quinn wasn't happy about having to tell her.

"He found someone who saw your brother."

Kayla's heart leaped. "Where? When? Who saw him? Are they sure?"

The questions tumbled from her excitedly. She'd hoped Foxworth could really help, that they were as good as they said, but to get this close in such a short time? They were miracle workers.

Dane leaned back in his chair, and she got the impression

he was mentally and physically backing away. But her excitement over the news made her put that on hold for the moment.

"Where?" she repeated, wondering why Quinn wouldn't just tell her.

And then he did, in a voice that held no pleasure or triumph.

"Here."

Kayla's breath caught. "Here? In Redwood Cove? But that's crazy. Why would he come back and not contact me?"

"Maybe he did, in his own, charming way," Dane said, and there was something dark and harsh in his tone.

She made the jump quickly. He thought Chad had done this. With no proof at all, even less than had been at the scene of the murders ten years ago.

She glared at him, wanting suddenly to prod him into saying it, even as she realized it was with the hope he would make her angry enough to start getting over him.

"What's that supposed to mean?" she asked him, her voice sharp.

"Depends on the answer to 'when,'" Dane said with a glance at Quinn.

Quinn sighed. Kayla turned back to him.

In a voice so gentle she knew the words were going to hold pain, in his view anyway, Quinn finally answered her.

"Last night. Just after 2:00 a.m. Near your house."

Chapter 24

Kayla felt like a suddenly punctured balloon. Deflated, limp. Pressure had been building up inside her until she'd felt as if she would come apart, and then, in less than ten words, Quinn Foxworth had burst the bubble she'd been living in.

Chad. Here.

Without contacting her.

Last night.

Near her home.

At about the time of the explosion.

"Who saw him?" It was Dane, speaking calmly, as if the world hadn't just collapsed.

Because it's only your world now. Not his.

"Troy Reid," Quinn said.

Kayla's head came up. "Troy saw him?"

This destroyed her tiny, lingering hope that it had been a mistake, that someone had only thought they'd seen Chad or had seen someone who looked like him. Troy had known Chad too well—he wouldn't make a mistake like that.

"Yes. And," Quinn added, "Teague said he was pretty upset when he told Troy what had happened. He wanted to know if you were all right, if you needed anything. He'll probably call you later."

"Where is my brother now?"

"We don't know," Quinn answered.

She frowned. "Troy didn't know? They were always best friends."

"He says he has no idea. Teague says he said he was completely surprised when he saw him—a little shocked even that Chad hadn't let him know he was back."

"The great Troy Reid caught off guard," Dane muttered. "I would have liked to have seen that."

There was a whiff of the old rivalry in his voice, and Kayla didn't know whether to be angry or secretly pleased about it. Maybe Dane hadn't shut things off as completely as it seemed.

"Now what?" she asked.

"We keep looking. You get some rest."

"But I—"

Dane cut her off. "You've been up all night, and you've been hurt, shocked and through hell. You need sleep."

She would have been happier about his interruption if he'd sounded more concerned and less like that impartial bodyguard she'd thought of earlier. But the thought of collapsing into bed was suddenly so appealing she thought if she closed her eyes she might doze off right here.

And then it struck her.

She didn't have a bed. Not anymore.

"Where?" She wished she hadn't sounded quite so forlorn.

"My place," Dane said.

"Or ours," Hayley put in.

"Neither," Quinn said, relieving her of that decision. "Until we're sure who's behind this, you should stay clear of anyplace you'd be expected to go."

Thankful that there was at least some doubt, somewhere, that Chad had done this, Kayla nodded.

"Where then?" she asked.

"We're a little short on safe houses in the area at the moment," he said.

"Speaking of things that have been blown up," Hayley said. There was a lighthearted note in her voice that seemed at odds with the words, and she and Quinn exchanged a glance that made Kayla smile despite her own turmoil, knowing the story of how they had met.

"There's an old motel over by Freedom Bay," Dane said.

"And Mrs. Clark's B and B," Kayla said. "Although I wouldn't want to cause her any problems."

"The motel, I think," Quinn said. "And you should take one of our cars, just in case."

He picked up his cell phone and pushed a single button.

"Rafe? We need a car. An anonymous one. Can we borrow yours?" A pause, then, "Okay, thanks."

He disconnected and looked at Kayla with a smile. "It looks like it couldn't get out of its own way, but looks are deceiving. More important, it blends."

"I'll be careful with it," Kayla said.

"I'll drive."

Her head snapped around to stare at Dane.

"I told you, I'm not leaving you alone until this is over." He looked at Quinn. "You have any problem with that?"

"None. I assumed," Quinn said easily. "We'll get you both some clothes and whatever else you need at the moment."

And just like that, she was dispensed with. Her next move decided by the men. She would have argued if she wasn't so tired. Too tired to even think.

Which told her, she supposed, that she shouldn't be arguing at all. Maybe it wasn't a male thing. Maybe it was the awake deciding for the half-asleep. And just as well.

Quinn hadn't been kidding, Dane thought. The slightly battered, decade-old silver coupe didn't look like much, but it purred like a big cat and shifted like silk, and when he put his foot in it from a stop sign he discovered it had some big dog tendencies, too—quick and powerful enough to bark the tires.

But most welcome for him was the fact that he didn't have to make an adjustment for his long legs. He and Rafe were about the same height, and he always felt a little cramped in most cars. Not this one, despite the fact that it seemed no bigger than any other average car on the road.

"A wolf in sheep's clothing," he murmured as they left the city limits and headed down the narrower part of the road through thicker trees and dappled sunlight.

"Sort of like its owner," Kayla said, the first time she'd spoken since they'd left Foxworth. "A little beat up on the outside but lethally effective."

Dane glanced at her, curious enough about what she'd said to set aside his determination to speak to her as little as possible. "Lethally?"

"Hayley told me he's the team sniper."

Team *sniper?*

Dane's perception of Foxworth as a do-gooder, strictly investigative-type organization shifted suddenly. They had—needed—a sniper?

"Teague wasn't kidding when he said Quinn kidnapped her. That really is how they met."

Dane knew her well enough to recognize she was feeling the urge to talk, to pretend things were normal between them simply because they were not. She kept going with the story, and he hoped she wasn't harboring the hope that pretending long enough could make it real. Yet he found it a relief himself; the strain of being with her was already beginning to wear at the edges of his control.

"Explosions, sieges, literal fly-by-night escapes and a sniper?" Dane said when she had finished the tale, shaking his head. "There's obviously a hell of a lot more to the Foxworth Foundation than I realized."

"Hayley said they do occasionally get involved in nasty situations. That this witness they helped knew of them because they'd rescued an American girl from a drug cartel. Took her right out from under the nose of some big drug lord."

"Sounds like something we have government people for," Dane said.

"But they didn't do anything. Bogged down in diplomacy and political haggling, Hayley said, and the girl nearly died. Would have, if they hadn't gone in and gotten her."

"Bet that made them unpopular in some quarters."

"Hayley said that's the best part. They're independent, not connected to any agency, and have extensive resources. They don't need anyone's approval to act."

"What about fallout afterward?"

"I guess some of those resources go to some really good attorneys," Kayla said.

"So they're not beholden to anyone, but there are many, many people beholden to them," Dane said.

"That's how it works."

"Sort of gives a new definition to balance of power, doesn't it?" he mused aloud.

"Exactly," Kayla said with a small laugh.

And Dane realized that somehow things had slipped back into normal. As if her pretending really had made it real.

He was going to have to be on guard, he thought. It would be very, very easy to let it happen, to let it all slide away like a patch of debris floating in a stream, forgotten once it was out of sight and replaced by clear, fresh water.

The motel, with a small café attached, appeared on the right, tucked back into the trees. The nearest other buildings had been left behind at least a mile back. Dane wasn't sure if that was good or bad, but Quinn had seemed happy enough with the choice, and with his new awareness of some of the unexpected skills of the whole Foxworth organization, he decided that was good enough.

He'd have to stay alert and aware, though. And right now, after the long, rough night, he was feeling a bit ragged. But it was Kayla who had been hurt, who needed rest; he was just going to have to manage.

He ordered Kayla to stay in the car with the doors locked while he went into the office. He found that the ever-efficient Hayley had called ahead for them, and he was back in moments with a key in his pocket. An old-fashioned key dangling from a ring that also held a heavy brass tag in the shape of an orca, that icon of the Northwest.

Then he walked to the café and ordered two of the largest coffees they had and a couple of sandwiches for later. Once they were in, he didn't want to come back out unless he had to.

The room was at the far end of a row of six, and Dane guessed it had been chosen specifically for that location; there were no vending machines, no laundry facility, nothing was beyond that last door, so no one had reason to be there except the occupants. He wouldn't be surprised if Quinn knew that already. Or had been able to find it out in the time it had taken them to get here; the Foxworth research capabilities were very impressive.

He parked the car near the opposite end of the building, as Quinn had suggested. He wasn't sure it would help if Chad—or whoever—came after them, but it might slow him down enough for them to realize he was there and give them time to escape.

He just had to be awake to realize it.

"We're down here," he said when Kayla gave him a puzzled look as he started to walk back along the row of doors. She looked more than just puzzled by his actions, but he wanted her inside and safe before he explained about the slight diversion of parking the car in front of a different room.

It wasn't until he had the door open and they'd stepped inside that she turned to look at him, then at the single room key, and asked the simple question that had apparently really been behind the deeper intensity of her expression.

"We?"

He steeled himself. "One room. Two beds."

She looked around, saw the two queen-size beds, and color crept up into her cheeks.

Two beds, he told himself. No problem. Sure.

Dane closed the door behind them, refusing to think about the hell he'd let himself in for.

Maybe he'd have no problem staying awake after all.

Chapter 25

"Do your folks ever fight?"

Dane blinked at the seeming non sequitur and at the oddity of it in itself; she knew his parents, they—

Damn.

It hit him abruptly. He was going to have to tell them. And his mother would be…maybe not pleased but relieved. And that would smart. It would probably be best to just let her think he'd finally seen the light, that he'd finally taken her advice after all these years.

"Do they?"

"No. They've been married thirty years."

"Are you saying they don't have anything to fight about anymore, or that they never did?"

He frowned. Was she really trying to make some sort of comparison between what was happening between them and a marital spat?

"Of course they did. When I was a kid they'd argue now and then, just not much anymore. They've learned how to deal. What's that got to do with anything?"

"They love each other more than any couple I've ever known. I just wondered if it was always smooth sailing."

Just like that she took the wind out of his sails. And reminded him of something he'd once learned that he'd shoved so far back into the "don't want to think about it" part of his mind that he indeed rarely did.

When he was nineteen, home from college for a visit, he'd

learned his parents had actually separated for a while. His uncle Alex, who his mother had always said needed a governor on his mouth, had let slip one day that Dane's father had once spent several weeks sleeping in his attic room. To this day he didn't know the full story of what had happened with them at the time relative newlyweds; neither of them would discuss it.

"Newlywed problems. We worked it out," was all his mother would say, "and because it was before you were born, it's not your concern."

"Working it out is *why* you were born," his father had quipped, earning him a simultaneous glare and blush from his wife. And that had embarrassed the still teenaged Dane enough that he dropped the subject forever.

He'd never told Kayla that, he realized. That was at the time when his long absences away at school, and the unrelenting peer pressure over loving someone younger at that stage of life, had stretched their relationship to its thinnest. Until now.

Only Kayla's unswerving loyalty had kept them going back then. The same unswerving loyalty she had to her brother. Could he really hold that against her when he had reaped the benefits? And hadn't she been just as loyal to him, even when he'd been the prime suspect in the attack on her?

And there it was, he thought. Just what he'd been afraid of. An hour alone with her in a motel room, and he was looking for reasons to backtrack, to change his mind, to go back to what they'd had, that loving, deep, and then passionate relationship that had been his foundation for so long.

"I'm going to go out and look around. Quinn said to make sure I knew what normal looked like here so I could spot anything different."

"Makes sense," she said, not calling him on the abrupt change of subject.

"I need you to promise me to stay here."

"I'll go with—"

"No."

It came out more sharply than he'd meant it to. She jerked back as if he'd raised a hand to her, and that hurt as much as if she'd actually slapped him.

"You're the target," he said. "The last thing we need is you outside advertising where you are."

She couldn't argue with that, he told himself.

"And you want to be alone," she said. "Away. From me."

No, she didn't argue, but she didn't leave it at that, either. She knew him too well.

"Yes," he said, not seeing the point in denying it. His brain knew the truth; they were over. His heart, gut and especially his body were taking a lot longer to get the message.

"I'll rap on the window first when I come back."

She didn't answer. He supposed there was nothing more to say. He set the lock, closed the door behind him, shoved the key into his pocket and just stood there for a moment.

In the short time they'd been inside clouds had rolled in, turning what had been a sunny day into the typical grayness. "Junuary" in the Northwest, he thought. Normally it didn't bother him; this time of year the sun rose at 4:30 a.m. and it didn't really get dark until nearly ten, so there was more than enough daylight. At 4:30 a.m., it seemed too much.

But that was in Kayla's house, where her bedroom windows faced—had faced—east. He wondered what was left of it now.

She'd wanted to go by, wanted to see just how bad it was, but he'd followed Quinn's advice to get her under wraps right away. It had been only advice, but something about the man, some air of knowledge, of command, made it hard to do anything else.

Dane knew he was ex-military, and he suspected that both

Teague and Rafe were also. He'd asked once if all Foxworth people were, and got, "Many, but not all," as his answer.

He wondered what a nonmilitary person had to do or be to make it into the Foxworth fold, what criteria they had. From what he'd seen of Quinn, it was probably very particular.

Dane walked around the building, trying to untangle his chaotic thoughts. He was usually more organized in his thinking, and this tumbling from one subject to the next, like a billiard ball bouncing off the sides of the table, was disconcerting. He knew it was all to keep from thinking about the one thing that was unbearable, but he couldn't seem to find anything strong enough to put it out of his mind.

He finished his circuit, trying to set the details in his mind. The faded red sedan parked behind the office was likely the clerk's, and he guessed whoever worked the next shift would park in the same place. The trees had been cleared enough to give a good fifteen feet of grass around the back of the building, and the parking area was a clear field of view out to the street.

He supposed it would be possible to come in through the trees and not be seen. It appeared to be open forest behind them, and fences weren't the norm out here. So if he assumed any approach would be from the rear, the only weakness he could see was the bathroom window. It was the only window in the room that opened to the back. It was high, but not impossible to reach. And it was small, but an adult could get through if they had time to squirm or were particularly athletic. The frosted glass prevented anyone from seeing inside but also declared exactly what room it was.

Once he had it set in his mind, he headed back. Kayla had opened the curtains in the front window, but thankfully she wasn't in sight. He tapped the window with his knuckles as he went by to let her know it was him.

When he unlocked the door and stepped inside, he saw

that she had pulled one of the two upholstered chairs off to one side, to where she could see through the opened curtains but not be seen except by someone right at the window or at an extreme angle. So she was, at least, taking this seriously. That relieved some of the pressure that had been building.

She was sitting in that chair and talking on her phone. She glanced up when he came in.

"You're not telling anyone where you are?"

The look she gave him was both answer and opinion.

"Sorry," he muttered as he locked the door behind him, stifling the urge to close the curtains; she was taking care and he didn't want to upset her more than she already was.

He walked back to the bathroom and checked the window that had caught his attention. There was a latch on the lower sash, but it was a bit flimsy and old, and he imagined it wouldn't take a lot to overpower or break it, even from the outside.

Warning was the best he could do, so he took the paper-wrapped glasses that were next to the ice-bucket on the dresser, unwrapped them and lined them up on upper edge of the lower sash of the window. There was just enough room for them to balance a bit precariously. He might not be able to stop somebody from trying to open that window, but at least he could make it a noisy proposition. He'd have to warn Kayla; it wouldn't take much to knock those off.

When he came back into the main room, Kayla was off the phone.

"Hayley is coming over. She's bringing clothes and tooth-brushes and stuff."

He tensed. "Clothes? She's not going to your place, is she?"

Kayla looked at him rather oddly. "No, she bought things. My stuff will need to be cleaned. If there's anything left," she ended sadly. "I gave her your sizes and preferences earlier."

"Oh." He tried to ignore the implied intimacy of that last

bit. She was still giving him that quizzical look, and he felt compelled to add, "I just didn't want her coming from there straight here. Quinn said arsonists like to revisit."

"And you thought he might follow her? When did you become Mr. Super Spy?"

"The moment somebody tried to kill you," he said.

She stared at him for a moment, then lowered her gaze. He saw the faint tinge of color appear in her cheeks. He knew her too well not to guess accurately what she was thinking.

"I don't want it to end that way," he repeated bluntly. "We'll see this through, and then we can both walk away clean."

Her head came up. "If we see this through," she said, "then the reason you're leaving will be resolved."

He'd thought of that. Repeatedly. But right now he was hurting too much to see hope there. "Unless it's not Chad. Then you'll go on and on searching until you've wasted your life on it."

"I promised you I'd accept what Foxworth found."

"What they've found is evidence your brother tried to kill you."

"Evidence someone did," she said, her defense of Chad immediate and automatic.

"I believe we've just arrived back at what they call square one."

For a long moment they stood there silently, the impasse almost tangible between them. He saw the pain in her eyes and guessed it was probably echoed in his. He would never have believed it would come to this, nor could he keep going. He would see this through, make sure she was safe. This would end—they would end—on his terms. And then he would start learning to live a life without her.

Somehow.

Chapter 26

The slamming of a car door and a bark sounded from outside almost simultaneously. Hayley, Kayla thought. And Cutter, apparently.

She walked to the window and saw that Hayley had also parked farther down the row of rooms on the other side of their borrowed car. She doubted anybody could have found them this quickly, but she supposed the precaution was wise.

A quick glance at Dane told her he approved. He seemed so different now, she thought with a growing qualm. He wasn't her laid-back, easygoing Dane anymore. He was edgy, sharp and...distant. As if it were already over, as if he were already pulling back, treating her as if she were merely someone he knew, not someone he'd spent ten years of his life with, not someone who had been his passionate and only lover for the last five of those.

She heard another bark and looked out the window in time to see Cutter jump from the back of Hayley's small red SUV to the ground. He raced ahead, coming to a stop at their door. How he knew which room they were in was beyond her.

"He must have picked up our scent or something," Dane said.

Kayla smothered the instant pang; they had always been so in tune they answered each other's unspoken thoughts.

The sound of scratching came at the door, then the doorknob rattled.

"I swear, if you gave him a key, he'd figure out how to

use it," Kayla said as she walked over to the door. She was grateful for the distraction; she simply couldn't bear thinking about a life without Dane. Especially because she'd done it herself, with her inability to let go of her faith in her brother.

For a long time it had seemed to her an unfair pressure. How could he expect her to give up her quest to find Chad? But now, faced with the price of that quest, she wasn't at all sure anymore that it was worth it. Chad was her brother and she loved him, but Dane was her entire future.

Or at least, he had been.

She turned the knob, but didn't have to pull the door open; Cutter took care of that. He pushed it back and came in as if he belonged. He greeted them both with nudges and licks and then sat before them, looking from one to the other. And as if he'd read the tension between them, he let out an audible sigh that sounded exasperated. If he was human, Kayla thought, he'd be shaking his head in disgust at them.

"That dog," Dane muttered.

And then Hayley was there, four shopping bags in hand. She stepped in, and Kayla closed the door behind her.

"Nice enough," Hayley said as she scanned the room.

"It's clean," Kayla said.

"Always my priority," Hayley said with a laugh. "I can put up with old and worn if it's clean."

"Especially the bathroom," Kayla said, forcing a smile in response.

"Speaking of which, careful around the window in there," Dane said, then explained what he'd done with the glasses.

"Good idea," Hayley said.

"It's the only vulnerable spot on that side."

"He's turned into quite the operative," Kayla said, trying to keep her tone even. "Quinn must have taught him a lot in a short time."

"Or he's just thinking of everything. When someone you love is in danger, it happens that way."

Kayla stopped herself from saying he didn't love her, not anymore. She didn't want to hear it, not aloud, not in her own voice, because that would make it too real. Besides, it wasn't true, not really. He couldn't turn it off just like that—it wasn't humanly possible. Dane might be the strongest man she'd ever known, in his own quiet way, but he wasn't a robot who could turn his emotions off at will. His love might be dying, but it wasn't dead yet. She wasn't sure that gave her much hope, but she clung to what flicker there was.

"His and her clothes," Hayley said, holding up two of the bags and tossing them on one of the beds. "Jeans and T-shirts, underwear, socks and shoes for you, Kayla, because yours are pretty messed up. Toothbrushes and toothpaste, razors, all that are in there too."

"Thank you," she answered.

Dane merely nodded; if he found anything uncomfortable about Hayley buying him underwear, it didn't show. Odd; if it had been reversed and Quinn had done the shopping, she would have been beyond embarrassed at the sight of the silky bra and panties she found in the bag.

Guys, she thought.

"He does still love you, you know," Hayley said quietly when Dane had gone to put the toiletries in the bathroom. "Look how he came running when you needed him."

"You don't understand," Kayla said tiredly. "That's just Dane. It's who he is."

She reached down and petted Cutter's silky head. There was something amazingly soothing about the action, as she'd learned after the explosion when she'd spent a long, quiet time huddled on the couch in Hayley and Quinn's living room, with the dog half in her lap. She'd finally gone to sleep, a surprisingly dreamless, peaceful sleep she'd never expected to manage.

Hayley held up the third bag. "Some books and magazines if you get bored."

"Thank you," she repeated. "When you said you'd help find Chad, I never thought it would come to this kind of thing."

Hayley laughed. "If there's one thing I've learned since going to work at Foxworth, it's that things rarely go how you think they will."

"Want to make fate laugh, make plans," Dane said as he came back.

Was that aimed at her? Kayla wondered. Was there an undertone of bitterness in the words? There was certainly a harsh note that wasn't like him. But then, nothing was normal anymore. Not in a world where they, of all couples, could be torn apart.

"Exactly," Hayley said. "Now, you should be okay here at least for a while. Quinn's working on a better location, but that takes a little time."

"How long do you think I'm going to have to hide?" Kayla asked, more than a little alarmed at the idea it might be more than a day or two.

"Until we find who did this," Hayley said, serious now. She might have been putting on a cheerful front, but she didn't make light of the situation.

"You really think I'm still in danger?"

"That's what we're trying to avoid. And to that end, I'm leaving you our portable burglar alarm."

Kayla blinked, looking around for some bag or package she hadn't seen. Then Cutter yipped, sounding very pleased with himself.

Or his assignment, Kayla realized.

"Cutter?" Dane said, sounding startled now.

"Cutter," Hayley confirmed. "He's better than any mechanical alarm system. And this way you both can get some sleep."

With an effort Kayla didn't look at Dane. And she was grateful when Hayley went on, giving instructions on how it would work.

"Walk him around and show him how things are now, so he'll know. Then he'll let you know long before anybody gets close enough to be trouble. And he'll show you where they're coming from."

Kayla shifted her gaze to the dog, who was watching intently. "Seriously?"

"Seriously. I can't explain it, and neither can Quinn. He just seems to know what to do."

Dane frowned. "Is he ex-military, too?"

Hayley laughed and scratched her dog's ears. "We've wondered, but we don't know. The vet says he's young, so we don't think so, but he sure seems to act like a trained war dog sometimes."

"So you haven't had him since he was a puppy?" Dane asked.

"No." Hayley smiled, and her voice went very soft. "He just showed up on my doorstep on the day I needed him most. You'll find he does that a lot. He just seems to know that, too."

Dane's mouth quirked. "You sure he's not an alien in a dog suit?"

"No," Hayley said and laughed.

The atmosphere in the room had lightened considerably, Kayla thought. Cutter was also, it seemed, a great distraction. And, she thought, he would be a buffer, something to focus on, to think about, besides the awful tension between her and Dane. Kayla wondered if that was part of the reason Hayley had brought Cutter. She wouldn't put it past her; the woman was not only kind and understanding, she was also perceptive.

"I brought some food for him and a couple of bowls," Hayley said, at last getting to the fourth bag. "He's good about only eating what he wants, so you can leave it full. Water's more important. And he's not above the occasional people-food treat, especially if you hand feed him, but don't overdo it."

"They allow dogs here?" Kayla asked, suddenly doubtful.

"They're allowing this one," Hayley said. Kayla wondered how they'd managed that and guessed it hadn't been cheap.

"He'll let you know when he needs out," Hayley went on. "He's very polite about it. He'll get your attention, then go sit by the door. Just let him go on his own, he'll be back quickly."

Dane shook his head, as if in wonder. "I suppose his... warnings are different?"

"Yes," Hayley said. "He won't leave you any doubt. If it's someone he knows, one of us, he'll give all the usual happy-dog signals. If it's not, if it's a threat, he'll act like he's going to jump out of his fur if you don't let him get at them."

"What about animals?"

"Normally, he gets as revved up as any dog when he smells or spots critters. But when he's on guard, oddly, no. He seems to know when it's people we're guarding against."

Dane shook his head. Hayley laughed.

"We've given up trying to figure it out. Especially because every day he surprises us with something new." She grinned. "Of course, just about the time we decide he really is that alien in disguise, he does something utterly doglike, like digging up the garden or dragging home a dead tree rat, and we slide back into reality."

Kayla and Dane both laughed in turn. It seemed impossible not to.

Hayley took something out of the bag slung over her shoulder. She handed it to Dane. Kayla thought at first it was a cell phone, but it only had four numbered buttons and a couple of larger ones—one was black with the standard on/off symbol and the other red.

"This is a Foxworth walkie-talkie. It uses rotating frequencies, but the signal is always scrambled, so no one can hear you except someone with another one of these. It has a range of about five miles. If you need anything, use it. But if something happens, if Cutter signals strangers coming, you use that red button. It broadcasts to everyone, and Quinn, Rafe and Teague all have them on them now."

"But if its range is only five miles…" Dane began.

"There will be somebody within that range at all times until this is resolved."

Kayla drew back slightly. "You mean you're guarding us?"

"We're keeping an eye on this place, yes."

"Twenty-four/seven?" Dane asked.

"Yes. Quinn's nothing if not thorough."

"But what about finding Chad?"

Kayla sensed rather than saw Dane's demeanor instantly shift; the tension was back that quickly.

"We're still on it. When one is watching, the other three—and me—are working on that."

"Sleep much?" Dane asked.

"On a case? Not so much," Hayley said. "If you turn on the TV, keep it down. Muted with closed captions would be better. Nothing to interfere with your alarm system."

She crouched down beside Cutter, who had given every appearance of following the conversation intently.

"All right, my boy," she crooned, "you know what to do. You watch, all right? Watch and warn."

The dog was on his feet instantly. In that split second he went from attentive, clever dog to…something else. Kayla couldn't describe it, exactly, but there was no doubt the animal understood the command. On alert, she supposed.

And she had to admit, it made her feel safer.

Chapter 27

"We should have gotten a dog," Kayla said.

Dane looked up from one of the magazines Hayley had bought—the latest issue of a trade magazine that was actually sitting at home on his desk unread. He usually read their main articles online, but he liked to have the print version for those occasions when he didn't have a connection or when his phone wouldn't do because the article had charts or graphs or other details he needed to see full size.

Odd. He usually would have felt unsettled by now, disconnected from the world he spent so much time in. Yet he felt no desire to check email, and no urge to check his online feeds. Nothing like a good old life and death crisis to push the online world down on your priority list.

Nothing like having your real world crumble to make the online world seem trivial.

Kayla was petting Cutter, who was curled up peacefully beside her on the bed farthest from the door. She'd spoken idly, he realized; in fact, she looked almost lulled by the dog's presence. He found it unexpectedly comforting himself. He'd had dogs as a kid but never any even remotely like this one.

And they had talked about it before, after she'd moved into the little house and he'd ended up practically living there himself. It would have been cozy, them and a four-legged kid. Like this moment had been, until she'd spoken. They had always been that way, happy just being under the same roof, even if they each were occupied with their own pursuits.

The memory wasn't soothing; it jabbed at him.

"Right," he said. "Then we could have fought over custody."

He saw her wince. Cutter's head came up sharply.

"That wasn't necessary," Kayla said. "I gave you your past tense."

She had, he realized. "Should have" not "should." No wonder he'd snapped back.

He had the grace to acknowledge the unfairness of that. He couldn't make such a point of it being over between them and then get in a mood about it when she acknowledged that point. Couldn't hold that it was okay for him to use the past tense when talking about them, then get upset if she did.

"Fine," he said and pretended to go back to the magazine.

He should be grateful, shouldn't he? That she was accepting, that she wasn't making a scene or making it even harder with weeping and wailing?

But that wasn't Kayla's way. It never had been. Her dogged determination wouldn't allow such time and energy wasters. She'd wept her soul dry when her parents had been killed, but he could count the number of times he'd seen her cry in the ten years since on his fingers, maybe plus a toe or two.

And usually on Chad's birthday, he reminded himself. On the anniversary of her parents' deaths she was quietly solemn, but on Chad's birthday she wept.

That stiffened his resolve.

Cutter let out a long-suffering sigh, as if he'd understood perfectly that they were again at a contretemps.

He'd done as Hayley had instructed—taken him out and repeated his own earlier circuit of the property. The dog had paused now and then, sniffing the air, and twice had veered off on his own to point his nose toward the woods around the motel. Dane had watched as the animal seemed to scan the trees and then the parking area, as if placing things in his mind.

The mysteries of the canine brain, he had thought at the time. This one's, at least. More on a whim than anything, he had let Cutter take the lead and take his time. And oddly, the dog had stopped in the same place he had—under the bathroom window of their unit.

How did he know? Scent again?

The dog looked up at the window, then around, for all the world as if he were judging how someone would approach that window from the trees.

At that point Dane had shaken his head and picked up the pace; when you started attributing human qualities to a dog, even a very smart one, it was time for some rest.

Yet rest, or at least sleep, eluded him. It was still afternoon, and he'd never been one for going to bed during the day.

Unless it was with Kayla.

Pain slammed into his gut, at odds with parts lower, which responded fiercely to just the thought. The memories of long, lazy weekend afternoons when they'd decided nothing on any agenda was more important than what they were doing, when they'd made love, rested, laughed, eaten and then started the cycle all over again.

Cutter's sudden movement jerked him out of the painful reverie. The dog got up, jumped to the floor and raced to the front window, his ears back, head down and a low, menacing rumble coming from his throat. Just his reaction sent Dane's adrenaline surging, and he wished he had some kind of a weapon. Not that he knew the first thing about guns, but even a baseball bat would be nice. He'd have to do something about that if this went on much longer.

So he did the only thing he could, he walked over to the window and peered through the crack in the drapes. He saw the man who had checked them into the room sweeping the walkway that ran in front of all the rooms. He'd apparently worked his way down here to the end.

"What is it?" Kayla's voice was a whisper.

"The manager," he said, reaching down to reassure Cutter, although he wasn't sure the dog would take his word that this man he didn't know was safe. But the animal shifted his gaze to him, looking as if he were evaluating Dane's ability to properly assess the potential threat.

Apparently Cutter found enough to satisfy him, and he stood down. Odd that that was the phrase that popped into his head, but it was the only one that seemed to fit.

"I wonder if he'll remember the guy," Kayla said.

"If he comes around again? I wouldn't be surprised."

"Hayley seems to think he can read minds."

"I wouldn't bet against it," Dane said, still watching as the man with the broom finished and started walking back toward the office.

They settled back into quiet, Kayla returning to the bed and Dane to the chair beside the small table. Cutter seemed to hesitate between them for a moment. Dane's gaze flicked from the dog to Kayla, who needed the comforting the dog seemed to bring.

He was wondering how to indicate to the dog he should go to her when Cutter made up his own mind in that direction and returned to his earlier position beside her. Giving her the companionship and comfort Dane could no longer give her.

Well, he could, technically. But he knew too well what would happen if he lay down on that bed with her. All his determination, all his good intentions would be seared away. The passion that ignited so quickly between them had never faded, but deep down he knew that if he gave into that fierce urge now, it would make it that much harder, that much more painful to disengage all over again.

Kayla at last stretched out, put her head on a pillow and

closed her eyes. After what she'd been through, he was amazed she'd kept going as long as she had. It wasn't long before he sensed she'd gone to sleep; he knew her so well, knew when the tension of her body changed, relaxed, when her breaths became deeper, more regular.

Cutter stayed there, his head coming up occasionally as he heard something. But whatever he heard, he apparently decided it wasn't a threat and put his head back down. He didn't, however, close his eyes. Dane wondered idly if dogs ever had trouble sleeping.

Perversely, now his own restless mind declared itself willing to shut off, and his eyes were more than happy about the idea of sleep. But now was when he couldn't, if for no other reason than he had to be awake to make sure Kayla was all right. She seemed to have suffered no serious aftereffects of the smoke, but Quinn had explained how with smoke inhalation damage sometimes took time to develop as the lungs reacted to the insult.

Then, of course, there was the fact that someone had tried to kill her.

He stayed in the not terrifically comfortable chair, fighting the urge to go lie down beside her. He tried to make himself stay awake, listening to her steady and apparently unimpaired breathing. But the long night and the stress of actually being suspected of the attack on her were catching up to him, and more than once he caught himself jolting awake.

It got harder. The room was getting warmer as the summer sun was now hitting the front of the building, and he weighed the dangers of opening a window against the dangers of him falling asleep. It wasn't worth it, he thought, and regretted the lack of air-conditioning in the room, although he accepted the practicality of not retrofitting this older place with it when simply doing just that, opening a window, would provide all the cool air necessary most of the year in this climate.

He shifted position, leaning forward and resting his elbows on his knees, so that if he dozed off he'd fall forward and wake himself up. It worked until his brain seemed to learn to balance even when asleep.

Maybe he should just get up and stay on his feet, he thought. If he kept walking, he'd have to stay awake. He'd have to be quiet or wake up Kayla, but—

A movement from the bed drew his weary gaze. Cutter was moving toward the edge of the bed, inching his way without actually getting on his feet. He slid off to the floor, as if he were being careful not to wake Kayla. He didn't seem alarmed or attuned to anything outside, so Dane waited to see if perhaps Cutter would go to the door to indicate he needed outside.

Instead, the dog came over to him and nudged his hand with his nose in apparent greeting. Then he plopped down at Dane's feet, as if he'd merely decided that now that Kayla was at last asleep, Dane was his job.

"If only you could keep me awake," Dane said to him quietly.

Cutter's head twisted to meet his gaze, and for an instant in the dog's dark eyes Dane saw something that looked amazingly like understanding. Dane nearly laughed at himself; he was getting as bad as Hayley and Quinn.

He reached down, scratching behind that right ear until the dog sighed happily. Now that was normal, he thought. Utterly doglike, as Hayley had said. He settled back in the chair, awake for the moment. He picked up the magazine but soon realized that was a mistake as his eyes began to fight to close again.

Maybe a cold shower, he thought. That might help. Might help more than just having trouble staying awake. He pondered the idea.

A tug on the leg of his jeans jerked him awake. He didn't

know how long he'd been out, but nothing had changed. The room was still too warm, the sun was still pouring around the edges of the curtains he'd closed in an attempt to foster the idea of cool darkness and Kayla was still asleep, still breathing evenly.

The only difference was the dog at his feet. The dog who had just tugged on the bottom of his jeans but now that he was awake had put his head down once more.

If only you could keep me awake...

His own words echoed in his head. And so did the memory of that moment when Cutter had given him that look that had seemed so full of an almost human understanding.

Maybe he'd been taught that, that "guard" meant someone else had to be awake, too. Could dogs learn something like that? His old Lilah had been a retriever, and she'd had her own skills that, to someone not used to them, could seem amazing in a dog. At least that was the answer he came up with. It had been in Lilah's blood, in her genes, that retriever nature.

Another memory hit him hard. The day he'd finally had to say goodbye to the dear old friend who had been there for him almost his entire life. He'd been seventeen, far too old to cry, and yet it had overwhelmed him. He'd retreated to the tree where he and Kayla had often sat, liking the feeling of being above the fuss below. She had found him there, and she, only she of everyone he knew, said and did the right thing. Which was nothing except simply taking his hand and holding it.

He'd known she would never tell, never taunt or tease him with his unmanly reaction to the loss of his childhood companion, and so he had let it out, tears and all.

And on his eighteenth birthday, she had told him that was the moment when she knew just how much she loved him. "Wait," he'd said, "I thought you said you liked how I was strong and stood up to Rod that time."

"I did."

"So do you want the strong type or the sensitive type?"

She had given him a look that seemed wise beyond her sixteen years. "Yes," she said.

He'd laughed. "Don't you think that's asking a lot?"

"Aren't I lucky I found it?"

The aches of regret and loss filled him now. Here he was, in a room alone with the woman he'd loved from that day forward. He'd experimented a little in college, as much because he felt he should as anything, but nothing had lasted. They all seemed lacking somehow.

And nothing had ever been able to erase the thought of the girl back home, who was, as she'd promised she would, growing up so that they could begin their life together.

As he watched her sleep, he drifted into memories, too tired now to fight them off. They floated through his mind, each with its own special pain attached. The first time he'd seen her, up in that tree. The day of her sixteenth birthday, when he'd stolen a minute to give Kayla her first real kiss. The day she turned eighteen and he'd driven home from college just to see her for a few hours on her special day, then turned around and drove back. The day she'd arrived at the same school herself, chosen mainly because he was there. The agony of waiting because he knew she wasn't ready, and then she turned twenty-one and had practically demanded he make love to her. And all the sweet, wonderful years since, when he'd counted himself more than lucky to have found the love of his life so early in that life.

He closed his eyes, knowing he had glossed over the horrible night that happened just days after she turned sixteen and the days of dealing with the aftermath. He didn't need to think about them again; they were etched so deeply into his mind he would never be free of them. Besides, if there was anything that could weaken his resolve, it was thinking again about what she'd been through.

He must have slipped too close to sleep because Cutter tugged on the leg of his jeans again. He snapped back to wakefulness and stared at the dog for a long moment.

"You really do get it, don't you?" he said softly, reaching out to lay his hand on the dark head.

The dog nudged his hand with his nose and swiped his fingers with his tongue. And as if satisfied he was awake and alert again, Cutter settled his chin back down on his front paws.

Dane shook his head half in wonder, half in disbelief and leaned back in the chair. His body was protesting the long stretch of sitting, but he was afraid he'd wake Kayla up if he moved around too much. Which reminded him of the careful way Cutter had slipped off the bed, as if he had the same fear but knew right now Dane needed his help more.

Damn, I'm tired. He's a dog.

But whatever the dog's intent, it worked. He was awake again. And belatedly he realized sunlight was no longer streaming around the edges of the curtains, and the room wasn't quite as warm. How long had he been lost in that reverie anyway? He reached for his cell phone to check the time, and as if the movement had triggered it, the phone vibrated on the table beside the chair; he'd turned off the ringer when Kayla had first gone to sleep. He grabbed it now before the buzz could wake her. Who was calling?

Quinn and nearly 3:00 a.m., he noted, answering both his questions at once.

He got up and walked into the bathroom before he answered.

"Everything okay?"

"Kayla's sleeping. I'm trying not to."

"Cutter can help you with that," Quinn said.

Dane's brows rose. "So he did mean to do it."

Quinn chuckled, obviously needing no further explanation. "That dog rarely does anything he doesn't mean to do."

Dane leaned against the sink, smiling wryly to himself. "I'm getting that feeling."

"Everything quiet?"

"So far."

"Good."

Dane sensed this was more than just a status check. "Something happen?"

"Somebody showed up at the house."

Dane straightened up. "At Kayla's house?"

"Yes. Teague was watching the place, just in case. Just after dark he saw somebody in a black watch cap sneaking through the side yard. He couldn't see him well enough to make an ID, but the moment Teague got out of the car he took off running back through the trees."

"You think it was Chad?"

"Don't know. Could have been a curious neighbor."

"But why would he run?"

"Good question. Teague's pretty fast, almost had him, but the guy darted down a few side yards and then out into open forest. He knew where he was going."

"So a local," Dane said.

"Seems that way."

"Or somebody who once was. Like Chad."

"Yes. And somebody also called the hospital to ask after Kayla but refused to say who he was."

Dane tensed. "To ask how she was or to find out if she was still there?"

"Both. Thankfully when he wouldn't identify himself, they didn't tell him anything. Said he got a little insistent, though. Enough so that they made a note of the number he was calling from."

He knew Foxworth and their capabilities better now, so he merely said, "And?"

"Landline listed to Franklin Warren."

"Rod's dad?"

"Any reason you can think of he'd be involved?"

"Zero. He barely knew Kayla. And he's in a wheelchair, so it surely wasn't him running away."

"What about Rod himself? Would he call?"

Dane frowned. "He's not a friend, not after that day I told you about. Kayla doesn't like him and neither do I, so I don't know why he'd call. But if he did, he'd have no reason not to say who he was. Unless he really was involved."

"All right." Quinn paused as if thinking. "All right, it's quiet now, we've got the house covered in case he comes back there and you've got Cutter inside and us outside if he gives you a warning. Why don't you try and get some sleep?"

"But Kayla—"

"She breathing all right?"

"Yes."

"Coughing?"

"Not since we got here. But they said she needed to be watched for at least twenty-four hours."

"News for you, buddy. It's been twenty-four hours and then some."

"Oh." He felt a little silly for not having put that together. "Sorry."

"Sleep deprivation will do that to you. Besides, Cutter will probably let you know if she starts having trouble. Hayley had some nightmares in the beginning, and every time she started getting restless or murmuring in her sleep, he woke her or me up."

"Someday," Dane said, "I'd like to hear that whole story."

"Someday," Quinn answered, "you might. Now get some sleep."

"Right."

Dane disconnected the call then stood there in the bathroom for a moment, pondering the likelihood of being able to follow that order thinly disguised as a suggestion. The likelihood of being able to sleep with Kayla just a few feet away.

He realized his ears were buzzing. In fact, everything above his ears seemed to be humming with that warning sound that told him he'd just about hit the wall. He'd been up nearly two nights straight; no wonder he was starting to feel wobbly.

He'd just have to hope he was tired enough.

Chapter 28

"How are they?" Hayley had stayed quiet as Quinn spoke to Dane, watching the area surrounding the motel while he was distracted with the call.

"She's been sleeping for a while. Breathing's fine, and no more coughing. I think she's probably okay."

"And Dane?"

"Hasn't slept at all. He's been too worried about her."

"That's good."

Quinn shifted to look at her. "It's good that he's so worried he hasn't slept since the day before yesterday?"

"Yes. He still loves her."

"Well, yeah, you don't turn that off by fiat," Quinn said.

"But this has been gnawing away at him for a long time. I was afraid it was too late, but now I don't think so. They can work on fixing things."

Quinn shook his head but with a smile at her. "Might be more important to find out who tried to kill her first."

Hayley shook her head. "Nothing's more important than that." She gave him a sideways look. "Which did you think was more important—getting those guys at the cabin or getting out of there alive?"

"Getting *you* out of there alive," Quinn said.

"Why?"

"Is this a trap?"

"Would I tell you if it was?"

He laughed. "You know damn well I was already half in love with you."

"Only half?" she asked sweetly.

"Yeah," he drawled, "the other half was Cutter."

Hayley grinned at him. "Oh. Well that's all right then."

"Love me, love my dog?"

"Exactly."

"Well it's a good thing I love you both then, isn't it?"

"It is," Hayley said, her voice going achingly soft. "A very, very good thing."

"Damn." Quinn sighed. "I'll be glad when Liam gets here to relieve us."

"Me, too," Hayley said. There was nothing particularly suggestive in her words, but something in her voice set him off.

"Hope he rested up on his days off," Quinn said gruffly, "because he's liable to be here the rest of the night on his own."

"And maybe longer," Hayley said, and Quinn felt his body clench with need at the promise in those words.

Quinn spent the next hour in varying states of discomfort as he made himself focus on the job at hand instead of the delectable woman beside him. And if Dane was in anywhere near the same condition inside that room, Quinn felt sorry for him.

It was going to be a long night.

Kayla's nightmare of smoke and fire took an odd turn as the splash of the firefighter's water began. Because on some level even her sleeping brain knew she hadn't been aware of that, that Mr. Reyes, bless him, had gotten her out and away before the fire trucks had actually arrived. But the watery sound was comforting nevertheless, and the nightmare shifted

in the nonsensical way dreams do, and she was adrift in a
boat, water lapping at the sides—

Her eyes opened.

Lapping.

The dog.

Cutter was getting a drink of water.

Reality rushed back, and there was enough of the nightmare clinging to it to make her jolt upright. She looked around
the strange room, placing things in her mind as best she could
in the dim light. A glance at the bedside clock told her it was
just after six. She was surprised at that—she hadn't expected
to sleep that long at all, not after napping through the afternoon and evening. Perhaps she'd been more stressed and trau-
matized than she'd been willing to admit.

She was reaching for the bedside lamp, then paused. She
glanced over at the other bed. Dane was there, stretched out
on his side, facing her but with his head half buried in the
pillow his arm was bent back under. His other arm was in
front of him, and it seemed his fist was clenched even in
sleep. She sighed.

She looked around again. It was well after sunrise this
time of year, but the motel faced west and the front window
was still in shadow. With the blackout curtains closed, it was
hard to tell what kind of day they were facing.

She nearly laughed at her own thought; she knew exactly
what kind of day it was going to be. Hellish.

She sat up and swung her legs over the side of the bed.
Cutter was there instantly, what light there was reflecting
off his dark eyes.

"Hi," she said softly, reaching to pet that silken fur. He
nudged her in turn, then tilted his head to lay it on her knee.
She found it absurdly sweet and endearing.

"I'd love a dog like you," she whispered to him, "no matter what Dane says."

"I'm not sure there is another dog like him."

Dane's voice came out of the dim light from the other bed, and she felt a start of embarrassment.

"Sorry I woke you," she said stiffly.

"You didn't."

"You've been awake?"

"Since I let him out a few minutes ago. Tried not to wake you."

"You didn't," she echoed. "I think his drinking did. I started dreaming of water."

"Better than fire."

"Yes." She suppressed a shudder.

"How do you feel?"

"Fine."

"No sore throat or need to cough?"

"Throat is a bit dry and scratchy is all."

"All right."

"You didn't have to stay up—"

"Yes. I did."

She wanted to see hope in that last statement, but looking at his face all she saw was the same emotionless resolution that had sounded in his voice. She lowered her head, looking at Cutter, once more stroking his fur for the comfort as much as the communion. Silence stretched out for a long moment before he spoke again.

"Somebody was poking around your house last night."

Her head snapped up. "What?"

"They had Teague watching it. Somebody showed up a little after dark."

"Who?" She had to force out the word because she wasn't sure she really wanted the answer.

"Don't know. The instant he saw Teague he took off running. He got to the woods and vanished. He obviously knew his way around."

"So of course it must have been Chad revisiting the scene of the crime," she said, her tone creeping beyond tense into sarcasm.

"Didn't say that," he said. But to Kayla, his expression was screaming, "Who else could it be?"

That she didn't have an answer for that made her even unhappier.

"I want to see my house," she said.

"Not yet."

"You're not my boss," she snapped.

He drew back slightly, and the sharp sound of her knee-jerk answer hung in the air. She drew in a long, deep breath.

"I'm sorry," she said. "That was uncalled for."

Dane, being Dane, accepted the apology graciously. Yet in the back of her mind was the knowledge that it was easier to be gracious when you didn't really care.

"You've had a very rough couple of days. Anybody would be a bit tense," he said. "And it wasn't my idea. Quinn thinks it would be best if you stayed away until we know more."

Kayla started to answer, then realized a quick agreement with that seemed to her to carry a subtext that she wouldn't listen to him, but she would to Quinn. And it would do no good to point out that she would listen to Quinn, or Hayley, because they were impartial; Dane definitely was not. But she had no desire to add any fuel to his mood; he already felt beyond her reach and it was breaking her heart.

"And you agree," she said after a moment, carefully keeping her voice even and hoping the words were safe enough.

"Yes."

"All right," she said, giving up on the desire for now. She still wanted to see her home, start assessing the damage, figuring out what repairs were needed; she wasn't about to let whoever had done this destroy her love for her little house.

But her relationship with Dane was just as damaged, if not more, and she wasn't sure it could be repaired.

And if that were true, then the house didn't matter.

Nothing else mattered.

Cutter was suddenly on his feet, alert and looking toward the front of the room. A second later his plumed tail began to wag, and he leaped across the room to the door. He looked back over his shoulder at them with that doggy grin on his face.

All the usual happy-dog signals, Hayley had said.

A tap came on the door. Cutter yipped. Dane was already there, peering through the peephole.

"Mr. Burdette, Ms. Tucker, I'm Liam Burnett," he called through the door. Kayla thought she caught a bit of a drawl in his voice. He sounded like her college roommate, who had been from Houston. "I just relieved Quinn and Hayley. And I have coffee."

"Well, that's tempting," Dane muttered.

As if he'd guessed at their hesitation, the man outside added, "Watch Cutter. He'll verify my ID."

It sounded silly, but Kayla couldn't deny the difference in the dog now compared to how he'd reacted when the motel manager had simply come by to sweep the walk.

"Hayley did say they had one more guy who'd be joining the crew—"

Even as she said it, her cell phone dinged, announcing the arrival of a text message. She went to grab it off the nightstand.

"It's from Hayley. She says Liam Burnett is on his way with coffee." She gave a little laugh. "She says Cutter will let us know he's okay."

"Well, he did that, didn't he?" Dane said as he reached for the doorknob.

For a moment, Kayla was startled at what she saw when

the man holding two cups stepped into the room. Liam Burnett looked like an earnest Boy Scout, almost too young to be drinking the coffee he was carrying. Maybe he was, she thought, noticing he had only two of the cups from the café.

The man handed the cups in their paper sleeves to the two of them, then crouched to greet the dog.

"Hey, you ol' hound. You doing your job right?"

The swipe of a pink tongue across the young man's cheek sealed the deal for Kayla. Obviously this was a known and appreciated person in the dog's life.

"Okay, he likes you," Dane said, obviously reaching the same conclusion at the same moment. As usual. Kayla blinked at the sudden pain.

"Dogs generally do. My family's raised them for years. But this guy, he's something special."

"We've noticed," Kayla said with the best smile she could manage.

"Texas?" Dane asked.

Liam grinned. "Yes, sir. Born and bred." Then he looked at Kayla and said, with that same sort of earnestness she'd seen in his face, "I'm sorry about your trouble. But if anybody can unravel all this, it's Foxworth."

"You sound confident."

"I am. Trust them to the wall and over," he said. "Quinn turned my life around when I was headed down a wrong path."

Kayla had trouble picturing this innocent-looking guy in trouble, but she took his word for it.

"Speaking of Quinn, he'll be around later," Liam said. "He had to go talk with Rafe—you've met Rafe, haven't you?"

Dane nodded. "Interesting guy."

"If by interesting you mean downright scary sometimes, yeah, he is," Liam said with a quirky grin that spoke of both respect and liking. "He's our sniper. And he's wicked good."

"So I've heard," Kayla said. "So what's your specialty?"

"Me? I'm the tech guy mostly. And the tracker."

"Tracker?"

"I would have found that guy last night," he said. "Teague's good, and tough as the ex-marine he is, but he's a city boy. He needed me. Or Cutter."

Foxworth, Kayla thought, was a much more interesting operation than their name and website would lead you to believe.

"I keep telling him a month out in the wilds with me would fix that, but he keeps saying no. He feels bad about losing that guy in the woods like that, so I'm guessing he'll take me up on it now."

The grin had widened, and somehow Kayla felt lighter than she had in days. Something about this young man's easy charm and innocent face brightened her outlook.

No sooner did she acknowledge that welcome fact than the new arrival's cell phone rang. He answered, and within moments the easy grin and innocent expression vanished. When he hung up and looked at them, he was all business.

"What is it?" she asked.

"Rafe turned up a homeless guy who'd been squatting in an abandoned building. Said some new guy moved in, ran him off."

"So?"

Liam looked uncomfortable, but he didn't dissemble. "The description matches Chad to a T."

Kayla's breath caught in her suddenly tight throat. She sensed rather than saw Dane tense and she felt her own suddenly accelerated heartbeat. She looked at him and saw the same knowledge in his eyes.

It really was coming to a head.

And she was coming face-to-face with the distinct possibility that the end of her quest also meant the end of them.

Chapter 29

"Where?"

Kayla focused on that question so that she didn't have to face the simple fact that now that her goal might actually be within reach, she wasn't sure she wanted it. This quest had consumed her for so long she wasn't sure what would be left of her when it was finally over, one way or another.

"Out off of Breakers Road," Liam said. "Quinn's heading over there. Rafe's staying on the building because somebody will need to watch the back entrance."

Kayla wondered if she'd had too much sleep; she couldn't seem to process this.

"An abandoned building?" Chad had friends here, he had her. This made no sense. "But why would Chad—"

"I don't know," Dane said. He didn't add, "And I don't care," but Kayla heard it anyway. Apparently so did Liam because for the first time he looked uncomfortable and excused himself to go back out to his car and to his guarding of the area around them. She wondered if he'd been warned. *Watch out. They're in the middle of a breakup so things are a bit intense....*

Kayla shook off the useless speculation. She looked around automatically. Without a word Dane picked up her phone and handed it to her. That was still working fine, it seemed, that communication without words, that knowing someone so well you knew what the slightest gesture meant.

She made herself concentrate on the phone, called up the

map app they both used and entered the location. The image that popped up told her little until she backed out a click and saw the surrounding area.

"The old tag arena!" she exclaimed.

"What?"

"You know, the place that used to be a skating rink ages ago, then it was a video arcade, then a laser tag arena?"

"Out by the gravel plant? I went there a few times."

She nodded. "And Chad used to spend a lot of his free time there, with Troy and their other friends."

"They closed down years ago, didn't they? I remember my dad saying it was because the home video game systems were getting so good, and my mom saying it was more because the kids were getting out of control."

"And Chad was furious. Especially because our parents wouldn't buy him one of the home systems."

"He ever heard of a job?" Dane said.

Kayla forced herself not to defend her brother; Dane had had a part-time job from the age of sixteen and had little patience for those who expected everything to be given to them. Or made their way through life on looks and charm. Most of the time she agreed with him. Except regarding Chad.

She'd always told herself Dane just didn't understand her brother, but now she was asking herself if perhaps she shouldn't have thought more about why she always made that exception for Chad.

"I don't think it was the games so much as a place to hang out with his friends," she finally said.

"You're right about that," Dane said, his mouth twisting wryly. "Believe me."

"What do you mean?"

"I was into the games," he said. "Chad and his buddies were into harassing the younger or smaller kids who were into the games."

She stared at him. "Harassing?"

"Intimidation might be a better word. Or bullying."

"Chad wouldn't—"

"I was there. He did it to me. Personally. Would have been worse if Troy hadn't finally pulled him off me."

"You never told me that!"

"Please. You never wanted to hear a word against him."

"What did he do?"

"Picked the weakest, littlest kids and extorted their game money from them. Threatened them if they didn't hand it over. Beat me up just to demonstrate what would happen if anybody resisted."

A memory flashed through her mind of the day they'd made that promise to each other to never let others determine who they were. The day she'd sworn to make the most of what looks she had yet never deny her intelligence, and the day he'd sworn to become tough and fit and yet never give up what he loved. He'd been sporting a bruised face and skinned-up knuckles that day, but he would only tell her he'd run into a bully.

Chad.

He'd never told her it was her brother who had done it.

And it obviously wasn't open for discussion now; he had taken back his phone and was making a call. Cutter's gaze shifted to her, and she realized he'd been watching them like a human would watch a tennis match, head moving side to side as each of them spoke.

"It's Dane," he said into the phone. "Kayla knows the place Liam told us about. Chad used to hang there when it was a video arcade."

He listened for a moment. Quinn, she guessed.

"Yes," Dane said into the phone. Then "Yes," again and more listening. Kayla barely managed not to demand to know what was going on. If Chad was really this close, she wanted to know, and she wanted to know now.

What she didn't know was what she would do about it. And again she felt the uncertainty she'd never expected. How could her goal of so many years be within reach, and yet she suddenly wasn't sure she wanted it?

"All right," Dane said and ended the call. He turned to look at her, and when he spoke it was with no more emotion than a police officer making a report. "Building appears empty right now. Quinn and Rafe checked the inside and there are signs someone's living there, but they can't be sure what belongs to the homeless guy until they question him further."

"Who is he? I hadn't heard of anybody local losing their home, not lately anyway."

"Don't know who he is, but Quinn said Hayley was making arrangements for him, getting him into a shelter Foxworth helps fund."

Kayla blinked. "They're into a lot of stuff."

"Seems that way."

"So now what?"

"They're going to watch the place, see if Chad shows up."

"I should go—"

"Quinn wants us to sit tight. With watching that place, your house and here, they're spread a little thin."

"Then we should go there now, and they could stop watching this place."

"There's nobody there now. There's no point. And if there are too many people around, it could spook him and they'd lose him again."

"You're assuming it is Chad," she said.

He said nothing, but she saw his jaw tighten and knew he was holding back whatever response had come into his mind.

"All right," she said, "I admit it sounds like it is. But that's why I should be over there."

"Quinn will call if he shows up. Then we'll decide."

Reluctantly she conceded. She wasn't used to doing nothing, and they had another discussion about the possibility of taking Cutter for a walk through the woods behind the motel. Dane seemed to waver on that one. Probably, Kayla thought sourly, because he and Cutter had bonded. Then again, the dog was generally more cooperative than she had been, and she had the grace to admit that much at least.

But in the end Quinn's caution won out, and except for letting Cutter out when he needed it the door stayed shut with the "Do not disturb" sign hanging on the outside knob. And Kayla tried not to think of other times when that sign would have had an entirely different intent, times when they had hung it on the door of a room specifically to avoid interruption of a long, passionate session of enjoying how in tune their bodies and their minds were.

It was an effort to keep from pacing the room. But when she did, Cutter seemed to get wound up, and Dane, who was trying to sleep a little more, always woke up. This time the dog was curled up beside Dane on the other bed, and she noticed in sleep Dane's arm had come to rest along the dog's side. It was a picture that would have once made her smile, made the love she felt for this man bubble up inside her to overflowing.

Now it just made her hurt more.

She welcomed the distraction later when Dane woke up and, after checking the time, suggested dinner; they'd been nibbling on the snacks Hayley had brought, but a real, hot meal sounded wonderful. Dane quickly put to rest her thoughts of actually going to the restaurant by saying they'd order it to go. She didn't really quibble, although the thought of even a temporary escape was very tempting, because it didn't seem fair to leave Cutter here all alone in a strange motel room. And at this point, she wasn't sure he wouldn't figure out a way to follow them anyway.

The meal of fish and chips they ended up with wasn't the best she'd ever had, but it wasn't the worst either, and under the circumstances she figured that was enough. Mindful of Hayley's words, she gave Cutter a couple of bites of fish, which he took delicately from her fingers, while he caught the fries Dane tossed him neatly in midair.

Later, Dane amused the patient animal by taking a rolled-up sock and tossing it for him. The room was too small for the dog to run, but he seemed to enjoy the challenge of catching the makeshift ball over and over.

When darkness finally came again, Kayla didn't know what she was going to do. She didn't feel at all sleepy, and she certainly wasn't relishing another night spent in this room, with Dane so near and yet so emotionally far away. Now Dane was playing tug of war with Cutter, the worse-for-wear sock standing in for a rope. As a buffer between them, the dog was serving quite well.

"You're right," Dane said when he finally called it quits and sat down. "We should have gotten a dog."

She didn't know whether to feel gratified at the agreement or pained at the reminder of that damned past tense. And before she could decide, Dane's phone rang. At this hour, it had to be someone from Foxworth.

After he said hello, he listened for a long moment before speaking again.

"Yeah, I got some sleep. Enough, anyway. I'm good. She needed the sleep more," Dane said. Kayla's gaze shifted to the dog, who was sitting, watching Dane as if he knew who he was talking to. "And you were right—Cutter helped me stay awake."

Part of her wanted to believe he'd stayed awake to watch over her because he still loved her. But another part of her

knew that was just who Dane was; if he took on a responsibility, he saw it through. And that's all she was to him now.

"No. She needs to be there." Kayla's breath caught at his
words. "I know. I'll keep her back. But if it is Chad, he may
only cooperate with her." Another pause, and then, "All right.
We'll bring him."

He disconnected the call, slipped the phone into his pocket,
leaned over and scratched Cutter's ear.

He did everything but look at her.

When he didn't speak, the words finally burst from her.
"What's happening?"

"Get the sweatshirt Hayley bought you."

"I don't need a sweatshirt. I need to know what's going on."

"You will. It's cooled off outside now, and you can't take
the chance of a cold when we're not sure your lungs are a
hundred percent yet."

She needs to be there, he'd said. "He's there? Chad?"

"Someone is. Rafe is watching the building now, and
Quinn's on his way."

She darted over to the shopping bag she'd set on the
dresser and yanked out the new, zip-front sweatshirt Hayley had thoughtfully provided. She pulled it on, turned back
and saw Dane watching her with a sad expression she'd seen
a lot of lately. It took her a moment to work out that it was
because she'd resisted his suggestion until she'd realized it
had to do with Chad.

I can't play second fiddle to your fixation any longer.

For the first time she realized just how much she had made
him feel that way. Now that it was too late.

His expression cleared and shifted into something painfully neutral, uncaring. "Quinn wants us to bring the dog.
And then stay clear until it's safe," he said in a businesslike
tone that matched the look.

He turned away then, walking to the dresser to pick up the

keys to Rafe's car. She wondered idly what Rafe was driving in the meantime and how many cars Foxworth had access to. And again she realized her mind was skittering for the safety of mundane, unimportant thoughts to avoid dealing with the biggest one of all.

"Let's go," Dane said.

Kayla shoved her hands into the pockets of the sweatshirt, mainly to hide how her hands had knotted into fists. It felt so close, so imminent. Ten years of her life, and it could all be coming together tonight.

It could all be coming apart tonight.

She said nothing as they left the room and walked to Rafe's car. Dane opened the back door and Cutter jumped in as if it were familiar territory. It probably was, from what Hayley had said. Kayla got in while Dane was doing that so that she wasn't faced with wondering if he would open the door for her as he usually did. He said nothing in turn—just walked around and got in the driver's side.

The silence continued as they drove through the night. It didn't surprise her. What was there to say now? The past ten years of her life had been aimed at this moment. She couldn't turn back now if she wanted to, despite the urge to call it all off. She'd set this in motion, and it was out of her control now.

And now she would have to live with the results.

Chapter 30

Dane hadn't been out this way in years, but not all that much had changed. The building still stood alone at the far end of what had once been a pasture of some sort. It was the size of a small barn, about a story and a half tall, with an even higher roof. The windows and doors were boarded up now, and it had the empty look of the long abandoned.

Memories stirred as he looked at it. It had been cavernous inside, a big, open space where the games had once stood in a random sort of array that had actually been carefully planned, with alcoves to give each game its own space and avoid the distraction of having a traditional pinball or shooting gallery competing with the latest alien invasion game. There had been an open, raised level across the back, about ten feet higher than the floor, where the offices were and where what security there had been often stood to overlook the space and keep order. They'd never responded quite quickly enough to stop Chad and his crew from their own form of entertainment, though.

Most of the youngest kids just quit coming. Many of the older ones, too. He himself had been too stubborn, refusing to let Chad deprive him of a favorite pastime. Although he was the same age, he'd been weaker and smaller then, the growth spurt that had taken him to over six feet yet to come. But he'd started working out, biking, running, getting strong. Oddly, he hadn't needed his new strength and confidence; they'd left him alone after that beating.

Or maybe it was that same new strength and confidence that had warned them off. He'd never really known, nor cared, as long as they stayed away.

He stopped the car about halfway down the long driveway and turned off the headlights. They were twenty yards from the building and still in the trees, where the darkness was nearly absolute. They were also at the spot where the driveway curved toward the building, and the headlights would have announced their arrival rather blatantly.

Kayla glanced at him.

"Quinn said to wait here," he said.

It was the first thing he'd said since they'd left the motel; they hadn't spoken at all on the drive. He'd been glad of it. The last thing he wanted to hear right now was her excitement at maybe seeing her brother again. He should be glad for her, he supposed, but selfishly he wasn't. Not when he thought about the price they both were paying for this obsession of hers. True, it could well be over soon, finally resolved, but too late. For them anyway.

Still, he felt compelled to warn her. "Quinn said if he's here, they'll have to call Detective Dunbar. Chad is still their prime suspect."

He wasn't sure, there in the dark, but he thought she winced. Yet she didn't speak or take her eyes off the building as they waited. Once Dane thought he saw a faint light through the upper window, as if someone had a flashlight inside, but it was quick and didn't repeat, so he wasn't certain.

Cutter was suddenly on his feet in the backseat, looking out the back window. A low rumble they'd heard before issued from his throat. If there was such a thing as a happy growl, this was it. Or maybe respectful, Dane thought.

"Quinn," Kayla said, recognizing the sound from that first day out at Foxworth just as he had.

And a moment later the big SUV pulled up beside them

and Quinn was there. And somewhat to Dane's surprise, Hayley was with him.

Dane got out and opened the car door for the anxious Cutter.

"Quiet," Hayley said to the animal as he jumped out. Obediently, the dog skipped his usual happy bark of greeting for her. But he danced at her feet until she bent down and hugged him, crooning about how much she'd missed him. Then he moved to Quinn, sitting at his feet and looking up expectantly.

"Ready to do a little work, buddy?" Quinn asked as he scratched the dog's ears.

Instantly the dog was back on his feet, tail up, ears alert, answering in the affirmative as clearly as if he could speak.

Quinn unclipped a small walkie-talkie that matched the one Hayley had given them from his belt. He keyed it and spoke.

"Rafe?"

"North side" came the laconic response.

"Cutter and I will be making the approach. Stand by, and stop anybody who leaves the building."

Instead of an answer, Dane heard a click, as if the man on the other end had simply pushed the talk button and released it. This was obviously not new to them.

"I want to go with you," Kayla said. "If Chad's in there, I need to see him."

"Not yet," Quinn said almost absently, clearly already focused on the task ahead. "Ready, boy? Let's go."

Dane understood Kayla's desire; he was feeling a bit antsy at staying here himself. But as he watched Cutter and Quinn move out across the open space between here and the building at different angles, as he saw the way Cutter raced ahead, then stopped, lifting his head into the faint breeze, sniffing, then turning his head and sniffing again, then respond to an apparent hand signal from Quinn, he realized they were a smooth-working team. And that Quinn Foxworth was far more than the executive or philanthropist he'd first thought he was.

"They've done this before, haven't they?" he asked Hayley softly.

"Yes."

"I should be there," Kayla said.

"No," Hayley said with a reassuring touch on Kayla's arm. "If you go in now, I'll go in after you, and if I go in Quinn will be mad, and trust me, you do not want to see that."

Dane couldn't help chuckling; he had no doubts that Quinn mad over Hayley putting herself at risk would be a fearsome sight.

"You've got your walkie-talkie?"

Dane nodded; he'd stuck it in his back pocket as they'd left the motel room.

"He'll call us when it's safe to come in."

Dane sensed Kayla was about to speak, but she apparently changed her mind. Just as well; if she'd insisted she'd be safe with her brother, he would have likely said something harsh. Perhaps the concept that someone had tried to kill her had finally penetrated.

Or perhaps the fact that Quinn had been armed had made her realize this wasn't necessarily going to be the joyous occasion she'd always hoped for.

For a moment he felt bad for her, so bad he almost went to comfort her, as he always had. But he kept going back to what he'd thought through yesterday as she'd slept. One of two things would happen here tonight.

One, Chad would not be there, whether it was because he never had been or because he had moved on or some other reason that didn't really matter. In which case Kayla would simply slide back into search mode, expending her time and energy and money on the endless quest.

Two, Chad would be there. And Kayla would be either delighted and lost in the happy reunion, or hurt to learn the brother she'd loved to exhaustion hadn't cared enough to keep in touch, maybe hadn't even thought about her all that much. Or worse, she'd be devastated if it turned out Chad had been guilty all along.

Whichever way it turned out, Kayla would be either continuing her search, or wrapped up one way or another in his return. And if it turned out he was back in legal trouble, if the police arrested him, she'd probably throw all that effort into defending him. Either way, the result for him would be the same.

He'd lost.

Maybe he'd never had a chance to win.

If there was anything Quinn had learned in the time since a finally generous fate had set Hayley and Cutter in his path, it was to trust them both. Right now, it was the quick, uncannily clever canine who had his full attention. He'd given up questioning how the dog seemed to always know what the mission at hand was, how he barely had to formulate a command before the dog was off and running, as if he'd already known what to do and had merely been waiting for the order.

This time was no exception. They made their entrance through a delivery door where the lock appeared to have been broken long ago judging by the weathering and rust buildup. Cutter had stopped just inside in that way he had, his head lifted, nose pumping as he processed scents, ears alert as he listened for the slightest sound with that hearing that was uncanny even for a dog. Quinn's eyes were already adjusted to the dark outside and only took a moment to change further for the deeper darkness inside the building. He kept his small, high-power LED flashlight in his pocket for the moment; he could see well enough to make out shapes in the cavernous space, and he didn't want to betray his location too soon.

In what seemed like only a few seconds, Cutter headed for the far left corner of the building with obvious purpose.

In the beginning, it had been a stretch for Quinn to trust the dog completely, to accept that he would find what they were looking for and warn of any impediments, human or otherwise. But now he knew better, and he followed without hesitation.

In the end, it seemed almost anticlimactic. Cutter signaled with a single, sharp bark that he'd found something. Quinn ran the last few feet and found Cutter at the entrance to one of the old game alcoves, one that was more walled off than the others, making it almost a private room. The dog was on his feet, his attention riveted on what—or who—was inside that space.

It was obvious the dog didn't sense a threat, but Quinn wasn't quite ready to cede full assessment of the danger to a dog. Yet. Cutter might be smart, as dogs go downright brilliant, but the concept of firearms or even knives as weapons was asking a bit much.

Now was the time for the flashlight. Quinn pulled it out and set it to spotlight mode, which was a wide, intense beam that could temporarily blind an opponent at night. With the light in his left hand and his sidearm as a precaution in his right, he made the move, leaning around the wall to look into the alcove.

The light flooded the small space like it was a stage.

Apparently Cutter had been right about the threat level. The man inside the alcove was huddled against the back wall, staring in apparent shock at the dog in front of him. He had a dark blanket pulled around him, making his pale face stand out even more. He wasn't moving, but his hands were hidden by the blanket so Quinn stayed wary, although the man seemed pinned in place more by the sight of Cutter than Quinn and the powerful flashlight. Quinn supposed the sudden appearance of a fifty-pound dog could do that, although the guy was looking at Cutter like he'd seen one too many werewolf movies.

Quinn registered all this in a split second. These were logistical details, the threat of the hidden hands, the lack of movement, the fear of the dog. Important, necessary, but not the overriding fact.

That was, simply, that they'd found him.

Because there was no doubt this man huddled in the blanket was Chad Tucker.

Chapter 31

"Guard, Cutter. Make a move and he'll tear your throat out," Quinn said pleasantly. Cutter growled for effect.

Kayla smothered a gasp at the threat. She was shaking, knowing she'd be unable to believe what she'd heard come over the small radio until she got inside and saw it for herself. Now that she was there, she wanted to rush forward those last few yards, but both Hayley and Dane were solidly between her and the goal.

And then Quinn was there, talking into his walkie-talkie.

"—pole out at the road, see if you can jury-rig some lights. Stay alert—this is a big place. Cutter hasn't triggered on anything else in here, but he's pretty focused just now."

"Copy," Rafe's voice came back.

Quinn turned to Kayla. "I've searched him for weapons, and he's clean, but I still want you to stay back far enough that he can't get his hands on you."

She started to say if it was her brother he wouldn't hurt her, but she held it back. "It's really Chad?"

"Yes."

She shivered again, her emotions a tangled mess of anticipation, excitement, apprehension and a tinge of fear. But overriding them all was the sense that it was finally done, her brother was finally home.

"Please, I need to see him."

"I know. Just don't let your emotions overrule common sense. We don't know the truth yet."

She nodded.

"He doesn't know you're here. I want to watch his reaction when he sees you. It may tell us something."

"All right."

She was aware Dane hadn't said a word, but that was better than having him make some comment that would tear her up even more inside. Still, she couldn't help glancing at him.

To her surprise, he softly said, "Go ahead. You've been living for this moment for ten years."

There was no criticism, no harshness in his tone, and for an instant he was the old Dane, solid, supportive, strong. Impulsively she reached out, took his hand and squeezed it. Then she turned and walked the last few steps to where that blessed dog who had begun all this sat.

Now that the time was here she was a shaky mess, she thought, pausing to pet the dog instead of hurrying forward. But finally she turned to face the culmination of ten years of faith, loyalty and determination. Quinn turned the bright light on him.

He was a huddled, dirty mess, with what looked to be a blanket tossed onto the floor beside him. He was unshaven, his hair scraggly and unkempt under a red baseball cap that had also seen better days. He put up a hand against the glare, blocking her view of his face. Kayla saw the hand was dirty. But it wasn't that that make her heart leap—it was the little finger on that hand, crooked and bent slightly inward, a souvenir from a long ago incident with a car door.

"Chad," she whispered, barely able to keep herself from ignoring Quinn's order to stay back.

Her first thought was that the computer-aged picture had been startlingly accurate. Her second was that good as it had been, it hadn't been able to show the haggard, haunted look in her brother's eyes. He was twenty-eight, but he looked ten years older. Ten long, hard years.

She realized that while he was lit up as if on a stage, she was still in shadow to him.

"It's me," she said.

He didn't answer, just sat with a hand still up to shade his eyes from the brightness of Quinn's powerful flashlight.

A second later a bank of lights far above came to life. Rafe, she thought, out at the power pole on the road. They only lit this corner of the spacious building, but it was enough that Quinn shut off the flashlight.

Chad dropped his hand then, and Kayla saw that although perhaps he didn't look quite as badly as he had in the flashlight's harsh beam, he still looked tired, dirty and worn.

And beaten. Broken. Smaller somehow. It was definitely Chad, although the cocky grin, the swagger, seemed gone. Even the dimple that had so charmed everyone seemed to have morphed into just a long crease in a tired face.

She wanted to go to him, wanted to throw her arms around him and hug him, but Quinn was close enough to stop her, as was Dane, and she had no doubts that they would.

She stared at her brother.

"Are you all right?"

It was, she supposed, a silly question, but it was the first thing that came to her mind.

"Is that your damned dog? Get him away from me."

For the first words she'd heard him speak in ten years, they certainly lacked something. Kayla looked at Cutter, who was sitting obediently, although he never took his eyes off Chad.

"If it wasn't for him, we'd never have found you."

"I don't like the way he's looking at me."

"He won't hurt you."

Chad looked doubtful, but he let it go.

"Who are these guys?"

His gaze shifted from Quinn to Dane, and he frowned. Kayla drew back slightly; did he really not recognize Dane?

Quinn stayed silent but glanced at Dane. She couldn't see what passed between the two men, but it was Dane who spoke.

"I'm the guy who tries to clean up the damage you leave behind," he said.

Chad's eyes widened. "Burdette?" He looked Dane up and down. "It sounds like you, but…"

"Ten years makes a difference. Whether you're going up—" Dane looked at Chad in a similar fashion "—or down."

Chad didn't even respond to the jab—there was no sign of the old rivalry. Her brother just seemed bewildered.

"You're still around?" he asked. "I mean, you two, together?"

"For now," Dane said.

Stung by the reminder Dane's words made clear, Kayla took a step forward. Dane put a hand on her arm, stopping her. She shook him off.

"Can't you see he's not a threat?"

"What I see is the guy who ran and left you to deal with everything by yourself. Even if he is innocent—and I'm not convinced—that makes him a damned son of a bitch in my book."

Somehow his words, even though they accused her brother, made her feel better. He was angry, yes, but he was angry on her behalf, and that gave her hope.

"I am innocent!" Chad burst out. "I swear, Kayla, I didn't do it. You have to believe me."

She turned back to her brother. "Then why did you run?"

"You know why. You know the police had me tried and convicted and on my way to the death penalty."

"All you had to do was tell them the truth, that you happened to get there right after, that's why your fingerprints were in the wet blood. You got scared and ran, that's all. Anybody would have."

Chad stared at her, looking nonplussed. Then, he smiled.

To her discomfort, Kayla noticed a faint trace of his old smugness, the kind he'd shown when he'd done something he knew he'd get away with. But it vanished the moment Dane spoke.

"Well, well," Dane said. "If only you'd thought up that story at the time, eh, Chad?"

Kayla flushed, but she couldn't deny Chad's reaction when it was right in front of her. Apparently her neat little story was just that, a story she'd made up to explain what had happened. Chad's expression made it clear that it wasn't the truth.

"I'm hungry," he said. "I can't even think I'm so hungry."

Tension filled Kayla as she wondered what he would have said if he could think. Would he have gone along with her version of events? Would he have let her believe what obviously wasn't the truth if only he'd been quick enough to grab at the out she'd given him?

"You don't need to think," Dane said, "just talk. Tell her the truth. She deserves that after standing by you for ten years."

"Can't we go someplace where I could eat?"

"You buying?" Dane asked, and Chad flushed.

"We can go someplace else," Quinn said, the first time he'd spoken since he'd turned the flashlight on for her, "but if we do, I'll be obligated to call the police first. I don't feel like explaining why we let a double murder suspect leave the scene where we found him."

Chad blinked. "You're not the police?"

"No," Quinn said. "But they can be here quickly enough. So now's your chance to tell your sister the truth. Maybe your only chance."

Kayla had been watching him carefully, looking for any trace of the young, carefree kid she'd known. She found nothing. And for the first time in her life, she wondered how much of Chad's cheerful bluster had been a facade. Maybe deep down he'd been as uncertain as she had once been, only he'd hidden it so well he'd never developed the real confidence of someone who'd learned their own worth as they built it. He'd never really grown up because he'd always pretended to already be there.

"I didn't do it," Chad said stubbornly. "They pissed me off all the time, but I didn't kill them."

Kayla should have felt vindicated. After all these years of believing just that, she should have been overjoyed at hearing it from Chad's own mouth. But she wasn't. Not that she didn't believe him; she could tell he was telling the truth. But she knew that look, that hangdog expression, all too well. His appearance may have changed, but his expressions had not, and the way he wouldn't look her in the eye was an old, familiar warning that her brother wasn't telling the whole truth.

"You always were a master of omission," Kayla said. "So what are you leaving out now?"

Chad seemed surprised. That she'd called him on it? She remembered that brief flash of smugness and realized sadly that he'd been feeling smug because, as always, she had come up with an explanation for him. His little sister would bail him out again, as she always had.

"Nothing," he insisted. He glanced at Quinn. "Who the hell is this? And who's she?" he said, looking past Quinn to Hayley. "Is that their dog? Can't you get him out of here? He keeps staring at me."

Kayla expected Quinn to answer, but he said nothing. Nor did Hayley, although she whispered something to Cutter, something Kayla guessed was a keep doing what he was doing because that's what he did.

Apparently this was all Kayla's now. "They and their organization found you for me," she said.

Chad's eyes flicked to Quinn again. "You're them? The do-gooders?"

Dane went very still. Kayla saw him exchange a pointed

glance with Quinn. Quinn gave a slight shake of his head. And suddenly Dane was on the offensive.

"Is that what your partner told you? That Foxworth was looking for you? That they wouldn't give up until they found you? Why'd you come back if you knew Foxworth was here? Did he tell you to?"

Chad frowned at the rapid-fire questions and shook his head as if he were having trouble sorting it all out. She understood that; she herself wasn't sure what Dane was about here.

"He didn't say anything about any Foxworth," Chad said. "Just said she brought in professional help this time, good help, and that I should get back here so we could figure out what to do."

"Well, well," Quinn said, echoing Dane's earlier comment as he glanced at him. "Nicely done."

"Learned a lot," Dane agreed, seemingly pleased at Quinn's praise.

Kayla was feeling a bit confused herself. "Learned what?"

"That he did just come back, which makes our homeless witness accurate. That he knew you had help this time, and that it was good help. So someone's reporting to him. Which brings us to the other thing he just admitted."

"I didn't admit anything," Chad protested.

"Sure you did," Dane said. "You admitted there *is* a partner."

Kayla realized she indeed had been a bit slow.

And that once more, Chad had deceived her, had lied to her face.

What that made her, she didn't want to think about.

Chapter 32

Kayla was shaken, Dane could see that. He had to remind himself again that seeing to her, comforting her, wasn't his job anymore. At the same time, that little voice in his brain was telling him it was only human kindness to comfort someone in distress—it didn't have to be personal.

Didn't have to become…intimate.

Except with Kayla it usually did. He didn't seem to have any amount of willpower she couldn't overcome, not by trying, coaxing, wheedling. That wasn't her way. She simply was who she was, who she always had been, and she was irresistible to him.

Or had been, until her obsession had finally pushed him over a line he couldn't cross and still live with himself.

And now here she was, face-to-face with the object of that obsession, and Dane could easily tell she wasn't happy with what she was seeing. He didn't blame her; his own dislike for her brother aside, it had to be a shock to see the wreck he'd become at only twenty-eight. He barely recognized the once-handsome, charming Chad Tucker in the dirty, skinny guy with badly cut, scraggly hair and sunken eyes before them now.

And he could see in Kayla's face that she knew he was, even now, still lying to her. Or at least not telling her the whole truth. Hayley had moved to Kayla's side and whispered something to her. Dane wondered if it had something to do with him because it was he Kayla glanced at for an instant before she turned back to Chad.

"Who is it?"

Kayla's words were flat, emotionless. Chad shifted uncomfortably.

"Who's helping you?" she asked again. And then, as the conclusion he'd reached a while ago struck her visibly, she added, horror echoing in her voice, "Is it whoever helped you that night? Helped you get away?"

Something about the way she said it got through to Chad. "You do think I did it! You think I killed them, don't you?"

He was nearly shouting, and Cutter let out a warning rumble. Chad drew back, glancing warily at the dog. *Good boy,* Dane thought.

"Atta boy," Hayley said to the dog, loud enough this time for Chad to hear.

"I've spent ten years of my life trying to prove you didn't," Kayla shot back at her brother. "With no help from you. Nothing but a note every few months to let me know you were alive."

"Or to keep you dancing on his string," Dane said. "So you'd be focused on looking for him, instead of—"

He cut off his own words as Kayla's head snapped around and she looked at him. It would be better if she got to that realization on her own. And she did it so quickly he knew she'd already thought of it before.

"Instead of thinking about who did do it, if he didn't?"

"Yes," Dane said simply.

"But why would he do that?"

"Good question," Dane said.

She whirled back on her brother. "Tell me the damn truth, Chad. Or are you so twisted now you can't?"

"I didn't kill them," he insisted.

Kayla made a small, harsh sound. Dane knew her so well

he could almost follow her thoughts. She'd waited so long to hear that from her brother, and now that she had, it only emphasized what he wasn't telling her. She seemed to finally realize he'd been playing her all these years.

She turned away, shaking her head slowly, like a wounded animal. It was more than Dane could take. He glanced at Quinn, but the man merely nodded; apparently he was satisfied with the way things were going. Dane looked back at Chad.

"Then why did you try to kill your own sister?" Dane demanded.

Chad gaped at him. "I didn't! I wouldn't."

He ignored the denial. "For that matter, how did you even know where she lives now?"

Dane didn't make a move toward the man, but Chad cringed backward anyway. He seemed shrunken, a long, long way from the swaggering, cocky bully he'd once been. He would have almost felt sorry for him—if not for the thought of Kayla nearly dying in her burning house.

"I don't know what you're talking about."

Kayla whirled back. "You were there. You were seen there."

When Chad looked away, still refusing to speak, Dane's disgust spilled over. "This is pointless."

"Yes, it is," Kayla said, surprising him with both her words and her tone; her voice was a harsh, bitter thing. She looked at Quinn. "You might as well call Detective Dunbar."

Quinn nodded. "Between us we'll find whoever it is he's protecting. Just like we found him. Of course, it'll go worse for him—" he jerked a thumb toward Chad "—because he refused to cooperate, but he's already in so much trouble it won't matter much."

"Wait, wait," Chad stammered. "Kayla, you can't do that. I'm your brother."

"You don't get it, do you?" Dane asked, almost astonished at the man's refusal to understand. "You think you're just going to take off again, run?"

Chad looked at him. His words were tinged with his old bluster, but Dane saw the doubt in his eyes. "She won't turn me in."

"This is for real, Chad. It's out of your hands, our hands. You won't tell your own sister, the woman who's stood up for you for ten damned years, the truth, but I bet by the time the police get done with you you'll spill it all."

"But—"

"And they'll realize quickly enough you didn't do it all on your own," Dane said. "You're not smart enough."

Chad let out a foul curse. "You always did think you were so smart."

"He didn't think it," Kayla said softly, "he knew it. Because he is."

A stab of pain at the quiet declaration shot through Dane as he glanced at her. But she wasn't looking at him; she was staring at her brother. This time he wasn't sure what she was thinking, only that she was; her expression told him her mind was racing.

"You two are the perfect couple," Chad said, that trace of bluster growing stronger. "You always thought you were better than everyone."

Dane almost laughed at that; Chad seemed to have a very different memory of their adolescence than he and Kayla had.

"If that's the way you feel about me, then why did you come back at all?" Kayla asked. She sounded flat, emotionless. "Why the notes even? Why bother?"

Chad shifted, as if her tone had made him uncomfortable, draining away some of his regained swagger. "You're my sister."

"And that obviously means less than nothing to you because you won't even tell me the truth." She looked at Quinn again. "Make the call."

Quinn nodded and pulled out his phone. Kayla again turned away.

"No!"

Chad's regained facade of confidence crumbled like the shaky structure it had been. Perhaps had always been, Dane thought. Chad wasn't inherently mean, like some. With the knowledge of maturity, something Chad had never achieved, Dane realized that behind the bullying exterior had likely been an uncertain, timid kid. It didn't excuse his behavior, but he understood better now than back then, when he'd only been angry and scared at being a target.

And out of that had come his resolve to change that, to become someone nobody would mess with. The pact made with Kayla that long-ago day, to defy the expectations of those who judged on appearance alone, had arisen out of her brother's bullying, although she'd never known it until today. So in a twisted sort of way, he supposed he owed Chad a thank you. He was who he was today in part because of him.

Kayla looked at her brother over her shoulder. "If you're telling the truth, if you didn't kill our parents, you're protecting who did. And you expect me to keep protecting you?"

"Kayla—"

"You're not worth it. And you're surely not worth what you've cost me. The man I've lost over you is worth a million of you. Ten million. I've been a fool to believe in you."

She turned and started to walk away. Dane watched her, feeling tangled inside, proud that she'd done it, sorry for the pain that had been in her voice and shaken by hearing her declaration of tremendous love and loss in the same sentence.

The sound of her footsteps echoed in the cavernous room. For a long, torturous moment that was the only sound. And then, finally, Chad broke.

"It was Troy!" he shouted.

Kayla stopped. Dane's head snapped back. His brows furrowed.

Kayla slowly turned around.

"Troy?" she said. "You seriously expect me to believe that?"

"It was him."

Cutter was on his feet, apparently reacting to the sudden upswing in tension. For the first time the dog looked away from Chad, while Dane himself was staring at the guy in disbelief. It echoed in his voice.

"Of all the people you could try to pin this on, you pick on the poster boy for goodness and clean living? The adults' favorite 'why can't you be more like him?' guy?"

"It was him," Chad insisted. "We were both there that night, but I only wanted the money. Troy was broke, I was broke, and his car payment was due and I wanted to buy a motorcycle, and I remembered dad's stash."

"You knew about the money in his desk?" Kayla looked puzzled.

"God, you didn't?"

Kayla shook her head. "I thought it was just all the important papers—birth certificates, insurance, that kind of thing."

"Yeah, they were in there, too. Troy was looking through it all, searching for more money." Chad shook his head. "I can't believe you didn't know he kept over five grand in there."

"How did you know?"

"I overheard him telling Mom about it, in case she ever needed it."

"So you snuck into the house intending to steal from your own father?"

Chad's smugness at her lack of knowledge vanished.

"Hey, I asked him for a loan, and he said no."

"Maybe because he knew you wouldn't pay it back?" Dane

suggested. He knew a whine was about to ensue as Chad opened his mouth to protest, and he was in no mood. He cut him off with an impatient question. "What happened?"

Chad seemed distracted by Cutter as the dog began to turn in place, sniffing and listening at every angle. But after a moment he went on.

"I don't know how they heard us. I thought they were up-stairs. But they walked in on us. Dad saw the money in my hand and saw Troy digging through the drawer. He yelled. And Troy freaked."

"Freaked? And killed both your parents?" Dane couldn't picture the always polite, charming Troy doing any of this. The guy had never been in trouble. He was the proverbial good kid, the one every parent wished was their own. Smart, well-mannered, polite—all those things adults treasured in teenagers.

"He did," Chad insisted.

Now if he'd said Rod, that he could believe. But Troy? He couldn't help thinking Chad was pulling this out of thin air, trying to save himself. Maybe Troy was just the first person to pop into his mind when cornered.

"Where'd he get the knife?"

Chad didn't look at him; he kept his pleading gaze on his sister. "It was him, I swear. I didn't know he'd brought a knife. I didn't even realize what was happening until it was too late. Until it was over."

Cutter growled, and Chad lowered his eyes to the dog un-easily. Kayla took a few steps back toward him.

"Why did you run?" she asked.

Chad's head came up. "Because I knew they'd suspect me. Troy told me I'd better get out of there. Because it was my idea to take the money, he said I'd take the fall. Besides, nobody would ever believe it was him." Chad flicked Dane a glance. "Because of just what you said. I was the one with a record."

"And he just stayed here? Went on with his life?" Kayla demanded.

"And you just let him?" Dane added.

"He sent me money." Chad's voice was resentful, and Dane wasn't sure who it was aimed at. Life maybe. He was the type. "He owed me for what he did."

"Owed *you?*" Dane nearly shouted it. "You were eighteen, technically an adult. Your sister was only sixteen!"

"It wasn't my fault! Once he found out about the money, there was no stopping him. Besides, he warned me to stay away, told me that they were still looking for me, that I was still the only suspect."

"And I suppose the thought that your good friend should confess and take the heat off you never occurred to you?"

Chad shifted uncomfortably, and Dane guessed it had indeed occurred to him more than once. "But he said we'd both go to jail," Chad whined, "and this way at least we both were free."

"If you call this free," Dane muttered, indicating Chad's sorry state with a tilt of his head.

"It wasn't my fault. I never—"

"You never thought anything was ever your fault," Kayla said. Dane had once thought he'd give anything to hear her say that, but there was such pain in her voice he took no pleasure in it now. "But you got our parents murdered as surely as if you'd used the knife yourself."

"I never touched them!"

"Your partner was right about one thing," Quinn said, breaking his silence. "In the eyes of the law you're equally culpable. You broke into a residence with the intent to commit a felony, and in the course of that felony, two people were killed."

"But I didn't mean for anything to happen to them!"

"And I'm sure the jury will take your good intentions into

account, right before they convict you of murder," Dane said, only realizing as he said it that he was buying Chad's story. It was too stupid, too ridiculous for him to have made it up. And it was just like Chad. His always-looking-for-the-easy-way selfishness had not only cost his own parents their lives, and nearly destroyed Kayla's, it had cost him the woman he'd loved. Restraint was beyond him at the moment.

"I can't believe this," Kayla whispered, sounding a little shell-shocked. "Or rather, I can, and it makes me sick. You make me sick. All these years I wasted, while all along you—"

She broke off as a low, threatening growl rumbled up from Cutter's throat. The dog whirled and took off at a head-down dead run toward the back of the building.

Quinn swore. "I knew something was up with him. I should have paid more attention."

Dane realized Cutter's restlessness hadn't been merely reaction to the tension. "He's headed toward the stairs," he said as the dog left the lighted area and disappeared into the shadows. "It's like a loft, and the office and storage rooms used to be up there."

"He heard something. Sensed something. And now he knows. Somebody must have gotten in when Rafe went to rig the lights." Quinn's voice turned sharp as he looked at Dane. "Get Kayla and Hayley outside, back to the car."

"What about him?" Dane asked, indicating Chad.

"Call Rafe on the walkie-talkie and give him an update. If Chad's stupid enough to run, Rafe'll take him out."

Then he was gone, running into the shadows after the dog who had known something was wrong long before they had.

"No," Kayla began when Dane took her arm.

Dane cut off her protest. "Let's go." He wasn't sure if she was protesting going or wondering just what Quinn meant by the lethal Rafe taking her brother out.

"But—"

A loud, explosive sound cut her off this time.

A shot.

Kayla gasped, then ducked instinctively. Chad yelped and hit the ground, cowering into a corner. Dane turned Kayla around and found Hayley had grabbed her other arm, and between them they propelled her toward the door they'd come in. But she still didn't seem to want to move.

"Don't you get it?" Dane demanded. "He's here. The guy who murdered your parents is here. And he's graduated from a knife to a gun."

Chapter 33

"Stay here. Keep the doors locked."

Kayla heard the words but couldn't seem to react. She was trembling—she could feel it, hated it, but couldn't seem to control it. There had been so much to process so quickly that now she felt as if her brain was trying to swim upstream through a rush of revelations she'd never expected.

Belatedly, she realized Dane wasn't getting into the car.

"What are you doing?"

"Quinn might need some help in there."

"Rafe is there."

"Yes. But he's got Chad to deal with, and obviously Troy is armed."

He took off back toward the building. She stared after him. When had her Dane become fearless? Heroic? Or had he always been, and it just hadn't been put to the test until now?

This was insane. He could be hurt—or worse. An image of Dane lying dead on the dusty floor of the old arcade nearly smothered her. The last, shaky vestige of naïveté about her brother crumbled away. She'd been a fool. And it had cost her the man she'd loved nearly half her life.

Her Dane.

Only he wasn't hers. Not anymore.

She'd been devoted to finding Chad, while for his part a few unsigned notes had been his sole effort at keeping in touch. She'd spent years searching for him, and if she'd found him earlier she would have channeled that time, energy and money into proving his innocence. Even as kids, she'd always been loyal to him, tolerating his behavior because she loved him and because every now and then he threw her a crumb of brotherly affection. Now, she doubted he even knew what the word loyalty meant.

But she did.

Loyalty was Dane, sticking with her for so long, despite taking second place to her foolish stubbornness. Loyalty was Dane, giving her chance after chance to move on, to make the life with him they'd always planned, always wanted.

Loyalty was Dane, who came running when she was hurt, even after he'd finally walked away, even after being suspected himself.

Loyalty…and love.

And she'd worn out that love, thrown it away, all for nothing. For a brother who at best had been a careless, self-centered fool and at worst a stupidly, willingly manipulated pawn who had cost the people who loved him the most their lives.

She glanced around. Hayley was in the back of the SUV, digging through what looked like a locker and occasionally stopping to speak into the walkie-talkie. Hayley apparently was serving as a coordinator.

While she sat here doing nothing, like the helpless female of some fairy tale. While the men were inside, likely dealing with a confirmed killer.

While Dane, even lacking the training the Foxworth men had, was in there.

A muffled crack jerked her out of her self-castigating reverie.

Another shot.

She'd had enough of sitting on the sideline, even though

it had only been a couple of minutes. She'd gotten everyone into this, after all. She scrambled out of the car and ran toward the building.

The moment he'd gone back through the door, Dane had heard Cutter's bark. In the echoing space it was hard to pinpoint, but it seemed to come from the back. And from above, so Dane guessed the dog was up in the raised loft. For a moment he hesitated but decided Quinn was a pro and would instinctively assess that Chad was the lesser threat and deal with the armed man first.

Dane ran back to where Chad had been hiding out. And collided with him as he darted out of the alcove.

Chad staggered back a couple of steps.

"Running, as usual?" Dane asked.

"He's got a gun," Chad said, a tremor in his voice.

"And that night he had a knife."

"I didn't know—"

"Spare me. You've put Kayla through hell for ten years. You're a coward, Chad. You always have been."

Another shot split the dark, the sound bouncing off the walls, making it sound like the crack and roll of thunder. Chad jumped, then tried to push past Dane.

And Dane indulged in the urge that had been prodding him since the moment they'd found Kayla's brother huddled here in a shameless heap, not caring what he'd done to his sister for years.

He launched a solid punch carefully aimed at Chad's lips and nose. The crunch was immensely satisfying.

Chad crumpled, wailing.

Dane left him there. And ran in the direction of the shot.

The halo of light Rafe had managed was fainter here, but after a moment his eyes adjusted and he could at least see to move, if not details and colors. He found Quinn crouched halfway up the stairs, head turned toward him. Then he saw some tension ease when he saw who was there.

"He's up there?" Dane whispered.

"Yes." Quinn's voice was even quieter. "He leaned out to take that shot, but it was nowhere close. He was just firing blind." Quinn glanced over toward the light. "Chad?"

"He tried to run when he heard the shot. I stopped him but probably not for long. We'll have to find him later." And he had no doubts Foxworth would do just that.

"Rafe's around. He won't get far. Kayla?"

"Locked in the car." Dane grimaced. "Whether she'll stay there..."

"Gutsy girl. Hard to find."

Dane couldn't deny that. And wondered if Quinn was making an observation or a recommendation.

"What now?" he asked.

"I think Cutter has a plan."

Dane nearly gaped at the man. Quinn was tough, smart and a former special forces operative, and he was trusting a dog to have a plan?

"I know, I know." Even in a whisper Quinn's wry tone was obvious. "I can only tell you that if I don't trust him, things get screwed up. If I do, things always seem to work out."

And so he crouched there, beside Quinn, waiting on a dog to make a move.

Kayla was nearly there when a shape reeled out of the door they'd used to enter. She stopped abruptly, nearly slipping on the gravel. The man started to run, half stumbling back the way she had come, toward the road.

Was it the man with the gun? Had he somehow escaped even the clever Cutter?

Then she saw the red cap. Chad. Running away as usual.

So intent on avoiding the consequences of his actions that he didn't even see her as he ran.

Without a second thought, she stuck a foot into his path and sent him sprawling.

He swore, rolled over, then finally saw her.

"Kayla! What the hell?"

Even at night, there was enough light for her to see that his mouth and nose were bloodied. The instinctive, automatic lurch of concern died almost instantly; her brother didn't care about her, never had, so she wasn't going to waste any more time worrying about him. Someone had given him his split lip and bloody nose, and it was the very least he deserved.

"You're through running, Chad," she said coldly.

"C'mon, sis, I've got to get out of here. I can't go to jail."

"You can, and you will. You're almost as responsible as Troy is."

"I'm not. I didn't know. It wasn't my fault."

"Shut the hell up, you coward. You're a useless piece of humanity, and I regret every second I spent worrying about you and searching for you."

"Hear, hear," came Hayley's quiet cheer of approval from just behind her.

She saw realization dawn on his face, realization that he'd finally lost his grip on his little sister. He rolled to his hands and knees, starting to get up.

"Oh, no you don't."

She let loose a short, quick kick Dane had taught her years ago, catching Chad hard just below the rib cage. His breath whistled out of him and he collapsed face down. Following part two of the lesson, Kayla came down hard, planting a knee just over his kidneys. He grunted. She ignored him.

"Nice job."

She jumped at the male voice coming out of the dim light

just feet away. But she calmed as she recognized the slight limp of Rafe Crawford as he approached.

"You were here?" she asked, startled. "Not inside?"

He nodded as he came to a stop and looked down at Chad. "Quinn'll handle it."

She wasn't surprised, now that she had a chance to think, that Quinn would want Hayley's, and her own, safety insured before anything. It fit with who the man was.

But that didn't ease her main worry. "Dane," she said.

"That boy'll do, don't worry," Rafe said. She had the feeling that from this man, that was the highest of praise. "And they've got Cutter," Rafe added. "It's taken us all a while but we've learned to trust that darned dog." He glanced down at Chad. "Besides, it didn't seem like you needed much help. And some things you need to do yourself."

She stared at the man. Saw a world of understanding in his eyes. And felt a small burst of pride that he had held back, trusting her to handle it. "Thank you."

"It had to be a tough call, him being your brother and all."

"I'm not sure who he is anymore. I'm not sure the brother I loved ever really existed."

Rafe only grimaced but managed to do it in a way that conveyed such empathy that she felt an easing of the pressure that had built inside her since she'd realized what her brother had become and only increased as she was forced to admit he probably had always been.

They were an amazing group, these Foxworth people, she thought. She bet each one of them had a story that would fascinate.

But much as she might want to know them all, in particular this laconic, obviously dangerous yet clearly understanding man's, right now she was only worried about one thing.

What was going on inside that building.

* * *

Dane heard faint steps above, on the landing. He wondered what Cutter was doing; it sounded like the man—Troy, he amended—was just walking around.

"Troy!"

The scrape from above made Dane think Troy had jumped, startled, just as he himself almost had at Quinn's sudden shout.

"Give it up, Troy. It's all over."

"Go to hell!"

Quinn glanced at Dane. Realizing what he was silently asking, Dane nodded. "It's him."

"What was that?" Quinn called out. "I couldn't hear you."

Dane frowned. Troy's words were perfectly clear. Then he realized Quinn was trying to lure him forward, out of the shelter of the hallway between the offices.

"I said go to hell."

"Still can't hear you. Acoustics are weird in here."

And where was Cutter? Dane wondered. He didn't expect to hear the dog's steps, but—

"Cops already know it was you, Troy," Quinn yelled. "There's nowhere to run."

"Who's running?"

There was another sound, a creak of the floor, toward the front of the loft. Quinn held out an arm to urge Dane back against the stairway wall. Dane didn't argue but pressed back, expecting to hear another shot any second. Instead, he heard a yell of surprise and a series of heavy thumps.

Troy rolled past them, somersaulting down the stairs.

At the top of those stairs, Cutter let out a woof of pure satisfaction.

At the bottom, Troy was now sprawled, groaning.

Dane looked up at the dog, who had clearly managed to

nudge Troy over the edge. Then at Quinn. The man grinned and shrugged. "Told ya' he had a plan," he said.

Then he headed down the stairs to where Troy had now rolled onto his side, still groaning pitifully.

Cutter headed down the stairs, stopping to give Dane a nudge with his nose.

"You are something else," Dane said. "I'll never call you just a dog again."

Cutter tilted his head quizzically. And Dane could have sworn he winked. But in the faint light it was impossible to be sure. And ridiculous to believe. Then the dog was gone, headed down to check personally on his handiwork.

And realizing the threat was over, Dane launched himself over the stair railing to the floor and began to run. Toward the door.

Toward Kayla.

Chapter 34

When she saw Dane burst from the building, she nearly cried in aching, heartfelt relief.

No, she *was* crying, Kayla realized. She started to wipe at her eyes, then stopped. She didn't care if he saw it. She was just glad Chad was facedown and couldn't see her; he was so self-centered he'd probably think she was crying for him.

Dane skidded to a halt. For a moment he just stared. She supposed she made quite a sight, kneeling on Chad's back, forcing him down as he flailed, trying to get up. For an instant she thought she saw something in his face, a flash of promise, or at least hope. She tried to quash it, afraid to believe.

He glanced toward Rafe, standing off to one side.

"Don't look at me," the man said. "She did it. Nicely, too. Didn't need my help at all."

Kayla saw disbelief warring with the realization that Rafe had no reason to lie to Dane. Did he really think, after what she'd learned tonight, that she'd just let her brother waltz away and go on the run again?

Why wouldn't he? she told herself. *Haven't you made it clear you'd forgive Chad almost anything?*

She noticed Dane flexing his right hand, then rubbing at the knuckles as he looked at her brother.

"It was you," she said. "You punched him."

Dane's gaze snapped to her face. There was a touch of recalcitrance in his voice when he said, "After what he's put you through for so long, it was the least I could do and still sleep at night." He glared at Chad. "And I'll do it again if he tries to get up," he added by way of warning.

Chad fell still, and his body went slack, as if he'd finally given up. Kayla barely noticed. She was too distracted by the leap of her heart in her chest. Dane had punched Chad for what he'd put her through. Was there some hope, some possibility that she hadn't completely killed his love for her?

"Quinn cleaning up?" Rafe asked.

Dane nodded, never taking his eyes off Kayla. She saw Rafe look from her to Dane, then back. He gave the slightest of nods before he spoke. Somehow it encouraged her.

"I'll just take care of this clown then," he said, indicating Chad.

Kayla stood up, releasing her brother. Rafe yanked him up to his feet and started walking him back to Quinn's SUV. When he got there, he reached in and turned on the powerful headlights, throwing a shaft of light all the way to the door of the building.

"Don't you want to go help him?" Dane asked. "I bloodied him up a bit."

"No."

He studied her for a long moment. "You finally have what you wanted."

"No." He drew back slightly. "What I wanted never really existed, did it?" she said.

"Little late realizing that," Dane said.

"Yes," she admitted. But she didn't dare voice the crucial question; was it too late?

A sound from the building turned them both around; the door opened again. First out into the swath of light was Cutter, who quickly turned to supervise the exit of the two men who followed; Quinn and a limping man cradling his right arm. Cutter then took up a position on the other side of Troy, keeping the man securely between himself and Quinn.

Until this moment, Kayla hadn't quite believed it. But as Troy gave her a sideways glance as the trio reached them, she saw it in his eyes. Not guilt, but a sort of deadness that she realized must have always been behind the charming smile.

"Why, Troy?" she asked, not even really expecting him to answer. "My parents always liked you. Everybody liked you."

"Except you."

Dane saw Kayla's eyes widen. There wasn't a trace of anger in Troy's voice or his expression, just coldness.

"That's why you did it?" she asked, astonished. "Because I turned you down?"

Troy laughed, and it was even colder. So cold Dane had to suppress a shiver. "You'd like to believe that, wouldn't you, sweetheart?"

"But why my parents? They were the ones trying to push you and me together, they liked you so much."

"All the parents liked me." The smirk on his face, even now, echoed in his voice. "It made life so easy."

The smirk widened, but Troy said no more. Cutter wasn't happy with the pause. He had moved, put himself between Troy and Kayla, a move she noted with affection for the clever dog. She resisted the urge to pet him, with the idea of not disturbing a working dog while he was working, which Cutter obviously was just now. He was watching Troy with an intensity that was almost unnerving even to her; she couldn't imagine what it must feel like to Troy.

Then again, after what she'd learned tonight, she wondered if he would even be affected.

"All this time I thought he was defending his best friend," Kayla said, feeling a bit numb, "and he was really telling the truth. He knew Chad hadn't done it."

"I'm guessing Detective Dunbar will get it all out of him," Quinn said. "He's got enough sore spots to work on. And the broken arm, of course."

Kayla saw Troy's expression change at the mention of the cop's name. "You've called him?" she asked.

"Hayley did," Quinn said. "He should be here momentarily. He'll have to look around, of course. Do a thorough investigation. Maybe call in forensics or something. Finding those bullets this idiot shot in a building that size could take some time. Probably take quite a while to get that broken arm set. Be a shame if it never was right again."

Dane and Kayla could see Quinn's wink. Troy could not, and he suddenly wasn't quite so smug. He took a step, as if to test the strength of Quinn's grip. Cutter whirled, growling. It was a dangerous, spine-tingling sound Kayla would never have imagined coming from the whimsical dog. But Troy heard it, and with one look at the dog's lethal-looking exposed teeth, he gave up whatever idea had entered his head. And went docilely as Quinn led him back to join Chad.

"Definitely an alien," Dane said.

She saw one corner of his mouth quirk upward. Something about that half-grin gave her hope. More, it gave her courage. If there was a chance, the slightest chance, now might be the only time she had to take it. She would have preferred a better place, inside somewhere, where it was warm and comfortable. But she knew things would likely get complicated once the police arrived. Statements, interviews, she knew too well how it all worked. It could be hours before she'd see Dane again.

She wasn't about to pass up this chance. She just didn't know where to start.

"I never would have thought Cutter could be so scary," she said instead.

"You should have seen him inside. He literally pushed Troy down the stairs. Felt like we were just there to clean up after he handled it."

She drew in a deep breath. "That must have felt familiar. You've been cleaning up for me for ten years."

He didn't answer and went very still. Then she heard him let out a long breath.

"We're going there right now?" he asked.

"I owe you too much to put it off."

"You don't owe me anything. Anything I did was my own choice."

"Why? Why didn't you just stay away once you left?"

He shifted his feet, looked to one side, then back at her. "It's hard to turn off a decade of feelings."

"Then don't." She stopped, aware her voice was shaking. "Kayla—"

"I understand. I wouldn't blame you, not a bit, if you really left now and never wanted to see me again. It's no more than I deserve. I took you for granted, assumed because you'd always been there for me, you always would be."

Again he said nothing. Dane had never been one to dodge serious discussions, so it worried her that he wasn't really participating in this one. But whether he spoke or not, whether he accepted it or not, he deserved this and more.

"You were right all along. I should have known. I had a blind spot for Chad, and I always have had. I'm so sorry it took me this long to wake up. That I had to see it for myself to realize he wasn't the guy I'd built him up to be in my mind."

"Well that's something," Dane muttered.

A car pulled up behind Quinn's SUV on the drive. Detective Dunbar got out, and she heard the crunch of his steady stride on the gravel as he walked toward Quinn, who had gone to greet him. Dane looked toward them, as if in his mind he was already over there, as if he was only staying here with her out of that innate courtesy she'd always admired.

She understood that, too. She wanted to be there herself, wanted to hear what they found out, wanted to know what had been behind the night that had destroyed life as she knew it.

"I want to know, too," she said, flicking a glance down

the drive. Then she said, very pointedly, "But this is more important."

Dane's head snapped around and he focused on her once more.

"It always was more important. I just lost track of that in my blindness."

She looked at him for a long moment. In the silence she felt a churning inside, as if her fear she'd lost him, her disappointment at Chad, her anger at herself were all battling each other, leaving her shakier than she could remember since that night ten years ago.

"This would be easier," she said, barely aware she was saying it out loud, "if we were in a tree."

Something flashed in his eyes then, something startled yet warm, and the feeble hope she'd nurtured glowed brighter for a moment.

"Want to go climb one?" he suggested.

"I would if it meant you'd listen."

"I'm listening."

She took in another deep breath, as if she were preparing to jump into the cold, deep sound.

"I love you. I have loved you since the day you climbed into that silly tree with me. I knew I was too young for you, but I waited. Then that night came, and you were there for me like no one else could be. I would not have survived it without you."

Here was where he usually would have protested, told her she was stronger than she knew, even back then. That she would have managed; she would have gotten through it. But this time he said nothing. And she didn't know if that was a good sign or an awful one.

She made herself go on. "I knew you could find someone else when you went off to college, but I still waited. When you came back to visit, I wanted to ask if you had, but I was so afraid of the answer I couldn't bring myself to do it. The two years between us meant nothing to me, but I knew it did to you. That I was probably still just a kid in your eyes."

"You were never a kid again after that night."

His quiet words sent a chill through her, stirring up memories that were always there but that she managed to control most of the time. That he'd spoken at all stirred that hope again.

"I never felt like one," she agreed.

"I did meet some girls at college," he said. He'd admitted this to her before but never added any details. He did now. "Some pretty, some smart, a few both. But all of them seemed...shallow next to you. They were carefree and careless. They had no idea how tough life could really be."

Kayla swallowed tightly. "Carefree must have seemed... appealing after all my drama."

He didn't answer, which, she supposed, was answer in itself. Now that she was finally seeing the whole picture, it seemed nothing less than miraculous that Dane had stuck with her so long.

"Kayla? Dane?" Hayley's voice held a world of apology at the interruption. "Sorry, but Detective Dunbar wants us at the station, ASAP. Time to start unraveling all this mess."

Kayla didn't think she was imagining Dane's relief.

Chapter 35

It was almost over.

Dane rubbed at his stubbled jaw. He knew he was pacing, wandering the anteroom of the small holding cell, but he was afraid if he stopped moving he'd fall asleep; it had been a couple of rough nights in succession. And by the time they'd arrived here at the small police station, it had been close to dawn. Besides, it kept him from looking at Kayla, where she sat huddled on one of the hard, plastic chairs along the back wall.

He supposed the sun was up now. He couldn't tell, down here in the back of the lower level of the building with no windows. They didn't have a jail of their own, and prisoners were transported to the county facility after being booked and processed here.

It was only luck—and Detective Dunbar—who had kept him out of this place himself, Dane thought. He could easily have been sitting in there, ink on his fingertips, awaiting transport to county jail. Silently he again thanked the man's instincts or whatever it had been that had made him decide Dane wasn't, after all, the fire bomber he was looking for.

Or maybe it had been Kayla.

Her defense of you was what they call spirited, Quinn had said.

She had never doubted him. Not for a minute. It was he who had fallen down on that particular job. Maybe he was the one who needed to make that up to her. Maybe he was the one who needed to give some reassurance.

Or maybe he was just looking for a way to still make this work, to keep this woman he'd loved for so long in his life.

A door opened, and Dane stopped midstride and turned. Kayla's head came up. Quinn stepped out of the secured area, the heavy, steel door closing behind him with a solid thud. He nodded to Dane, but it was Kayla he went to, crouching beside her chair.

"Chad's talking now. Detective Dunbar made him see the wisdom of coming clean, for his own sake."

"His own sake. All he cares about."

She sounded hollow and, worse, broken. Just the bitterness in her voice made Dane's chest tighten. He hated that she could sound like that, that after ten years of searching, of never giving up, it seemed she finally had.

He hated that she could still make him feel that way. That she could make him feel that strongly.

That she could make him feel.

"What about Troy?" Dane asked.

"He's a tougher nut," Quinn said. "But he took those shots at us, so he'll be on his way to county on attempted murder charges when Dunbar is done questioning him. That should soften him up a little."

"I still can't believe it was Troy. He was always the quintessential charmer."

"I'm no expert," Quinn said, "but I think that man's been a puppet master for a long time."

"So you think he manipulated Chad?"

"I think he's gone beyond that to controlling," Quinn said.

"Chad was easy prey for that," Kayla said, the bitter edge back in her voice. She'd come a long way in the past few hours, now seeing the truth about her brother for the first time.

"Do you want to talk to him?" Quinn asked her.

Kayla hesitated, then stood up. She seemed to sway slightly, and Quinn steadied her with a hand on her shoulder. Something sparked through Dane, something hot and unsettling. Not jealousy because he'd never seen a man more in love with his woman than Quinn was with Hayley. But that was his place. Kayla was his—

He broke off the automatic thought. No, she wasn't. Not anymore, no matter what his automatic, long-ingrained reaction to another man touching her might be.

"I want to hear his explanation," she said, sounding a bit stronger now. She looked up at Quinn. "Do you think he's telling the truth?"

"Probably not all of it," Quinn said, "but what he is telling is true, I think. He's too shaken not to. Dunbar is good."

Quinn glanced at Dane, one eyebrow lifted in query. Dane nodded; he wanted to hear this, too. Chad had cost him everything; he had the right to know what had really gone down that night and why.

Shaken, he thought after a few minutes on the other side of that steel door, wasn't a strong enough word. Chad looked like he'd shrunk to child size.

He wasn't behind bars per se—the small room was screened, not barred. But it was clearly a cell, and Chad clearly knew it. He was willing to talk to his sister, although Dane suspected it was an effort to regain her sympathy and enlist her help in saving him from the consequences of what he'd done.

From the consequences of who he was, Dane amended silently as Chad again gave them the same version of that night's events that he had back at the abandoned arcade. Kayla listened, expressionless, although Dane knew that hearing about it all again had to be excruciating. It was hard enough for him to listen to Chad's repeated excuses, his declaration that he'd had no idea, that he'd only wanted the money.

"Why?" Kayla finally said, asking again the ultimate question.

"I told you, they walked in on us. Startled us."

"Please," Dane said. He'd stayed quiet throughout the long, rambling discourse, but now he was unable to stop himself. "Troy could talk squirrels out of trees, and you expect us to believe he murdered two people because he was startled?"

"But he had the money in his hand and was reading Dad's papers. He was caught red-handed."

"Papers?" Dane asked, brows furrowing. "Even after he had the money? What papers?"

Chad looked blank. "I don't know."

"I think I do."

Detective Dunbar's voice came from the doorway behind them. The detective walked into the room, wearing the expression of a man who'd figured out a puzzle.

"I went back through the old evidence files. There was a list of the papers from the desk that were booked as evidence because of blood spatter." He glanced at Kayla, as if to see if she was okay with the blunt description. She gave the slightest nod of her head, so he continued. "The investigators at the time thought it was just a result of the fight. And because the killer wore gloves, there were no prints, even if we did go back and look with better technology now."

"I already told you Troy had gloves on," Chad said, that whiny note that had always irritated Dane creeping back into his voice. Dunbar ignored him, which made Dane like him even more.

"One set of those papers had more blood than the rest, indicating they were on top of the desk. Or closest to the attack."

"Meaning they were what Troy was holding?" Kayla asked, getting there quickly.

Dunbar nodded. "There was a void in the pattern, indicating perhaps a thumb holding them and that they were on top."

"What were they?" Dane asked.

"Insurance," Dunbar said. "Life insurance."

Kayla frowned. "I remember that. It took a long time for the insurance claim to come through because the police had the papers. Dad's attorney had to step in."

Dane remembered that, too, but he was focused now on something else. "Wait, are you saying there's a connection? Between the insurance and the murders? That makes no sense—Kayla got the money."

He didn't mention that she'd spent a goodly chunk of it hunting down her brother. Or the painful fact that she'd accused him of being after it himself. But he saw her wince and suspected she was thinking just that.

Detective Dunbar looked at Kayla. "According to those papers, you and your brother were equal beneficiaries."

"Yes," she answered.

"What did you do with the money?"

"Wasted too much of it looking for him." She confirmed Dane's suspicion about her thoughts, indicating Chad with a jerk of her head, not even looking at him.

"Including his half?"

She looked startled. "No. Of course not. I never touched his."

Dane saw Chad perk up at this. He was thankful they were separated by that metal screen, or he likely would have punched him again. As if he'd sensed it, Dunbar moved them over to the far side of the room, where Chad couldn't listen to every word.

"Chad's half is still sitting in a beneficiary account," Kayla explained.

Dunbar looked as if the number-one thing on his list had just been checked off. "Okay," Dane said, still baffled, "I get that there's a tempting pile of money there, but—"

Dunbar held up a hand. "Here's what I think went down.

Troy—and if that guy's not a pure sociopath I'll be surprised—sees the insurance papers in the desk. Realizes that with their folks dead, Chad comes into a hundred times what he had in his hand. And knows he's got Chad under his thumb."

Kayla gaped at him. "You think he killed my parents so that Chad would get that money and he could manipulate him out of it?"

"So when Troy called Chad a tool, he meant it literally—is that it?" Dane asked.

"If I'm right, yes."

"I always wondered why Troy stayed friends with Chad." It made perfect, if twisted, sense, Dane thought. Except for one thing. "But Chad ran and never collected. And if he had contact with Chad all this time, why did he wait so long? And why was he sending him money, which helped him stay away?"

"Yeah, that hung me up, too. I figured at most he'd give it a cooling-off period, until things settled, before he brought Chad back."

"But Chad was the only suspect you were looking for," Kayla said. "He couldn't have collected the money, could he?"

"Not likely while he was the suspect, and especially not if he was convicted. This state has a pretty solid Slayer Statute. But that would mean it would go to the next likely beneficiary. If Troy convinced Chad to make that him, gave him power of attorney on that account or something…"

Dunbar let it hang with a shrug.

"And he could," Kayla said. "Chad's that weak-minded."

Something in her voice, something steely and solid, told Dane she truly had reached the end when it came to her brother. He was a little puzzled; he should be glad, but he was feeling a bit numb. Had the love that had guided his life for a decade truly died, or was he just afraid to believe after having been burned so many times?

He made himself get back to the matter at hand. "So why the wait?"

"I did a bit more digging. You knew Troy's dad died shortly after the murders?"

Dane nodded. "Cancer. Troy was—or seemed—pretty devastated."

"So was his mother," Kayla said. "She just wasted away afterward. He even moved back home to take care of her. Everybody thought that was so noble of him."

"A million dollars buys a lot of nobility," Dunbar said.

Dane blinked. "What?"

"His father had a million dollar life insurance policy, too."

Kayla's eyes widened. "And taking care of his mother likely meant taking care of the money, too."

Dane's mind leaped ahead. It was crazy, but so was this whole thing. "So you think it was just coincidence that Troy's dad died during the...cooling-off period after the murders, as you called it?"

"Had to be. It's the only explanation for why they never went ahead with it. Troy didn't need the money by then."

Kayla's eyes widened. "I remember once, when his father was still alive, Troy saying how his dad's illness was sucking up everything. He said it as if he were worried about his mother doing without, but it was probably just himself he was worried about."

"Makes sense. Things must have been tight, and anything extra would have gone to his father's care. Time, attention, money, everything. A guy like Troy wouldn't take to that very well. He's got that entitlement mentality to the bone."

"So that triggered the theft of Kayla's dad's stash?"

"I'm betting if we dig deep enough, we might find some

other thefts, too. Buddy burgs, we call them—stealing from friends' homes."

"And then when his dad died and the insurance came through, he didn't need that anymore," Dane said.

"Or Chad's," Kayla said.

"He has been living pretty high," Dane said.

"And," Dunbar added, "sending money to Chad. To keep him on the string, if my theory is right. I'll put the financial guy on it in the morning, but I wouldn't be surprised if he's run through most of that money in the last ten years."

Kayla shuddered visibly. "So now he needed Chad's."

"Did Troy know you hadn't touched it?"

She nodded, her expression grim. "The subject came up a time or two when we would run into each other. It seemed casual at the time, but now I see he was checking to make sure it was still there."

"So there were two options," Dunbar said. "Chad comes back, somehow proves his innocence and collects and Troy manipulates the money out of him. Or..."

He hesitated, looking at Kayla as if not sure he wanted to finish. Dane did it for him.

"Or he tells Chad to come back knowing he'd be arrested and convicted." Kayla sucked in an audible breath. She had to be reeling from all this, Dane thought, but he made himself finish. "Much easier to just be the secondary beneficiary."

"Unless Kayla fought it," Dunbar said as Dane had just gotten there himself. "He did it, didn't he?" he asked, staring at Dunbar.

The detective looked at Dane. Then, slowly, he nodded. "That's my guess."

Kayla glanced from Dane to the detective and back, looking a little shell-shocked. "What?"

"I'm betting the insurance policy or your folks' will said that if one of you died, the other got what was left of that money. Troy would have to fight that, as long as you were still alive."

Dane saw the realization dawn. Her voice shook as she spoke it. "Troy threw that fire bomb. He brought Chad back to collect one way or another and tried to kill me. He planned it all along."

Dane would have done worse than kill Troy if he'd been able to get at him just because of the look on her face. She'd been betrayed by her brother and a man who was supposedly a friend.

And by he himself?

He shoved aside that thought as another occurred to him. "Why was Troy there at all tonight?"

Dunbar studied him for moment. "I think you already know."

"To clean up the other lose end," Dane said slowly. "Chad."

Dunbar nodded as Kayla gasped yet again. "I think he knew things were falling apart. Once he realized Foxworth was never going to stop, he decided to cut his losses. And the only person who could throw suspicion on him for the murders was Chad."

"My God," Kayla breathed. "Is he really that…evil?"

"Just how sure are you," Dane asked sourly, "that Troy's mother died of natural causes?"

Dunbar's brows raised, and he gave Dane a slight nod of salute. "I'll be looking into that," he said. "It would explain why he got so cocky, if he'd already gotten away with it once."

"My God," Kayla said again.

She swayed on her feet. Dane caught her but with, he told himself, no more personal involvement than Quinn had shown before.

It really was over. There was nothing left to do but pick up the pieces of their lives, separate them and move on.

Chapter 36

He'd forgotten they'd both come in one car, Dane thought as they arrived back at Foxworth. It would have been easier if they each had their own, but then, none of this was going to be easy.

It hit him suddenly. Where was Kayla going to go? Back to the house, which was so damaged? Maybe even still smoldering?

He glanced over at her as she slid out of the other door of Quinn's SUV. Hayley was already at the back, opening the hatch for Cutter. She and Kayla had been in quiet conversation for a few moments after they'd left the police station; had they been discussing what would happen now, where Kayla would go?

He should offer his place, he thought, but the idea of having her in his apartment, so near and yet so far, was more than he could handle just now. Maybe later, when he'd had some sleep and was steadier, he could deal, but now? No way.

Cutter jumped to the ground, and Hayley closed the hatch. If the dog was tired, as the rest of them were, it didn't show. His head and tail were up, and he trotted off toward the back of the building.

"Rounds," Quinn said as he walked around the front of the car. "He seems to think it's part of his job to inspect and secure everything whenever we've been gone for a while."

Kayla smiled at that, but it seemed halfhearted.

"He's amazing," Dane said.

"Yes, he is," Hayley said, then added with a grin up at Quinn, "and so's Cutter."

Quinn's smile at that was like a punch to Dane's gut. He'd been like that once. Happy in his life, confident in Kayla's love and enjoying her teasing him like Hayley had just teased Quinn.

"Come along, dear," Hayley said, linking her arm through her fiancé's.

"What?" Quinn looked surprised.

"Just come inside, Quinn. Now," she added when he still hesitated.

Dane didn't know what she did, but the man suddenly glanced at him and Kayla, and realization dawned; she was trying to get him to leave them alone.

"Oh. Yeah. Right."

They vanished inside the Foxworth building, leaving the two of them standing there in the growing morning light. Saying nothing.

Rafe, having parked the Foxworth vehicle he'd borrowed because they had his, came up to them. His brain fogged by weariness, it took Dane a moment to realize Rafe needed his keys back. He dug into his pocket and handed them over with assurances it was in the same condition it had been in.

"No new dings? Too bad," Rafe said. "Adds to the sleeper effect."

"Don't mention sleep," Dane said.

"We could all use some," the lanky man agreed. He turned as if to go, then turned back. "You two have something special. Don't blow it."

And then he was gone, leaving them standing there once again in awkward silence.

"We did have something special," Kayla finally said. "And I'm the one who ruined it."

"You did what you thought you had to do."

"That's no defense for what I did to you. And I'll pay for it every day I have to go on without you."

He didn't have an answer for that. And he didn't like the sound of it, put flatly into words like that.

"I love you, Dane Burdette. I have loved you more than half my life. And I will love you for the rest of it, whether you love me or not."

"Kayla—"

"So is that what I'm facing? A life spent knowing I ruined the best thing I ever had because I was such a fool?"

This was it. All he had to do was say he was sorry and walk away. Quinn and Hayley would see to her, he knew that. But he stood there in silence, letting the painful question hang in the air unanswered.

He was vaguely aware of movement out of the corner of his eye. Cutter, he thought, finishing his "rounds." The dog headed for the front door of the building, stopped suddenly and spun around to look at them. Then he started toward them.

The dog came to a halt and sat between them, looking from one to the other with an expectant expression.

"Hey, Cutter," Dane said, reaching down to scratch the ears of the dog who'd started all this.

When he straightened, as if she didn't want to get too close to Dane, Kayla crouched in front of the animal, stroking his head. "Thank you," she said to him. "For everything."

Cutter made a low sound that wasn't a growl or a woof but still managed to be commanding. Dane supposed it was how he got sheep to do what he wanted—that is, if he'd ever really seen a sheep.

The dog moved then, getting up and walking behind Dane. He looked over his shoulder at the animal, curious about what he was up to. Cutter leaned suddenly, pressing his full weight into the back of Dane's legs, forcing him to take a step forward. Just as he had with Troy at the top of the stairs. Only now, he was pushing Dane.

Toward Kayla.

Dane jerked around, startled, staring at the dog. And Cutter met his gaze with a look he would swear was impatient.

Cutter moved back between them. Sat again. And yipped.

Dane knew he was losing it then because that yip had sounded for all the world like "Well?"

The dog's gold-flecked eyes seemed to pin him, and Dane knew with a certainty that had no explanation that, in Cutter's mind, he and Kayla were supposed to be together, and he was holding things up.

"Look, Cutter, it's complicated."

The dog woofed then, sounding disgusted.

"What are you, a matchmaker or something?"

The dog glanced over his shoulder at the door Quinn and Hayley had gone through.

"Taking credit for them, are you?"

He nearly laughed then; was he really talking to—and worse, trying to divert the conversation with—a dog?

"Hayley said he picked Quinn for her. And made it happen."

Kayla's soft words brought his head up. But she was looking at the dog, not him. He looked back at Cutter's intent expression.

"I wish you could fix us, boy," he said to the dog. "I mean, the worst is over now, so the problem is over except for Chad's in trouble and she—"

"Doesn't give a damn," Kayla said, cutting him off.

"Even if that's true," he said to the dog, "after ten years, I just can't go on. But I can't give up either."

Wait. He hadn't meant to say that.

"I've always assumed we'd be together. Forever. So how can I quit on that now that the only problem we had is—"

He stopped himself this time. That was *not* what he'd meant to say. What the hell was going on?

"Look, Cutter, it's just that I got so tired of coming in second. I used to think it was making us stronger because nothing this bad could happen to us again, and if that's true then we've been through the worst and made it, and we'll always know that if there are problems in the future."

He stopped again, realizing he had somehow shifted focus in the middle of that rambling explanation, that he'd gone from convinced it was over to explaining why it wasn't.

To a dog.

"That's what you're saying, isn't it?" Kayla said to Cutter. "That we belong together."

Something in her voice, the tiniest quaver, sent a ripple up Dane's spine. A ripple that reminded him of the heat of their passion, and the deep, sweet softness of snuggling with her in the night and the joy of waking with her in the morning.

"You think I should listen to a dog—is that what you're saying?" Dane asked, aware of the sudden huskiness of his voice as the memories flooded him.

"I think you know as well as I do this is no ordinary dog."

Dane sighed. Because when it came right down to it he couldn't deny one simple fact.

Cutter was right.

He reached down and ran a hand over the dog's soft fur. "You're right, Cutter-dog. We do belong together. We have since that day I first climbed that tree between our houses to find out why that skinny neighbor girl with the big eyes was hiding up there."

He was talking to Kayla now more than the dog.

"I waited for her to grow up, I waited until I finished school, then I waited for her to find her brother."

"All good things…" Kayla said softly.

"Come to those who wait? Personally, I'm of the opinion

that good things come to those who quit just waiting and do something about it."

"You may be right. So are you going to do something?"

He gave up the pretense of talking to the dog. He straightened up and met her gaze head-on. He wasn't sure, but he thought she was holding her breath.

He'd been right about one thing. He was through waiting.

He held out a hand. Kayla took it. The moment their fingers touched, the electric jolt seared away the pain, the doubt, the determination.

Yes, Cutter had been right. They belonged together. They always had.

"Now, I think," Hayley said.

Quinn looked at her, wondering where women got that sixth sense about people and their emotions. But he knew better than to disagree with her because he knew she was almost always right.

He opened the door and leaned out. And found out that, of course, Haley was right again. There was no mistaking the passionate kiss going on for anything other than two people putting things back together.

"Cutter! Get in here," he yelled.

The dog hesitated, looked from Dane to Kayla, then gave a satisfied nod and got up. He trotted toward the building, his tail up and waving with every step like a banner carried by a victorious army.

An army of one, Quinn thought, smiling at the old saying. Whoever had begun it had probably never thought of it being one dog.

When Cutter was back inside, Quinn took another look at the two people outside, standing in a shaft of morning sunlight, wrapped in each other's arms.

"Good job, dog," he said. "Time to leave the rest to them."

Cutter woofed.

"They'll do it," Hayley said. "They came close to losing it, but they'll rebuild."

Quinn knew she didn't mean just Kayla's house. Which Foxworth had already made arrangements to have repaired.

"Have I told you lately I love you?" he asked.

"Me or Cutter?" she teased.

"Yes," he answered, glancing around for the clever animal who had brought them together.

Cutter was curled on his bed in the corner of the office sound asleep.

Resting up, Quinn thought, for his next adventure.

* * * * *

She needed to tell him—needed to be honest with him about the little she did remember. But before she could open her mouth, his lips pressed against hers.

And whatever thoughts she'd had fled her mind. She couldn't think at all. She could only feel. Desire overwhelmed her. Her skin tingled and her pulse raced.

He kissed her with all the passion she felt for him.

Then his palms cupped her face, cradling the cheek she'd touched looking for a scar. And he pulled back.

"I'm sorry," he apologized, and his broad shoulders slumped as if he'd added to that load of guilt and regret he already carried. "I shouldn't have done that…"

"Why did you?" she wondered aloud. With a bruised face and ugly scrubs stretched taut over her big belly, she was hardly desirable.

Those broad shoulders lifted but then dropped again in a slight shrug. "I wanted you to remember me—to remember what we once were to each other."

PROTECTING
THE PREGNANT
PRINCESS

BY
LISA CHILDS

First published in Great Britain 2013
by Mills & Boon, an imprint of Harlequin (UK) Limited,
Eton House, 18-24 Paradise Road, Richmond, Surrey TW9 1SR

© Lisa Childs 2013

ISBN: 978 0 263 90357 7
ebook ISBN: 978 1 472 00716 2

46-0513

Harlequin (UK) policy is to use papers that are natural, renewable and recyclable products and made from wood grown in sustainable forests. The logging and manufacturing processes conform to the legal environmental regulations of the country of origin.

Printed and bound in Spain
by Blackprint CPI, Barcelona

Bestselling, award-winning author **Lisa Childs** writes paranormal and contemporary romance for Mills & Boon. She lives on thirty acres in west Michigan with her two daughters, a talkative Siamese and a long-haired Chihuahua who thinks she's a rottweiler. Lisa loves hearing from readers, who can contact her through her website, www.lisachilds.com, or snail-mail address, PO Box 139, Marne, MI 49435, USA.

For my parents, Jack and Mary Lou Childs.
Alzheimer's disease has stolen her memories of their
long life together, but he is still her hero—loving
and protecting her. While her mind doesn't always
remember him, her heart will never forget that he is the
love of her life.

Prologue

Heat scorched his face and hands, but Aaron Timmer ignored the pain and ran headlong toward the fire. His breath whooshed out of his burning lungs as his body dropped, tackled to the ground.

"You damn fool, what the hell are you thinking?" asked the man who'd knocked him down.

"We have to save her!" As her bodyguards, saving her was their responsibility. But she had become more than just a job to Aaron.

"It's too late." The house—the *safe* house—they had stashed her in was fully engulfed. The roof was gone, and flames were rising up toward the trees overhead. Leaves caught fire, dissolving into sparks that rained down onto the blackened lawn surrounding the house.

"We shouldn't have left her." But Aaron's partner, Whitaker Howell, had insisted that she would be fine— that no one could have possibly figured out where she was.

Obviously someone had.

He rolled over and swung his fist right into Whit's hard jaw. His knuckles cracked and stung as blood oozed from them. He shook off the pain and pushed away Whit's limp body. Then he turned back to the burning frame of the house, debris strewn wide around the yard from the explosion.

It was too late. She was gone.

Three years later...

BLOOD SPATTERED THE ivory brocade walls of the Parisian hotel suite. Holes were torn through the paper, causing plaster and insulation to spill onto the hardwood floor. Some of the holes were big, probably from a fist or a foot; others smaller and blackened with gunpowder. The glass in the windows was broken, the frames splintered. Shots had been fired. And there had been one hell of a struggle.

Aaron's heart hammered against his ribs, panic and fear overwhelming him as he surveyed the gruesome crime scene.

A whistle hissed through clenched teeth—not his but Whit's, the man with whom he'd vowed to never work again after that tragedy three years ago. But a couple of months ago he'd been offered an opportunity too good to pass up. Only after he'd accepted the position as a royal bodyguard had he learned that he was actually going to share that assignment with his former business partner and friend.

That safe house explosion had destroyed whatever bond they'd formed in war, fighting together in Afghanistan. After the fire, they had only fought each other. So Aaron should have walked away from this job. He should have known how it would end.

"She put up one hell of a fight," Whit said, his deep voice almost reverent with respect. "But there's no way they survived..."

Aaron shook his head, refusing to accept that they

were gone. *She* couldn't be gone. Charlotte Green was too strong and too smart to not have survived whatever had happened to her.

What the hell had happened to her?

To them? Charlotte Green was also a royal bodyguard for the princess of St. Pierre Island, an affluent nation near Greece.

Aaron and Whit had retraced their steps from their missed flight home, back to the hotel they'd been booked into in Paris. The suite had been destroyed. But despite the amount of blood pooled on the hardwood floor, the Parisian authorities had found no bodies. No witnesses. No leads at all. And no hope for survivors.

King Rafael St. Pierre nodded in agreement with Whit Howell's statement of resignation. Aaron clenched his fists, wanting to punch both men in the face. He couldn't strike the king though, and not just because he was paid generously to protect the ruler of St. Pierre. He couldn't hurt the man because Rafael was already hurting so much that he probably wouldn't even feel the blow.

Whit, on the other hand…

For the past three years Aaron had wanted to do much more than just strike the man. He had damn sure never intended to work with him again. But when they'd both been hired, separately, to protect the king, neither had been willing to give up the job—a security job they'd been lucky to get after what had happened to the last person they'd protected together.

The king was fine, though. Physically. Emotionally, he was a wreck. The man, once fit and vital, was showing every year and then some of his age in the slump of his back and shoulders and in the gray that now liberally streaked his dark hair. Clearly Rafael St. Pierre was beside himself with grief.

Despite how far he and Whit went back, to a friendship forged under fire in Afghanistan, Aaron never knew exactly what his ex-business partner was thinking. Or feeling, or if Whit was even capable of feeling anything at all.

As dissimilar as they were physically, Whit being blond and dark-eyed and Aaron dark-haired with light blue eyes, they were even more unlike emotionally. Aaron was feeling too much; frustration, fear and grief battled for dominance inside him. But then anger swept aside those emotions, snapping his control. He shouted a question at both men, "How can you just give up?"

Whit's head snapped back, as if Aaron had slugged him. And the king flinched, his naturally tan complexion fading to a pasty white that made him look as dead as he believed his daughter and her female bodyguard to be.

Whit glanced at the king, as if worried that the once so powerful man might keel over and die. They could protect the ruler from a bullet but not a heart attack. Or a broken heart. Whit turned back to Aaron, his intense stare a silent warning for him to control his temper.

He had to speak his mind. "Charlotte Green is the best damn bodyguard I've ever worked with." Before she'd gone into private duty protection, she had been a U.S. Marshal. "She could have fought them off. She could have protected them both. She devoted herself to protecting the princess. She went above and beyond the responsibilities of her job."

And to extremes that no other guard could have or would have gone.

"It isn't just a job to her," Aaron continued, his throat

thick with emotion as thoughts of Charlotte pummeled him. Her beauty. Her brains. Her loyal heart. "She considers Princess Gabriella a friend."

"That's why she would have died *for* her," Whit pointed out, "and why she must have died *with* her."

Aaron's heart lurched in his chest. "No…"

"If they were alive, we would have heard from them by now," Whit insisted. "They would have reached out to us or the palace."

Unless they didn't think they could trust them, unless they felt betrayed. Maybe that was why it was easier for Whit and the king to accept their deaths; it was easier than accepting their own responsibility for the young women's disappearances.

"No matter how fierce a fighter she was," Whit said, "Charlotte Green is gone. She's dead. And if the princess was alive, we would have had a ransom demand by now."

The king gasped but then nodded in agreement.

Aaron shook his head. "No. We need to keep looking. They have to be out there—somewhere." He couldn't have been too late again. Charlotte Green couldn't be gone.

Chapter One

Six months later...

Like a sledgehammer shattering her skull, pain throbbed inside her head—clouding her mind. She couldn't think. She could barely feel...anything but that incessant pain. Even her hair hurt, and her skin felt stretched, as if pulled taut over a bump. She moved her fingers to touch her head, but she couldn't lift her hand.

Something bound her wrist—not so tightly that it hurt like her skull hurt, but she couldn't budge her hand. Either hand. She tugged at both and found that her wrists were held down to something hard and cold.

She forced open her eyes and then squinted against the glare of the fluorescent lights burning brightly overhead. Dark spots blurred her vision. She blinked over and over in an attempt to clear her vision. But images remained distorted. To her it looked like she had six arms—all of them bound to railings of a bed like an octopus strapped down to a boat deck. A giggle bubbled up with a surge of hysteria, but the slight sound nearly shattered her skull.

The questions nagging at her threatened to finish the job. *What the hell happened to me? Where am I?* Because she had no answers...

She also had no idea why she was being held down—restrained like a criminal. Or a captive…

She fought against the overwhelming fear. She needed to focus, but her head wouldn't stop pounding and the pain almost blinded her, like the fluorescent light glaring down from the ceiling. It was unrelenting, and reminded her of the light in an interrogation room or torture chamber.

That light was all she could discern of her surroundings. Flinching against its glare, she looked down, but she couldn't see more than a couple of feet in front of her—not because of the pain but because she couldn't see beyond the mound of her belly.

Shock turned her giggle into a sharp gasp. *I'm pregnant?*

No…

Her swollen belly must have been like her seeing six hands, just distorted and out of focus. She wasn't pregnant…

In denial of the possibility, she shook her head, but the motion magnified her pain. She closed her eyes against the wave of agony and confusion that rushed over her, making her nauseous. Or was that sick feeling because of the pregnancy?

How far along was she? When had it happened? And with whom?

She gasped again, her breath leaving her lungs completely. Not only couldn't she remember who the father of her unborn child might be but she couldn't even remember who *she* was.

AARON HELD OUT his phone to check his caller ID, surprised at where the call was coming from. Sure, as desperate as he'd been he'd reached out to everyone he thought might be able to help. He had called Charlotte's ex-partner with the U.S. Marshals. He'd tried calling her aunt, but there must not have been any cell reception in whatever jungle she was building schools or orphanages. And he'd called this man…

"Hello, Mr. Jessup." This man was America's version of royalty—the ruler of an empire of news networks and magazines and newspapers. Nothing happened anywhere without his knowing about it—unless a more powerful man, like King St. Pierre, had covered it up. "Thank you for calling me back."

Aaron was surprised that the man would speak to him at all. He was the last client of the security firm in which Aaron and Whit had been partners. He had hired them to protect the most important thing to him. And they had failed…

"Don't thank me yet," the older man warned him. "Not until you see if the lead pans out."

"You have a lead?"

"Someone called in a tip from a private sanatorium in northern Michigan, wanting to sell a story about Princess Gabriella St. Pierre being committed to the psychiatric facility."

From that destroyed hotel room to a private sanatorium? Given what she'd seen, what she must have gone through, it almost made sense. A tip like this was why Aaron had refused to give up. That and a feeling deep in his gut—maybe his heart—that told him Charlotte Green wasn't dead. She couldn't be dead—somehow he'd know if she was.

"Is she alone?" he asked.

"She's got a royal entourage," Jessup said, "including a private doctor and nurse."

Royal? But the king swore he knew nothing of their

disappearance. And a man couldn't feign the kind of grief he was obviously experiencing.

"And a security detail?" Aaron asked. Or at least one very strong woman.

Stanley Jessup grunted. "Yeah, too much of it according to the source."

Hope fluttered in Aaron's chest. Was it possible? Had he found them both? "Is one of the guards a woman?"

"I don't know." The man sighed. "I'm getting this third hand—from the editor of a magazine who got it from an ambitious young reporter. I don't have details yet, but I'm going to check it out."

"Why?" The question slipped out.

Stanley Jessup grunted again, probably around the cigar he usually had clamped between his teeth. "It's a story—a damn good one since it involves royalty."

If only Stanley knew the real story…

But the women had been checked into that Parisian hotel under aliases. To prevent the paparazzi from hounding the princess, Charlotte had developed several alternative identities for them. She had been that thorough and that good.

Still was—she couldn't be dead. Aaron had already lost one woman he thought he might have been falling for—Stanley Jessup's daughter.

"Why call me?" Aaron asked the newsman. "Why talk to me at all?"

"I don't blame you or Whit for what happened three years ago," Jessup assured him. "Neither should you."

Stanley, despite grieving for his daughter, might have found a way to absolve them of any culpability. But Aaron hadn't.

"Do you want me to call you back after I get more details?" Stanley asked. "I'm going to talk to this young reporter to verify he really has a source inside the sanatorium. Then I'll see if he can get a picture to prove it's actually her."

"No," Aaron replied. He couldn't trust anyone else to do that. No one else would know for certain which woman she really was. "Just tell me the name of this psychiatric hospital."

"Serenity House," Stanley divulged freely. "I'm going to have that reporter follow up with his source, too, Aaron. Anything Princess Gabby does is newsworthy, and this story is a hell of a lot more exciting than her attending a fashion show or movie premiere. And she hasn't even hit one of those in a few months—maybe longer. In fact, she's kind of dropped off the face of the earth."

Or so everyone had believed. But if it really was her...

"I know I don't have any right to ask you for a favor..."

"You said that when you called the first time," Jessup reminded him, "when you asked me if I'd heard anything recently about the princess."

"So I definitely don't have any right to ask you for a second favor," Aaron amended himself.

"That's BS," Stanley replied with a snort of disgust. "You can ask me anything, but I have the right to refuse if you're going to ask what I think you are."

"I'm not asking you *not* to run with the story," Aaron assured the man. He knew Stanley Jessup too well to ask that. "I'm just asking you to run in place until I get there."

"So hold off on printing anything?"

"Just until I get there and personally confirm if it's really Princess Gabriella."

Stanley snorted again. "Since she was ten years old, Princess Gabriella St. Pierre's face has been everywhere—magazines, newspapers, entertainment magazines." Most of those he owned. "Everybody knows what her royal highness looks like."

Everyone did. But unfortunately she was no longer the only one who looked like her. The woman committed to the private sanatorium wasn't necessarily Princess Gabriella.

"Just hold off?" Aaron asked.

Stanley Jessup's sigh of resignation rattled the phone. "Sure."

"And one more favor—"

The older man chuckled. "So what's this? The third one now?"

"This is important," Aaron said. "I wouldn't have bothered you if it wasn't…" If Charlotte wasn't missing, he would have never been so insensitive as to contact Stanley Jessup again. He hated that probably just the sound of his voice reminded the man of all that he had lost: everything.

"I can tell that this is important to you," the older man replied. "So what's this third favor?"

Maybe the most important. "If Whit calls, don't tell him what you've told me."

"About the explosion not being his fault?"

Aaron snorted now. It had been Whit's fault; he'd convinced him that the safe house was really safe. That was why he couldn't trust another woman's safety to his former partner. "Don't tell him about Princess Gabriella."

"He'll read it for himself."

"Let him find out that way, and let *me* find out first if it's really the princess." Or Charlotte.

"You don't trust Whit?"

Not anymore. Whit had always cared more about the money than Aaron had. Maybe he cared too much. Maybe he'd been bought off—three years ago and now. Both times there must have been a man on the inside. Aaron hated to think that that man was one he'd once considered a friend—a man at whose side he'd fought. But war had changed so many veterans. Whit had changed. Maybe he'd gone from killing for his country to killing for the highest bidder.

"Promise me," Aaron beseeched his old client.

Jessup grunted. "You make it all sound so life and death. She's just a spoiled heiress who's probably been committed to this private hospital to get cleaned up or dried out."

Aaron had only interacted with the princess for a couple of months before her disappearance. Even at parties she'd never had more than a few sips of champagne and she had never appeared under the influence of drugs, either.

If this really was Princess Gabby at Serenity House, she wasn't there for rehab.

She stared at the stranger in the mirror above the bathroom sink. The woman had long—very long—caramel-brown hair hanging over her thin shoulders. And her face had delicate features and wide brown eyes. And a bruise on her temple that was fading from purple to yellow.

She lifted her hand and pressed her fingertips against the slightly swollen flesh. Pain throbbed yet inside her head, weakening her legs. She dropped both hands to the edge of the sink and held on until the dizziness passed. She needed to regain her strength, but even more she needed to regain her memory.

She didn't even recognize her own damn face in the mirror. "Who are you?" she asked that woman staring back at her through the glass. She needed a name—even if it wasn't her real one. She needed an identity. "Jane," she whispered. "Jane Doe."

Wasn't that what authorities called female amnesiacs…and unidentified *dead* female bodies?

Drawing in a shaky breath, *Jane* moved her hand from her head to her belly. Her flesh shifted beneath her palm, moving as something—*somebody*—moved inside her.

She didn't recognize her face or her body. What the hell was wrong with her? Maybe that was why she'd been locked up in this weird hospital/prison. Maybe it was for her own damn good. Her belly moved again as the baby kicked inside her, as if in protest of her thought.

"You want out of here, too," Jane murmured.

A fist hammered at the door, rattling the wood in the frame. The pounding rattled her brain inside her skull.

"Come out now, miss. You've been in there long enough."

The gruff command had her muscles tensing in protest and preparation for battle. But she was still too weak to fight.

The door had no lock, so it opened easily to the man who usually stood guard outside her room. Unlike the other hospital employees who wore scrubs, he wore a dark suit, and his black hair was oily and slicked back on his big, heavily featured head. His suit jacket shifted, revealing his holstered weapon. A Glock. As if familiar with the trigger, her fingers itched to grab for it.

But she would have to get close to the creep and if she got close, he could touch her, probably overpower her before she ever pulled the weapon from the holster. A cold chill chased down her spine, and she shivered in reaction.

A nurse moved around the guard. "You're cold," she said. "You need to get back into bed." The gray-haired woman wrapped an arm around Jane and helped her from the bathroom to the bed. The woman had a small, shiny metal nameplate pinned to her uniform shirt. *She* had a name: Sandy.

Jane found herself leaning heavily against the shorter woman. Her knees trembled, her legs turning into jelly in reaction to the short walk. With a tremulous sigh of relief she dropped onto the mattress.

"Put the restraints on her," the gruff-voiced guard ordered. He spoke with a heavy accent—some dialect she suspected she should have recognized if she could even recognize her own face right now.

"No, please," Jane implored the nurse, not the man. She doubted she could sway *him*. But the woman... "Sandy, please..."

The nurse turned toward the man, though. "Mr. Centerenian, do we have to? She's not strong enough to—"

"Put the restraints on her!" he snapped. "You remember what happened to her the last time you didn't..."

Deep red color flushed the woman's face and neck. But was her reaction in embarrassment or anger?

What had happened the last time Jane hadn't had on the restraints? She hadn't simply fallen out of bed...if that was what he was trying to imply.

Jane doubted the bruise on her head had come from a fall since she had no other corresponding bruises on her shoulder, arm or hip. At least not recent ones. But she had a plethora of fading bruises and even older scars.

More than likely the bruise on her face had come from a blow. She glanced again at the holster and the gun visible through Mr. Centerenian's open jacket. The handle of the Glock could have left such a bruise and bump on her temple. It also could have killed her.

From the loss of her memory and her strength, she suspected it nearly had. This man had attacked a pregnant woman? What kind of guard was he? He definitely wasn't there for her *protection*.

The nurse's hands trembled as she reached for the restraints that were attached to the bed railings.

"Sandy, please…" Jane implored her.

But the nurse wouldn't meet her gaze. She kept her head down, eyes averted, as she attached the strips of canvas and Velcro to Jane's wrists.

"Tight," the man ordered gruffly.

Sandy ripped loose the Velcro and readjusted the straps. But now the restraints felt even looser. The nurse snuck a quick, apologetic glance at Jane before turning away and heading toward the door. Sandy couldn't open it and leave though. She had to wait, her body visibly tense, for the man to unlock it.

Mr. Centerenian stared at Jane, his heavy brows lowered over his dark eyes. He studied her face and then the restraints. She sucked in a breath, afraid that he might test them. But finally he turned away, too, and unlocked the door by swiping his ID badge through a card-reading lock mechanism. The badge had his intimidating photograph on it, above his intimidating name.

Jane Doe was hardly intimidating. What the hell was her real name?

Once the door closed Jane was alone in the room,

and she struggled with her looser restraints. She tugged them up and down, working them against the railings of the bed, so that the fabric and Velcro loosened even more. But she weakened, too.

Panting for breath, she collapsed against the pillows piled on the raised bed and closed her eyes. Pain throbbed in her head, and she fought to focus. She needed to plan her escape.

Even if Jane got loose, she didn't have the ID badge she needed to get out of the room. But then how could she when she didn't even have an ID? Of course she was a patient here—not an employee.

But the slightly sympathetic nurse didn't have one, either. The only way Jane would get the hell out of this place was to get one of those card-reading badges off another employee.

The guard was armed, and Jane was too weak and probably too pregnant to overpower Mr. Centerenian anyway. So whatever employee or visitor stepped into her room next would be the one she ambushed.

Images flashed behind her closed eyes, images of her fists and feet flying—connecting with muscle and bone, as she fought for her life.

Against the guard?

Or were those brief flashes of memory of another time, another fight or fights?

Who the hell was Jane Doe really?

Chapter Two

A sigh of disappointment came from the man standing next to Aaron. "It's not Charlotte," he said.

The guy wasn't Whit Howell. Aaron had managed to leave him behind on St. Pierre Island. But this man had met him at the airport in Grand Rapids, Michigan. Once Aaron had dealt with his anger over the guy flagging his passport to monitor his travel, he had made use of him…for the fake credentials that had gotten Aaron on staff at Serenity House. Problem was that the U.S. Marshal had insisted on coming along.

Jason "Trigger" Herrema pushed his hand through his steel-gray hair. "Damn, I'd really hoped she was still alive."

"You and me both." The only difference was that Aaron wasn't entirely convinced that this woman wasn't Charlotte. Through the small window in the door of hospital room 00, he couldn't see much more than her perfect profile: slightly upturned nose, delicately sculpted cheekbone, heavily lashed eye.

Charlotte's partner didn't think it was her because Charlotte Green hadn't had a perfect profile…until she'd taken on the job of protecting the princess and had plastic surgery to make herself look exactly like the royal heiress. Because they had already shared the same build and coloring, it hadn't even taken much surgery to complete the transformation.

Aaron had seen a before photo of Charlotte; she'd had one of her and her aunt on the bedside table in her room in the palace in St. Pierre. She'd had a crooked nose from being broken too many times and an ugly, jagged scar on her cheek from a wanted killer's knife blade. It was no wonder her old partner didn't recognize her now.

But it had to be Charlotte.

Aaron couldn't look away from her; he couldn't focus on anyone but her, which was exactly how he had reacted the first time he'd met the tough female bodyguard. Even more than her beauty, he'd been drawn to her strength and her character. And even lying in that bed, she was strong—she had to be to have survived the attack in the hotel room in Paris.

"I need to talk to the princess," Aaron said. Obviously Charlotte hadn't told her old partner about her surgery, so neither would Aaron. If she had wanted the U.S. Marshal to know about her physical transformation, she would have informed him already. Maybe she hadn't trusted this guy. And if she hadn't, Aaron didn't dare trust him, either. "Someone needs to keep an eye out for the goon that was guarding her door."

They'd waited until the muscular man had slipped outside for a cigarette. "And maybe check around to see if Charlotte's been visiting her." He doubted it. If this was the princess and Charlotte knew she was here, she would have broken her out of this creepy hospital long ago.

Unless Charlotte wasn't who Aaron had thought she was. Unless she was the one keeping Gabriella here…

The Marshal nodded in agreement. "I can ask some of the nurses about her visitors and keep an eye out for the big guy."

"The princess knows me," Aaron said, "so I'll talk to her."

Trigger glanced inside the room again. "Just because she knows you doesn't mean you're going to get any information out of her."

"Maybe not," Aaron agreed. "But maybe she can shed some light on what happened in Paris—"

Trigger interrupted with an urgent whisper, "And what happened to Charlotte!"

"Exactly," Aaron said with a nod. "I have to try to find out what she knows."

Trigger's shoulders drooped in a shrug of defeat, as if he was already giving up. "Don't expect much. I doubt that girl knows anything. I worked with Charlotte for four years, and I never knew what was going on with her."

"I had a partner like that, too," Aaron muttered beneath his breath as the U.S. Marshal headed toward the nurses' station.

Was it possible that Whit had sold out? Was he the one behind what had happened in Paris?

And what about Charlotte? Had he been wrong about her, too? Maybe she'd had her own agenda where the princess was concerned.

Only one way to find out...

He clutched his fake ID badge and swiped it through the security lock beside the door. After a quick glance around to make sure no one was watching him, he slipped inside the room and shut the door at his back.

She didn't awaken; she didn't even stir in her sleep

or shift beneath the thick blankets covering her. Was she all right? Or heavily sedated?

If she was Charlotte, then whoever had brought her here would have had to keep her subdued somehow. Drugs made sense.

He stepped closer, checking for an IV, but there was nothing. However, her arms were strapped to the bed railings.

"Are you all right?" he whispered, reaching out to touch her. He tipped her face toward him. He'd been able to tell the women apart—because Gabriella was younger with a wide-eyed innocence. And because Charlotte had made his heart race. But now his heart slammed against his ribs when he noticed the angry bruise marring her silky skin. "Oh, my God…what the hell happened to you?"

This injury was not from the struggle in the hotel room. Much of the bruise was still brilliant with color; it was a recent wound.

Despite his hand cupping her face, she didn't react to his touch. Her lids didn't flicker; her thick lashes lay against her high cheekbones. He ran his fingertips along the edge of her jaw toward her throat to check for a pulse. But as he leaned over her, his arm brushed against her stomach and beneath the blanket, something shifted, almost as if kicking him.

It wasn't just her body beneath the heavy blankets. Or at least it wasn't the shape of her formerly lithely muscled body; it had changed due to the rounded mound of her stomach.

"Oh, my God!" He felt as if he had been kicked—and a hell of a lot harder than that slight movement against his arm.

This woman was pregnant. So she couldn't be Charlotte, who had been adamant about never becoming a mother. She had to be the princess. But he hadn't known…he hadn't realized…that the princess must have already been carrying a royal heir when she and Charlotte disappeared.

While he stared down at her stomach, she moved. Suddenly. Her hands wrapped tight around his throat, pushing hard against his windpipe. Despite the pressure he managed to gasp out one word, "Charlotte."

He had no doubt now—he had found *Charlotte*. And if her death grip was any indication, she wasn't happy that he had.

"CHARLOTTE…" she whispered the name back at him. It felt familiar on her lips. Was it her name? Or had she used it for someone else?

She wanted to ask the man, but for him to reply, she would have to loosen her grip. And then she wouldn't be able to overpower him. She'd caught him by surprise, playing possum as she had; otherwise she never would have managed to get her hands on him.

He was nearly as big as the other guard. But his body was all long, lean muscle. His hair was dark, nearly black, and his eyes were a startlingly light blue. His eyes struck a chord of familiarity within her just like the name he'd called her.

Did she know him? Or had she just seen him before in here? He had one of those name badges clipped to what was apparently a uniform shirt. It was a drab green that matched the drawstring pants of what looked like hospital scrubs. So he obviously worked here.

She needed that badge to escape. She needed to escape even more than she needed to know who the hell she was. But her grip loosened, as his hands grasped hers and easily pulled them from his throat. She cursed her weakness and then she cursed him. "You son of a bitch!" She wriggled, trying to tug her wrists from his grip. But his hands were strong. "Let me go!"

"I'm trying to help you," he said, his voice low and raspy—either from her attack or because he didn't want to be overheard.

"Then get me the hell out of here!"

"That's the plan."

Her breath shuddered out in a gasp of surprise. "It is?"

"It's why I'm here, Charlotte."

"Why—why do you think I'm Charlotte?" The question slipped out, unbidden. And now she silently cursed herself. If Charlotte was the woman he'd intended to free, then she should have let him believe she was Charlotte.

Hell, maybe she was.

His eyes, that eerily familiar pale blue, widened in surprise. "You're not?"

God, now he wasn't sure, either.

She should have kept her mouth shut, but maybe she had done that as long as she had physically been able. Her voice was raspy, as if she hadn't used it much lately. Or maybe someone had tried choking the life out of her, too.

She needed to get the hell out of this place. But should she leave with a stranger? Maybe he posed a bigger threat than the man with the Glock.

He studied her face, his gaze narrowing with the scrutiny. "Princess Gabriella?"

"Pr-princess?" she sputtered with a near-hysterical giggle. "You think I'm a princess?" Maybe it wasn't that ridiculous a thought, though. It was almost as if she had stumbled into some morbid fairy tale where the princess had been poisoned or cursed to an endless slumber.

Except she wasn't sleeping anymore.

"I don't know what the hell to think," the man admitted, shaking his head as if trying to sort through his confusion.

Maybe it wasn't the blow to her head that had knocked out her sense since he couldn't understand what was going on, either.

"Please," she urged him, "get me out of here." She glanced toward the window in the door, where the burly Mr. Centerenian usually stood guard. "Now."

"I need to know," he said. "Who are you? Gabby or Charlotte?"

Gabby? The name evoked the same familiar chord within her that Charlotte and his eyes had struck. It must have been a name she'd used. "Does it matter?" she asked. "Would you take one of us but leave the other?"

And why couldn't he tell the difference between the women? Was she a twin? Was there someone else, exactly like her, out there? Hurt? In danger? As freaking confused as she was?

He shook his head. "No, damn it, I wouldn't. You know I wouldn't leave either of you here."

Either of you...

Where was the other woman? Locked in another room in this hellhole? Jane's breath caught with fear and concern for a person she didn't even know. But then she didn't even know herself.

"But why won't you be honest with me?" the man asked, and hurt flashed in his pale blue eyes. "Don't you trust *me?*"

It was probably a mistake. But the admission slipped

out like her earlier question. "I don't even know who you are."

"Damn it, you have every right to be pissed, but it was the king's decision to make that announcement at the ball. He wouldn't listen to me…" he said then trailed off, and those pretty eyes narrowed again. "You're not talking about that. You're not just mad at me."

Maybe she was.

He definitely stirred up emotion inside her. Her pulse raced and her heart pounded hard and fast. Her mind didn't recognize him, but her body did as even her skin tingled in reaction to having touched his. An image flicked through her mind, of her hands sliding over his skin—all of his skin, his broad shoulders bare, his muscular chest covered only with dark, soft hair.

Then her fingers trailed down over washboard abs to…

Her head pounded as she tried to remember, but the tantalizing image slipped away as a ragged breath slipped between her lips. Despite the pounding, she shook her head and then flinched with pain and frustration. "No. I really don't know who you are."

He sucked in a sharp breath, as if her words had hurt him even more than her hands wrapped tightly around his throat had.

"Don't feel bad," she said with a snort of derision. "I don't know who I am, either."

"You don't?" His dark brows knitted together, furrowing his forehead. "You have amnesia?"

She jerked her head in a sharp nod, which caused her to wince in pain again. "I don't know who I am or why I'm here. But I know I'm in danger. I have to get the hell out of here."

Even if leaving with him might put her in more danger…

The door rattled. And she gasped. "You waited too long!"

While this man was probably stronger than the one who usually guarded her, this man was unarmed. He would be no more a match for the Glock than she had been.

The door creaked as it swung open. The man spun around, putting his body between hers and the intruder—as if using himself as a human shield.

"Timmer, we gotta go," a male voice whispered. "He's coming back."

A curse slipped from Timmer's lips. "We have to bring her with us."

"There's no time."

Anger flashed in those pale blue eyes. "We can't leave her here!"

"If we try to take her out, none of us will be able to leave."

The man—Timmer—nodded.

She grabbed him again, clutching at his arm. "Don't leave me!" she implored him.

"I'll be back," he promised.

"Hurry!" urged the other man, who hovered yet outside the room. "He's coming!"

Timmer turned back toward her, and taking her hand from his grasp, he quickly slipped her wrists back into the restraints and bound her to the bed.

He obviously hadn't intended to help her at all. Maybe it had all been a trick. Some silly game to amuse a bored guard…

As her brief flash of hope died, tears stung her eyes. But even in her physically weak state, she was too strong and too damned proud to give in to tears. She wouldn't cry. And she damn well wouldn't beg.

"I will come back," he said again, so sincerely that she was tempted to believe him.

But then he hurried from the room. Before the door swung completely shut behind him, she heard a shout. Voices raised in anger. Maybe even a shot.

She flinched at the noise, as if the bullet had struck her. As if they had sharp talons, fear and panic clutched at her heart. She was scared, and not just because if he were dead, he wouldn't come back and help her.

She was scared because she cared that he might be hurt, or even worse, that he might be dying. She'd had only a faint glint of recognition for him—for his unusually light eyes and for his skin...if that had been his body in that image that had flashed through her mind. However, she didn't remember his name or exactly how she'd known him.

She had known him very well; she was aware of that fact. Her stomach shifted as the baby inside her womb stirred restlessly, as if feeling her mother's fear and panic.

Or her *father's* pain?

AARON HAD STEPPED into it—right into the line of fire. The burly guard had caught him coming out of the room. The door hadn't even closed behind him yet, so he couldn't deny where he'd been—where he had been ordered never to go. Only a few employees were allowed into the room of the mysterious patient. Room 00.

Since he probably couldn't talk his way out of the situation, especially with the guy already reaching inside his suit jacket for his gun, Aaron tried getting the hell *out* of the situation. He ran away from the guard, in the direction that Trigger Herrema had already disappeared.

Some help the U.S. Marshal had proven to be...

With that guy as her partner, it was no wonder that Charlotte had left the U.S. Marshals and become a private bodyguard.

Was she now, despite her adamant resolve not to, about to become a mother? Or was that pregnant woman actually Princess Gabby?

He needed to know. But even more than that, he needed to get her the hell out of this place. He couldn't do either if he were dead.

Shouting echoed off the walls, erupting from the guard along with labored pants for breath. But he was either too far away, or the guy's accent too thick, for Aaron to make out any specific words. But he didn't need to know what the man said to figure out that it was a threat.

He skidded around corners of the hospital's winding corridors, staying just ahead of the lumbering guard. With a short breath of relief, he headed through the foyer to the glass doors of the exit. He would have to slow down to swipe his name badge through the card reader in order to get those doors to open.

But he never made it that far. Shots rang out. That was a threat he understood. He dropped to the ground. But he might have already been too late. Blood trickled down his face and dropped onto the white tiled floor beneath him.

He'd been hit.

Chapter Three

"You could have killed him," the woman chastised the guard, her voice a hiss of anger. "You could have killed other employees or patients. You were not supposed to use that gun. Again."

Through the crack the door had been left open, Aaron spied on the argument. Despite the man's superior height and burly build, he backed down from the woman. She was tall, too, with ash-blond hair pulled back into a tight bun. The plaque on her desk, which Aaron sat in front of, identified her as Dr. Mona Platt, the hospital administrator.

"That man is not an employee," the guard replied, his accent thick.

Aaron tried to place it. Greek? St. Pierre Island was close to Greece.

"He's a new hire," she replied, "who passed all the security clearances."

She had checked. She'd used her computer to pull up all of his fake information. He needed to know what other information was on her system, like the identity of the woman in Room 00. Or if not her identity, at least the identity of the person who had committed her to Serenity House.

Keeping an eye on the outer office where the two of them argued, Aaron moved around her desk and reached for her keyboard. He needed to pull up the financials. A place like this didn't accept patients for free. Someone had to be footing the bills.

Dr. Platt hadn't signed off her computer before leaving the room. And not enough time had passed since she'd left her desk that the screen had locked. He was able to access the employee records at which she'd been looking. But he needed *patient* records. However, he didn't know the patient's name. And if she was telling the truth, neither did the patient.

"He's not a nurse aide," the guard argued. "He could be a reporter."

"Not with those credentials," the administrator argued. "They're real. He passed our very stringent background check."

"Then he's not a reporter," the man agreed with a sigh of relief.

"That isn't necessarily a good thing," she warned him. "Since he had a legitimate reason for being here, he's more likely to go to the sheriff's office to report your shooting at him."

Aaron couldn't involve the authorities—couldn't draw any media or legal attention to the woman in Room 00. No matter who she was, it was likely to put her in more danger if her whereabouts became widely known.

"He can't go to the police if he can't leave," the man pointed out.

Aaron suppressed a shudder. Maybe instead of looking for information, he should have been looking for an escape. There was a window behind the desk, but like every other window in the place, it had bars behind the glass.

"We can't hold him here," she said. "Someone could report him missing, and we don't want the state police coming here asking questions. Or worse yet, with a search warrant."

"It is too dangerous to let him go," the man warned. "He could still go to the police."

"Yes, because you shot at him," she admonished him. "That was dangerous—for so many reasons!"

"I couldn't let him get away!" the man replied. "He was in *her* room."

"And she couldn't have told him anything," the administrator assured him. "*She* doesn't know anything to tell."

"But he must have recognized her…"

Aaron had but he still wasn't certain which woman she was. Her trying to strangle him had convinced him she was Charlotte. But part of Charlotte going above and beyond, besides plastic surgery, to protect the princess had been teaching the royal heiress how to protect herself. And Princess Gabby had never needed more protection than she did now.

So as not to draw their attention back to him, he lightly tapped the computer keyboard. But he wasn't certain what to enter. To pull up patient records, he needed the patient's name.

"All our employees sign a confidentiality agreement," the administrator reminded the guard. "He can't share what he saw with anyone without risking a lawsuit from Serenity House. Shooting at him was totally unnecessary."

"I still need to talk to him."

"You will only make the situation worse," she said. "If he does go to the authorities, I will be informed."

So she had a contact within the sheriff's office.

"Will you have enough warning for us to get her to a more secure location?"

"I don't know."

"You were paid handsomely to keep this location secure," the man said, his already gruff voice low with fury. "And since you have failed, I will handle this, and him, in my own way."

The guard wasn't going away. Instead of punching keys in the computer, Aaron needed to figure a way out of Serenity House—first for him and then for the patient in Room 00.

Room 00. He typed it in and the screen changed, an hourglass displaying while the computer pulled up records. He was almost in…

"What the hell are you doing?" the woman demanded to know as she slammed open the office door with such force it bounced off the wall and nearly struck her.

Aaron hit the exit key as he leaned across the keyboard, reaching for the box of tissues. He pulled one out and pressed it to his head. "I'm bleeding. That crazy son of a bitch was shooting at me."

He glanced behind her but the man was gone. Somehow she'd gotten rid of the goon—apparently with just a look as he'd overheard no words of dismissal. Maybe Aaron would have been in less danger if he'd gone with the guard because there was something kind of eerie about this steely-eyed woman.

"Yes, that was bad judgment on his part," she said, sounding nearly unconcerned about the shots now. "But maybe it wasn't uncalled for."

"Dr. Platt, I've done nothing to warrant an *execu-*

tion." He edged around her desk, toward the door. She blocked it, but as a trained bodyguard, he could easily overpower her—physically. Mentally, he didn't trust her—given the doctorate of psychology degree on her wall and her overall soulless demeanor.

"You entered a room that every employee," she said, "newly hired and long-term—has been warned is strictly off-limits."

He hadn't actually attended an orientation. But the guard posted at her door had certainly implied Room 00 was off-limits. "I thought I heard a yell for help. I was concerned—"

"Then you should have summoned the guard or the nurse who are authorized to enter that room. That is protocol," she stated, her voice cold with an icy anger. "By going inside yourself, you violated protocol."

"I wasn't thinking," he said. "I just reacted."

"You reacted incorrectly," she said. "And because of that, you can no longer be on staff at Serenity House." She held out her hand.

He moved to shake it, but she lifted her hand and ripped the ID badge from the lanyard around his neck. "You're fired, Mr. Ottenwess," she said, addressing him by the name on that ID badge.

"I would appreciate another chance," he said. "Now that I'm fully aware of the rules, I promise not to violate them again."

She shook her head. "That's a risk I can't take. And frankly, Mr. Ottenwess, staying here is a risk you can't take. I talked the private security guard out of interrogating you. But if he sees you again, I'm not sure what he might do to you."

Shoot at him again. And maybe the next time he wouldn't miss. The only thing that had nicked Aaron's cheek had been a shard of a porcelain vase that the guard had shot instead of him.

The burly guy had disappeared, but Aaron suspected he hadn't gone far. How could he get past him again to access Room 00?

"That's why I'm having my own guards escort you off the premises." As silently as she'd dismissed the private guard, she must have summoned her own because two men stood in the doorway.

"This isn't necessary," Aaron said. "I can show myself out."

"Actually you can't," she reminded him, "without your badge you can't open any of the facility doors—not to patients' rooms and not to exits. They will show you out." She barely lifted an ash-blond brow, but she had the two men rushing forward. Each guy grabbed one of his arms and dragged him from her office.

Aaron could have fought them off. They weren't armed. But he didn't want to beat them. He wanted to outsmart them. Or he had no hope of helping the woman in Room 00.

JANE HAD JUST resigned herself to the fact that the man, that the voice in the hall had addressed as *Timmer,* wasn't coming back...when the lock clicked and the door opened. She fought to keep her eyes closed and her breathing even, feigning sleep as she had when he'd entered the first time. Or at least the first time that she remembered.

"Is she really out?" the gruff-voiced guard asked someone.

Soft hands touched her face and gently forced open one of Jane's eyes. She stared up at the gray-haired nurse who dropped her lid and stepped back before replying, "She's unconscious."

"Did he hurt her?" Mr. Centerenian demanded to know.

"Who?" the nurse asked, her voice squeaking with anxiety. Over Jane or over lying to the guard?

"Someone was in her room," the man explained.

"He wouldn't have been able to talk her," Nurse Sandy easily lied again. She obviously hadn't been anxious about lying to him. "I gave her a sedative earlier, like you requested. She's completely out and oblivious to her surroundings."

Jane fought to keep her lips from twitching in reaction to the nurse's blatant lie. Wouldn't the guard remember that the nurse had given her no medication?

If only this woman had access to a door-opening name badge, Sandy could prove an even more valuable ally because Jane suspected she would help her escape if she could.

Of course the other man—*Timmer*—had promised he would return. Could he? Was he physically able to return?

"Good," the guard grunted. "And he won't get another chance to talk to her."

She held in a gasp as fear clutched her heart. Had one of those shots struck the man?

"Why—why won't he?" the nurse nervously asked the question burning in Jane's mind.

The guard did not answer, just issued another order. "Leave now."

"But—but I should stay to monitor her—"

"Leave now," Mr. Centerenian repeated.

The lock clicked again and the door opened with a creak of hinges and rush of cool air from the hall. It closed again, shutting in the stale air that smelled faintly of the cigarette smoke that always clung to the guard.

Had Mr. Centerenian left with Nurse Sandy? Was Jane alone again?

She nearly opened her eyes but then the guard spoke again. Since the older woman had left, he wasn't talking to the nurse.

Jane peered through a slit in one lid and saw that his cell phone was pressed to his ear. He spoke in a language she couldn't place but somehow understood. She interpreted his side of the conversation.

"There is a problem," he said. "Someone got inside her room tonight. He saw her..."

Mr. Centerenian grunted in response to whatever the person he called told him and then agreed, "Yes, it is no longer safe to keep her here. I will bring her and your unborn child to the airport tomorrow night to meet your private plane."

Who the hell was the guard talking to? Who was the father of her unborn child? She had suspected it was the man who'd snuck into her room. If not him, then who?

She barely restrained her urge to attack the guard and demand that he tell her who he was talking to, who he was bringing her to meet. But she couldn't risk getting hit again. An apparent blow had already cost her too much—of her strength and her mind.

And she needed all she had of both to escape before the guard brought her to the airport. She feared that if she got on that private plane, that she would have no hope of ever regaining her freedom.

She couldn't trust that the man who had snuck in would keep his word to return and help her. She didn't know if he even could—if Timmer had survived his confrontation with the guard. She waited but Mr. Centerenian said nothing of the man he'd caught in her room.

Was he alive or dead?

And who the hell was he or *had* he been to her?

PAIN EXPLODED IN Aaron's stomach, sending his breath from his lungs in a whoosh. He doubled over, hanging from the arms holding him back. Not that he couldn't have broken free had he wanted to fight. But as he writhed around in an exaggerated display of pain, he lurched forward and *accidentally* fell against the guard who was using him as a punching bag.

"And don't come back unless you want more of that," the man warned as he pushed Aaron back. He pushed him through the gate he'd already opened that led from the building to the employee parking lot.

The lot was behind the big brick building and dimly lit. The few parking lights flickered and cast only a faint glow that reflected off the windshields and metal of the cars filling the lot. Darkness was gathering, pushing the last traces of daylight into night.

The gate snapped shut behind him and the lock buzzed. That gate and the one between the guest parking lot and front entrance were the only ways through the sixteen-foot-high fence surrounding the building.

Serenity House was a freaking fortress—more prison than hospital. If Charlotte was the woman in Room 00, it was no wonder that she hadn't managed to escape yet—despite her skills. Of course if she'd been telling him the truth, she'd forgotten all those skills…except for how to strangle him. Only she hadn't been as strong as the woman he remembered—as the woman with whom he'd made love one unforgettable night.

Images flashed through his mind. Moonlight caressing honey-toned skin and sleek curves. His hands following the path of the moonlight. Then his lips…

And her hands and her soft lips, touching him everywhere. Passionate kisses, bodies entwined…

His breath shuddered out in a ragged sigh as he shook off those skin-tingling memories. That had been one incredible night. And even though they'd used protection, it wasn't foolproof.

Was that baby she carried his? The dates would probably be about right. But was the woman?

He would find out soon. For the sake of the guards who watched him yet from behind the gate, he stumbled across the parking lot with the drunkenlike stagger of a boxer who'd taken too many hits.

Aaron had driven separately from the U.S. Marshal, which was good since Jason "Trigger" Herrema had left him without a backward glance. Some partner Trigger must have been to Charlotte. No wonder she was so strong and independent. And no wonder she had resigned from the U.S. Marshals for private security.

But Charlotte Green wasn't the only one with skills. Aaron clutched the ID badge he had lifted from the guard who'd hit him. The guy had seemed too arrogant an SOB to admit or even realize that Aaron had taken the badge off him. At least not right away. But he might eventually figure it out. So Aaron had to act quickly.

But not too quickly that they were waiting and ready for him to try something. He also needed backup. Obviously he couldn't count on Trigger, the man, so he needed another kind of trigger—one on a gun.

He hurried toward his vehicle, which was a plain gray box of a sedan that he'd rented at the airport. His gun wasn't inside but back at the cottage he'd found in the woods near Serenity House. He hadn't rented it; he hadn't needed to—it had looked abandoned or at least out of season for the owners. The cottage was close enough that he'd figured they would be able to run there if they weren't able to reach his vehicle.

But now that he had seen Charlotte or Princess Gabriella or whoever the hell she was and realized how weak she was, he suspected that outrunning anyone was out of the question.

He needed wheels and a very powerful engine. Maybe he should have gone for fast rather than nondescript when he'd rented a car. Just as he was considering his choice, shots rang out—shattering the rear window. He ducked down, easing around the trunk toward the driver's side. Maybe if he kept the car between him and Serenity House, the guards wouldn't have a clear shot—if they were the ones shooting. But he'd seen no weapons on them. Then the driver's side windows shattered, bullets striking first the rear window and then the front window.

"I'm not getting the deposit back on this rental," he murmured as he clicked the key fob to unlock the doors. He could have just reached through the shattered window and unlocked it himself, but he didn't want to raise his head too high for fear that it might be the next thing a bullet hit.

He didn't even know where the hell the shots were coming from. Serenity House? Or somewhere in the parking lot behind him?

He ducked down farther, suspecting the shots might have been coming from behind him. Maybe he had his answer about where the hell the private security guard had gone. Instead of standing sentry outside Room 00, he'd set up an ambush outside Serenity House.

With the door unprotected, Aaron had the best

chance to free Charlotte or Princess Gabriella. But he couldn't go back inside. Shots kept firing, and he knew it was just a matter of time before one struck him. He had to get the hell out of here while he still could.

Chapter Four

Shots rang out, echoing inside Jane's aching head. She reached for her gun, but it wasn't on the holster. Hell, she wasn't even wearing the holster. Instead her fingers encountered the soft mound of her burgeoning belly. Of her baby…

She jolted awake, as if fighting her way out of a nightmare. But she awakened *to* the nightmare, not *from* it. She still couldn't remember who she was or how she had wound up trapped in this strange hospital jail. But she hadn't forgotten that she needed to get the hell out of here.

And not to that private airport. She couldn't let the surly Mr. Centerenian take her there. When? Tomorrow night? Tonight? She had no idea how long she'd been asleep. She wore no watch, and there was no clock for her to mark the seconds, minutes or hours.

Given the urgency of her situation, how had she fallen asleep? Was she the one to whom the nurse had really lied? Had Sandy actually slipped her a sedative? But Jane didn't feel groggy from drugs. She was just tired—either because of the concussion or the pregnancy.

The baby shifted inside her, kicking against her ribs

as if trying to prod her into action—reminding Jane that she had someone besides herself to protect now. No matter who the father was—*she* was the mother. Something primal reared up inside her, clutching at her heart and her womb. A mother's instinct, a mother's love. This was *her* child.

Her baby girl. She felt it with a deep certainty that the baby she carried was a girl. Had she had an ultrasound? Even though she didn't remember the process, maybe she remembered the results.

"Okay, baby girl, I don't know how we got here," she murmured. "But that doesn't matter right now. What matters is that we're getting out."

She just had to figure out how. She tugged on her wrists, fighting to loosen the restraints. Maybe that man—Mr. Timmer—hadn't tightened them as much as she'd feared. Or maybe the nurse had returned and loosened them while Jane had been sleeping. Either way, she had enough play to slip one hand free. Just as she reached out to undo the other strap, the lock beeped. And hinges creaked as the door opened.

Damn it! Maybe she had slept too long. Maybe she'd slept away a day and any chance she'd had of escaping this nightmare of captivity.

SHE WAS STILL HERE.

Aaron's breath shuddered out with a sigh of relief. He had worried that they might have moved her already, that they probably had just minutes after he'd been discovered in her room. But then maybe they didn't realize those last shots—fired at him in the parking lot—had also missed him.

As he studied her, his relief ebbed away, and his concern returned. She lay, her body stiff and unmoving beneath her blankets. Maybe when they hadn't managed to get rid of him, they'd decided to get rid of her instead. Was she dead? Or just playing dead like she had the first time he had come into her room?

He moved toward the bed, hoping that she would reach out to strangle him as she had last time. She wasn't strong enough to hurt him but it proved she was still strong enough to fight.

He opened his mouth to whisper her name but had no idea what to call her. Was she Charlotte or Princess Gabriella? He wished he knew. Since he wished she was the woman he had already begun to fall for, he called her, "Charlotte..."

Her eyes opened wide with shock, but probably at the sound of his voice rather than any recognition of her name because she said, "I thought you were dead."

"So did I," Aaron admitted.

If the Marshal hadn't shown up in the parking lot when he had, those shots probably wouldn't have stopped until Aaron had been hit. And killed. But Marshal Herrema's car pulling into the lot had sent the shooter into hiding. Aaron suspected he would come out again—just hopefully not until Aaron got *her* to safety.

"We have to get out of here," he said, reaching for her restraints.

But she already had one arm free and quickly freed her other arm. "I thought you were shot," she said. "I was sure I heard gunshots."

"You did," he confirmed.

"The guard with the Glock?" She swung her legs over the bed but hesitated to stand.

"Yes." She knew guns. She had to be Charlotte, or had Charlotte taught Princess Gabriella to identify firearms? "He caught me coming out of your room."

She glanced toward the door, her caramel-colored eyes widening with fear. "After catching you, I'm surprised he would leave my side for a second—even for his nicotine fix."

Her fear made him think she was the princess. Because he'd never seen fear on Charlotte's face. Passion. Anger. But the fear had been Gabriella's.

"I came up with a distraction to get him away." Trigger, in a short dark-haired wig that made him, from a distance, look like Aaron. "But we don't have much time." Before the guard either gave up trying to catch Trigger or caught him and figured out he wasn't Aaron.

She gestured at her hospital gown. "I won't be able to just walk out of here dressed like this, and I don't think I have anything else to wear. There's no bureau or closet in here."

He'd noticed that the first time he had broken into the room. There had been no sign of her belongings—nothing to provide a clue to her identity or a wardrobe for her departure. So he had come prepared. He handed her the wad of clothes he'd had clenched under his arm. She unfolded the drab green shirt and pants. He'd stolen the scrubs from the employee locker room. He reached for her arm to guide her from the bed, so that she could change.

She stood but swayed on her bare feet.

Aaron grabbed her. "Are you all right?"

The blow to her head had obviously stolen more than her memory. Would he be able to get her out without assistance? Maybe he should have brought along a wheelchair.

She drew in a deep breath and, using his arm, steadied herself. "I'm fine."

"Do you need help getting out of the gown?" he

asked. And images flashed through his mind of another time he'd undressed her…

"No. I can manage myself." She hadn't lost her stubborn independence. She had to be Charlotte.

"Turn around," she ordered him, her modesty misplaced. If she was Charlotte, he had already seen every inch of her naked. He had already caressed and kissed every inch of her naked skin.

But he obliged her and turned back toward the door and kept watch through the small window to the hall. For a big building—three stories of brick and mortar—the place was surprisingly quiet and nearly deserted. Where were all the other patients and visitors? Locked up and locked out?

"Actually I can't manage," she corrected herself. "These damn ties are knotted in the back. Can you undo them?"

He drew in a deep breath to steady his suddenly racing pulse, and then he turned to face her again. She stood with her back toward him, her long hair pulled over her shoulder so it would be out of the way. She had already pulled on the pants and stepped into the slip-on shoes. Her arm over her shoulder, she contorted as she tugged on the straps binding her inside the hospital gown.

"You're making it worse," he observed and gently pulled away her fingers. Forcing his fingers to remain steady, he unknotted the ties and parted the rough cotton fabric.

Baring her back reminded him of lowering the zipper on another kind of gown—one of whisper-soft silk that had slid down her body like a caress—leaving her bare but for a tiny scrap of lace riding low on her hips. She wore no bra now, either. Maybe she thought turning away from him protected her modesty. But he could see the side of her full breast and the nipple puckered with cold. But the rounded mound of her belly drew his attention from the beauty of her breast.

This was another kind of beauty.

One that stole away his breath. Was the baby she carried his? That was only possible if she was Charlotte. While he suspected that she was, he wasn't certain if that was merely wishful thinking on his part rather than fact. Hell, not even she knew for certain who the hell she was—if he could believe her claim of amnesia.

She tugged the scrubs shirt down over her breasts and burgeoning belly. The cotton stretched taut. He should have found her a bigger size, but he'd grabbed what he could from the first accessible locker. He'd acted quickly then because they didn't have much time.

"Are you ready?" he asked, the urgency rushing back over him. Trigger might have already been caught. Time was running out. "Do you have everything?"

"There's nothing here," she said. "We shouldn't be here, either." As she turned toward him, she swayed again and clutched at his arm.

"You're not fine," he said, disproving her earlier claim. "You're weak and dizzy."

"I will be fine," she amended herself. "Once we get out of here. Let's go." And then instead of holding on to his arm for support, she was tugging on it to pull him toward the door. "You still have your badge?"

He shook his head even as he pulled the ID from the lanyard around his neck. "Not mine."

This was probably better. Since it belonged to one of the Serenity House security guards, it had access to more areas than Mr. Ottenwess's badge had.

"I was fired."

"Then how did you get back in?" she asked, her golden-brown eyes narrowing with suspicion.

He lifted the badge toward the lock. "I grabbed this off the guy throwing me off the premises." His stomach clenched in protest of the blows it had taken to provide the distraction. He could have fended those off and would have had he not needed that damn badge.

Her brow furrowed now—with suspicion. "Who are you?"

He sucked in a breath of disappointment. "You still don't remember me?"

"I don't remember anything before I woke up in this place." But she looked away from him as she said it, as if unable to meet his eyes.

Why? Because she lied? But why lie about having amnesia? Was she playing him for a fool?

What the hell was going on? Was this whole disappearance just a way to get the princess out of the obligation the king had announced at the ball? That was what Rafael St. Pierre and Whit had suspected until they'd seen the hotel suite.

But Aaron had believed Charlotte too honest for subterfuge. Had he been wrong about her?

It wouldn't be the first time he had let his attraction to a woman cloud his judgment. The last time his lapse had cost that woman her life.

He had to be more careful—had to make certain that nobody died this time. Because, given all the bullets that had already been fired at him, it just might be him who wound up dead this time.

JANE HELD HER breath as she waited for him to swipe the badge he'd stolen through the lock. But he hesitated, his gaze fixated on her. Even though she wasn't looking at him, she knew those pale blue eyes were staring at her. He wasn't touching her, but yet she *felt* him. Her skin heated and tingled as it had from just the brush of his fingertips as he'd untied her gown.

She closed her eyes and drew in a steadying breath. But that was a mistake because that fleeting image she'd had earlier of him returned—even more vividly. She not only felt him. She *saw* him. Naked.

Her face heated with embarrassment over that being the only thing she remembered about her life before she had woken up in this place. That was why she'd lied to him. How could she admit to knowing what he looked like naked—*magnificent*—but not what his name was?

She'd only heard that voice from the hall refer to him as Timmer. But she didn't even know if that was really his name or a cover he'd used to gain access to this creepy place.

Hell, she didn't even know what *her* name was.

But none of that mattered right now.

"We have to get out of here," she urged him. "Mr. Centerenian, that armed guard, called someone—I don't know who—earlier, and they made plans to take me to some airfield—to get me out of the country." She had no idea what country they were in, but that didn't matter, either. What mattered was not getting on that private plane to a new prison.

He nodded, either in understanding of the guard's plan or in agreement with the need to get out of here because he swiped the badge through the card reader.

She held her breath until the lock buzzed and a green light flashed on the card reader. She reached for the door, but his hand was already on the handle. Her fingers connected with the back of his hand, with his hard knuckles and warm skin. And she tingled again from his touch, just as she had when he'd undressed her. Attraction had chased chills up and down her spine then. Now apprehension did as he opened the door to the hall.

Would the guard catch them as he'd caught this man last time?

Now that Timmer had unlocked the door, he was done hesitating. His hand wrapped tight around her arm. Maybe just to steady her. Or maybe to make sure that she didn't get away from him.

He pulled her down the hall behind him, as if keeping himself between her and whatever threat they might encounter. As she followed him, she noticed the bulge beneath the scrubs at the small of his back. He wasn't unarmed this time. Since she'd seen him last, Timmer had acquired a gun. Was it his or had he taken it off the burly guard?

Was that where Mr. Centerenian had gone? Disarmed? Or dead?

Maybe this man, whom she'd once known intimately, was just resourceful. Or maybe he was dangerous.

The threat actually came from behind them as someone yelled, "Stop!"

The man increased his speed, nearly dragging her as Jane obeyed the command and tried to stop. It wasn't a male voice yelling but a familiar female voice. Nurse Sandy caught up to them and clutched at Jane's free arm.

"Stop!" But the older woman spoke to the man. "You can't take her."

"I can't stay," Jane told her. "That guard—the one who hurt me—he's going to take me out of here. Out of the country. I can't leave with him."

"You can't leave with this man, either," the nurse

said. "Unless…" Sandy stared intently into Jane's eyes. "Do you know him?"

"I—I—"

"Of course you don't," the woman answered her own question. "You don't even know who you are."

"Tell me," Jane implored the nurse. "You know. Tell me!"

She shook her head. "I can't. And I can't let you leave." She held on tightly to Jane's arm as the man tugged on her other arm.

Feeling like the rope, pulled taut to the point of fraying, in a game of tug-of-war, Jane summoned all her strength and wrestled free of both of them. "I have to get out of here!"

"Don't leave with him," the woman implored again. "You don't know him."

As if the adrenaline coursing through Jane had awakened the baby, she shifted inside her womb. Or maybe she was trying to send her mother a message. "I think I knew him—that I would know him if I had my memory."

"That doesn't mean you should trust him," the nurse said. "If he was on the up-and-up, he would have come here with the police—not all by himself."

"I didn't come alone," the man replied. There had been the other one in the hall, warning Timmer to leave before the guard came back. "I brought a U.S. Marshal with me."

At the mention of a Marshal, Jane shivered—her blood chilling. Who the hell was the Marshal? And how would she know one? Was she a wanted criminal?

"You don't have a warrant or any legal reason to take her," the nurse said with absolute certainty.

"There's no time to get before a judge and get one," he replied.

"There isn't," Jane agreed. The guard had already made plans to take her away. This man wouldn't have had time to obtain a warrant.

And then whatever time they had had ran out because someone else shouted. The burly guard lumbered toward them. Mr. Centerenian wasn't alone—two other, slighter men followed close behind him. When they caught sight of Jane with Timmer, they surpassed the guard.

As he had before, Timmer stepped between Jane and the threat—bracing himself as if to take a blow. But he dodged the fist thrown at him and instead threw one of his own with such force that he dropped his would-be assaulter to the ground.

The guy grunted and clutched his head while his co-worker stepped over him, his arms already swinging. Jane's protector braced himself with a wide stance, but instead of throwing another punch, he kicked out. His foot connected with the man's jaw, sending him backward over the guard already sprawled on the ground.

Who the hell was Timmer? What kind of experience had equipped him to break in and out of secure facilities and beat up men nearly as big as he was?

But before Jane could ask him any questions, the guard usually posted outside her door lifted his weapon and stared down the barrel at him. Mr. Centerenian wouldn't shoot her—not when he had plans to take her away.

His intent was clear. He was going to kill the man who had tried to help her escape. And if he succeeded, her chances of ever regaining her freedom would be dead, as well. But she cared less about getting away than she cared about Timmer. No matter who or what he was—he had mattered to her.

Chapter Five

Aaron reached for his gun, but he was too late. Metal scraped his spine as someone pulled the weapon from the waistband of his drawstring pants. He'd been so focused on the guards rushing him that he'd forgotten about the nurse. But it wasn't her. The older woman had flattened herself against the corridor wall to avoid the fight and the bullets that would inevitably fly.

The barrel of the guard's gun pointed right at Aaron's face—his own gun probably pointed at the back of his head. Either way, this wasn't going to end well for him.

A shot rang out, reverberating off the walls. He flinched at the noise and in anticipation of the pain. But he wasn't the one who cried out with it. The burly guard uttered a foreign curse as he dropped his gun from his bleeding hand. One of the Serenity House guards reached for the discarded weapon, but another shot rang out. And another curse as blood spurted from torn knuckles.

"What the hell!"

Aaron repeated the sentiment. "What the hell—" He whirled toward the shooter who stood beside him. Recognition and relief clutched his heart, squeezing it tight in his chest.

Charlotte.

"Let's go," she said as she backed quickly down the hall.

He shook his head at her and then addressed the guards. "Toss your ID badges over here."

Their eyes hard with rage and hatred, they just stared up at him.

Another shot rang out and Charlotte gestured at them with the gun. "Do as he says or the next bullet I fire will do some serious damage!"

They tugged off their badges—the two who still had theirs—and tossed them onto the floor.

"You, too," she warned the other.

"I don't have it!" the man exclaimed, casting a vicious glare at Aaron.

Charlotte's lips curved into a small smile. "You took his?"

Aaron nodded. He leaned over and grabbed up the badges and the gun.

"Now let's go," she said.

He wanted to, but he couldn't leave yet. Trigger might have taken off on him earlier, but he had returned. "Where's the Marshal?" he asked the first guard she'd shot—the man who wore the suit instead of hospital scrubs.

The man was still cursing beneath his breath while he clutched at his bleeding hand. "Who?"

"We have to get out of here," Charlotte urged him. Clutching his arm with her free hand, she tugged impatiently.

"The Marshal," Aaron repeated. It wasn't the only question he wanted to ask the man; he wanted to know who the hell he was working for, too. But first he had to know if the Marshal was all right. "The man wearing the wig to look like me—where is he?"

The guard shrugged. "He's gone…"

"We should be gone, too," Charlotte said.

She was right. More guards or the police could have been called and were already on their way. His other questions and answers would have to wait until he got Charlotte safely out of Serenity House.

Aaron agreed with her—with action. Keeping an eye on the guards to make sure no one followed them, he steered her through the lobby to the exit doors. A quick swipe of his badge had the doors sliding open, but then an alarm blared. The noise was louder even than the shots that she had fired, causing him to flinch and for his heart to slam into his ribs.

The doors stopped and began to close. Aaron gently pushed Charlotte through the narrowing gap. Then he turned sideways and tried to squeeze through behind her. The metal edges of the glass doors scraped against his hip and shoulder, threatening to crush him as the doors continued to close. But he made it through the narrow space just before it closed completely.

Alarms sounded outside, too. Aaron swiped his badge through the card reader in the gate, but the red light kept blinking. And the alarms kept blaring.

Charlotte squinted and grimaced—probably in more pain from the bruise on her head than in fear. She'd been almost too weak to stand up back in her room. The physical exertion might be too much for her. But before Aaron could reach for her, she lifted her gun toward the lock and fired at it—in sheer frustration and anger. Sparks ignited from the machine, glinting off the metal. "It won't open."

Not now. He couldn't even try another badge since

the reader caught fire. And there was no way he could get Charlotte over the gate—not with the men rushing through the lobby behind them.

He glanced through the fence, to where a car idled in the front lot. "Stand back!" he shouted at her, as the engine revved.

Tires screeched as the car headed right toward the gate. And them.

JANE LIFTED HER gun and aimed it at the windshield. It was already broken, the glass shattered. She couldn't get a clear target, only the vague shadow of a man behind the wheel. This shot might not be as nonlife-threatening as the other shots she had fired. But before she could squeeze the trigger, a hand closed over hers and shoved down the gun.

"Don't shoot!"

The car kept coming, right at them. She struggled to lift her arm, but her strength wasn't back yet. She couldn't overpower a man like this—one so strong he'd easily fought off two men. Timmer's arms closed around her, lifting her off her feet. Her legs flailed, but she didn't kick at him. He was already moving, carrying her away from the fence.

Metal crunched as the car careened through the gate, crumpling it and the fence around it. She screamed—more with frustration than fear. Would she ever be able to escape?

Then the man changed direction, carrying her toward the car instead of away from it. Timmer opened the passenger's side rear door and pushed her inside, onto the backseat. Had the nurse been right? Had Jane been a fool to trust a man she didn't know, or at least that she couldn't remember?

Before he could climb in beside her, the guards reached him—tugging him from the car as it backed away from the building. The gate tangled beneath it, sparks flying as the car dragged it across the asphalt.

"Stop!" she screamed at the driver. "Don't leave him!" Her mind couldn't recall more than how he looked naked, but her heart—which beat frantically with panic—remembered him. Had she loved him? And if she had, how could she have forgotten him?

And if the man behind the wheel was the partner of the other man, why wasn't he helping him? Instead he glanced into the rearview mirror and studied her. "Charlotte?"

It felt more familiar—more right—than it even had the first time that Timmer had called her that name. But was it hers?

She remembered the weapon clenched in her hand and lifted it again, training it at the back of the man's head, she told him again, "Stop!"

"Charlotte," he repeated with the same certainty she had heard from Timmer when she'd tried to strangle him.

She cared less about who she was than his safety right now, though. Ignoring the driver even while she kept her gun trained on him, she turned back to the fight going on inside the gate. The man didn't need her help this time. Hell, he wouldn't have last time if she hadn't pulled his weapon before he'd had the chance.

He had the guard's gun, but he used his feet and fists, knocking down the guards as easily as he had inside the building. Then he ran toward the car, jumping inside the door she'd left open for him.

"She's Charlotte," the driver told him, turning from behind the wheel to look at his backseat passengers.

"How the hell is she Charlotte looking like that—looking exactly like Princess Gabriella?"

"Get out of here!" Timmer ordered him, pointing toward the guards rushing toward them.

As the car backed away, a tall woman ran out of the building. It wasn't the nurse but another woman, one who shouted with an anger that was more intense than Mr. Centerenian's. Her shouts were clearly audible through the broken windows. Had every window of the car been shot out? When?

The woman yelled, "Don't let them get away!"

Jane shivered.

Timmer pulled the door shut and wrapped an arm around her shoulders. "Are you all right?"

"Not yet," she murmured. "Not until we're far away from this place."

But they didn't go far—just a few sharp turns on dark back roads and the car pulled up in front of a cottage. Headlights glinted off dark windows. The place looked abandoned.

"Where are we?" she asked. "Are we still on the grounds of that horrible place?" She shuddered at the thought. She wanted—she *needed*—to be much farther away.

"They'll be checking airports and train stations," Timmer replied as he opened the back door again and stepped onto the driveway, gravel crunched beneath his shoes. He held out his hand for her. "This'll give us some time…"

"Time for you to explain what you're up to this time, Charlotte," the driver said, his voice gruff with bitterness. He reached over the seat and caught her arm before she could slide out.

Her fingers were grasped in the other man's hand—

leaving her feeling again like that rope in a demented game of tug-of-war. And that rope was getting even more frayed as exhaustion overwhelmed her.

"You're not going anywhere until you tell me what I want to know," the driver said. With his free hand he dragged off a dark wig, revealing coarse-looking iron-gray hair.

The man was threatening despite or maybe because of the fact that he seemed vaguely familiar. She may have known him before but definitely not as intimately as she had known the younger man. And she had certainly never trusted this man.

It was nothing—*what she remembered*—so damn little that it made her laugh. She wasn't all that different from the baby she carried—starting out all over again—with no past.

At least no past that she could clearly recall…

"You think this is funny?" the man asked, a vein beginning to bulge in his forehead with frustration that she wasn't taking him seriously.

No. But now that she had started laughing, she couldn't stop. It was all so ridiculous—how could she have forgotten *everything?*

"What's so damn funny?" he demanded to know, his voice sharp with anger.

She gasped for breath and tears rolled down her face. But she couldn't stop.

"What's wrong with her?" the driver asked the other man.

"She doesn't remember anything, Trigger."

Like his roughly lined face, the name struck a chord with Jane. A very unpleasant chord that had her breath catching in her throat.

"What do you mean?" Trigger asked. "You don't even know what I was going to ask her."

"The only thing you should be asking her about is what happened in Paris or where she's been the past six months." Timmer's light blue eyes narrowed with suspicion. "Unless you're here for some other reason than breaking her out of that psychiatric hospital?"

Paris? Six months lost? Timmer had also mentioned some things earlier—about princesses and kings and announcements. Jane wanted to know about those things and so much more. But she didn't want to talk in front of this man—this guy named Trigger. She tugged on her arm, but he held tightly to her yet, refusing to release her.

"I—uh," he stammered, "there is some other information I need from Charlotte."

Timmer tugged on her other arm, trying to pull her free of the driver. "She's not Charlotte."

"I know she doesn't look exactly like her," Trigger said. "But her voice…"

Timmer chuckled. "The princess is so adept at learning languages that she picks up the dialects of the people she spends the most time with. So of course she picked up her American accent from Charlotte and sounds just like her."

So there was another woman out there that not only looked like her but sounded like her, too?

Trigger shook his head, obviously still unwilling to accept Timmer's explanations. "But the way she holds a gun…"

"Charlotte taught her how to shoot. She taught her how to defend herself."

So despite the certainty with which Timmer had said her name, he wasn't really sure who she was. Or at least he now appeared positive that she was the princess when earlier he'd seemed convinced she was Charlotte. Until Jane reclaimed her memory—and all of her memories—she had no idea which of these two women she actually was.

"Since they were that close," Trigger persisted, "maybe Charlotte talked to her about some of our old cases."

Timmer groaned in obvious frustration with the other man's stubbornness. "You yourself said that Charlotte kept everything to herself. You doubted the princess would know anything."

Jane dragged in a deep breath as her own frustration overwhelmed her. "I don't know *anything*. I don't even know who I am."

The guy studied her face intently. "Then it's possible she's Charlotte and that Charlotte had a nose job and that scar fixed…"

Jane wanted to reach a hand up to her nose and her cheek. But she couldn't move her hands. She was trapped, her arms bound as effectively as the restraints had tied her up and made her helpless.

But Jane wasn't helpless. While her memory was gone, her common sense was not. She moaned and sagged against the seat, faking a faint.

AARON'S HEART SLAMMED against his ribs as he watched her go limp. He reached inside the car and caught the woman up in his arms, tugging her free of Trigger's grasp. Careful to not hit her head against the roof, he lifted her through the door and carried her toward the house. She was light but she wasn't limp. Her body was still tense. With fear? Was she so frightened that she couldn't relax even in unconsciousness?

Her actions back at Serenity House hadn't been fearful. More fearless.

But maybe the fight she'd put up had exhausted her to the point of passing out. He needed to get her inside. He needed to get her away from Trigger.

The car headlamps illuminated the entrance to the tiny clapboard and fieldstone house. Aaron didn't bother searching for a hidden key to the front door, and he didn't waste time walking around to the back door that he'd unlocked earlier that evening. Instead he lifted her higher in his arms and kicked open the front door.

"I could've gotten that for you," Trigger said, as he hurried inside after them. He pulled a sheet from a couch and stood there, waiting for Aaron to lay her down.

Aaron didn't want the U.S. Marshal anywhere near her, so he held her yet in his arms. "Why did you really flag my passport?" he asked. "What was your real reason for wanting to find Charlotte?"

"You called *me*," Trigger reminded him. "You wanted *my* help to find her."

Because he'd thought that if she was in trouble—or hiding the princess from her controlling father—that she would have reached out to friends. It was only now that he realized she and Trigger may have been partners, but they had probably never been friends.

Not like he and Whit had once been friends. But that seemed like a lifetime ago now.

"I know why I called you," Aaron said. "But why did you agree to help find her? What information did you want from her?"

Instead of answering Aaron's question, Trigger asked one of his own. "You really don't think she's Charlotte?"

Aaron finally settled her onto the couch. The headlamps shining through the open door illuminated her flawlessly beautiful face. "Look at her. *Really* look at her. What do you think?"

"She's been missing for almost six months. She could have had plastic surgery," Trigger said, stubbornly clinging to that possibility.

She'd actually had the surgery long before she'd disappeared, but Aaron felt compelled to continue lying to the Marshal. "Is Charlotte the kind of woman who would ever get plastic surgery?"

"What I knew of Charlotte, no," Trigger admitted. "The woman had no vanity. She cared about nothing but keeping people safe. And because of that, she might have had it, so she could protect the princess."

Charlotte's former partner knew her better than he thought he had.

But then Marshal Herrema shook his head. "That would be extreme, though, even for Charlotte. But even if it's Princess Gabriella, she might know something. Maybe Charlotte talked about…"

"About what?" Aaron asked. "What do you want to know about?"

Trigger shrugged. "An old case."

"If it's old, why does it matter now?"

"The witness is missing."

"Just now?" Could that case have had something to do with what had happened in Paris? Had someone gone after Charlotte to find out where the witness was?

Trigger sighed. "The witness has actually been missing for a while, and it's important we find her."

If she'd been missing before Charlotte disappeared, wouldn't he have already contacted her? And if Charlotte hadn't told him then, she must have had her reasons for keeping the witness's location secret from her former partner.

"Charlotte left the Marshals a few years ago," Aaron recalled. "How would she know anything about where this witness is now?"

"They got close."

Like she and Princess Gabby had.

"If anyone knows where she is, Charlotte does," Trigger said.

Aaron gestured at the unconscious woman on the couch. "That's not Charlotte," he lied. At least he was pretty damn certain he was lying.

"But since that woman was her friend, Charlotte might have talked about her. Or maybe the princess overheard Charlotte talking to the witness…"

"It wouldn't matter if she had," Aaron said. "She has amnesia. She doesn't remember anything now."

"Not even you?"

He shook his head. "No. She may never get her memory back." That was another lie because he was determined for her to remember. Him.

"Amnesia is her excuse for forgetting," Aaron continued. "What's yours?"

"What?"

"We had a plan," he reminded the Marshal. "After we got her out, you were going to go to the police and have them get a warrant to seize Serenity House records to find out who the hell put her in that place."

Trigger stared at the sleeping woman for another minute, as if he was having an inner debate about whether or not she was Charlotte. Aaron recognized the look since he'd been having that debate within himself since he'd found her in Room 00. Finally Trigger shook his gray head, turned away and walked toward the open door. "I'll go to the county sheriff and see what I can find out," he agreed. "Do you want me to bring anything when I come back?"

He didn't want the Marshal to come back. "I have everything we need in the trunk." He followed the Marshal out to the rental car and groaned when he saw the fresh damage on it. "I'm definitely not getting my deposit back," he murmured as he got the box of food and clothes. Then he told the Marshal, "You've got my number. Call me as soon as you talk to the sheriff."

Trigger nodded and got back behind the wheel of the running car. When he drove off, he left the cottage and property in total darkness. Aaron stumbled his way to the open door and stepped into the blackness inside the home. As he did, a cold barrel pressed hard against his temple. Had the guards already tracked them down?

Maybe they should have followed Charlotte's instincts and gotten far away from Serenity House. He'd gotten her out, but he hadn't done a very damn good job of keeping her safe. He shifted the box to one arm, so he could nonchalantly reach for his gun.

"Don't move," a raspy voice warned him, "or I'll kill you."

Chapter Six

"You don't want to kill me," the man told her.

Timmer was right. She didn't want to kill him. But he was the only thing that stood, literally blocking the door, between her and freedom. And she suspected that she needed to leave before the other man returned.

What had he been saying about a case and a missing witness? And why had his mentioning those things had her heart beating heavy with dread and fear?

"I won't kill you," she promised, "as long as you do what I tell you. Hand over your gun and don't try to stop me from leaving."

"You can't leave," he said.

"Why did you go to the trouble of breaking me out of that place?" she asked. "Why take me out of one prison cell if you only intended to put me in another?" That was why she'd been determined to not get on that plane to only the devil knew where—the devil who claimed to be the father of her unborn child. She shuddered.

"This isn't a prison cell," he replied.

"Then let me leave."

"And go where?" he challenged her. "Do you have any idea where we are?"

"Too close to that horrible hospital." She shuddered again.

"Do you even know which state we're in?"

"We're in the U.S.?" The question slipped out, revealing too much of her ignorance. Hell, talking to him at all when she should have been running from him was showing her ignorance. She couldn't trust him— not when she couldn't remember who he was to her— besides that he was an old lover.

He nodded, his head moving against the barrel of the gun she held on him. She eased back a little, not wanting to hurt him. "We're in Michigan."

Michigan. She'd been in Michigan before. Hadn't she?

"And," he continued, "this place is a temporary shelter."

Despite her earlier threat, he moved. His eyes must have adjusted to the faint light as thick clouds moved away from a sliver of the moon. He set the box down on a table and rummaged inside it. If he'd been looking for a weapon, he would have pulled the gun from the waistband of his pants. Instead he pulled out a small box and a wad of paper, and he moved again—to the fireplace. The paper rustled then caught the flame from the match he struck. The paper ignited the logs that had been left in the hearth.

Warmth and light spilled from that wide brick hearth, tempting her to leave the bone-chilling cold of the open doorway and approach it. But then she'd be approaching him, too.

"We'll stay here," he said, "until we figure out our next move."

"Our next move should be getting out of this place," she said. They needed to leave before the older man returned or those guards from the hospital tracked them down.

"We have no vehicle," he pointed out.

She shouldn't have let the other man leave with the car, but she hadn't wanted to deal with him and his insistent questions, either. That was why she'd faked the faint. "I can walk."

"You're not strong enough," he said.

Pride lifted her chin. "I'm strong—"

"You just—" He stopped himself and laughed. "You didn't really faint. You staged that whole thing, so you could get the jump on me. I helped you escape Serenity House. Why won't you trust me?"

Serenity House? That was the name of the psychiatric hospital? How ironic when she'd felt anything but serene there.

"Because I don't know who you are," she reminded him.

"My name is Aaron Timmer."

She shrugged. "Your name means nothing to me." But that was a lie. *Aaron* felt right, like it fit him—like she had once fit him.

He sighed with obvious resignation. "You really don't remember anything."

"I need more than your name," she explained. "I need to know who you are. What kind of person can break in and out of a secure facility and steal an ID badge and fight off trained guards…?"

"A trained bodyguard," he replied.

"Bodyguard?" she asked, the title striking a chord within her. "For hire?"

"Yes, I'm a professional bodyguard. I used to have my own security business." He sighed again. "Well, with a partner, but that didn't work out. Now I protect only one person."

"Me?"

"No."

She smiled. "Good. Because if you were responsible for protecting me, you're not that great at your job."

He flinched as if she'd struck a nerve.

She nearly apologized, but then she didn't know the whole story. Didn't even know if what he was telling her was just a story and not the truth.

"If you're someone else's bodyguard, why are you here?" she asked. "Why did you come looking for *me?*"

AARON HAD ANSWERED her earlier questions because he wanted to jar her memory—wanted to say something that would have her remembering everything. So he'd been honest with her. But being honest now would gain nothing. She didn't know how he'd felt about her. Because she'd left the palace the morning after they'd made love, he hadn't even had time to figure out how he'd felt about her before she and the princess had disappeared.

"Why did you track me down?" she repeated her question. Then she drew in an audible breath and asked, "Or aren't I the woman you were looking for?"

"You're the woman I was looking for," Aaron assured her.

Her brow furrowed in skepticism. "I'm Princess Gabriella?"

"No," he said, correcting her. She was nothing like the princess, who he'd found to be rather timid despite having lived her life in the bright glare of the media spotlight. "You're Charlotte Green."

Her brow furrowed even more with confusion and skepticism. "You convinced the other man that I wasn't."

"I wasn't sure he can be trusted."

"I'm sure he can't," she said.

"You remember him?"

"I don't have to remember him to realize that he can't be trusted," she said. "I'm not sure I can trust you, either."

"I'm telling you the truth. You're Charlotte Green." He had no doubt. She may have forgotten who she was but she hadn't forgotten *what* she was. She wasn't just defending herself as she'd taught Princess Gabby; she was using her talent and experience to protect herself. She'd even used it to protect him back at Serenity House. "You're a bodyguard, too."

"I'm a bodyguard." She said it as if trying on the job title to see if it fit.

"Now," he said. "Before you went into private security, you were a U.S. Marshal."

"That's why that other man was talking about a case and a witness," she said. It was as if she was trying to fit together puzzle pieces to get a picture of her forgotten past.

He studied her face, looking for any flicker of recognition—to see if she remembered any of what he was telling her. "He thinks you know where she is."

"I don't know…" She lifted her free hand and rubbed her swollen temple as if her head was throbbing. "I don't remember…"

"That's okay," he assured her with a twinge of guilt for overwhelming her with information. It was obviously too much for her to process all at once. "He was talking about an old case. You may not know anything about that witness anymore."

"But the other guy—*Trigger*—" she uttered his nickname with such derision it was almost as if she did remember him "—said that the witness was a friend of mine."

"I haven't known you long," he admitted, "but it seems like you tend to become friends with the people you protect."

"Do you get close to the people you protect?" she asked.

He glanced back at the flames flickering in the hearth, and with a flash of pain he remembered another fire. "Sometimes too close and then it hurts too much when you lose them."

"Who's lost?"

He wouldn't talk about his old case with her. That wasn't her memory to recover, and it was one he wished he could forget. "Princess Gabriella."

"Is that who you were protecting?" she asked.

Aaron shook his head. "No, you're her bodyguard. Do you know what happened to her?"

She swayed as if her legs were trembling, as if she were about to pass out again. Or for real this time. Because she still tightly clutched the gun, he walked slowly and carefully toward her—trying to be non-threatening. But she didn't let him get close. Instead she moved around him to stand in front of the fireplace. She trembled yet, shivering.

Cold air blew through the open door, stirring sparks in the fire. So she stepped back from the hearth, as if afraid of getting burnt.

Aaron shut and locked the door, but because his kick had broken the jamb, he also moved a bureau in front of it to keep the wind from blowing it open again.

"Are you okay?" he asked, as he joined her by the

couch in front of the fireplace. "Is your memory coming back?"

She shook her head and grimaced. "No. It's almost like it's slipping farther away. If you're so sure I'm Charlotte and not the princess, then you're saying I had plastic surgery to look exactly like her? That's why you and that other man—that Marshal—didn't know for certain which one of us is which?"

Firelight flickered across her face, illuminating her perfect features—her breath-stealing beauty. "When you started protecting Princess Gabriella, you had plastic surgery to look like her. When I met you, you had already had it done—the two of you are pretty much identical." But only Charlotte had stolen his breath— not the princess.

"So identical that you couldn't tell us apart? What makes you so certain that you're right now?" she challenged him.

"I was wrong to doubt myself before," he said, self-disgust overwhelming him. "I should have known immediately that you were Charlotte."

"Why should you have known?" she asked.

He had to *tell* her. He just hoped she wouldn't laugh as she had at her old partner. Or worse yet deny that it had ever happened. "I should have known who you were right away because we were lovers."

LOVERS.

Those images—of his naked skin rippling over hard muscles—flashed through Charlotte's mind again. He wasn't lying to her. But maybe he didn't know the truth. "How can you be sure?" she asked.

He chuckled. "No one hit me on the head. I haven't lost my memory. We made love." He glanced down at her stomach, as if trying to gauge if the child she carried was his.

Was he the father? Another man claimed the baby was his. But she couldn't be any more certain that he was right than she could be sure of anything in this crazy situation.

"Why would Princess Gabriella's bodyguard have plastic surgery to look exactly like her?" she prodded him. This was one answer she knew but needed to draw him to the same conclusion she had.

"To protect her," he automatically replied, probably thinking she was stupid in addition to having amnesia.

"How?" she persisted. "By *fooling* someone into thinking that she was the princess even though she wasn't? By stepping in for the princess in the case of danger?"

He gave a slow nod, his blue eyes narrowing.

"Well, then," Jane said, bringing home her point, "when the bodyguard is pretending to be the princess, isn't the princess pretending to be the bodyguard?"

His jaw dropped open, as if he were appalled at the thought of being fooled into making love with the wrong woman. "No. I would have known. You're very different from the princess."

"You told the other guy that Charlotte taught the princess how to act like her."

"Just how to shoot and defend herself," he clarified, "but you're not Princess Gabby."

"How can you be so certain," she wondered, "when *I* don't know which woman I am?"

A muscle twitched in his jaw as if he was clenching it. "I wouldn't have gotten involved with a client."

"I thought you weren't the princess's bodyguard."

"I wasn't. I'm her father's bodyguard, so I wouldn't

have gotten involved with his daughter." His gaze dropped from hers as he made this claim.

She'd struggled to trust him before, but now she knew she shouldn't. "You're lying to me."

"Not lying—leaving something out."

Somehow she suspected she could relate—that she'd kept secrets of her own and had kept them so well that she couldn't even remember them now—when she so desperately needed to remember.

"What are you leaving out?"

"Something that happened before I met you." He uttered a ragged sigh. "Something that has nothing to do with you."

He sounded as if he believed that, but still she doubted him. He might not be aware of it, but she felt as though she had had something to do with it—something to do with whatever had his shoulders slumping even now with a heavy burden of guilt and regret. Guilt and regret overwhelmed her now. Her legs weakened and began to shake.

He reached for her, his hands on her arms steadying her. "Sit down," he advised, as he helped her settle onto the couch on which he'd laid her earlier. "You're probably starving. Let me get you something to eat."

"I don't need food," she said even as her stomach growled and the baby shifted inside her.

He headed back to the box and ripped open a plastic bag and then passed it to her. "It's just crackers. But there's soup in here, too. I can see if the stove works or heat it over the fire."

More out of reflex than hunger, she ate a couple of crackers. "This is fine," she assured him. "What I really need is my memory back. Since you didn't know for certain if I was Charlotte or the princess, you didn't know where *either* woman was."

"No," he said. "You've been missing for the past six months."

"I disappeared in Paris?"

"You remember?"

She shook her head. "You mentioned it in the car. It sounded ominous."

His jaw tensed again. "The hotel suite was trashed. There was evidence of gunshots. And blood. You must have been attacked."

She touched her swollen temple. "This isn't six months old."

"Do you have other scars or bruises?"

"Lots of them," she said. Either she'd been assaulted or tortured...maybe from someone trying to find out where the princess was. She had to be Charlotte. How would a princess, no matter how good her teacher, know how to shoot as she had? And the very thought of her being a princess was really utterly ridiculous...

He grimaced as if feeling the pain she must have felt when she'd gotten all those marks on her body. "You had some scars and bruises before you disappeared."

"I did?" She lifted her hand to her cheek, but the skin was smooth. It hadn't always been. She could almost remember running her fingertips over the ridge of a jagged scar.

He reached out and ran his fingertips along her cheekbone, as well. "You remember the scar..."

Her skin tingled from his fleeting touch. And she involuntarily leaned closer, wanting more—wanting to be closer to him. "I don't know if it's memory or instinct," she admitted. "Like with the gun, I didn't necessarily remember how to shoot—I just *knew*."

"That's how I know you're Charlotte. You can be sure of that, too," he said. "Princess Gabby has never even been in so much as a car accident. She would have no scars."

"We don't know that anymore," she said. "We don't know what happened to her." She could be dead, and that horrible thought overwhelmed Charlotte with grief. The princess must have been her friend. "How could I have failed to protect her?"

"You don't know that you failed her. You don't know that she's gone," he said, trying to offer her hope—which she feared might prove false. "Until the hotel in Paris called about the damaged suite, we thought that you two had run away."

She snorted derisively. "I must be at least thirty years old. I doubt we would have run away like teenagers." Then she remembered what Aaron had said when he'd first come into her room at the psychiatric hospital. "You thought I would be mad at you about some announcement the king had made…?"

He contorted his mouth as if biting the inside of his cheek—as if trying to grapple with what he'd done. Or what he'd allowed to be done. "The king is old-fashioned."

"He's a king—that's pretty archaic."

"To us Americans, yes," he agreed, "but in St. Pierre, he is the absolute authority. The ruler. He treats his daughter the same way he does his country. From the day she was born, she was betrothed to the prince of a neighboring island."

Anger flared inside her. "That is barbaric."

"I think she was resigned to marry Prince Demetrios," Aaron said. "But then the night of the ball…"

His pupils enlarged, darkening his pale blue eyes, as he remembered something.

The night they'd made love?

"What happened the night of the ball?" she asked.

"The king cancelled Gabriella's betrothal to Prince Demetrios."

"That's great—"

"And promised her to another," Aaron continued as if she hadn't spoken at all. "He changed her engagement to Prince Malamatos, whose country has more resources and wealth."

A curse spilled from Jane's lips—a curse she doubted a princess would know. "The king sounds like a selfish son of a bitch. Why would anyone work for him?"

"He's a powerful man who's used to getting what he wants."

"But his daughter disappeared before he could arrange her marriage," she said. "He must be furious."

"At first he was," Aaron admitted. "But then when the hotel notified us, he was devastated. He loves his daughter."

She snorted in derision of a man claiming to love someone he tried so hard to control. Jane's heart swelled with sympathy and concern for the princess. "But if Gabriella was alive, wouldn't you or her father have found her before now?"

"It took me six months to find you," he said with a heavy sigh of frustration.

"But you weren't looking for me," she said. "You were looking for the princess."

"The king and his other bodyguard—they're looking for the princess—I was always looking for you."

Her pulse stuttered and then raced. "Because we were lovers?"

"I know that blow you took gave you amnesia, but…"

"It bothers you to think that I forgot." She needed to tell him the truth—that one of the few memories she had was of him.

"And I haven't been able to get you—and that night—out of my mind." He reached out again, to touch her belly.

The baby shifted, kicking against his palm. If she believed the conversation between the guard and whoever he'd called, this baby wasn't Aaron's. She belonged to another man. She needed to tell him—needed to be honest with him about the little she did remember. But before she could open her mouth, his lips pressed against hers.

And whatever thoughts she'd had fled her mind. She couldn't think at all. She could only feel. Desire overwhelmed her. Her skin tingled and her pulse raced.

He deepened the kiss, parting her lips and sliding his tongue inside her mouth. He kissed her with all the passion she felt for him.

She moaned, and he echoed it with a low groan. Then his palms cupped her face, cradling the cheek she'd touched looking for a scar. And he pulled back.

"I'm sorry," he apologized, and his broad shoulders slumped as if he'd added to that load of guilt and regret he already carried. Or, actually, she had added to it. "I shouldn't have done that…"

"Why did you?" she wondered aloud. With a bruised face and ugly scrubs stretched taut over her big belly, she was hardly desirable.

Those broad shoulders lifted but then dropped again in a slight shrug. "I wanted you to remember me—to remember what we once were to each other."

Confession time had come. "I remember," she admitted, "that we were lovers."

"You remember me?"

"I remember making love with you." And after that kiss she wanted to do it again—wanted to cling to the one good memory she had of her life before waking up in that horrible hospital.

Desire heated his blue eyes. "I haven't been able to forget—not one single detail of that night. But you have amnesia—"

"That's all I remember. You—just you…" She pulled him back to her and kissed him desperately. He was the one connection to her past—to who she was. She needed him close—as close as a human being could get to another.

He kissed her, too—with his lips and his tongue and with a passion that matched hers.

Putting aside her weapon, she slid her hands over him—as she had in that vivid memory. In the dreamlike vision, he had worn a tuxedo. She'd undone his bow tie and all the studs on his pleated shirt. Now she had only to pull his scrub shirt over his head and push down his drawstring pants.

But he groaned and pulled back again. "We can't do this…"

"Why not?" she asked and then teased him. "Worried that I might get pregnant?" Or was he disgusted that she was? To find out if that was the case, she pulled off her shirt.

But the passion didn't leave his face. Instead his pale blue eyes softened with awe, and he reached out trembling hands, running his palms over her belly.

She needed to tell him that the child probably wasn't his. But before she could open her mouth, he was kissing her again. His hands moved from her stomach to her breasts. When his thumbs flicked over her nipples, she cried out with pleasure. Her desire for him was so intense that she lost all control—lost all sense of time and place as she had lost her past. He was that one link to who she was—her anchor in a storm of emotion and doubt. She needed him like she needed air.

She pushed him back onto the couch. Then she wriggled out of her pants and straddled him, taking him deep inside her. She cried out again, passion overwhelming her.

"Charlotte," he said with a deep groan. Muscles tensed in his shoulders and arms as he held her hips. He thrust gently, as if trying not to hurt her.

But she was beyond pain. Pleasure was all she felt in his arms, with him buried deep inside her. And finally he joined her in ecstasy, groaning gruffly as he filled her. She collapsed onto his chest, which heaved with pants for breath. But instead of relaxing like she had, his body tensed.

"Someone's here."

She tensed, too, as she heard gravel crunching beneath footsteps on the driveway. "It's probably that Marshal coming back."

"No. We have a signal he's supposed to give if it's him. Someone else is here."

"Maybe the owner of the cottage…" But she doubted it. They'd been found. And they might not even have time to get dressed and armed before the person, who rattled the door now, caught them.

Chapter Seven

Damn it. Damn him!

Aaron cursed himself for doing it again—for letting his emotions distract him. And his emotions for Charlotte were stronger than he'd ever had before. For anyone else. After helping her pull on her clothes, he pressed her down in front of the couch, even though the thin fabric and wooden frame would provide little protection from a barrage of bullets.

But he wouldn't give the intruder time to aim his gun. The minute the door opened he vaulted over the couch and tackled the dark figure, dragging him to the floor. He threw a punch, eliciting a grunt of pain. But the man swung back, striking Aaron in the jaw.

To block more blows, he locked his arms around the intruder's. Trying to break free of Aaron's hold, the guy bucked and rolled them across the floor toward the fire. The wood floor was hard beneath Aaron's bare back, scratching his skin. He'd only had time to pull on his pants before the stranger had broken the lock on the door. As they wrestled, Aaron's bare foot struck the hearth. Pain radiated up his leg, distracting him so that the man loosened his grip and swung his fist again.

In the light of the fire, Aaron recognized him. But

just as he said his name, "Whit," his former partner's dark eyes widened with shock before closing completely as he slumped forward—collapsing onto him.

Charlotte stood over the man, clenching the barrel of her gun in her hand. She'd struck Whit's head with the butt of the weapon, just as she had probably been struck when she'd lost her memory. "Who is he?"

"You don't recognize him?" Even if she had amnesia, Princess Gabriella probably would have. The young woman had seemed fascinated by her father's other bodyguard.

She studied the man's face before shaking her head. "No. Should I?"

"You've known him as long as you've known me," Aaron said, trying to prod her memory. But if making love hadn't brought it back…

"And how long is that?" she asked. Maybe the heat from the fire flushed her face or maybe she was embarrassed that she didn't remember how long she had known her lover.

"We met you just a couple of months before you and the princess disappeared," he replied. "His name is Whit Howell."

"And who is he?"

Aaron got up from the floor and stood over his old friend's unconscious body. "He is also one of the king's bodyguards."

"You work with him?"

He had sworn to himself that he never would again. But he had needed a real job—something more challenging than guarding white-collar secrets for corporations or vaults for banks. Choking on the self-disgust welling up in his throat, he just nodded.

"So we can trust him?" She dropped on her knees

beside Whit and felt for his pulse. Her breath shuddered out in a ragged sigh. "I didn't kill him."

"Good." Relief eased the pressure he hadn't even realized was squeezing his chest. No matter what he had become, Whit Howell had once been his friend. "But we really shouldn't trust him."

"Why not?"

Aaron shrugged. "It's kind of like your former partner—nothing I can prove—"

"If I could remember, I probably could prove that I can't trust that man," she said, glancing through the open door. "Your friend has a car out there. Grab his keys and let's get the hell out of here before the other guy comes back."

Aaron shook his head. "We can't leave yet." Maybe she was wrong about Trigger and the guy would come through with a subpoena for Serenity House's records. But he needed another answer right now and only one man could give him that. "I want to talk to Whit and find out how the hell he found me."

"If you two work together, didn't he know where you were going?"

"No. I made sure he didn't know," Aaron said. He had used a family emergency as his reason for leaving St. Pierre. Maybe Whit had checked out his story and discovered his lie. But how the hell had Whit tracked him down—not just to Michigan—but to this very cabin?

She glanced again out the open door. But darkness enveloped them in the impenetrable cocoon of night; morning was hours away yet. "We can take him with us and question him when he wakes up."

Aaron lifted Whit from the floor but just to drop his heavy body onto the couch. "I don't want him coming along with us. I don't want him to know where we're going." He already knew too much about Aaron's whereabouts.

She expelled an unsteady breath. "You *really* don't trust him."

"Not as far as I can throw him." He pointed toward the box. "There're some smelling salts in there. Can you find them?"

"Smelling salts?" She arched a golden-brown brow, as if offended. "You planned on me fainting?"

"You did," he retorted.

"Not for real."

The thought flitted unbidden into his head: What else had she faked? Amnesia? Desire? He shook off the idea; he didn't have time to deal with the consequences.

"There are some clothes in the box, too," he said. "You should probably change into something warmer." Spring nights were cold in Michigan, as a bitter gust blew through the open door.

She glanced down at the wrinkled scrubs and nodded. Then she lifted out the bundle of clothes. "Looks like some of these are yours."

"Yeah." Another cold gust blew through the open door, sending sparks shooting up the chimney. He caught the shirt and jeans she tossed at him.

"Here are the salts," she said, passing over a bottle.

"I'll take these." She held on to a sweater and pants. "And change in another room."

"Why?" It wasn't like he hadn't already seen every inch of her. Again.

She pointed toward the man on the couch. "I didn't kill him, remember? He could come around even before you use those on him."

And Whit did. When a door to another room closed

behind her, the man shifted on the couch and groaned, struggling to regain consciousness. Aaron dragged on his jeans. He grabbed up the ID badges from Serenity House that he'd dropped on the floor in front of the couch when he'd torn off his clothes earlier. He might not need them again. But just in case he did…

As his head popped through the collar of the heavy knit shirt he pulled over his head, he came face-to-face with Whit. The guy's dark eyes were open and staring up at him. His brow furrowed with pain and confusion.

"Who hit me?" he asked, with another groan. "And what the hell did he hit me with?"

"Charlotte hit you with the butt of a gun," he replied matter-of-factly. After all, Whit wouldn't have followed him if he hadn't discovered he was chasing down a lead to her whereabouts.

"You found Charlotte?" Whit scrambled up from the couch and peered around the dimly lit room, as if looking for the female bodyguard. "And she's armed?" He slid his hand into his jacket, reaching for his own gun.

Aaron caught his arm. "What the hell's wrong with you?"

"What's wrong with you?" Whit asked. He pointed at the scratch on Aaron's forehead. "Did she do that? Did she shoot you?"

"It's nothing," he said, touching the mark on his head to remind himself. He'd forgotten all about the shard from the broken vase hitting him. "And she didn't do it. She isn't dangerous."

Whit uttered a bitter laugh. "There's no one more dangerous for you." He shook his head with disgust. "This is why you shouldn't have given me the slip back on St. Pierre. Family emergency—my ass."

"You were supposed to stay there and guard the

king," Aaron reminded him. As if he'd needed another reminder of why they were no longer business partners. "Who's protecting him? You didn't bring him with you?" He grimaced at the thought of the king in the line of fire. It was bad enough that Charlotte had been.

Whit shook his head. "He's still on St. Pierre, ensconced in the palace, with Zeke Rogers reinstated as head of his security in our absence."

"Zeke?" Aaron hadn't trusted the former mercenary and apparently neither had Charlotte since she'd recommended the king replace the man. "Is that wise?"

"With the guys we brought on as backup palace security, the king is safe," Whit assured him.

Were Aaron and Charlotte safe now that Whit knew where they were? Aaron asked the question that had been nagging at him since Charlotte had hit Whit over the head. "How did you find me?"

"Stanley Jessup."

Disappointment tugged at Aaron. Obviously the other man hadn't forgiven him. "He had promised me that he wouldn't tell you where I was."

It had been the most important of all the favors Aaron had requested of their former client.

"I forced it out of him," Whit defended the media mogul. The legendary businessman had never been forced into doing anything he hadn't wanted to—except for burying the ashes of his only child. "I told him you were playing white knight again, and that you were probably going to get yourself killed."

Even though Aaron had only gotten the scratch on his head and some bruises on his stomach, he couldn't deny that he had had some close calls. "None of that was Charlotte's fault. She's a victim in all this."

Whit shook his head. "No. Gabby is the real victim in all this. Did you find *her?*"

"No."

A muscle twitched in Whit's cheek, as if he'd tightly clenched his jaw. "Did Charlotte tell you what she did with her?"

Aaron hadn't been hit with anything other than that shard of glass or porcelain, but his head was beginning to ache. "What do you mean? What would Charlotte have done with Princess Gabriella? Do you think she's hidden her because of the king arranging another marriage for her?"

That muscle twitched in Whit's cheek again. "I thought so—at first," he admitted. "But even though Gabby might have been upset with her father, she loves him too much to make him worry this way. If she was all right, she would have contacted somebody by now."

"What makes you think Charlotte has anything to do with the princess not being able to contact anyone?" he said, wondering about Whit's suspicions. Was it Whit's cynicism talking or his own guilty conscience?

"She was the last one to see Gabby alive, so of course she had something to do with her disappearance. And I'm going to find out exactly what," Whit vowed, his dark eyes raging with anger and determination. "Where the hell is she?"

"She can't tell you anything," Aaron said, edging between Whit and the door which Charlotte had shut behind herself. Everyone wanted information from Charlotte. He wanted only Charlotte.

Whit was no longer the man who never gave in to—hell, even appeared to—have emotions. The anger bubbled over into pure rage. "She is damn well going to tell me what she did to Gabby!"

"She can't tell you anything!" Aaron shouted to get through to the stubborn man. He had never seen Whit so out of control. Maybe Charlotte had hit him too hard, like she had been hit too hard. "She doesn't remember."

Beneath the blond hair falling over his brow, furrows of confusion formed deep ridges. "Doesn't remember? What the hell are you talking about?"

"She has amnesia."

Whit stared incredulously at Aaron like he had just announced a spaceship landing on the island of St. Pierre. "What the hell—"

"She has a concussion," he explained. "She doesn't remember *anything*."

Whit snorted. "That's damn convenient. What doesn't she remember?"

"Anything. She doesn't remember anything." But him. "She doesn't even know who she is—if she's Charlotte or Gabby."

"And you fell for that?" Whit asked with a grimace of disgust.

"Why would she lie about something like that?" he asked because he had wondered, as well.

"Because the woman has lied to you about *everything*," Whit said. "Hell, she was lying to you before you even met her."

"What the hell are you talking about?" Aaron's stomach churned with a sick feeling of foreboding. "What has she lied to me about?"

That telltale muscle twitched in Whit's cheek. "Josie."

He fisted his hand, tempted to strike Whit again for even daring to mention the name of the woman who had died under their *protection*. "Josie? She didn't even know Josie Jessup."

"When Charlotte was with the U.S. Marshals, she staged Josie's death and relocated her," Whit said matter-of-factly, as if he was speaking the truth and not the wild fantasy that it had to be.

Aaron shook his head. "No. We were there—we both saw that house blow up."

"But we didn't see Josie in the house when it blew up," Whit pointed out. "Her body was never recovered."

"But her DNA…"

"Charlotte planted it and had a coroner identify the remains of a cadaver as Josie," Whit explained. "It was her last case before she discovered who her own father was. Then she realized she wouldn't ever have to work again if she played her cards right."

Aaron couldn't accept what Whit was saying. "Josie is dead."

"Nope," Whit corrected him. "She and Charlotte let you believe that."

"*You* let me believe that!" And of all the people who had known about Josie going into the witness relocation program, his best friend should have been the one to tell him the truth. *Then*. Not now…

Now it was too late—to undo the damage that had been done to their friendship—too late to restore the trust that Aaron had lost.

"When you saw how much he'd been suffering, you would have told Stanley Jessup," Whit said. "And no one could know where she was."

"Do you know?"

"Charlotte is the only one authorized to know her whereabouts," Whit replied. "Not even Charlotte's partner with the U.S. Marshals knows."

So Josie had to be the witness that Trigger had wanted to question Charlotte about—the one he claimed had gone missing. But how could he know that if he'd never known where she was?

"But I don't care about Josie," Whit said.

The admission surprised Aaron because he'd thought the other man had been as attracted to the American princess as he had been. Well, he'd thought that until Whit had talked him into leaving her momentarily unprotected. Now Aaron knew why he had—if he believed what the other man was telling him. Now. More than three years after the fact.

"I care about Gabby," Whit admitted. "I want to know what Charlotte did to her. Let me talk to her! Now!"

Aaron was afraid that talking wasn't all Whit intended to do to Charlotte. And Aaron hadn't found her only to lose her again.

But then had he ever really had her? Betrayal struck him like a fist in the gut. Did he have any idea who she actually was?

THIS MAN, THIS stranger who'd broken into the cottage—he knew Charlotte. He knew her better even than the man with whom she'd made love because Whit Howell knew all her secrets. All the secrets she hadn't really wanted to remember.

Aaron had been in love with another woman—so in love with her that he'd turned on his best friend. He'd given up his business. His life. He had been so in love with Josie Jessup that he would have never been able to fall for another woman.

No matter what feelings Charlotte might have had for him, they would never be returned. And now she heard the suspicion in his voice as he questioned his emotional friend.

"Why do you think Charlotte would hurt the princess? They were so close. She had surgery to look like her, to protect her!"

Charlotte closed her eyes, and the image was there—of her face. But it wasn't her face at all. The golden brown eyes were wide and full of innocence and naïveté. And the skin was so smooth, completely free of lines of old scars or stress. Princess Gabriella St. Pierre had spent her life so sheltered that she'd been completely unaware of what the world was really like.

It would have been so easy to take advantage of that youth and innocence. So easy to dupe her...

"Charlotte Green had surgery, so she could take over Princess Gabriella's life and her inheritance."

Aaron's derisive snort permeated the door behind which Charlotte stood. "That might have worked if everyone wasn't aware that she'd had that surgery. Everyone in the king's inner circle—his business associates, lawyers and financial advisors—knows Princess Gabriella has a doppelganger."

"Charlotte isn't just a doppelganger."

"No," Aaron agreed. "She's her bodyguard and her friend."

"She's her *sister*."

"No."

Charlotte silently echoed that denial. Sisters grew up together or were at least aware of each other's existence. Charlotte hadn't been until her mom had finally conned the wrong person and wound up dead, leaving behind documents that Charlotte had never seen before, documents that had proved that her mother's outrageous lies had actually been the truth.

"Why do you think they looked so much alike?" Whit asked.

"The surgery—"

"Hadn't changed her height or build or coloring," Whit pointed out. "Even before the surgery they'd looked eerily similar."

"How do *you* know?" Aaron asked and then bitterly answered his own question, "Oh, that's right, you met her before…when you helped her stage Josie's *death*."

Jealousy kicked Charlotte in the stomach just as the baby did. Why had she given in to her attraction to him even though she had known that he had already given his heart to another? She patted her belly soothingly.

Apologetically…

"She's good at staging murder scenes," Whit said.

"Like Paris?"

"Maybe that wasn't staged," Whit said. "Maybe that was a real murder scene. Maybe she killed Gabby."

"I don't think—"

"No, man, you don't!" Whit accused him. "You *feel*. And you let those feelings cloud your judgment. That's why you couldn't know about Josie."

"Why couldn't I know about *Charlotte?*" he asked, his voice gruff with anger. "Why didn't you tell me that she's the king's daughter, too?"

"Because King St. Pierre didn't want anyone to know."

Charlotte flinched, feeling rejected all over again. Her father hadn't wanted his dirty little secret to come out. But he'd been happy to use her to protect the daughter he had wanted. The one he had loved.

"And that's why she did this," Whit explained. "With his legitimate heir dead, he'll be forced to acknowledge his illegitimate one—if he wants to continue his reign in St. Pierre."

"Charlotte wouldn't do something like that," Aaron protested, but his argument had weakened, his voice lower now with doubt.

She had to nearly press her ear against the wood to hear him.

"You don't know Charlotte Green at all," Whit said, almost gently. "You have no idea what she's capable of…"

But Charlotte finally did—as all of her memories came rushing back over her. They struck her like blows. And as the pain overwhelmed her, she wanted to strike back.

FISTS CLENCHED AT his sides, Aaron struggled for control. He wouldn't hit Whit—despite his gut-wrenching need to pummel the other man until he took back every last word he'd uttered.

"You have no proof to back up all these wild accusations." His head reeled from them, making him wonder if he had been hit harder than a graze. "Why should I believe you?"

"Because I always had your back," Whit said. "Because we were closer than friends—we were like brothers."

"Until Josie…" Losing her had cost them their friendship. But then they hadn't really lost her.

"There was nothing between me and her, you know," Whit said.

Aaron had thought there'd been, and he'd resented Whit for acting on the attraction Aaron had struggled to ignore. Because he'd wanted to be professional, had wanted to keep her safe. And all these years he'd thought he'd failed. "It doesn't matter now."

Because he realized those feelings for Josie hadn't been real. He'd liked her, had admired her beauty and brains, but he hadn't loved her. He'd only loved one woman, but now that might have been a lie, too.

If he were to believe Whit…

"What you're saying is wrong," Aaron pointed out. "None of it makes sense."

"Greed always makes sense," Whit insisted, his words an unwitting reminder of how much money had mattered to him. His background was completely opposite Aaron's; Whit had grown up poor with a single dad who'd struggled to support them. Whit had been denied all the things he'd wanted. Had he gotten sick of going without all the things that money could buy—all the things he'd always considered so important?

"But if she'd intended to pull the switch, why had she talked the king into hiring us?" Aaron wondered.

"Maybe the king's head of security had been on to her," Whit suggested. "Maybe she thought we would be easier to dupe than the guard who'd known Gabriella her whole life."

At Serenity House, Aaron had had his doubts about her identity. And she and the princess had disappeared just a couple of months after he and Whit had been hired. "I can't believe this…"

"Let's ask her," Whit suggested. "Get her out here to explain herself."

She wouldn't be able to explain what she couldn't remember. But was Whit right? Had her claim of amnesia just been a trick? Was it all a trick? His legs didn't feel quite steady as he walked across the room to that closed door. "Charlotte?"

She didn't reply. She had probably heard every word of their conversation—why hadn't she come out earlier to explain herself? He reached for the knob, but it wouldn't turn. She'd locked him out. Like he had the front door, he kicked the door until it broke free of the jamb.

Cold air, flowing through an open window, hit him in the face like a shotgun blast.

"She's gone?" Whit asked, leaning against the broken jamb behind Aaron.

He shut his eyes as dread pummeled him. "Tell me you didn't leave the keys in the car."

Whit cursed profusely. They both turned toward the front door—just in time to see the flash of a gun as it fired directly at them.

He'd been such a fool—such a damn fool to fall for her lies. To fall for her. And now he was about to become a dead fool…

Chapter Eight

As he had just minutes ago, Aaron knocked Whit to the ground again. Bullets flew over their heads and filled the room. Stuffing burst from the holes in the couch and wood splintered—in the furniture and the walls behind them. And the sound was deafening, rattling the windows and shaking the pictures off the walls.

It wasn't a handgun firing at them—more likely a machine gun or some other automatic rifle. Even if they could get off a shot, they were outgunned.

"We have to get the hell out of here!" Aaron said. When he'd first found the cabin, he had scoped it out and knew all the exits. He dragged Whit across the floor with him, toward the back door. It was the one he'd left unlocked earlier. But instead of reaching up to turn the knob, he just kicked it open as he had the others.

"She took my car, man," Whit reminded him, as they rolled across the back porch and tumbled down the steps.

Aaron kept low to the ground as they edged around the corner of the cottage. How long before the shooter stormed inside and discovered them gone? Minutes? Seconds? "And your gun?"

"I have my gun on me." It glinted in that sliver of

moon. He had it drawn, clutching it tightly in his hand. "She had her own. She hit me with it," Whit reminded him.

"That's not her gun shooting at us." Where was Charlotte? They hadn't heard the car start; she may not have driven off before the gunman arrived. She could have been somewhere out there—in the line of fire? Or kidnapped again. "We have to make sure she's okay."

"She's okay," a female voice whispered. "This way…"

Aaron turned to follow the shadow moving toward the trees, but Whit caught his arm.

"Don't trust her," he warned, lifting his gun so that the barrel pointed toward her.

Aaron knocked the gun down. "She's not the one shooting at us."

That person had moved to the back of the building. More shots rang out, hitting the ground near them.

They ran toward the woods. Aaron easily caught up to Charlotte. She wasn't as strong as she wanted to be, and her gait was unsteady. He caught her around the waist, almost carrying her through the small thicket of brush.

"I parked the car over here," she said.

It idled in the dark, its lights shut off. The engine was quiet. No wonder Aaron hadn't heard it drive up or drive away.

"You stole my car," Whit accused as he opened the driver's door and slid in behind the wheel.

As she scooted across the backseat in front of Aaron, she nodded. "I took it. But when I saw the other car driving toward the cottage, I came back." She turned to face Aaron, her gaze steady, as if she was trying to tell him something else. "I came back…"

Before she could explain herself, the back window exploded behind her. Aaron pushed her head down below the seat.

Whit slammed the car into Drive and pressed hard on the accelerator. Gravel sprayed from under the wheels as the car fishtailed, nearly careening into the trees surrounding it.

Aaron checked Charlotte. Shards of glass caught in her hair, cutting his fingers as he brushed them out. "Are you all right?"

"Do you care?" she asked, and she drew back, settling into the corner and probably for more than protection. Obviously she'd heard quite a bit of his discussion with Whit before she'd climbed out the window and stolen the only means of escape.

But she came back, he reminded himself. And somehow he suspected she meant more than physically.

"What the hell is this road?" Whit grumbled as the car bounced over deep ruts.

As well as the cabin, Aaron had scoped out the area surrounding it before he and Trigger had gained access to Serenity House. "It's the public access road to a lake."

"A lake?" Whit repeated. "So if I keep going we're going to hit water?"

And the road was unlit, the surrounding woods dark, blocking out that faint sliver of moon. They might not even see the lake before it was too late and the car was going under.

"Turn around," Charlotte advised.

But bright lights came up fast behind them—blinding in the rearview mirror.

"Get down," Aaron said, as he pulled Charlotte onto the floorboards behind the front seats. He covered her with his body, protecting her from flying glass and gunfire.

But if they were forced off the road into the lake, he wasn't sure he would be able to save her then. He wasn't sure he would be able to save himself in dark, cold water.

But hell, he already felt as though he was drowning—going under from all the information Whit had given him—from all the secrets his old partner had revealed. Aaron was already drowning in emotion, so water couldn't hurt him much more.

SHE HAD ALREADY hurt him enough—with all the secrets she'd kept from him. She couldn't accept this, too—his using his own body to protect hers. But maybe he wasn't really protecting her—maybe he was protecting the child he thought was his.

And there was one more secret she'd kept from him. "I'm sorry," she murmured, turning her face into his neck as he crouched over her.

His heart thumped fast and hard in his chest; she felt each beat of it against her back—beating in rhythm with hers. They would have been perfect for each other—if he hadn't already loved another woman.

But Charlotte was used to that—used to being rejected for someone sweeter and prettier—someone more uncomplicated and open. Her own father had rejected her in favor of her sister, choosing Gabriella as his heir even though Charlotte was his firstborn.

She covered the rounded swell of her belly. She didn't care who the father of her child was; she wouldn't reject her. Charlotte would never deem a baby unworthy of her love.

But Aaron probably would—were he to learn the

truth. She needed to tell him—needed to tell him *everything*. Because she remembered...

But she couldn't talk into his neck as they huddled in the backseat. She had to wait until they got to safety. If that was even possible...

"You have to do something," Aaron ordered his former friend. "If we go in that water, we'll be sitting ducks. He'll just wait until we surface to shoot us dead."

"You don't think I know that?" Whit snapped, his voice gruff with frustration.

"We're braced back here," Aaron said. "Put on your seat belt and then slam on the damn brakes. Hard."

"He'll rear-end us," Whit said.

"Yeah," Aaron agreed. "And maybe he'll knock himself right through the windshield or at least the hell out."

Charlotte nodded her approval of the plan. They were safer on land than in the water—had more options for escape.

But then the car screeched to a stop, and the other car struck them with a sickening crunch of metal. Despite Aaron holding her tight, she shifted against the seats and her shoulder jammed into the console.

"Are you okay?" Aaron asked.

She managed only a nod.

Then Whit shoved the car into Reverse and stomped on the accelerator. Bumper ground against bumper, as the pursued became the pursuers.

Aaron rose up, and his gun glinted in the headlamps of the other car. But instead of becoming a target again, he took aim and fired. Again and again.

If he didn't hit his target, he would become one. And the driver of the other car had a clear shot at him. Charlotte reached up, trying to pull him down—trying to protect him as he had protected her.

The metal crunched against metal again. Rubber burned, enveloping the cars and woods in a thick, acrid smoke. Charlotte blinked furiously against the sting, fighting off the threat of tears so that she could see—so that she could make sure Aaron was all right.

But there was another crash that flung Aaron's body into the back of the front seat. He grunted and struggled for the grip on his gun. But it flew into the front, leaving him unarmed and vulnerable.

Charlotte pulled her weapon from the back of her jeans, but by the time she surged up—it was too late. There was nothing she could do...

"Is HE REALLY gone?" Whit asked, as he stood over Aaron's body. Instead of gazing down at his friend, he stared off down the road in the direction the other vehicle had disappeared.

Aaron scrambled to his feet. He'd had to crawl out of the crumpled rear door of the backseat he'd shared with Charlotte. The trunk was totally crushed, and the quarter panels had buckled. "For now."

"Do you think you hit him?" Whit asked.

Aaron shook his head. "If I did, it wasn't fatal or even painful enough to stop him."

"It got him to leave though," Whit remarked.

"He'll be back." Every time the mysterious gunman had fired at Aaron, the man had come back for another round.

Whit moved back toward the open driver's door. "Then we should get the hell out of here."

Aaron wanted to make sure Charlotte was okay first. He reached back and helped her out of the twisted metal. "Are you all right?"

He found himself reaching out automatically to her

belly, placing his hands on her to check her baby as if he had the right. As if the baby was his…

Was it?

They'd used protection that night—and they had only been together just that one night. Until tonight…

And letting her distract him had nearly taken all their lives. The baby moved beneath his palms, kicking against her belly.

"I'm fine," she said. "But Whit's right. We need to get out of here before he comes back."

"We're going to need time to find a safe place," Aaron said. He couldn't risk her and her unborn child getting into the line of fire again.

"Got it," Whit said.

Doubt knotted Aaron's stomach muscles. Over three years ago he had lost his trust of this man. And learning that Whit had lied to him hadn't exactly worked to regain that trust. "You just got here." Hadn't he? "How do you already know of a safe place to stay?"

"Stanley Jessup."

"He found you a place?" All he'd given Aaron was the name of the hospital where Princess Gabby might have been committed. Okay, he'd given him a hell of a lot.

"His place."

"Stanley Jessup has a place here?"

Whit nodded. "He rented something. He's here. Guess he wanted to see for himself if this story was as big as that freelance reporter claimed it would be."

It was a hell of a lot bigger, and Aaron didn't even know the half of it. The woman who did was, of course, keeping quiet. Keeping her secrets…

So many damn secrets…

And he had so many questions. He kept them to himself during the bumpy and rigorous ride in the damaged car to the cottage Stanley Jessup had rented. It was nothing like the cabin Aaron had found in the woods near Serenity House.

The contemporary tower of metal and glass sat on a dune overlooking Lake Michigan. Waves rushed to the dark shore below, breaking apart on the rocks. While Whit had gone inside the house, Charlotte stood on the overlook deck, her arms propped on the railing.

Aaron joined her on that deck that overlooked the beach far below. But he kept a careful distance from her. "Don't you have anything to say?" he wondered out loud.

Like sorry?

Charlotte shrugged. "I've been waiting for the inquisition. It sounded like your friend has a lot of questions for me."

"More like a lot of accusations." He glanced toward the house, where a shadow moved behind one of the walls of glass. "Is that why you ran?"

Or was it because she'd gotten caught in a web of her own lies?

"Does it matter why I left?" she asked. "I came back..." Her tone was just as distant as it had been before.

"It matters to me," he said. Why she'd left and why she'd returned...

Even knowing how much she'd lied to him, she mattered to him. Self-disgust over what a lovesick fool he was turned his stomach.

"I was overwhelmed," she said. "It all came back. All my memories."

"Had they ever really been gone?"

She sucked in a breath, as if offended that he wouldn't

trust her. Given what he'd learned, how the hell could he trust her? No matter what she told him now…

"I didn't remember anything," she insisted. "But you…"

His heart—his stupid, traitorous heart—clenched in his chest. "I can't believe you," he said. "I can't believe anything you tell me now."

"But you can believe *him?*" she asked. "Hasn't he lied to you, too?"

He found himself defending his old friend. "Because you made him."

"Does anyone make Whit Howell do something he doesn't want to do?" she asked with a bitter chuckle.

No. But she didn't need the confirmation. She already knew.

"So you do remember everything now?" he asked.

"No," she replied with a shaky sigh of frustration. "There are still holes in my memory."

"Paris?" They needed to know what had happened there, if they were ever to learn Princess Gabriella's fate.

"I remember someone bursting into the suite, guns blazing. I remember fighting for my life. And then I woke up in that damn hospital." She touched her stomach. "Pregnant…"

That was a hell of a hole. How many months had she lost?

He drew in a breath, bracing himself for the answer before he even asked the question. "Do you remember who the father of your baby is?"

Her reply was a flat, unemotional "No." As if it didn't matter to her.

And it mattered like hell to Aaron. "So it might not be mine?"

She shook her head. "She's probably not."

He had known about the child for less than twenty-four hours but losing her—losing the possibility that she was his—hurt like hell. The loss twisted something inside Aaron, tied his emotions up in a tight knot.

"When Mr. Centerenian, that guard, called whoever the hell his boss is, he referred to the person as the father," she explained.

That breath he'd drawn in to brace himself stuck in his lungs, hurting his chest. "So you knew that I wasn't the father before I broke you out of Serenity House? Before we…" He couldn't call it making love—not now that he had confirmation that only his feelings had been involved.

"I was confused and scared. I had no idea what was going on. I didn't even know who I was. You were the only one I recognized, making love with you was the only thing I remembered."

She turned toward him and closed the distance between them. Wrapping her arms around him, she clung to him as if she cared—as if his feelings might not have been all one-sided. "I needed you…"

Aaron released the breath he'd held, but the pressure in his chest didn't ease. And the rest of his body tensed with attraction to her. No matter how many secrets she'd kept from him, no matter how many lies she'd told him—he still wanted her.

But he resisted the urge to wrap his arms around her and hold her close. Because he couldn't think with desire overwhelming him. He couldn't be objective when his emotions got involved; Whit had been right about that. *Damn him!*

So Aaron caught her shoulders in his hands and eased her away from him. "But now you have your memory back," he reminded her. "You don't really need me anymore."

He suspected Charlotte Green had never needed anyone. She was tough and independent. And those very traits that had drawn him to her were what would keep them apart.

"I still don't know who committed me to that horrible hospital."

That same person was the father of her child. "You have no idea who it could be?"

She had been in the princess's world longer than he had. She would know all the king's enemies. Not that he couldn't think of a few after the king's announcement at the ball the night before the princess and her bodyguard had left for Paris. But had the person who'd committed Charlotte to Serenity House realized she was Charlotte or had he mistaken her for Princess Gabriella?

She shook her head. "All I know for certain is that it wasn't me. I don't have some master plan to take my sister's place as princess of St. Pierre. I don't want that kind of life."

"You don't want a life of wealth and privilege?" he asked skeptically. "You just wanted her face?"

She skimmed her fingertips across her cheek that used to be marred with that horrific scar.

Aaron had only seen that one photograph of her face before the surgery, but the scar had haunted him, reminding him of the pain she must have endured when the injury had been inflicted. That snapshot had been of her and her aunt, their arms around each other—both looking, as Whit had said, eerily similar to Princess Gabriella, even before the surgery.

She tapped her cheek. "I did this to protect her—to keep her safe. I wouldn't have done anything to hurt

Gabby. Not like her father continuously hurt and betrayed her."

"*Her* father? But the king is your father, too."

She shook her head. "He's my employer. Not my father. And if not for Gabby, he wouldn't even be that. I wanted to protect her."

Maybe Whit was right again. Maybe Charlotte had hidden Gabby from the king—to thwart his plans to marry off the young princess. He studied her face, looking for any sign that she might be lying when he asked, "Where is she?"

She shook her head. "I don't know…"

Aaron shouldn't believe her—given how easily and often she'd lied and kept information from him in their brief past. But he wanted to believe her. He needed proof to do that. "I'll go back to Serenity House."

He had almost gotten into the administrator's records once. With more time, he could break into the system. Or maybe there was another way he could find out. He pulled his cell from his pocket and checked the call log. He hadn't missed any, though—not even during the shoot-out. "Trigger was going to try to get a warrant for their records. I'll see what he found out—"

Charlotte knocked the phone from his hand. The cell flew over the railing and dropped far to the beach below, breaking apart on the rocks.

Staring down at the pieces of metal and plastic glinting in the faint light of that crescent moon, he murmured, "What the hell—"

"Don't you get it?" she asked with impatience. "He can't be trusted."

"You remember him?"

"I remember that Trigger is actually short for Trigger *Happy*. He's a loose cannon. And there's another reason I didn't tell him where Josie is," she said. "He can be bought and the people looking for her have deep pockets."

He gasped. "She's still in danger?"

She turned away, looking out at the waves rushing toward the shore. "Too many people now know she's still alive."

He glanced toward the house but no lights had come on inside. Whit must not have woken Stanley Jessup yet. "So we can tell her dad the truth?"

"No," she said. "You shouldn't have been told, either. Every person that learns the truth puts her in more danger."

Aaron nodded.

He didn't like that he'd been lied to—that people thought he'd failed to protect his client. But if lying to him had kept her safe, he would make peace with the fact.

"Do you think that could have been Trigger shooting at us tonight?" he asked. It would explain why he hadn't called; why he hadn't come back…

She nodded, and her tangle of golden hair fell across her face. "If Mr. Centerenian hadn't found us, it could have been Trigger. He's one of the few who knew where we were."

"The only one who wasn't there when the shooting started," Aaron pointed out.

"But how did Whit know where we were?" she asked.

"Stanley Jessup told him," he reminded her.

"But he knew *exactly* where we were," she pointed out. "He knew we'd already broken out of Serenity House and broken into that very cabin to hide out. How did he know that?"

Aaron had wondered that himself and had fully intended to find out how—but then the shooting had started. "You think that Whit could be working with Trigger?"

"Or someone else he's had following you," she suggested, "maybe from the minute you left St. Pierre."

"But they shot at him, too."

"But he didn't get hit, did he?"

"You're saying I shouldn't trust the man I've known for so long." When sometimes he felt like he'd only known her ten minutes.

"Do you trust him?"

"Damn it…" His curse was his admission. He couldn't trust Whit. When she'd staged Josie's death, Charlotte hadn't known Aaron. But Whit had—he'd known how much it'd hurt him—how much it had hurt him to think he'd failed her. But he'd let him suffer anyways.

Whit was not really his friend.

"I should contact the authorities myself then," he said since he couldn't trust that the U.S. Marshal had.

"Serenity House might be the biggest employer around here. Someone at the sheriff's office could tip them off," she pointed out. "Then they'd have time to destroy the records."

She was smart, since Dr. Platt had insinuated as much when he'd been listening to her conversation with the private guard. He needed to accept that he could trust no one. "I'll go to Serenity House alone."

"No," she said. "I'm going with you."

"We barely got you out of that place," he reminded her. "We can't risk taking you back there."

"I know who I am now," she said. "I know how to take care of myself."

Even when she hadn't known who she was, she'd still known how to defend herself. And him.

"What about your baby?" he asked. Her baby. Not his. Why did it hurt so much to lose what he'd never really had? What he hadn't even realized he'd wanted? "Don't you want to take care of him?"

"Her," she corrected him—almost automatically. Every time she'd talked about the baby, she'd referred to her as a girl.

"You had an ultrasound," he realized. "You know what you're having?"

"If I had an ultrasound, I don't remember it," she said. "But I know…" She was already connected to her child.

"Then you know you have to stay here—where she will be safe." He didn't wait for her agreement. He didn't care what she said. She damn well wasn't going back to Serenity House with him.

Hoping that Whit had left the keys in his car again, Aaron headed toward the driveway. That sliver of moon led him toward the banged-up vehicle. It had a sticker on the crumpled rear bumper that identified it as being from the same rental company as Aaron's car. Whit wasn't going to get back his security deposit, either. With the rear quarter panels nearly pushed into the tires, it was a wonder that the thing was drivable at all.

But it had to make another trip. Aaron needed to discover the truth about how Charlotte had wound up in Serenity House. And he figured he was only going to trust it was true if he learned it for himself instead of trusting what someone—anyone—told him.

Charlotte had raised more doubt in his mind. About her. But mostly about Whit.

Could he trust what his former business partner had

claimed? And how had the man found him at the abandoned cabin tucked away in the woods?

Sure, he'd been with him when the shots had been fired. But that didn't mean he didn't have an accomplice—either the Marshal or some mercenary he'd hired. Had he wanted to kill Aaron and take Charlotte for ransom since he was one of the few who knew she was really royalty?

Had Whit known where to find them because he was the one who'd put her in Serenity House?

Aaron opened the door and the dome light glinted off the keys hanging from the ignition. After what had happened at the cabin, Whit really should have been more careful. Aaron slid behind the wheel and reached for the keys. But he didn't turn them. Because the barrel of a gun pressed against his temple.

He really should have been more careful.

Chapter Nine

In the rearview mirror, Aaron met Whit's gaze. "This is the second damn time that someone I thought I could trust pressed a gun to my head and threatened to kill me."

"I haven't threatened you."

Aaron pointed toward his head. "Guess it's kind of implied by the gun to my temple."

Whit pulled it away. "I thought you were her. I figured she'd give you the slip on the beach and try to steal the car again."

"Sure, she stole it. But she came back," Aaron reminded him.

"Probably to make sure we didn't get away from the guys she hired to kill us."

Aaron snorted. "She speaks highly of you, too."

"So she's talking now?" Whit scoffed. "Passing all the blame off on me?"

Aaron turned around to face his old partner. "She doesn't know who's to blame."

Whit snorted now. "Yeah, right."

"You didn't see her in Serenity House," Aaron said, flinching as he remembered how scared and confused she'd been. That was why he'd momentarily mistaken her for Princess Gabriella. "She was tied down to a bed. She had been beaten up and bruised. She didn't do that to herself."

"So who did it?"

Possibly Whit. He knew, as few people did, that Charlotte Green was a royal heir. "I'm going back to Serenity House to find out."

"You're just going to walk inside and politely ask them for the princess's records?" Whit scoffed. "At least I'm assuming they thought she was the princess since that's the tip the freelance reporter passed on to Stanley Jessup."

"How did the reporter get that tip?" Aaron hadn't bothered asking Jessup who his source was because the media mogul was a die-hard newsman and fanatic defendant of the First Amendment. He would never reveal a source.

"Someone on staff at Serenity House tipped off the young reporter," Whit explained. "Do you want me to wake up Stanley and get the reporter's contact information? He's some young kid fresh out of community college, but he's got great investigative skills. He's been following you around since you got here."

The kid was very good because Aaron usually figured out when he was being tailed. But maybe three years of being bored out of his mind in corporate security had dulled his instincts. "So that's how you knew where I was tonight?"

Whit nodded. "What? Did you think I planted a GPS chip in you like a dog?"

Aaron chuckled.

"I thought about it," Whit teased, reminding Aaron of the friend he had once trusted with his life. "But I thought you'd notice. And you probably wouldn't believe that you were abducted by aliens, and they implanted it."

Aaron snorted with derision. "I'm not that big a fool."

"You are if you think you're going to just waltz right back in there." Whit crawled over the console and dropped into the passenger seat. "I checked that place out. It's got higher security than most federal penitentiaries."

"That's why whoever kidnapped Charlotte put her in that place."

Whit stared at him with respect. "So how'd you get her out?"

Aaron pulled one of the ID badges from his pocket, grateful now that he'd grabbed them from the cabin. He suspected they hadn't been deactivated—just that during their escape someone had sounded an alarm that sealed all the doors and gates.

"I used this to get out, and I'll use it to get back in. It's like a key that'll let me through all the locked doors and gates." He dug deeper into his pocket. "I should have a couple more of these." He'd taken three.

"We only need one more," Whit said, holding out his hand—palm up, "for me."

Aaron's pocket was empty. "I must have lost them back at the cabin…"

"When we were getting shot at," Whit finished for him. "It's okay. Instead of splitting up and having me play the diversion tactic, we'll have to stick together at the hospital."

He was tempted. But he'd be a fool to trust anyone again. "Like I told Charlotte, it'll be better if I just go in alone."

"And she agreed to that?" Whit asked skeptically.

Aaron nodded. "She knows it's not safe for her to go back there."

"It isn't safe for you, either," Whit pointed out. "I should be the one to go back in alone. Let me do this…"

Aaron shook his head. "No."

Whit uttered a ragged sigh of resignation. "You still don't trust me."

"Right now I don't know who to trust," he replied, "not after years of being lied to."

The sigh became a groan. "God, man, I would have told you the truth if I could have. But you wouldn't have been able to watch Stanley Jessup suffer like he had and not tell him that his daughter wasn't dead. And the people after her needed to see him suffer to believe she was really gone. Don't you get that?"

Anger and resentment overwhelmed Aaron. "I get that you didn't trust me to do my job—to protect our client, and you let me suffer these past three years thinking that I'd failed."

"It wasn't like that…"

"It was exactly like that," Aaron retorted. "You didn't trust me. So how can you expect me to trust you?"

"Then don't let me go in alone," Whit negotiated. "But let me go in *with* you. We have always worked well together—in Afghanistan and running our own security business. Hell, look what we did tonight. You pulled me out of the line of fire."

"And you drove us here, to safety," Aaron had to admit.

Whit uttered a wistful sigh of nostalgia. "It was like old times…"

Aaron chuckled. "Yeah, getting shot at—running for our lives. It sure was like old times."

Whit chuckled. "I didn't say they were all good times."

"Okay, you can come along," Aaron allowed.

"You've finally decided you can trust me again?"

Aaron turned the keys in the ignition and pointed at the lightening sky. "I'm sick of arguing about it. We're wasting time. Our best chance of getting inside and finding the records is going to be now—before the more heavily staffed first shift starts."

The rental car's ignition whined but didn't turn over. However, another engine fired up, breaking the quiet of the late night. Lights momentarily blinded Aaron until the car passed them. And as it passed, Aaron recognized the profile of the woman driving the sports car.

"Charlotte…" She must have taken a car from the garage of Stanley Jessup's rental home. "I thought she agreed to stay here. Out of danger…" Aaron turned the keys again, but the engine refused to start. "Now she's going off with no backup…"

"Damn her," Whit said, pounding his fist against the dash. "She's getting away."

"She's not getting away," Aaron said. "She's going back to Serenity House. She's risking getting caught all over again."

Whit pounded the dash again—this time right in front of Aaron. "She told you she was staying here, too. Why would you believe anything *she* tells you?"

But, Aaron realized, she'd never actually said the words—had never agreed not to go back to Serenity House. Whit's pounding the dash must have knocked something loose because the car finally started.

"We have to beat her back there." Or she would walk alone into danger—just as she had so many times before.

Whit shook his head. "How many times do I have to tell you that you can't trust Charlotte Green?"

"I know I can't trust her," Aaron admitted. But he didn't want to lose her, either. And if she walked back into Serenity House alone, he worried that he would.

SHE HAD BEATEN them to Serenity House. The car she'd borrowed from the garage was faster than the battered rental. As damaged as Whit's car had been, she'd have been surprised if it had started up again let alone been functional enough to follow her. And even though she hadn't known exactly where she'd been going to get back to the horrible hospital, she'd found street signs that had guided her.

She bypassed the front lot to drive around the fenced-in grounds and the building to pull the borrowed Camaro into the employee lot in the back. She parked far from the gate that led to the building. If she were to be discovered, she wanted to be close to the street so no one could block the car from leaving.

Night shift must have been skeletal because there weren't that many cars in the lot. Or maybe, after her escape, some of the employees had quit for fear of getting involved in a police investigation. Maybe she should have gone to the authorities as Aaron had wanted.

But if Serenity House had influence over them, the police might have brought her right back here. Because of the holes in her memory, she didn't know if she had been legally committed to the hospital. Maybe a judge had ordered her confinement. And the authorities would have to uphold the judge's order.

That was why she'd had to go back. She couldn't stand one more minute of not knowing how she had wound up here. But she had a sick feeling that she wouldn't like what she learned. What if the king had orchestrated her disappearance?

What if he'd resented her intrusion into his life and her interference with Gabriella? He had spent years denying her existence. When she'd showed up to protect his real princess, he had agreed begrudgingly. And only because of all the attempts that had already been made to abduct the princess. Since the day she'd been brought home to the palace, Gabriella St. Pierre had been the target of kidnapping and extortion plots.

His enemies had wanted to use Gabriella for leverage—forcing King Rafael to agree to their political or business demands. And everyone else had wanted to hold the princess ransom for money because her father would have willingly paid a huge sum for her safe return.

If Charlotte had been kidnapped by mistake—which might have been the case—he wouldn't have paid a dime for her return. He would have just let her rot. Here.

Why had she wound up in a psychiatric hospital? Had it all just been a case of mistaken identity?

She turned off the car and reached into her pocket, pulling out one of the security badges she'd stolen from Aaron. Growing up with a con artist mother had had some benefits. She'd taught Charlotte to pickpocket at an early age. Not that Bonita had relied on pickpocketing to support herself. She'd just used the wallets she'd *found* to meet the men she'd wanted to meet.

Charlotte flinched with a twinge of guilt that she'd used Aaron to get what she'd wanted. Of course she'd wanted to hug him, had wanted to apologize for keeping so many secrets from him. But now that he knew his beloved Josie was alive, he wanted nothing to do with Charlotte. So when he'd pushed her away, she had pulled the badges from his pocket. She'd only intended to take one, but the lanyards had been tangled together. She had left him one…if he could get here to use it.

But dawn was already burning away the night with a low-hanging fog. Getting in now, before the day shift began, was Charlotte's best bet to go unnoticed. Because she'd been cold, she had kept on the scrubs under the warmer clothes Aaron had packed in the box for her.

He was such a considerate man—always more concerned about others than himself. It was no wonder that, even knowing his heart had already belonged to another, she'd begun to fall for him. He had reminded her of her missionary grandparents and her aunt. Always trying to save the world and uncaring of their own comfort or needs.

Her mother had been the exact opposite. And Charlotte had grown up worrying that she would become more like her than the others—since her father was also a selfish bastard. How could he have made that announcement at the ball? Cavalierly passing Gabriella from one man to another like a possession with no thoughts or feelings of her own…

Just as Charlotte had been imprisoned here—with no concern for her comfort or her feelings. She stepped out of the vehicle and peeled off the sweater and then wriggled the jeans down her legs. The exertion zapped what she had left of her strength, which had already been diminished by being restrained to a bed. And either the pregnancy or the concussion had stolen the energy she used to have.

Her legs trembled beneath her weight. Maybe she just wasn't accustomed to standing anymore. Or maybe she dreaded going back inside the hospital that had served as her prison. She tucked the stolen gun in the waistband of her pants and tugged the shirt down over it. At least now she wasn't unarmed.

But if she was caught…

She wouldn't be just tied down to that bed again. She would be taken to that airfield and whisked away on a private plane to some other prison. One from which she would probably find no escape.

And no one to help her.

If she were taken again, would Aaron even look for her this time? Or was he so angry over her lies and lies of omission that he would consider it good riddance if she went missing again?

Or would he think that she'd just taken off on her own? That she'd duped him yet again?

She glanced back toward the street, wanting to wait for him. Wanting him to come for her. But she had no way of knowing if he was coming—if he were even able or willing to come after her.

And she couldn't wait any longer. This was her last shot to find out who had abducted her—to find out the identity of the father of her baby.

"WE'RE TOO LATE," Aaron said as he pulled into the employee lot and parked beside the Camaro, which was in a space farthest from the building. Even once he'd gotten Whit's rental car started, he should have known it would never catch up to the faster vehicle Charlotte had taken. "She's probably already inside."

She must have taken the extra two badges from him when she'd hugged him. God, he'd been a fool again—to think that she'd actually been apologizing to him for all the secrets she'd kept from him.

But she'd only been playing him to get what she wanted. Access to Serenity House. After what she'd gone through—being tied down and beaten—why would she want to go back inside?

And would he be able to get her out again?

He shut off the vehicle and turned toward the three-story brick building. Lights shone in only a few windows, the rest of the rooms eerily dark.

Serenity House had been anything but serene earlier that evening—it had been like a war zone with gunfire and fighting and yelling. Hell, there had even been the vehicle knocking down the fence. But as they'd passed the front entrance, he'd seen that gate and fence had been repaired, so it appeared as though nothing had happened. And now it seemed that hardly anyone was around—guards, staff or patients.

Whit stared at the black Camaro as if trying to determine if it was the one that had raced past them earlier. "I have to admit that I'm surprised she came here at all. I figured she'd just keep driving."

"She wants to find Princess Gabriella every bit as much as you do," Aaron said. That had to be the reason she would risk going back inside. Now he understood why she'd been so protective of the princess. She hadn't been just doing her job. She'd been guarding her sister.

Whit shook his head. "I doubt that…"

"She said she doesn't want to take Princess Gabriella's place."

"She's said a lot of things."

"Actually she hasn't," Aaron said, compelled to defend her. "It wasn't that she lied to me. She just didn't tell me things."

"A lie of omission is still a lie," Whit persisted.

"I guess you'd know."

Sick of arguing with his old partner, Aaron stepped out of the car and slammed the door. "We have to find her."

Despite her skills, Charlotte needed him. She wouldn't be able to get in and out of Serenity House alone. Remembering the shots that had been fired at him earlier in this lot, Aaron moved cautiously toward the building.

Whit's footsteps followed him, the other man sticking close and keeping his voice low. "She's already beaten us to whatever we might find here."

"You don't know that." She could have been stopped at the gate. Maybe the ID badges they'd taken had been deactivated. Maybe they wouldn't open the locked gates and doors.

Disappointment and frustration made Whit's whisper gruff. "Princess Gabriella isn't here."

Aaron had already checked that out; he knew it was true. Obviously Whit had learned the same from Stanley Jessup's young reporter's source. "But maybe whoever put Charlotte here took Princess Gabriella, as well."

"I doubt both of them survived what happened in Paris," Whit replied.

"We don't know what happened in Paris."

"She does…"

Aaron was done arguing. He ignored the other man and hurried toward the gate.

"Stop," Whit ordered in a harsh whisper.

Recognizing the urgency in Whit's voice, Aaron froze and crouched lower to the pavement, wary of getting shot at again. He turned back to Whit, who was pointing toward one of the few other cars parked in the lot.

Like the fog rising up from the ground, steam covered the windows, but it didn't conceal the dark shadows of two people sitting inside the front seat.

Had Charlotte already been grabbed—before she'd even made it to the building?

With just a look and a jerk of his head, Aaron communicated with his old partner. They each took a side of the car—Whit on the driver's side and Aaron the passenger's. That was probably where Charlotte would be sitting if she were inside the vehicle.

He could only see the shadows through the fogged-up windows. He couldn't tell if the passenger was actually Charlotte. And he had no clue who the driver was. The U.S. Marshal? One of the guards?

Neither shadow moved. They must not have noticed him pass behind the vehicle on his way across the lot. Why were they just sitting there—long enough to steam up the windows?

Were they talking? Arguing?

He heard neither, nothing except for the mad pounding of his own pulse in his ears. Foreboding chilled him more than the cool gusts of wind. Something wasn't right. It had to be Charlotte…

Whit moved as silently and quickly as Aaron did. Each had his weapon clenched in his hand, the barrel glittering in the first light of dawn streaking across the sky.

Maybe he could grab her and pull her to safety before the driver even realized they were sneaking up on them. With his free hand, Aaron grabbed the handle and jerked open the door. And the passenger fell out— onto him. Blood—thick and sticky—dripped from the woman's body—saturating his shirt. And he realized it wasn't steam fogging up the windows but a spray of blood.

They were too late.

Chapter Ten

"This is why you don't want to help me," a soft voice murmured from the cover of the enveloping fog.

Startled, Aaron jerked—knocking the body off him so that it dropped onto the asphalt and rolled over. With the hole in her face from the bullet she'd taken in the back of her head, the woman was nearly unrecognizable but for the gray hair.

But she wasn't Charlotte, who stepped from the fog and approached the car.

"You're all right," Aaron said, breathing a sigh of relief that she hadn't been in the car—or entered the hospital yet.

She shook her head in denial, but he figured she was referring to her emotional state rather than her physical condition.

"It's Sandy. The nurse who took care of me," Charlotte said, identifying the woman. "She tried to help me, and look what she got for her trouble. Dead."

"Driver's dead, too," Whit informed them. He flipped open a wallet he'd taken off the body. A curse whistled between his teeth.

"What?" Aaron asked.

"It's that kid," Whit replied, "the young investigative

reporter who approached one of Stanley Jessup's editors with the story about Princess Gabriella being here."

"The nurse must have been his source," Aaron said, leaning inside the car to see that the reporter had also been shot in the back of the head like the woman.

They had probably been meeting in the parking lot to discuss what she'd witnessed that evening when someone had executed them. He suspected that their killer had been hiding in the backseat, like Whit had back at Jessup's rented cottage.

"That's why they were killed, Charlotte," he told her, trying to ease her guilt. She hadn't asked to be kidnapped and held hostage in this place. "It had nothing to do with you."

She shrugged off his reassurance. "It had everything to do with me. It wouldn't have happened if I hadn't been here. They would both still be alive."

He couldn't absolve her of guilt she was determined to hold on to—just as Whit hadn't been able to absolve him three years ago when he'd thought Josie had been murdered on their watch. The only thing that might help her was learning the truth.

"Then we need to find out who put you in here," he said, "because that's who's really responsible for these deaths."

"We don't know that," Whit said, his dark gaze narrowed with suspicion as he stared at Charlotte. Maybe he'd taken her claim of responsibility literally.

As Aaron lifted the nurse's body back into the car, he noted that her skin was already cold. "She's been dead awhile," he said. "They were probably killed shortly after Charlotte and I broke out of here. And our only lead to finding out who is behind all this is in that hospital."

He gestured back at the three-story building. But Whit continued to study Charlotte. He obviously thought she was a more viable lead. But if she knew who'd put her in this place, she would have no desire to go back inside.

Instead she drew in an audible breath and started across the lot toward the building.

He caught her arm. "You can't go back in there."

She pointed back at the car with the blood-spattered windows. "It's not any safer out here."

"She's right," Whit miraculously agreed. "We should all stick together."

Aaron figured his old partner just didn't want Charlotte getting away again before he'd had a chance to interrogate her. But, even though they didn't trust each other, maybe they would all be safer if they stayed together.

Because wasn't the saying *to keep your enemies closer...*

CHARLOTTE ACHED WITH the desire to throw her arms around Aaron's neck and cling to him. She was afraid, but her inclination had less to do with fear and more to do with relief. When she'd first realized that was blood dripping down the car windows, she'd thought that Aaron might have been inside—that he might have beaten her there using some back roads and...

Her breath hitched with a sob she held inside. She'd learned at an early age that tears were a waste of time. They had never swayed her mother from doing what she'd wanted and had never made the selfish woman care about her. She doubted crying would make Aaron care, either.

He was already in love with another woman. But

why hadn't he pressed her for Josie's whereabouts? Ironically, she was close. That was why Michigan had sounded familiar to Charlotte because she had brought Josie here for her new life.

It would be even more ironic if this was where Charlotte lost her life. But Aaron was determined to keep her safe. That was why he was still here—because it was his job. Even more than that, it was his honor. He was the kind of man who enjoyed playing white knight to helpless damsels. He was a true hero—in wartime and peace. That was why Charlotte had been so drawn to him.

But she was no damsel in distress, so she should have known that they could never be…

"Are we doing this?" Whit asked, breaking the silence that had fallen between them as she stared up at Aaron's handsome face.

His gaze was locked with hers, as if he was trying to figure out what she was thinking. Or plotting…

Aaron nodded. "Yeah, we're doing this."

"What's the plan?" Whit persisted.

"We go in the employee entrance, but we bypass the locker room and cafeteria and take the back stairs up to the administrator's office."

Whit whistled in appreciation. "You know the layout of the place."

"I interviewed here and then worked a day before I even tried getting inside her room," Aaron explained.

A grin tipped up a corner of his sexy mouth. "And then I got tossed out on my ass after I got caught coming out of her room."

"I thought you weren't coming back," she remembered with a flash of the panic she'd felt then. "I thought you'd been shot."

"Not yet," Aaron said with a glance back at the car where two people had been shot. "But we have to make this quick. Get in, get into the administrator's records, and get the hell out!"

"Good plan," Whit mused.

The first test was getting past the lock at the security gate. They all breathed a sigh of relief that a swipe of the card turned the light from red to green.

"I thought they might have deactivated them." Aaron spoke aloud the fear she'd been harboring, too. "Guess they didn't think we'd be stupid enough to come back."

But they were wrong. It probably was very stupid to return to the place they'd barely escaped the first time.

No one accosted them between the employee entrance and the stairwell to the second floor and the office suites. But the administrator's office was not empty. A light glowed behind the frosted glass in the door, and a machine buzzed inside, the floor vibrating with the low drone of it.

"She's shredding papers," Charlotte said, her stomach lurching with a sick feeling of hopelessness.

"The records are online," Aaron assured her—giving her hope as he had in the parking lot. Trying to make her feel better.

He was such a damn good man. That was why she reached for the door handle, trying to enter first. Whoever had put her in this place wanted her baby; she doubted anyone would shoot at her. But Aaron apparently wasn't willing to take that chance. He held her back, and with a nod at Whit, the two men burst through the door with their weapons drawn.

The woman standing behind the desk wore a power suit and had an air of authority—even with her ash-blond hair falling out of the bun on top of her head and dark circles blackening the skin beneath her eyes. She had to be the administrator. She confronted them with a hard stare and slight smile—more triumphant than fearful. She had definitely suspected that they would come back.

"It's too late," Dr. Mona Platt, per the nameplate on her desk, said. "I wiped the hard drive. Everything's gone…"

Charlotte shook her head. She would not be denied. She had gone too long without knowing what had happened to her. "Everything's *not* gone," she pointed out. "You're still here."

"I'm not going to tell you anything," the woman stubbornly insisted.

"You'll talk to us or the police," Aaron threatened her.

"What will I talk to the police about?" Dr. Platt asked, waving her hand over the paper shredder. "There is nothing to talk about."

Charlotte's anger flared, energizing her as her pulse raced. "You held me captive in this place!"

The woman's thin lips pursed into a tight line of defiance and denial. "I don't know what you're talking about."

"You restrained me to a bed," Charlotte accused, "and had a guard posted outside my door with a gun."

"We do not employ armed guards at Serenity House," the administrator replied prissily.

Aaron snorted at that claim.

Charlotte pointed to the bruise on her head. "Mr. Centerenian nearly killed me with that gun!"

"Mr. Centerenian was not employed by Serenity House."

"Who was he employed by?" Whit threw the question out there. "Who paid him and who paid for this woman's stay here?"

"I cannot violate doctor-patient confidentiality clauses," Dr. Platt persisted. "Or the privacy law."

"I am the patient!" Charlotte snapped. "So you're going to damn well tell me who paid you to keep me here!"

"I will not—"

Charlotte lifted her gun and pointed the barrel directly at the woman. "You will tell me!"

"You won't shoot me."

"I wouldn't be so sure of that," Whit warned the doctor. "She can't be trusted."

"And since I was confined to a psychiatric hospital, I must be out of my mind." She moved her finger to the trigger. "I could probably use an insanity plea to get out of jail time."

"Then you'd wind up spending the rest of your life in a place like this," Dr. Platt threatened.

"At least I'll be alive…"

The woman's eyes narrowed with her own temper. "You should be thanking me."

A laugh, at the woman's audacity, burst out of Charlotte's lips. "God, lady, you should be committed here yourself instead of running the place. What the hell do you think I should be thanking you for?"

Dr. Platt pointed toward Charlotte's belly. "You should thank me for your baby. You owe me for its life."

"What the hell are you talking about?" Aaron asked the question before Charlotte could.

She pressed her palm over her stomach, as if her hand alone could protect her baby from this crazy woman. "You—you did this? You impregnated me?"

The doctor shook her head, knocking more brittle

blond strands of hair loose from the bun. "I was supposed to—with special sperm. But you were already pregnant. I didn't tell *him* that, or he would have had me terminate it. You have me to thank for your baby."

"My baby…" But it wasn't just *her* baby. It was Aaron's baby, too. Even though they had used protection that one night they'd been together, it must have failed…because he was the only man she'd been with recently. In a long while, actually. She turned toward him, and when she met his gaze, she knew he *knew*.

AARON WAS GOING to be a father. The baby was *his*.

The thought stole his breath away for a moment.

Whit had no such problems. "Who is *he?*" he demanded to know.

"The father?" Dr. Platt asked with a sniffle of disinterest. "I don't know." And she obviously didn't much care. She turned toward Charlotte. "Do you remember? Or are you still suffering from amnesia?"

If the look on Charlotte's face was any indication, she knew—with as much certainty as he knew. The baby was his. But that wasn't Whit's question.

So the tenacious Mr. Howell repeated it. "Who is the man who paid you to make her pregnant with his sperm? Who brought her here?"

"That guard—the one with the gun—Mr. Centerenian is the one who brought her here," Dr. Platt replied. "And he hired a private nurse, too, who only took care of the princess."

"The princess…" Whit murmured the words.

"I am not Princess Gabriella," Charlotte replied.

The woman laughed now. "And you don't think you belong here? You've either still got amnesia or you're crazy."

"Who I am is Charlotte Green," she said, "bodyguard to Princess Gabriella."

When Dr. Platt continued to stare at Charlotte like she was crazy, Aaron said, "It's true. She's a former U.S. Marshal and professional bodyguard." The woman didn't need to know that she was also royalty. "This man—Mr. Centerenian—brought you the wrong woman. He and his boss kidnapped the wrong woman."

Dr. Platt shrugged. "It doesn't matter to me. None of these outrageous claims of yours has anything to do with me or Serenity House."

"It has everything to do with you," Aaron argued, because she was the only one who could tell them what they needed to know. "You took money to hold a woman hostage. You're an accessory."

"That man brought her here," she stubbornly repeated. "I had no idea that she had been kidnapped."

Whit swore. "Bullshit!"

"That gorilla with the gun is not the one giving the orders," Aaron said. "And he's not the one paying you. I hope his boss paid you a hell of a lot for what you're going to wind up giving up for it."

She arched a brow, her interest finally piqued. "Giving up?"

"Your hospital," Aaron said.

"Your freedom," Whit added.

"Your life," Charlotte murmured. "If I have anything to say about it…"

She didn't mean it. Aaron was almost certain that she didn't. That she was just upset. Understandably so for all she'd had to go through.

"You're threatening me," Dr. Platt accused, as if she were the victim.

Charlotte stepped closer to her, and even though she

was six months pregnant and weak, she was a far more dangerous woman than the administrator realized. "I'm not just threatening," she warned the woman.

Aaron put his hand on her arm, pulling her back before she vaulted over the desk and throttled the administrator. He told both women, "We need to know who that man is."

And if Charlotte killed Dr. Platt, they might never figure it out. Or at least be able to prove it.

"You're already in trouble here," Aaron pointed out, "so you might as well tell us what you know."

"Come on," Whit urged her.

Aaron felt them coming before he heard them. There were enough of them that there were vibrations on the floor beneath his feet. He reached for Charlotte even before the door burst open and the armed men stormed into the office. He pushed her behind him, taking cover behind a filing cabinet, and raised his weapon.

The administrator didn't have magical powers, but somehow she had summoned the guards as silently as she had last time Aaron had been in her office. Maybe she had a secret button somewhere on her desk, or maybe she had a remote alarm in her pocket.

Or maybe she hadn't summoned them at all because the first bullet they fired went through her forehead, spattering her brains on the wall behind her. There was no need to check her for a pulse; there was no way she could have survived that shot.

Then the guards swung their weapons toward them, and the office erupted with gunfire. Aaron fought hard to stay between Charlotte and the men as he returned fire. But she moved around him, taking her own shots. Aaron was so concerned about her that he hadn't even noticed that Whit was down. He'd been hit.

Aaron's heart slammed against his ribs as he noticed the blood. And in that moment of distraction, one of the guards lunged toward him with gun blazing…

Chapter Eleven

"Her guards don't have guns, my ass," Whit murmured as Aaron carried him from the building. Sirens wailed in the distance.

Charlotte's hand shook as she swiped the badge through the lock on the gate. "Maybe we should wait for the police," she said, "or at least for an ambulance."

Whit had lost a lot of blood. But that hadn't stopped him from saving her and Aaron. He'd taken out the last guard. But none of the men who had stormed into the office had been the one who'd struck her with the gun and stolen her memory. Where was Mr. Centerenian?

"We should wait for an ambulance," Aaron agreed.

Whit shook his head. "It's a through and through, and I can move my arm so it didn't hurt anything in my shoulder."

"Then you should be able to walk," Aaron grumbled, but he continued to carry his friend across the lot. And they were friends again.

Enlisting Whit to help her stage Josie Jessup's death and forbidding him to tell Aaron had destroyed their friendship. Whit had obviously resented—maybe even hated her—for it. And for three years Charlotte had regretted what her job had cost the two men. That was why she'd convinced the king to hire them both for bodyguards. She'd wanted them to work together again.

But she had never imagined how well they would have to work together. They had kept each other alive in that office, and they'd kept her alive. She wasn't certain who else had survived. Not the administrator. But some of the guards might have.

And Mr. Centerenian was out there, somewhere. So she clutched her weapon close and kept a watchful gaze on the area around them. She hoped she wouldn't have to use her gun, though, because if she had to, she would need to make the one bullet she had left count.

"Put him in Jessup's car," she ordered as she fumbled for the keys and unlocked the doors. "We need to get out of here fast."

They all squeezed into the sports car, Whit bleeding on the leather seats in the back. Charlotte passed the keys to Aaron, who drove.

"He's lost a lot of blood," she whispered, leaning across the console. Warmth radiated from Aaron, chasing some of the chill from her body. "We should take him to the hospital."

"No," Whit protested from the back. "Just take me to Stanley Jessup's. And make sure nobody follows you this time."

Aaron cursed him, but he took the route toward the lake and the house sitting high on the dune above it. "If you die, you stubborn ass," he threatened, "it's on you."

"Actually it'll be on you," Charlotte remarked with a faint chuckle as Aaron carried his friend into the house.

"I'm fine," Whit promised.

Charlotte reached for the door just as it opened, and she came face-to-face with an older man. His hair was thick and wavy and pure white despite the fact that he wasn't even out of his fifties yet. And his gaze was green and piercing. She didn't need an introduction; she knew exactly who he was. Her stomach flipped, and then the baby kicked as if in protest of Charlotte's lurch of guilt.

"What the hell happened?" the older man bellowed. "Did you shoot him, Aaron?"

Aaron chuckled. "No. Can't say I haven't been tempted, though. Where can I put him? He's all dead weight."

"I'm not dead yet," Whit weakly murmured.

"Over here," Stanley Jessup said, leading them toward a den. "Lay him down on the couch and I'll call for a private doctor."

The media mogul understood the need for discretion. Over his head, Aaron met her gaze—as if trying to convince her to tell the man about his daughter.

She was tempted. Never more so than now that she carried a child of her own. But she couldn't risk Josie's safety. Not even to ease her conscience.

"Do you need a doctor, too, your highness?" Mr. Jessup asked, his voice gruff with concern.

If only her own father had ever cared about her like a virtual stranger cared…

She shook her head at the self-pitying thought as much as in reply to his question.

"This isn't Princess Gabriella," Aaron said.

"I told you I wouldn't run the story until she got out of danger, but the story's too big…" His gaze focused on her rounded belly. "I can't sit on it anymore. The young reporter who has a source at the hospital is ready to run with his story."

Thinking of the horrific fate that had befallen that

poor kid and the nurse who had tried to help her, Charlotte sucked in a breath of pain and guilt.

"I'll call the doctor," Stanley interrupted himself. He
grabbed a cell from his pocket and punched in some
numbers. Then he lowered his voice as he issued com-
mands to whoever answered his call.

"Are you all right?" Aaron asked, his focus on her
rather than his bleeding friend now. "You're extremely
pale."

His concern was back. But was he concerned about
her or was he concerned about his child? *Of course,
it's the baby.*

She was worried about the baby, too, and what could
have happened with all the bullets flying. She could
have easily been shot, just as Whit had. Fortunately
for her—*unfortunately for Whit*—the guards had been
more focused on firing at the men than at her. She suspected they'd had orders not to harm her baby. Because
whoever had employed them mistakenly thought the
baby was his…

The administrator had been right. But unfortunately
Charlotte hadn't had the chance to thank her before the
woman had been killed.

She should have listened to Aaron and stayed behind
the first time he'd brought her to this house. But she
hadn't wanted to be alone with Stanley Jessup almost
as much as she'd wanted to learn who had kidnapped
and imprisoned her in the mental hospital.

Having spent most of her professional life in dangerous situations, she hadn't had any qualms about risking her life again. After all, she had survived all those
previous dangerous situations, so she'd proven that she
could take care of herself.

But it wasn't just her anymore. She had someone

else to think about now—someone who wasn't a client or a witness but someone who was actually a physical part of her. Someone whose life depended on Charlotte staying alive and healthy.

As the enormity of that responsibility struck her, her knees began to shake, and she started trembling all over in reaction.

"Charlotte!" Aaron called out to her, his voice sharp with alarm. Then he repeated his earlier question, "Are you all right?"

"I—I need to sit down," she said. "Just rest for a little while, and I'll be fine." But before she could find a chair to sit on, Aaron swung her up in his arms. Black spots swam across her vision and dizziness threatened to overwhelm her. She clutched at Aaron's broad shoulders and his neck, holding on to him tightly.

"Where's a bedroom?" he asked Jessup, who'd just slipped his cell phone back in his pocket.

Even knowing that Aaron was only concerned about the baby and her health, Charlotte's pulse jumped at his question—at the idea of Aaron wanting to carry her off to a bedroom. But now that he knew how much she'd kept from him—that she'd kept Josie from him—she doubted he would ever want her—*Charlotte*—again.

Her head pounded with frustration and exhaustion, and she closed her eyes as the hopelessness washed over her. She did just need some rest—just a little—to get back her energy and her will to fight.

"Top of the stairs," the older man directed them. "There's a nice guest suite a couple of doors down the hall on the right."

She didn't care if it was nice or not. Hell, anything was nicer than Serenity House. She expected to fall asleep the minute her head hit the pillow. But when

Aaron laid her down on the bed, she tensed—unwilling to drop her arms from around his neck. She wanted to cling to him again—wanted to make sure that they had both really survived the shoot-out at Serenity House.

"After he takes care of Whit, I'll have the doctor come up to check you out," he assured her.

"You can't tell him…" she murmured as sleep tugged at her lids, bringing them down.

"I'm sure since Stanley Jessup called him, the doctor will be discreet. He won't be spreading any rumors about Princess Gabriella being pregnant."

"Gabby isn't…" Actually she didn't know that; she hadn't seen her sister in months. She had no idea how she was, and the panic must have shown on her face.

Because Aaron assured her, "Don't worry about Gabby or the doctor."

She shook her head, frustrated at his misunderstanding. "No doctor." She didn't need a doctor. She just needed sleep.

And Aaron. She needed Aaron. He was the father of her child, but she had to accept that was all he would ever be to her.

As if he couldn't stand her touch or feared she was picking his pockets again, he pulled away, albeit gently, from her grasping arms. He headed toward the door with the explanation: "I need to check on Whit. Make sure he stopped bleeding."

They had pressed a makeshift bandage, of his own handkerchief, to his shoulder, but the thin swatch of fabric hadn't done much to stem the blood loss.

So much blood…

Charlotte shuddered as she recalled the horrific crime scene they'd left. So much devastation.

Who was responsible?

"I need to talk to Mr. Jessup, too," Aaron continued with a heavy sigh.

Fighting to stay awake, she murmured, "You can't tell him about Josie…"

"It's been almost four years now," Aaron said. "What makes you think she might still be in danger?"

She placed her hands over her belly to soothe the baby's frantic kicking. Or was that her stomach churning with jealousy? And guilt churned along with that jealousy. Trigger had been telling the truth—she and Josie had become quite close. Charlotte should be worried about her friend—not Aaron.

"Trigger," she reminded him. "He wants to know where she is."

"You're sure it's her whose whereabouts he wanted to know?"

"My last case." Seeing how close Josie had been to her father had compelled Charlotte to want to get to know her own father.

It hadn't taken her long to realize that King St. Pierre would never be the father Stanley Jessup had been to his daughter. But Charlotte had stayed because of the bond she'd formed with her sister. It wasn't just outside dangers that she'd wanted to protect Gabriella from…

But now she focused on another friend. "There must be a reason Trigger wants to find Josie now. Somebody might have figured out she's alive and hired him to find out where she is."

"We haven't seen Trigger since we broke out of Serenity House," Aaron reminded her. "I don't think Josie's in danger."

"We can't be sure. Don't tell her dad."

"I won't," he promised, as he closed the blinds to shut

out the morning sun. "Don't worry. Just sleep. You're safe here. No one will hurt you."

It was too late. Someone already had. Aaron had with how easily he walked away, leaving her alone and aching for him.

Aching for a love that would never be hers...

HER LAST LUCID thought wasn't for her own safety but for someone else's. How could he have doubted—even for a minute—that her intentions weren't honorable?

Sure, he'd let Whit and all his cynicism and doubts get inside his head, but he had never considered Charlotte with his head.

He had always connected with Charlotte with his heart. That was how he'd known—no matter how morbid the crime scene in Paris was—that she wasn't dead. Because he would have known...

"She's not the princess," he told Stanley Jessup again, as he joined the older man at the bottom of the contemporary metal and glass staircase. It was a wonder he hadn't slipped carrying Charlotte up them. But then he'd been totally focused on her—on protecting her and their unborn child.

The media mogul snorted. "How big a fool do you think I am? That girl's the princess."

She was a princess. Just not the princess that Jessup thought she was.

"That girl is the princess's bodyguard," he divulged. It wasn't like it was a secret that could be kept any longer. "She had plastic surgery to look exactly like her."

Stanley Jessup whistled in appreciation of Charlotte's dedication. "Even you guys wouldn't have gone to those extremes to protect someone."

"She did." Because Princess Gabriella was her sister.

But that was a story Stanley Jessup didn't need to have because he wouldn't be able to *not* print it.

"Are you sure?"

"I've seen them both together. To people not that familiar with them, they're virtually identical." But if you really knew them, they were nothing alike.

So who had kidnapped Charlotte thinking that she was Gabriella? Someone who hadn't known either of them that well. And where was Princess Gabby?

"Doesn't matter who she is," Jessup said. "There's a hell of a story here. She was held hostage in that hospital for months, apparently. Whit got shot in that place."

Aaron glanced into the den where the doctor treated his old friend. The former war hero cursed profusely and creatively as a needle penetrated his skin, stitching up the wound.

Jessup reached for his phone again. "I'll call that young reporter and get him over here to brief us with what he knows."

Aaron shook his head. "That won't be possible."

"You need to get over this need for confidentiality," the media mogul scoffed. "There's really no such thing anymore."

"I'm not talking about the story," Aaron said. "I'm talking about the reporter. He can't come here." He swallowed hard on regret. "I'm sorry…"

The older man groaned. "I've heard that tone from you before. Heard that damn from-the-depths-of-your-soul apology. What happened?"

"I don't know for certain," he admitted. "But we found him and his source…"

"Dead?"

He nodded.

"Who did that?"

"Probably the same men who shot Whit." Four of them had stormed the administrator's office. Two had looked like the Serenity House guards he'd fought earlier—probably why they'd been so determined to shoot him. If not for Whit, Aaron might have been lying on the couch. Or in a morgue. "We left before the police arrived but we need to know what they know."

"And since you left the scene of a crime, you can't very well just waltz into the sheriff's office and ask?"

Aaron shook his head. "Only two of the men shooting at us were hospital guards." Despite Mona Platt swearing her security force was unarmed. "I don't know if the other two men worked for the hospital or someone else." Since they'd shot her first, and fatally, he heartily suspected someone else.

"The sheriff's office?"

Aaron shrugged. "We can't trust anyone." He had learned that the hard way. He couldn't even trust the woman who carried his baby. He still felt as though she had secrets, things she'd remembered but hadn't shared with him.

GUNSHOTS ECHOED INSIDE her head and blood spattered everything, blinding her with red. She shifted against the bed, fighting to awaken from the nightmare.

But it hadn't been just a dream. It was real. All of it had happened. All the death. The destruction. The senseless murders.

She could see Whit again, taking the bullet—getting knocked to the floor as blood spurted from his shoulder. But then it wasn't Whit she was seeing. It wasn't a blond man with dark eyes. Instead it was a dark-haired man with eerie light blue eyes that were wide, staring up at her in confusion as the life seeped away with the blood that pooled around him.

"Aaron!" she screamed his name, jolting awake with her heart pounding frantically with terror.

"It's okay," a deep voice murmured. And strong arms wrapped around her in the dark. "I'm here."

She clutched him close, realizing quickly that he wore no shirt. His skin was bare and damp beneath her fingers. And water trailed from his wet hair down his neck and chest. "Are you…"

Naked?

"I'm here," he assured her. He pulled her closer, so that her body pressed tightly against his. Rough denim covered his lower body. He must have only had time to pull on his jeans when he'd heard her scream.

"I thought it was you," she said, "who got shot. I thought you were dead."

"I'm fine," he said, skimming his hand over her hair—probably trying to tame the tangled mess. "How are you?"

Still trembling in reaction to her awful dream and filled with shame that she had let so many people believe their loved ones were dead. Maybe that was why she'd been so compelled to quit after Josie's case.

"Charlotte?" He eased back and tipped up her chin, his blue-eyed gaze intent on her face. "Are you all right?"

She nodded. "I'm just not quite awake yet. And it seemed so real…"

"It was real," he said. "The shooting was real. It just wasn't me."

"It was Whit," she said, remembering. "Is he okay?"

Aaron chuckled. "Sleeping off the painkillers the doctor gave him. But he'll be fine. We were lucky," he said, his voice gruff with emotion, "that we all survived."

"You told Mr. Jessup about the reporter?"

He nodded.

"I'm sorry." She pressed a kiss to the rough stubble on his cheek. "I know how hard that can be…"

Even if the people she'd told hadn't always lost their loved ones to death, they had lost them all the same. Her lips were still on his face, but he turned his head until they brushed across his mouth.

And he kissed her.

He knew Josie was alive, but he kissed *her.* Dare she hope that he cared? But then he pulled back.

"We need to talk," he said, "about the baby. About us…"

"Us?" She couldn't give in to the hope lifting the pressure from her chest. "When you learned how many things I'd kept from you—" *Josie* "—I didn't think you'd be able to forgive me."

"I don't know that I have," he admitted.

And he didn't even know that she still kept one secret from him.

"I feel like you're holding something back yet," he said.

Maybe he did know.

"Aaron…"

"But I know this isn't the right time for us to talk," he said. "We still don't know what happened to Princess Gabby. Or who kidnapped you. Or who shot all those people and had us shot at…"

She had leads. Thoughts. Suspicions. But when she opened her mouth, he pressed his fingers across her lips.

"So I don't want to talk," he said. "I want to celebrate

that we're alive." And he replaced his fingers with his mouth, kissing her deeply.

She moaned.

And he pulled away. "I'm such an idiot. You're exhausted. You've been through hell…"

"But none of that stops me from wanting you." She was surprised, though, that he wanted her since he knew that the real love of his life was still alive. But maybe he'd accepted that he couldn't be part of Josie Jessup's life without putting her in danger, so he'd decided to make do with the mother of his child.

"Charlotte…" he murmured her name with such regret.

He couldn't love her. She had to remind herself of that—so that she wouldn't fall even deeper for him than she already had.

"I shouldn't take advantage of you," he said, "like I did back at that cabin—"

She pressed her fingers over his lips now. "If anything I took advantage of you back there."

"You didn't even know who you were then."

"But I knew who you were." Strong and loyal and trustworthy. He would be a wonderful father—a far better father than she had ever known.

"I wish I knew who you are," he murmured wistfully.

"I told you—"

"I know your name," he said, "but I don't think I've ever really known you. And I'm not sure if you'll ever let me know the real you."

She didn't want him to just know her. She wanted him to love her. So she made herself vulnerable to him in a way that she never had for any other man. She didn't trust him enough to give him the words of love, but she showed him her love. With her lips and her tongue.

He lay back on the bed and groaned. He let her bring him to the brink before he turned on her. Pulling off her clothes, he kissed every inch of skin he exposed. And he pressed her back into the pillows and used his mouth to bring her beyond the brink—until pleasure tore through and she moaned his name again.

He joined their bodies, thrusting gently inside her— as if afraid that he might harm their unborn child. His slow and easy strokes drove her up again, with tension winding tight inside her. She clutched at his back, then slid her hands lower, grasping his tightly muscled butt. But he refused to rush. And each slow stroke drove her a little crazier—until she just dissolved with pleasure and emotion.

Then he groaned and filled her. "Charlotte…"

She was the woman whose name he uttered when pleasure overwhelmed him. She wanted to hope it meant something—that it might indicate they could have a future. But she had had her hopes dashed too many times to entertain any now. He flopped onto his back beside her and curled her against his side. But she couldn't look at him—couldn't let him see how much she cared. So she gazed around the room. The curtains were still drawn tight over the blinds—shutting out whatever light might be outside. "How long did I sleep?"

"Probably not long enough," he said. "You were exhausted. I should have let you go back to sleep instead of…"

"I must have spent months in that bed in Serenity House," she reminded him. "I shouldn't ever be tired again."

"But, even before what we just did, we had quite a night," he pointed out. "A night we were damn lucky to have survived."

And that was the only reason they had made love—in celebration of that survival, and for a wonderful while, she had been able to replace the pain and fear with pleasure. But now it all came rushing back along with her nightmarish memories of the night.

Her breath shuddered out in a ragged sigh as she remembered it all. "That was just one night? You got caught in my room and then came back to break me out all in the same night?"

"Yes."

Now she remembered something else—the guard's phone call. "Mr. Centerenian's boss is coming here tonight—to some private airfield. The guy who kidnapped and tried to impregnate me is going to be here."

"The guy who thought he was kidnapping and impregnating Princess Gabriella," Aaron pointed out. "This has nothing to do with you."

"She's my sister," Charlotte said with pride. "It has everything to do with me." It was her responsibility to keep the real princess safe.

Aaron shook his head. "I'll take it from here. I'll figure out which airfield they'll be using, and I'll meet him there."

"You're not going alone."

She didn't want to risk the baby's safety again, but she didn't want the baby's father putting his life at risk without backup he could trust, either.

"Absolutely not," he said. "I will not let you put yourself and my baby in danger again."

Chapter Twelve

Aaron momentarily took his gaze from the airfield to glance at the woman sitting in the passenger seat. She had come along. While he had admitted to himself and to Whit that he didn't know her as well as he should, he was already intimately familiar with her stubbornness.

If he had forbidden her to join him, she would have stolen another car from the garage and tracked down the airfield on her own. At least now, going together, it would be easier for him to protect her.

But she hadn't come along thinking that he would keep her safe. If anything she might think she needed to protect him…

But more likely she didn't trust him to tell her what he discovered on his own. And she wanted to know who'd locked her up in a psychiatric hospital. But what were all her motives? To keep Gabriella safe? They didn't even know where she was. Or so that Charlotte could take revenge on the person who had stolen nearly six months of her life?

Studying the dark airfield through the car windows, Aaron wasn't certain they would discover anything. They had been parked outside it since night had first begun to fall, and there were no lights illuminating the single runway or the steel hangar beside it. There was no vehicle parked near the hangar, either. They had parked Stanley Jessup's car on a farmer's access road to his fields that surrounded the small, private airport.

"This place looks deserted," he mused aloud.

He had no more than uttered the words when lights flashed on—bright beams of light pointing up into the night sky—to guide a plane to ground.

"He was here—that guard from the hospital—he's been here the whole time," Aaron said with a glance at Charlotte. "You knew it?"

She nodded.

"But there's no car anywhere around here…" So they'd shut off the Camaro's lights and waited in the dark for him to drive up.

"You said it's the only private airfield in the area," she reminded him. "He's here…"

Aaron nodded with sudden realization of how they'd missed him. "He must have parked his car inside the hangar."

Charlotte reached for the door handle. "We need to get inside there, too."

Aaron grabbed her arm, stopping her from stepping out. "No. *We* don't."

"We can't let him get on that plane and just fly away," she said. "He's the only lead we have left."

The reporter was dead. The nurse. The administrator. And if any of the armed men from the office had survived, they weren't talking yet. Stanley Jessup had developed a source in the sheriff's office. The small town was overwhelmed and bringing in state and federal authorities to take over the investigation. While that would be better for him and Whit and Charlotte, it would take too long for the investigation to yield any results.

"I will go," he clarified. "You will stay here."

"So he can sneak up on me, grab me and force me onto the plane?" She shuddered at the thought.

"You're armed," he reminded her. "I doubt he could force you to do anything." And that was part of the reason he'd agreed to let her come along with him. She really could take care of herself.

So was she more worried about him? That he'd take a bullet without her being there to protect him? Maybe she had feelings for him, too. Or was she just trying to keep alive the father of her baby?

"We decided to stick together," she reminded him. "That's what kept us alive in the administrator's office—sticking together."

"Glad Whit didn't hear you say that." They'd snuck out of the house while the other man had still been sleeping off his painkillers. Hopefully they would be back before he ever woke up.

Her lips curved into a faint smile. "He's in no condition to be here with us."

Aaron pressed his palm over her stomach. "Neither are you."

"I'm pregnant," she said. Then she dragged in a shaky breath and repeated, "I'm pregnant." She expelled the breath and said, "I'm not sick or injured."

Now he moved his hand to the bruise on her temple. "You were hurt," he pointed out the yet to heal injury. Thinking of the pain she'd endured, the fear over her lost memory and months of imprisonment, his stomach clenched as if he'd been punched in the gut again. "And you're lucky to be alive."

"I am alive," she said.

But what about Gabriella? Learning her fate was

probably what compelled Charlotte to put herself at risk again.

"And now I remember who I am," she added. "And I know what I know—how to take care of myself."

"And others…" He patted her belly again and nodded. "Let's get in there while the plane's landing." When the guard was distracted with the plane, they would be able to get the jump on him.

CHARLOTTE WINCED AT every snap of twig and rustle of grass beneath their feet as they moved stealthily toward the hangar. It was so damn quiet, and so damn black but for those lights beaming into the sky. She stumbled in the dark, would have tripped and gone down, but for Aaron catching her arm and steadying her.

She waited for him to use her clumsiness as a reason to insist on her returning to the car. But instead he kept his hand on her, keeping her close to his side.

Heat and attraction radiated between them. He may not trust her. Hell, he may not ever be able to forgive her, but he did want her. He'd proven that back at the house—proven it in a way that had her still feeling boneless and satiated.

The man was an amazing lover. If only he could really love her—*deeply* love her…

She shook off the wistful thought. It must have been the hormones—due to the pregnancy—that had her hoping for things she knew weren't possible. She had never been the romantic type.

She had always been a pragmatic person. She knew how the world really worked—her mother had made certain of that.

Now she had to make certain that the threat against

Princess Gabriella was gone. She clasped her weapon tightly in her hand.

Aaron reached for the handle to the back door of the steel hangar. He tested the lock and nodded.

The idiot guard wasn't as careful here as he'd been at the hospital. Mr. Centerenian would have never left the door to her room unlocked.

Charlotte lifted her weapon and nodded that she was ready. Aaron opened the door and stepped inside first, keeping his body between her and whoever might be in the hangar. Like her, he probably doubted that there was only one man meeting the plane—after all the men who had stormed into the administrator's office.

But the hangar was quiet and filled with light from the door open onto the field. One man stood there, staring up at the sky. A cigarette tip glowed between the fingers of his left hand. A white bandage swaddled his right hand.

"It's him," she whispered.

The man tensed and dropped his cigarette. Then he reached for the gun in the holster beneath his jacket. Before he could withdraw it, the drone of an engine broke the quiet. Mr. Centerenian turned his attention to the lights in the sky.

The plane was coming. The plane that Charlotte was supposed to leave on—to God knew where. A brief moment of panic clutched her heart. But she reminded herself that she wasn't going to be leaving—at least not on anyone's terms but hers.

As the guard stepped outside the hangar to watch the plane begin its descent, they moved through the shadows and edged closer to that wide-open door. But Charlotte clutched Aaron's arm—holding him back from going any farther. They ducked down below the side of the black SUV parked inside the hangar—keeping it between them and the guard.

She held tightly to Aaron's arm, making sure he stayed down. They couldn't be detected before the plane landed, or the guard might wave it off. And then they might never learn who had orchestrated her kidnapping. She had to know...

Her heart beat with each second that passed before the tires touched down on the airstrip. Calling it such was generous. It was obviously used mostly for crop dusting—not private planes coming from foreign countries. That had to be where Mr. Centerenian's boss came from. Was it someone working for her father? Dread welled up inside her at the thought. The plane bumped along the rough runway before finally coming to a stop.

The engine wasn't killed though; it continued to drone on even as the door lifted on the side. "Get her!" a voice yelled from inside the plane. "We can't stay here."

"I—I can't get her," Mr. Centerenian yelled from the entrance to the hangar. Obviously he was afraid of being too close to his boss when he gave him the bad news. "She got away."

"You lost her?"

He shook his head in denial of any culpability. "No. She got away from the hospital. She escaped."

"You were there so that would not happen," the boss reminded him—his voice terse with anger and frustration. "You need to find her! Now!"

"What are they saying?" Aaron asked, his breath warm as he whispered in her ear.

She shivered. "They're talking about me." And until he'd asked, she hadn't even realized the men had been speaking another language. Charlotte had been multilingual since a very young age.

Her grandparents had been missionaries. Whenever Charlotte had gotten in the way of her mother's latest scam, she'd been left with her grandparents—in whichever country they were working in—trying to take care of starving children and orphans.

Her mother had resented their concern for other children—had resented that they'd spent all their time and money trying to take care of everyone else in the world. At least her aunt had understood, and after her grandparents died, Aunt Lydia had taken over their good work.

And in her own way, Charlotte had thought she was honoring her grandparents, too—by taking care of people in trouble, by protecting them like they'd wanted to protect all those underprivileged children.

The plane engine cut out. "We are not leaving here until we find her," the man ordered the guard. He stomped down the steps to the ground. He wore a silk suit, and his hair was as oily and slicked back as the creepy guard who worked for him.

A breath whistled between Aaron's teeth as he recognized the guy the same time Charlotte did. Prince Linus Demetrios had been promised Princess Gabriella's hand in marriage. They had been betrothed since the day she'd been born—until the king had rescinded that promise. The day of the ball at the palace—the night she and Aaron had made love—the king had promised Gabriella to another man, a wealthier, more influential prince from another neighboring country.

And sometime during that night, someone had slipped a note under Gabby's door that she would die before she would ever marry Prince Tonio Malamatos. That was why Charlotte had whisked them off to Paris the next morning—under the ruse of meeting with designers to begin work on the princess's wedding gown.

"She could be anywhere," the guard protested. "Surely she must have contacted the authorities by now. They'll be looking for us!"

"Princess Gabriella is mine," the prince said. "We're not leaving without her and my baby."

Despite Aaron's arm on her shoulder, trying to hold her down, Charlotte jumped up. "This baby is not yours!"

"Gabby!" The prince hurried forward, his arms outstretched as if to hug her close.

She lifted the gun and pointed it directly at his chest. He had to be the one who'd threatened her sister as well as kidnapping Charlotte. "I am not Gabby, either."

"Yes," the prince insisted. "You are my sweet, sweet Gabriella."

She shook her head. "'Fraid not."

"She kept saying that," the guard related. "Kept saying that we'd grabbed the wrong woman."

Prince Demetrios shook his head, but his swarthy complexion paled in the bright lights of the airstrip. "No. That's not possible."

"I'm Charlotte Green," she said. "You know that—now that you see me."

His voice lacked conviction even as he continued to insist, "It can't be…"

"You've seen us together," she reminded him, "at the ball." Because Gabriella had thought she could trust him. As well as being engaged since birth, they had been friends that long, too. She'd felt horrible over what her father had done.

One of his heavily lidded eyes twitched as anger

overwhelmed him. "I prefer not to remember that night and all its betrayals."

Now she wanted to calm him down, to make him see reason. If he hadn't kidnapped her, she might have almost felt sorry for him. In one night he'd lost the life he'd known—the one he'd planned—just like she had when she'd lost her memory. "Gabby and I had nothing to do with the king changing his plans."

"Suddenly my country—my wealth—was not sufficient for his daughter," the prince griped with all wounded pride. "For you…"

"I am not Gabriella," she said again, her voice sharp with irritation. "I am her bodyguard." And her sister. "You know we look exactly alike. I had plastic surgery to look like her, so that I could protect her from situations like this, from her getting abducted."

"Where is she?" Aaron asked the question. "What have you done with her? You must have mistaken her for Charlotte. Did you kill her?"

"Of course not! I would never kill anyone," he protested. "That was not part of the plan."

"What was the plan?" Aaron asked. "To kidnap and rape a woman?"

That eyelid twitched again. "I would never harm the woman I love. I was helping her. Her father put her in an impossible situation, and I gave her a way out. Since she's carrying my baby, the king cannot possibly make her marry another man."

"She's not carrying your baby," Aaron said. "She's carrying mine."

The prince sucked in a breath of outraged pride. "That is not possible."

"She was already pregnant when you grabbed her in Paris," Aaron explained. "She's carrying my baby."

Charlotte's heart warmed with the possessiveness in Aaron's voice. He had claimed her baby. If only he would now claim her…

"It doesn't matter whose baby I'm carrying," she said. "I'm not Gabriella."

The prince turned toward his guard. "Could it be? Did you grab the wrong woman in Paris?"

The guard shook his head. "There was only one woman in that suite."

ONLY ONE WOMAN. Aaron couldn't even consider the implications of that claim. "There was so much blood, so much destruction," he said. "The authorities believe someone died there."

The guard nodded. "I lost a friend because of this woman. I could not hurt her then…because I had my orders to not harm the princess." He lifted the gun he clutched in his nonbandaged hand. "But if she's really not the princess…"

"I'm not," she said, "but I am the woman holding a gun on your boss. And I'm not so sure that you're going to be all that accurate shooting with your left hand. So if your bullet misses, mine won't."

The prince shuddered at her cold pronouncement and so did Aaron. She would have no qualms about pulling that trigger—about taking the life of an unarmed man.

"You're not my sweet Gabriella," the prince said, his voice choked with disappointment. "Where is she?"

"Where you will never get to her," Charlotte vowed with a conviction that had disappointment clenching Aaron's heart in a tight fist.

He realized that she had known all along—or at least as soon as her memory returned—exactly where Princess Gabriella was. Obviously because she had stashed her there…

Charlotte pushed the barrel of her gun against the prince's skinny chest. "You're going to be locked up for the rest of your life."

Maybe she didn't know—maybe that was simply what she meant—that he wouldn't be able to get to Gabriella through the prison bars he would be behind.

"I told you that I harmed no one," Prince Demetrios insisted.

"You were the one who killed my friend," the guard said, clutching that gun tightly. The murderous intent in his eyes revealed how much he wanted to pull that trigger, how much he wanted to take Charlotte's life— after having already taken her freedom and her memory.

"There are a stack of bodies back at Serenity House," Aaron said, "thanks to you."

The prince turned toward his employee. "Mr. Centerenian? What are they talking about?"

The guard tensed. With guilt? But he claimed, "I have killed no one…*yet.*"

"That nurse was killed." Charlotte addressed the prince instead of his employee. "The one you hired to take care of me. Sandy…"

"And the young reporter the nurse tipped off about your kidnapping," Aaron added. "And the administrator you paid to impregnate the princess with your sperm."

"She didn't do it," Charlotte hastened to add when the prince's dark gaze lowered to her stomach. "Is that why you ordered her and the others killed? To cover your tracks?"

"Bullets were flying everywhere," Aaron said. "It was a wonder that Charlotte wasn't hit, too." Or him. It was bad enough that Whit had been.

The prince shook his head—his pride appearing every bit as wounded as it had over losing his fiancée. "I am not a killer," he said.

"You didn't pull the trigger yourself," Charlotte agreed.

"But you must have had your goon do it," Aaron finished for her.

The prince glanced toward his guard again. Even he must have begun to suspect him. "I told you to take her and to keep her safe."

Aaron gestured toward the bruise on her head. "He did that to her. He nearly killed her—despite your orders. You don't think he could have hurt anyone else?"

The prince glared at his employee. "I did not tell you to kill anyone."

"You are a fool," the guard remarked with pure disgust. "You will spend the rest of your life in prison. You do not understand that you can't leave loose ends."

"So you shot them?" Charlotte asked. "You killed all those people."

"The reporter and that stupid nurse," the guard agreed. "And now all of you. I will not spend my life in prison for some lovesick fool."

And he raised his gun and fired.

Chapter Thirteen

"Nice shot," Charlotte remarked, as the guard clasped his other hand. Aaron had used a bullet to knock the gun from the guard's hand.

But the man didn't stop—he charged at Aaron and tackled him to the cement floor of the hangar. His breath audibly whooshed out of his probably almost crushed lungs. Mr. Centerenian was much larger than Aaron but more fat than muscle. Aaron was the more experienced fighter. He tossed him off with a kick and a punch. Then the guard swung back. But Mr. Centerenian screamed in pain when his bloodied fist connected with the cement floor since Aaron had rolled out of his line of fire.

The two men continued to grapple with each other. But another man made his move, stepping back from Charlotte and heading toward the plane.

She caught him by the back of his jacket. "You're not going anywhere...except behind bars."

The tall man turned slowly toward her. Then he moved, as if to lunge at her.

But she lifted her gun and pressed it into his chest again. "I told you that I will shoot you," she said. "Given

what I went through—the months I lost—because of
you, I really should kill you."

"I thought you were Gabriella…"

"And that makes me want to pull this trigger even
more," she said. Anger and dread surged through her
with the thought of Gabby enduring what she had. The
pain. The confusion.

First her father had betrayed the princess. And now
the man she had considered a lifelong friend had betrayed her, too. Despite Gabby having grown up with
the palace and the money, Charlotte was really more
fortunate; she had learned early to count on no one. To
trust no one.

She'd also learned that it was safer to love no one.
But she'd messed up there. First she'd fallen under the
spell of her sister's sweetness. And then Aaron's irresistible charms…

"Is she all right? Is she safe?" Prince Demetrios
asked, his pride forgotten as he pleaded for information.

Gabby had considered him a friend when it seemed
obvious now that he'd been more of a stalker.

"I need to know," he asked, his voice cracking with
emotion. "I have loved her my whole life. I need to know
that she's all right."

Whatever sympathy she'd fleetingly felt for the man
was gone. She cared only about making sure Gabby was
safe now. "And I need to know everything you know. I
need to know every damn thing that you were behind."

"I told you," the prince said, his voice rising so that
he sounded more like a whiny child than a grown man.
The king had been right to end this betrothal—for so
many reasons. "I only wanted Gabby—wanted us bound
together for life."

"And instead so many people lost their lives," she mused and glared at him with condemnation.

"I didn't know that Mr. Centerenian shot the nurse and a reporter."

"And the administrator," Charlotte added.

"And my friend." Aaron jerked the beaten guard to his feet and shoved him toward the prince. "Make him tell us everything."

"I did," Mr. Centerenian insisted. "I told you that I cleaned up the mess he left. I killed the nurse and the man she kept sneaking away to meet. I did not kill anyone else."

"Then you hired those men to kill the administrator," Aaron said. "And try to kill us."

"No," the guard protested. "I knew Dr. Platt would not talk. And she had promised to get rid of any evidence that could lead back to the prince or me."

"Someone killed her," Aaron said. "So you didn't need to worry about that evidence after all. Or about her testifying against you."

"I told you—she would not talk."

Charlotte believed that—the woman had seemed quite stubborn. But she'd obviously had her price. Prince Demetrios had found it; someone else might have been able—if they'd had deep enough pockets. "I don't know about that. But I do know that, with all those bullets flying in that office—" she patted her stomach "—we could have been killed, too."

The prince gasped in horror. He was a sick man. But apparently he was not a killer.

"I had orders to not harm you," Mr. Centerenian said, "or I would not have been paid."

She touched the bruise on her temple now.

"Kill you," he amended himself. "I could not kill you. But had I known who you really were…"

She would have been dead. But even with all those bullets flying, none had come close to her. Maybe the shooters had just had qualms about killing a pregnant woman. Or maybe they'd had orders. At any rate, she believed someone other than Mr. Centerenian and Prince Demetrios had hired them.

Why?

"WHAT ABOUT THE parking lot?" Aaron asked the guard as an officer loaded him into the backseat of a state police cruiser.

He had called the authorities from the phone they'd found in the hangar. And the only reason he and Charlotte weren't being loaded into cruisers themselves for questioning was because of the threats of Stanley Jessup's influential lawyer. They had called the media mogul, too.

The older man had gone above and beyond all the favors Aaron had asked of him. Well, except for telling Whit where he was. But he had only confided in the other man because Whit had convinced him that Aaron was in danger.

Stanley Jessup was a hell of a lot more forgiving than he would have been. If someone had failed to protect his daughter, Aaron wouldn't have cared if the guy put himself in danger. Hell, he would have preferred it. Instead Stanley kept helping them—with doctors, lawyers and a safe place to stay.

But no place would ever be really safe if there was another shooter out there.

He asked the guard again, "You shot at me in the parking lot, right?"

Mr. Centerenian shook his head and then boasted, "I would not have missed had I been shooting at you."

Aaron could have pointed out that he had missed him in the hall. That he'd hit a vase instead of him. But this man didn't matter anymore. He apparently wasn't behind the shooting in the administrator's office.

So who was?

The prince was being loaded into the back of a separate police cruiser. Charlotte stood beside him, facing the prince instead of Aaron.

"You said that you'd tell me where Gabriella is," the prince implored her. "We had a deal…"

"The deal was," she corrected him, "that you would tell me everything you know—"

"And I did," he interjected.

"And I would tell you that she was all right—not where she is," Charlotte reminded him of the details of their agreement. "She's all right."

"But you won't tell me where she is?"

She shook her head, and the long waves of golden-brown hair rippled down her back. "I won't tell anyone where she is."

But she knew. Aaron heard the certainty in her voice. All this time he and Whit had been concerned about Princess Gabriella and Charlotte had known exactly where she was.

Whit was right. Again. When was he going to learn that he couldn't trust Charlotte Green?

"Don't ask me," she said as she stood beside him, watching the police cars leave the airstrip.

"I know better than to think you'd tell me anything," Aaron admitted. "But you should tell the king. He's been out of his mind worrying about her."

"Of course he has."

Aaron winced at his insensitive remark. "I'm sure he's been worried about you, too," he amended himself. "It's just that I didn't know then that you're his—"

"Bastard?" She shrugged, as if she didn't care, but he suspected she cared a lot. "Doesn't matter. I don't matter. Only the legitimate heir matters. Gabriella is the only child he can profit from—using her to further his empire with money and power. That's why I won't tell him where she is."

"But aren't you using her, too, then?" Aaron pointed out her double standard. "To get back at him for never acknowledging you?"

Her eyes, the same golden-brown of her hair, darkened with anger. "I wouldn't use Gabby. I only want to keep her safe."

"Is she?" Aaron wondered. "We don't know who's behind the shooting in the administrator's office."

"If we believe Mr. Centerenian and the prince's claims that it wasn't one of them," she said.

"We shouldn't," Aaron agreed. "We shouldn't believe or trust anyone." That fact had been driven home to him time and time again—with every lie and omission Charlotte had uttered.

Charlotte nodded. "And that's why I won't tell the king where Gabby is."

"That's the reason you're telling yourself," Aaron agreed. "To justify not telling him. But we both know that's not the real reason."

"Let's forget about my reasons," she said, "and focus on the reason that someone would have been shooting at you in the parking lot—"

"So I wouldn't be able to come back for you," he pointed out. That was what he'd figured at the time. Now he wasn't so certain...

"The guard said he didn't do it."

"And we trust what he said?"

She shrugged. "He admitted to two murders. Why wouldn't he admit to trying to kill you? What difference would it make at this point?"

"It would answer the rest of our damn questions," he said. "Well, not all of our questions."

Because she refused to tell him where Princess Gabriella was...

"If we figure this out, if I'm sure she's safe," Charlotte said, "I will consider revealing her location."

He nodded. "So we'll figure this out. If not the guard, who else would want to shoot at me?"

"And Whit," she said. "He was hit in the administrator's office."

"You were shot at, too," he reminded her.

"You stood between me and gunmen, kept me behind the filing cabinet," she said. "So no one really shot at me." But she had shot back.

If she hadn't, he and Whit probably wouldn't have made it out of that office alive. They probably would have wound up as dead as the administrator had.

"Just because you didn't get shot, doesn't mean you weren't the target," he pointed out. "But if you weren't, the shooting seems like more work of the prince."

Or was there someone else out there that Aaron had been too naive to consider? Just like he had been naive to think that Charlotte had finally started being honest with him.

"What about Trigger?" she asked. "Where has he been since he dropped us at that cabin?"

"Maybe the guard got rid of him like he had the reporter and the nurse," Aaron said. But then why wouldn't he have admitted it as he'd admitted to the other two murders?

Charlotte shook her head. "I doubt it. Trigger is like a cat with nine lives. He's out there. Somewhere."

CHARLOTTE SHUDDERED AT the thought. She hadn't liked working with the older man. Mostly because he had been a first-class jerk and a male chauvinist. But also because she hadn't trusted him.

Trigger had reminded her too much of her mother— both were totally concerned with their own welfare and no one else's.

If he'd ever had a daughter, he would have sold her, too. She'd suspected he would have sold a witness's location, and that was why she hadn't told him where Josie Jessup had been relocated.

She had only told one person where Josie was— just in case something ever happened to her. And she'd thought the two women would be good friends.

Had Trigger figured that out? Had he figured out where she'd stashed Gabriella? And if they'd convinced the man that she was Gabriella, then he would think that Gabriella was Charlotte Green, his ex-partner.

"I have a bad feeling," she said.

"You're not feeling well?" Aaron asked, reaching for her arm to steady her. "We should get you back to the house."

He led her toward the car and helped her into the passenger's seat.

No matter how angry he was at her—and she suspected he was furious since she hadn't told him she knew where Princess Gabby was—he was still courteous with her. Because of the baby?

"I may have put Gabby at risk," she admitted, hating herself for what she'd done. "And not just Gabby but Josie, too."

"What have you done?" he asked.

"I told Gabby where Josie is," she admitted. "If Trigger finds her…" He wasn't beyond torturing her to discover where the witness was hidden—especially not if he was being paid handsomely to find her.

"You're the only one who knows where Gabby is," he said.

Now she couldn't tell him what she had done. Aaron would probably never forgive her for putting the life of the woman he loved in danger. And she knew better than to reveal a witness's location to anyone. But she had never felt closer to another human being than she had her sister.

Until now.

To soothe herself more than her baby, she rubbed her hands over her belly. Aaron had given her this child, but yet she didn't feel as close to him. Because one woman—a woman she herself considered a friend—had always stood between them.

"Josie's fine," Aaron said. "She's safe."

His empty assurances hung in the air between them as he drove the distance back to Stanley Jessup's rental house. He pulled the car up next to the dark house and turned off the engine. "We'll ask Whit to help us get to the bottom of who is behind the other shootings."

After his taking a bullet for Aaron back in the administrator's office, she now trusted the king's other bodyguard—as much as she let herself trust anyone. But would Gabriella?

The man had hurt her…because he had let her go. He had just stood there, the morning after the ball, and had silently watched her leave for Paris, to design her wedding gown to marry another man. Like Charlotte with Aaron, Gabriella had hoped for more with Whit Howell.

"I'm not sure we should include Whit," she said, remembering that Gabby had claimed to want nothing more to do with him.

"The doctor said the bullet didn't strike anything vital," Aaron assured her. "Once the painkillers wear off, he'll be fine—determined to go again."

"But maybe he shouldn't…"

He studied her face in the darkness. "You still don't trust Whit?"

She held her breath, unwilling to admit her real problem with Howell—sisterly allegiance.

"You trusted him enough to involve him in faking Josie's death."

And not Aaron. She needed no further assurance that he would never get over not knowing that Josie hadn't really died.

"I can understand you not trusting me back then," Aaron said, surprising her with his words and his closeness as he leaned across the console separating their seats. "You didn't know me that well."

She hadn't known Whit then either, so she'd trusted Josie's judgment on which one of her bodyguards to include in her plan. Josie hadn't wanted to put Aaron in the untenable position of having to lie to her father. She'd said he was too nice to have to deal with that burden. They hadn't realized that they'd given him a far heavier burden of guilt to carry in thinking that he'd failed to protect Josie.

"But you know me now, Charlotte." His hands covered hers on her belly, and he entwined their fingers, binding them together just as their baby did. But then he leaned even closer, and his lips brushed over hers with teasing, whisper-soft kisses.

Her breath caught in her throat as desire overwhelmed her. The man's kisses stole away her common sense as effectively as that blow to her head had stolen her memories. All he had to do was touch her and she wanted him, the need spiraling out of control inside her.

But it was more than want. More even than need. It was love.

Aaron pulled back and asked, "So why do you still not trust me?"

Because he could hurt her more than anyone else ever had. Because she wanted more from him. She wanted his love. But he wasn't talking about their relationship.

"I get why you didn't tell me about Josie," he said. "But you should have told me about Gabriella." He stepped out of the car and slammed the door behind himself.

Gunshots echoed the slam. The windows burst, glass shattering as bullets hit them.

Shards struck Charlotte, stinging her skin, but she didn't duck yet. Because she was looking for Aaron. He'd disappeared. Had he been hit?

Her door creaked open, and a strong hand grasped her arm, pulling her from the car. Just like Paris, she was getting grabbed again. And just like Paris, she wouldn't go without a fight.

Chapter Fourteen

Aaron grunted as her elbow struck his chin. "Stop it," he said. "I'm trying to help you."

It was probably too late for him to help Whit. He couldn't believe he hadn't realized it before. He should have known...

Charlotte gasped in shock, and her struggles ceased. "You're all right?"

He nodded, his chin rubbing against her silky soft hair. Physically he was fine. For the moment...

"Trigger must have followed us," she said, whispering since the gunshots had stopped. "He must have found this place."

"I'm not so sure it's Trigger." He had a horrible feeling that it was someone else.

She peered around the car, looking for the shooter. "Who else...?"

"Maybe a man who lost his daughter..."

"The king?" She shook her head in rejection of that idea. "Rafael doesn't care enough about either me or Gabriella to—" She gasped and turned to him with wide eyes. "Josie's father?"

"I was a fool to ask for his help," Aaron said. "It must

have brought all those feelings rushing back—all his pain and resentment."

"No…" She shook her head, her brow furrowing with confusion. "It doesn't make any sense…"

"Stanley Jessup gave me the tip that brought me here," he reminded her. Sure, Aaron had asked the man to flush out any leads to Princess Gabriella's whereabouts. And in doing that, he might have given the grieving father the perfect opportunity to take his revenge.

Charlotte expelled an unsteady breath. "And he came, too."

"And more than that, he told Whit that I was here—getting us both in the same place." Another gunshot rang out, pinging off the metal roof of the sports car. "It has to be Jessup."

Charlotte shook her head. "No, it has to be someone else." She ducked low as shots pinged off the fenders. "Josie talks about her dad all the time." Her voice carried a faint trace of wistfulness. "She told me what a good man he is…"

"Josie was the center of his universe," Aaron said. "She meant everything to him." His baby wasn't even born, and he could identify with those feelings. Maybe because he already had those feelings for Charlotte. If something had happened to her…

She clutched her gun in her hand, but she seemed reluctant to aim it in the direction from which the shots had come. Maybe she was reluctant to take a shot and hurt a man who had already been through so much pain. "But I didn't think he blamed you two for what happened—or what he thinks happened to Josie."

"I blamed us," Aaron reminded her. "I ended my partnership—my friendship—with Whit."

For no reason. Whit had only been doing his duty—keeping Josie safe. And now Aaron might never have the chance to regain the friendship he had stupidly and stubbornly given up.

"I have to get in that house," he said, fear and desperation clawing at him as it had when he'd stood outside that burning house over three years ago and thought he'd been too late to save Josie. "I have to make sure that Whit—that Whit is…"

She must have picked up on his hopelessness because she squeezed his arm reassuringly. "Whit Howell is resourceful," she reminded him. "And he's smart. Maybe he figured it out in time."

"Whit was out," Aaron said, and he hated himself for really doing what he'd thought he and Whit had done three years ago—leaving someone alone and vulnerable who had needed his protection. While he hadn't actually failed Josie, he had failed his friend—the man who'd risked his life to save Aaron's more than once. "He was out cold on those painkillers—a sitting duck for Stanley Jessup to take his revenge."

The gunfire continued to come, bullets striking the car and the asphalt driveway near them. "But why is he shooting at *me?*" Charlotte asked. "Do you think Whit told him how I was involved?"

"No." He shook his head. "If he knew his daughter was still alive, he wouldn't be shooting at all," he told her. "Maybe he's using you to try to flush me out."

Or maybe Jessup intended to take Aaron's family from him the way that he thought his family had been taken from him.

"Let's flush *him* out," Charlotte suggested, raising her gun. "You need to get in that house. You need to check on Whit." Even though she hadn't always seemed to trust his friend and vice versa, she was concerned about him—enough to risk her own safety. She rose up and fired off a round of shots in rapid succession, giving Aaron the time and the cover to sprint toward the house.

Keeping low, he ran toward the windows of the den and, heedless of the glass, jumped through them. A hard fist struck his jaw, knocking him down onto the floor. He hit the hardwood with a bounce and popped up again to strike back. He swung his gun like a bat, hitting out with the handle. Blindly—because he couldn't see anything but a big shadow in the total darkness.

The man's eyes must have adjusted better to the dark because he caught Aaron's weapon and tried to wrest it from his grasp. Aaron was stronger, though, and retained control of the gun. He twisted it around and pressed the barrel against the temple of the man.

"Just shoot me then, you son of a bitch," the guy said with a snarl of rage and hatred.

Aaron uttered a deep laugh of pure relief. "You're alive!"

"Yeah," Whit grumbled, almost as if he wasn't entirely convinced that he lived yet. "But I feel like crap from the painkillers, and then I get attacked. By you..."

"I didn't think it was you," Aaron explained. "I thought you got shot again."

"The gunman's out there," Whit said, as more gunfire shattered the night. His voice dropped with suspicion. "Where's Charlotte?"

"She's not the shooter." But he'd left her alone with him. Panic clutched Aaron's stomach. "She's out there. She covered me, so I could get in here to check on you."

Whit snorted. "So you both thought I was dead? Some confidence—"

He grabbed Whit, inadvertently clutching his bad

shoulder and eliciting a cry of pain from his friend. But he didn't have time to apologize—not with Charlotte out there alone. "Where's Stanley?"

"He went down to the police station to help you out," Whit said. "He thought you guys might get booked no matter what his lawyer said to the authorities."

"Are you sure he really left?" Aaron asked. "You weren't still out of it?"

Whit shook his head. "No. I was clearheaded—even offered to go with him, but he said no."

"He wanted you here," Aaron said, "so that he could take his revenge on us together."

Whit snorted again. "Revenge?"

"Because of Josie."

Whit lifted a hand to his head, as if trying to clear it of the aftereffects of the painkillers. "But Josie's not dead."

"Her father doesn't know that," Aaron pointed out. "He thinks she's dead and he probably blames us. He hired us to protect her, and we failed."

Whit opened his mouth again but only a groan escaped. And Aaron hadn't even grabbed his shoulder again. "But it doesn't make any sense…"

"In *his* eyes we failed," Aaron said.

"In your eyes, too," Whit admitted. "It was what you thought. You don't think that's really Stanley Jessup out there?"

Aaron was afraid that it was, and he was afraid that he had left Charlotte out there alone with the madman.

WITH ALL THE shots flying, Charlotte had no way of knowing if Aaron had made it safely inside the house. She had heard breaking glass. Was it from bullets or from a body flying through a window?

It was too dark for her to see anything. And tonight there wasn't even a sliver of the moon that had been out the previous evening. She could see nothing of the house. Or the gunman.

Was it only one? Was it Stanley Jessup?

Josie had been so convinced that her dad was a good man. But he had made enemies—with the stories he'd run on all his media outlets. Good men didn't make enemies, did they?

But then even if he was a good man, he could have let his grief and loss drive him over the edge. If all that mattered to him now was vengeance, he wouldn't rest until both Whit and Aaron were dead.

Maybe Whit was already dead.

Aaron would be devastated if he was. Just as he had blamed himself for Josie's death, he would blame himself for Whit's. Maybe even more so because they had been estranged, their friendship destroyed because of her.

She was the one whom Aaron needed to blame. Not himself. The burden of guilt should be hers to bear—not his.

If he wanted to kill the person responsible for him losing his daughter, Jessup should be trying to kill her—not them. She moved around the back of the car and kept low behind the hedges that lined the driveway. She made it to the garage. Her foot struck some shells, sending them skittering across the asphalt.

This was where the man had been standing when he'd fired round after round at the Camaro. And at her and Aaron. Where had he gone?

She clutched her gun in her hand and spun around, looking for him.

"Over here, Charlotte," a gruff voice murmured.

Whose voice? Whit's? It wasn't Aaron because her pulse didn't quicken. Charlotte's heart didn't warm with hope and love. And the baby didn't move in her womb in reaction to her father's voice.

"You looked." The voice was closer now and clearer as the man taunted her. "When I said your name, you looked. I knew it was you." He hid yet in the shadows. "Just from the way you held a gun, I knew it was you."

"Trigger."

All of her lies had destroyed Aaron's trust so much that he had begun to suspect everyone of having ulterior motives. But her gut—and maybe the baby moving inside it—had convinced her it was her old partner.

"That Timmer guy made me doubt myself though," he admitted. "So I went back to Serenity House and talked to the administrator—flashed my U.S. Marshal badge to get her talking."

"She wouldn't have told you anything," Charlotte said, remembering how stubborn that woman had been.

"She didn't realize she was telling me anything," he said, his voice still taunting her from the darkness. "She just answered my questions about your scars. Well, her face answered them with her reaction. She just confirmed what I already knew though."

She didn't bother trying to deny who she was. She just asked, "Did you hurt the man inside the house?"

"What man? The old, rich guy left a while ago," he said.

So maybe he didn't even know about Whit. Maybe that could work to their advantage. If the men realized she needed help in time...

Before it was too late...

"I waited here for you and Timmer to come back," Trigger said. "My source with the state police department told me that they let you two go but arrested some royal subject and his goon bodyguard. So I figured you two would be heading back."

"Then you waited for us and started shooting?" she asked. "What if you'd hit me? How was I going to tell you what you wanted to know then?"

"They don't call me Trigger for nothing," he said with unearned arrogance. "I know how to handle a gun. I only shoot what I mean to."

She could have argued that point with examples. But she just nodded—regardless of whether or not he could see the motion in the dark. "What about those men in the administrator's office? Weren't you worried about them shooting me?"

He chuckled. "What would make you think I had anything to do with that? Didn't they kill that woman?"

"After you questioned her about me," she pointed out. "You spooked her. That's why she was destroying records when we got to her office. That's why you killed her, so she wouldn't admit that she already talked to a U.S. Marshal. Were you trying to get rid of any trace that you'd even been there? That you'd even tracked me down?"

"That lady didn't really matter one way or the other," he said offhandedly. "I told the guys to take the shot if they got it."

How had a lawman become so callous about life? Was it that they had faked so many witnesses' deaths that he didn't realize that some deaths were *real?*

"And me?" she asked.

"They weren't supposed to shoot you," he assured her. "I just paid them to get rid of the men with you."

"Those men are better than you realized," she said with pride. "Or maybe you knew how good they are and that's why you hired the guys but stayed out of the line of fire yourself." Even now he stubbornly stayed in the shadows, so that she couldn't get a clear shot at him. He was both a bully and a coward.

He chuckled again. "They can't help you now."

Her heart slammed into her ribs. Had he killed them? Was it already too late for her to save the man she loved? Was it too late for her to tell Aaron that she loved him?

Her feelings probably wouldn't matter to him. But she needed to say the words—needed to let him know how much he meant to her. And she needed the chance to tell him.

It didn't matter that she didn't have the shot. She lifted her gun to fire into the darkness.

"I wouldn't do that," Trigger warned. And he finally stepped from the shadows. Or at least he dissipated the darkness when he screwed back in the bulb of the porch light under which he stood. His gun wasn't pointed at her though.

She could have taken the shot. But Trigger was Trigger *Happy*. His finger was already pressed to the trigger of his gun while the barrel of it was pressed against Aaron's temple.

"I know you, Charlotte," he said. "There was no way in hell you would tell me what I want to know to save yourself. I could press this gun to your head and you would let me pull the trigger before you'd ever give me the location of the witness."

She nodded. "True. I won't reveal the location of a witness." Any witness, but most especially one with whom she'd bonded like she had Josie. It was no wonder that Aaron had fallen for the woman. She was smart and funny and sweet. And she deserved to live her life in peace—not with the constant threat of danger.

"But I think if it comes down between his life and hers, you'll pick his," Trigger said.

Aaron laughed. "You don't know her as well as you think you do."

"I think you're the one who doesn't know her," Trigger said. "She loves you. Even when she didn't really know who *she* was, Dr. Platt confirmed the amnesia wasn't a trick, Charlotte knew that she loved you."

She had wanted Aaron to know her feelings, but she'd wanted to be the one to tell him. And how had Trigger so easily recognized what had taken her so long to realize?

"I saw it on her face," he continued talking to Aaron. "She won't let me kill you."

The guy was a hell of a lot smarter than Charlotte had given him credit for.

"So before I pull this trigger," Trigger warned her, "you better tell me what I need to know. Where is Josie Jessup?"

Need to. Not want to know…

This was about more than money to Trigger, which made him even more desperate and dangerous. He would pull that trigger.

"Don't tell him," Aaron said. "Let him shoot!"

Charlotte flinched with the realization that the man she loved still loved another woman—so much that he was willing to give up his life for hers.

But Charlotte wasn't willing to make that sacrifice.

Aaron might never be hers. But he belonged to someone else—he was the father of the baby she carried.

And he would be a good father—the kind of father a little girl needed.

"I'll tell you," she said. "I'll tell you what you want to know."

IT WAS A trick. Charlotte Green wouldn't give up the location of a witness. Not for her own life. And not for anyone else's.

Aaron knew that as well as the U.S. Marshal did. The older man tensed and buried the barrel of his gun even deeper into the skin of Aaron's temple.

"You're going to tell me?" Trigger asked, his voice cracking with suspicion. "Really?"

"Let him go," she negotiated, "and I'll tell you."

Trigger laughed. "You always treated me like I'm an idiot. You really think I'm going to take your word that'll you tell me where she is once I release my leverage?"

"Do you think it matters?" Aaron asked. "Do you really think she's going to give you Josie's real location? She could tell you anywhere. Could set you up to walk into a booby-trapped house and get your head blown off. You just said she thinks you're an idiot." He snorted. "Sounds like she's right to think that."

"Aaron—" she protested.

It probably wasn't his smartest move to goad the man holding a gun to his head. But then he'd never been all that smart where Charlotte was involved.

Apparently neither had Trigger since the guy actually thought she loved Aaron. Sure, she was attracted to him. Their attraction was so strong that the air between them fairly sizzled when they got close. But love was something else. Love implied need. And Charlotte

Green had never needed anyone. She took independence and self-sufficiency to an extreme.

"You better not give me the wrong location," Trigger threatened. "Because I'm bringing him with me and if your directions don't lead me to Josie Jessup, he'll get that bullet in his head."

That had no doubt been his plan all along—to put a bullet in his head and one in Charlotte's, too. He couldn't leave behind any witnesses.

But he couldn't kill Charlotte until he knew for certain she'd given him the correct location.

Charlotte lifted her hands above her head, as if she were being held up. "All right, I'll tell you the truth."

She met Aaron's gaze, hers dark with frustration. And something else…pain.

How had he hurt her? He was trying to help her. Didn't she realize?

"Ironically she's not that far from here," she said. "She's in Michigan, too." She named a city just a few hours north of where they were. Then she added a number and a street name.

Trigger grabbed Aaron's arm and jerked him along with him, dragging him toward his vehicle. But the gun never left his temple. It would no doubt leave a mark even if the guy didn't shoot.

"You can't take him with you," Charlotte protested. "I gave you what you wanted."

"But as the man pointed out, you can't be trusted, Charlotte." He pushed Aaron through the passenger's side of his car, keeping his gun barrel tight against his temple. "He's my insurance that you're telling the truth. If you are, I might let him live."

The barrel vibrated as the man laughed with amusement over his own sick joke. "And if you are lying to me," Trigger said, "I'll be back. I'll find you again. And the next person I'll take away from you will be your kid."

Charlotte gasped with obvious fear, and her palm protectively covered her belly.

"It'd be a shame for him to be raised without a father anyway," Trigger said, turning the proverbial knife. "Look what it did to you."

Aaron saw the pain cross Charlotte's face, and he wanted to hurt Trigger for hurting her. He wanted to make the man suffer as he was making her suffer.

Didn't she realize that Aaron had a plan? Didn't she trust him?

No. She wouldn't tell him where Josie was. She wouldn't even tell him where Princess Gabriella was. He doubted she had given Trigger the real location. Maybe that was the reason for the pained look on her face.

Guilt.

She thought she had sealed his death warrant.

Aaron tried to catch her attention, tried, with his gaze, to convince her not to worry. But then he did have a gun pressed to his head. And the U.S. Marshal's real nickname wasn't just Trigger. But Happy…

He was laughing yet, still amused by his sick joke. He shoved the barrel harder into Aaron's skin. "Start the car, damn it!"

He obliged, turning the key and shifting it from Park to Drive.

"And no crazy stunt driving like the other night," Trigger warned, pressing a hand over the bump on his forehead.

"That wasn't me," Aaron assured him. "That was my friend. Whit."

Trigger's brow furrowed. "The guy who got shot at the administrator's office?"

Aaron nodded, knocking the barrel a little loose.

"I'm glad the son of a bitch got shot then."

Aaron pressed on the accelerator, easing the car away from where Charlotte stood, staring helplessly after them.

"She really loves you," Trigger remarked. "Didn't think the ice princess had it in her. But she gave up the witness location."

"How do you know it's the real one?" he asked again, wanting the guy to be doubtful and nervous.

"You better hope it is," Trigger threatened, "or you'll be paying the price for her lies."

"Maybe you'll be paying the price," Aaron remarked. "It could still be a trap. That place is three hours away— gives her three hours to have authorities in place to grab you."

"We're not going there," Trigger said, fishing a phone out of his pocket. "All I needed was to get the address. I don't need to go there."

Aaron glanced into the rearview mirror where Charlotte's figure was getting smaller and smaller. She stood there when she needed to be getting on the phone, needed to be getting Josie to safety.

Unless she'd done as Aaron had suspected, given Trigger a false address.

"So this person who must be paying you a pretty penny, he or she won't be upset if you send them into a trap?"

"What?"

"Like I said, you really don't think Charlotte Green gave up the actual location of a witness…especially one she considers a friend?"

Trigger glanced back, too—just distracted enough that he gave Aaron a chance to reach for the gun. But they barely grappled with it before a shot rang out— shattering the windshield.

And ending a life…

Chapter Fifteen

The gunshot shattered the eerie silence that had fallen once the car pulled down the driveway of the rental house. Brake lights flashed on that car, and a horn blared.

A scream tore from Charlotte's throat. He'd shot Aaron. He'd shot him.

She'd thought Aaron had had a plan. That was the only reason she'd let them pull away. Otherwise she might have risked a shot; she would have tried to hit her old partner. But with his finger already on the trigger, there was no way he wouldn't have pulled it—even if just by reflex.

But at least then she would have had the satisfaction of taking out the Marshal herself. A satisfaction she still intended to have.

Tears streaming down her face like rain off a rock, she ran down the driveway—heading toward the stopped car. She bypassed the driver's side. She couldn't see Aaron—like she'd seen those other shooting victims. Instead she headed toward the passenger's side, jerked open the door and pointed her gun inside. Her finger trembled as she moved to squeeze the trigger.

"You can't kill him twice," a male voice remarked. The man sprawled in the backseat.

And Trigger slumped over the dash, a bullet in his head and his blood sprayed across the shattered windshield.

"Aaron!" she screamed his name, trying to peer around the other man to the driver's side. But it was empty—no one sitting behind the wheel.

Then warm hands closed over her shoulders, twirling her toward him—pulling her tight against a strong chest. "Shh…" a deep voice murmured into her ear.

She shivered and trembled in reaction to the horror she had just endured over thinking him dead. "You're alive!"

"I'm fine," he assured her.

But blood had spattered the side of his face when Whit had killed Trigger. Seeing it on his face had her stomach lurching with fear over what could have happened, over how that blood could have been his.

She pulled back and swung her palm at him, striking his shoulder hard enough to propel him back a couple of steps. "You're an idiot! How could you do that? How could you risk your life that way?"

"We had a plan," Whit said. His face twisted into a grimace of pain as he crawled from the backseat and joined them on the driveway.

"What kind of plan?" she asked, anger eclipsing her earlier relief. "A suicide pact?"

Whit pointed toward the front seat. "Only one who wound up dead was the bad guy."

She stared hard at the king's blond bodyguard. Even though she had worked with him to stage Josie's murder, she hadn't trusted him. Maybe because he'd agreed to keep a secret from a man he'd claimed was his best friend.

"I'm really not a bad guy," he said.

She threw her arms around him, hugging him tight. He grunted with pain.

And Aaron protested, "Why are you hugging him? I'm the one who risked my life."

"You're not helping your cause with that," Whit said, as he awkwardly patted Charlotte's back. "I think that could be why she's pissed at you."

"Well, I'm not exactly thrilled with her, either," Aaron admitted.

"Lovers' spat?" Whit teased.

"She doesn't just know where Josie is," Aaron said. "She knows where Princess Gabriella is too."

Whit's hands clenched on Charlotte's shoulders, pulling her back. "You know? Have you known all along?"

She uttered a shaky sigh and stepped back—away from both angry men. "Just since my memory returned."

"Since then?" Whit seemed more appalled than Aaron had been.

Aaron had just seemed betrayed. It would be a miracle if he ever trusted her again. And now that he knew where Josie was…

She expected him to leave soon. She glanced inside the car again. "We need to call the police."

"And probably Stanley Jessup's lawyer," Aaron added. "To help us explain everything that's happened and how a U.S. Marshal wound up dead."

"I had to shoot him," Whit said, "or he was going to kill you."

That feeling of panic and loss struck Charlotte again. She had nearly lost him. Not that she still wasn't going to lose him. He would be a part of his child's life. But he probably wouldn't be a part of hers.

And that was fine. She had never envisioned for herself the fairy-tale, happily-ever-after ending.

"You saved my life," Aaron said, and patted his friend's shoulder in appreciation.

Whit groaned in pain. "Damn it! Stop doing that!"

"I'll leave the two of you alone," Charlotte said, "to bond again." But she didn't make it two steps before Whit stopped her, with his hand on her arm.

"You're going to tell me where Gabby is."

She shook her head. "I haven't talked to her in six months. I need to make certain she still is where I sent her. And I have to find out if she's ready to see anyone yet."

"It's been six months," Whit reiterated. "Why would she need more time before she would want to see anyone?"

"She felt betrayed," Charlotte reminded him. "She's hurt and she's scared. And it may take more than six months for her to get over it." Because she suspected it would take more than six months for Aaron to get over her betraying him.

"I'll call her," she offered. Actually now that the threat against Gabriella was gone, Charlotte couldn't wait to see her sister again. They had so much to talk about—like the fact that Gabby was going to be an aunt.

Hell, she didn't even know that Charlotte was her sister. The king had forbidden her to tell the younger woman the truth. He hadn't thought Gabby was strong enough to handle that, but he'd had no problem passing her from potential bridegroom to potential bridegroom.

Charlotte should have ignored his threat to fire her if she told the truth. Because, by keeping that secret, she had betrayed the princess just as everyone else had. Charlotte was done keeping secrets; it was time for her to be honest with her sister. It was too late for her to be honest with Aaron.

As she headed toward the house, she felt both men watching her. With resentment…

And her heart ached with loss. Aaron was alive, but he would never be hers.

"God, that woman is infuriating!" Whit exclaimed, staring after Charlotte.

"Yes, she is," Aaron agreed wholeheartedly, as he rubbed the blood off his face.

Whit slapped him on the shoulder now. "You're a lucky man."

"What?" His friend must have lost more blood that he'd thought. "Are you okay?"

"Yeah," Whit assured him, "I'm just a little jealous. Okay, a lot jealous."

He studied his friend's face. Dawn was approaching, lightening the dark sky, so that he could see more clearly now. Apparently more clearly than Whit could see. "You're not making any sense."

"She loves you," Whit said.

"What?" he asked. Whit must have heard Trigger's claims and believed the madman.

Whit slapped his shoulder again. "Is that one more thing she kept from you? Her feelings?"

"She doesn't love me," Aaron insisted. "She doesn't even trust me." And how could you love someone you couldn't trust? The thought made his heart ache with loss.

Whit blew out a ragged breath. "She gave up Josie's whereabouts for your life."

Aaron shook his head. "No. She must have made up that address she gave him—just to buy us all some time to get Trigger under control."

Whit shook his head. "No. That is really Josie's address." Whit must have had the window cracked when he'd crouched down in the backseat of Trigger's car.

"No one but Charlotte knows where she stashed Josie," Aaron reminded him. That was why the U.S. Marshal had gone to such extremes to get the information from her. "So how would you know if she told me the truth or not?"

"I followed her the day that she moved Josie," Whit admitted.

"You really cared about her?"

"Not as much as you did, but yeah," Whit said. "She was an amazing lady."

"Is," he corrected him even though he was still getting used to the idea himself of Josie Jessup being alive. He'd wasted more than three years on guilt and anger.

"You never acted on your feelings for her," Whit said with absolute certainty. They hadn't taken shifts but had watched her together.

"She was a client," Aaron reminded him. "We were paid to protect her." And he would never cross that line.

"Her protection was why I followed Charlotte that day—to make sure that no one else followed them."

And that was why Aaron had struggled to understand why Whit had talked him into leaving the safe house the day it had exploded. Because he had always been vigilant about protecting their clients.

Whit nodded. "I had to make sure that Josie would be safe."

"Charlotte made sure of that," Aaron pointed out. So he could no longer resent her for keeping that secret from him. She'd just been doing her job. Actually she'd gone above and beyond because Josie had become a friend of hers. No matter how tough and independent she acted, Charlotte allowed herself to get close. To be vulnerable...

"Charlotte was kind of a client, wasn't she?" Whit asked, as if testing his former partner. "Being the king's daughter and all."

"I didn't know that she was," he reminded Whit and himself of another secret to which he hadn't been privy. And his resentment returned.

"Doesn't matter if you knew that or not, I guess," Whit continued. "As the princess's doppelganger bodyguard, she was still part of the job detail."

Wondering where his friend was heading with his comments, Aaron only nodded his agreement.

"And yet you acted on your feelings for her," Whit said.

Aaron arched a brow, wondering how Whit knew.

"Her kid is yours, right?"

Aaron nodded and then grinned with overwhelming, fatherly pride. "Yes."

"So your feelings for her are obviously stronger than your feelings were for Josie," Whit concluded.

"Josie was a friend," Aaron said.

"And Charlotte?"

His everything. "I don't know what she is. Or how she feels."

"She loves you."

Aaron's heart warmed with hope, but he didn't dare believe Whit's declaration. He wouldn't believe it until Charlotte herself told him her feelings.

But he suspected that was another secret she wasn't willing to share.

GABRIELLA HADN'T ANSWERED. But the phone hadn't rang and rang, either. Instead Charlotte had heard a message that the number she'd dialed was no longer a working exchange. It probably meant nothing more than that the minutes had run out on the disposable cell Charlotte had given her.

But who had Gabriella been calling? No one else knew where she was. And the few who'd thought they had, had actually mistaken Charlotte for the princess.

Unless Gabriella had used those minutes trying to reach her. When the men had burst into the hotel suite in Paris, she had destroyed her phone—making certain that there had been no way those men could track down the real princess. "Where are you?" she asked aloud, her voice echoing in the eerie quiet of the bedroom where she and Aaron had made love just hours before. The sheets were still tangled and scented with the sexy musk of Aaron's skin. Of their lovemaking…

She trembled with need. But it was a need she suspected would go unanswered. He was probably already on his way to Josie.

"Here you are," a deep voice murmured.

She glanced up to find him in the doorway, leaning against the jamb and studying her. "You were looking for me?" she asked and then realized his probable reason why. "Are the police here?"

"On their way," he confirmed. "So is someone else."

So instead of going to her, he was bringing Josie to him? That was even more dangerous.

"You called her? You can't do that," she said. "Someone could have traced the call. You could have put her in danger."

"Her who?" he asked, his brow furrowing with confusion. He still bore the round mark of the barrel of

Trigger's gun on his temple. "I don't know where Gabriella is."

"Not Gabby," she said, "Josie. You can't call Josie."

"Of course I can't," he agreed. "I don't have her number," he said.

Relief shuddered through her, and she hated herself that she wasn't just relieved her friend was safe but relieved that Aaron hadn't immediately tried to contact her. She hated this petty jealousy. It had to be the pregnancy hormones making her so emotional and crazy—because she had never acted like this before. But then she had never been in love before, either.

"I didn't even know I really had her address until now," he said.

She waited for him to leave then—to rush off to the woman he really loved. But he stayed where he was, staring at her so intently it was as if he was trying to see inside her.

"What?" She self-consciously lifted trembling fingers and ran them across her cheek. But the scar wasn't there anymore. She had nothing to run her fingertips along like she used to.

"Why did you give him her real address?" he asked, all narrow-eyed curiosity.

She shrugged, but the tension didn't leave her shoulders. She knew why she had. "I couldn't risk your life."

"But by telling him, you risked hers."

Guilt and regret clutched at her. She hated that she'd done that—hated that she'd been so weak.

"Why would you do that?" he asked.

"I—I shouldn't have done that," she regretfully admitted. "I shouldn't have told him."

"Trigger is dead," he assured her—a slight shudder moving his broad shoulders as he must have relived that moment when Whit had shot the man holding a gun to Aaron's head. "It doesn't matter now what you told him."

She released a shuddery breath. "True. It doesn't matter."

"Except it does," he said. "To me."

He was asking a question she was too afraid to answer. Earlier she'd thought that she should tell him her feelings—that she should because if something had happened to him, she would want him to know that she loved him.

But Trigger was dead. The prince and his henchman arrested. Nothing was going to happen to Aaron. But something bad could happen to her. She could tell him she loved him, and he could reject her.

So she cast around for any reason that she could keep her feelings to herself, like the fact that he loved another woman. "Now that you know where she is, are you going to go see her?"

"And risk someone following me?" He shook his head. "I wouldn't put a friend's life at risk."

Like she had.

"A friend?" The question slipped out, and she hoped it didn't reveal her jealousy. "Is that all Josie is to you?"

He nodded. "We were friends when she *died*."

"Just friends?" she asked. "You gave up your business because of what happened to her."

"What I thought happened to her," he said. "I didn't think I was too good at my job then so giving it up seemed like the right thing."

"And Whit?"

"I guess, subconsciously, I knew he was keeping something from me," Aaron said. "So I didn't trust him.

I didn't want anything to do with someone I couldn't trust."

And that was her reason for not telling him her feelings. He didn't trust her. After all the secrets she'd kept from him, she didn't blame him; she wouldn't trust her, either.

Since she had given up a witness's location, no one could trust her. Maybe it was good that she hadn't gotten in touch with Gabriella. The princess was safer without Charlotte knowing exactly where she was.

Sirens in the distance drew her attention. And she remembered something else he'd said. "Who, besides the police, is on their way?" she asked. "Stanley Jessup's lawyer?"

They would probably need him to help clean up and explain the mess they'd made in this small Michigan town. She doubted anyone would believe their convoluted tale of doppelgangers and kidnappings and amnesia and royalty.

"King St. Pierre is on his way," Aaron said.

Panic struck her. She was in no condition to deal with that man. Not now. Maybe not ever again. "What?"

"I called him," Aaron explained. "He needs to know what's going on."

"Why?" she asked. "So he can fire all of us?"

"You're his daughter."

She laughed. "Not to him, I'm not. I'm just an employee—like the two of you. You two were hired to protect him, and instead you came here—"

"He wanted us to find the princess," Aaron said. "He was all right with using his old security detail again. Why did you want them replaced?"

"I wanted you and Whit to work together again," she said. But she couldn't take all the credit with a clear conscience. "Actually Josie suggested it. She felt bad that her needing to disappear caused a rift in your friendship."

He grinned with obvious affection for the other woman. Just friends? Really?

"But I didn't entirely trust his current people, either," she admitted. "Especially Zeke Rogers." The former mercenary had given off a bad vibe. "The king hadn't done a very good job vetting them."

Kind of like how he hadn't done a very good job of vetting future sons-in-law—putting Gabriella and Charlotte in danger.

"Rogers headed up the king's security detail for years," Aaron said.

"That's why he should have had them more thoroughly checked out," she said. "He didn't know their backgrounds—their vulnerabilities."

"He knows ours now," Aaron said with a heavy sigh. "Guess that Whit and I can start up our business again if he fires us."

"He will," Charlotte warned him. "You found him the wrong daughter."

Just like she was the wrong woman for Aaron. She couldn't tell him her feelings. But it was okay. She had her baby. She would give her all her love.

Chapter Sixteen

Aaron waited for it but the words didn't come. So he asked the older man point-blank, "You're not firing me?"

Using Whit's gunshot wound as an excuse, Aaron had taken the meeting alone with the king. The gray-haired man paced the den of Stanley Jessup's rental home. His gaze kept going to the blood smeared on the leather couch. "Why would I fire you?"

"I followed this lead on my own," he sheepishly reminded him. He'd put himself in danger because he'd trusted the wrong people and hadn't trusted the right ones.

The king absolved him of any culpability, just as Stanley Jessup had. "You didn't think you could trust anyone."

"But shouldn't I have trusted you?" Aaron asked. Maybe he wanted to get fired. Because if Charlotte wasn't working at the palace, he had no reason for being there.

The king shrugged but even that had a regal edge to it. "Charlotte doesn't trust me."

"She probably won't tell you where Gabriella is," Aaron admitted. "But it's just to keep her safe." He believed that now, where before he'd thought it might have been out of spite that she wouldn't tell her father where his chosen daughter was.

But given how the first man to whom Rafael had promised his daughter had nearly killed Charlotte, he didn't trust the man's judgment. Even if arranging marriages was fine in his realm, Aaron hated to think of anyone marrying for any reason but love.

That was why he hadn't already asked Charlotte. He didn't want to marry her just because they were about to have a child together. He wanted to marry her for the reason his own blissfully happy parents had married—true love.

"You are a loyal man," the king praised him. "I will not fire you or Whit Howell. I believe it is my good fortune to have you as part of my security detail."

"And what about Charlotte?" he asked. Would he fire her as she suspected?

"She is not just a bodyguard," the king said. "She is my daughter."

Aaron was surprised by the man's admission. "You're claiming her now?"

Rafael St. Pierre's shoulders sagged with his heavy burden of guilt and regret. "I should have always claimed her."

"You should have," Aaron wholeheartedly agreed. "You don't deserve her."

"Do you?" the king asked, calling him on his hypocrisy. "I'm assuming you're the father of her baby?" No matter how busy the man had been ruling his country, he must have remained aware of what was going on with his daughters.

Aaron nodded. And now he realized the purpose of

this meeting. Today the king was just a father asking a man his intentions toward his pregnant daughter.

It didn't matter that Aaron, like Charlotte, was in his thirties. Heat rushed to his neck, and nerves mangled his guts—and he was every bit as nervous as a teenager who'd gotten his young girlfriend pregnant.

"I love her," he said. "And I'd like to marry her. But I don't know if she'll have me."

The king was not going to get away with arranging a marriage for his oldest daughter. But if he were to do that, he would undoubtedly choose someone with more wealth and means than Aaron had.

But no one could offer her the love that Aaron could. "I don't know if she can trust anyone to love her."

"Because of me." The king readily took the blame, his shoulders sagging even more with the additional burden. "I will talk to her for you."

Aaron flinched. "Championing me may not help my situation at all." If that had even been the man's intentions...

"She will not listen to me," Rafael agreed, "because she hates me."

Aaron shook his head. "If she hated you, she wouldn't be so hurt that you rejected her."

"I had more reasons for treating her how I did," the king said in his own defense. "But I really had no excuse for putting my country before my child."

Aaron couldn't absolve the man of his guilt—not when his actions had so badly hurt the woman he loved.

"Charlotte deserves to come first," he admonished the man.

The king studied Aaron's face through narrowed eyes. His eyes were a darker shade of brown than his daughters' warm golden brown. "Does she come first with you?" he asked.

"Yes," he answered from his heart.

"Does she know that?" the king wondered.

Given the way she'd treated him earlier, Aaron doubted it.

"Not yet." But he would make certain that she would have no doubts that she was the only woman for him.

CHARLOTTE WAITED OUTSIDE the door to the den where the two most important men in her life were locked inside together.

"Are you worried?" Whit asked and pointed toward the closed door. "About what's going on in there? Do you think your daddy is getting out the shotgun to force Aaron to the altar to make an honest woman of you?"

At the outrageous thought, she uttered a short, bitter chuckle. "I doubt that's happening."

"You don't think your father would defend your honor?" Whit asked.

"No."

"Do you want me to defend your honor?" Whit offered sweetly. "I could rough up Aaron for you."

"Since you only have one arm working right now," she reminded him, "I don't like your chances."

He shrugged then grimaced at his own gesture. "Well, I offered. So what do you think they are talking about in there?"

"Gabriella." That was the only daughter the king would worry about and rightfully so. "I'm worried about her, too," she admitted. "I couldn't reach her on the phone earlier."

All his teasing aside, Whit anxiously asked, "But she should be fine, right?" He nodded in response to his own question. "Of course she's fine. We neutralized all the threats against her."

"She's Princess Gabriella," Charlotte said. "There will always be threats against her."

A muscle twitched in his cheek as he tightly clenched his jaw.

"People will want to kidnap her for her father's money or his power," she said. "She's always in danger. And then there was that note shoved under her door the night of the ball."

"What note?" he snapped, as if he should have seen it himself. As if he'd been with Gabby...

"It threatened her life," she said. "It promised that she would die before she would get the chance to marry Prince Malamatos. It was why we left for Paris the next morning." When Charlotte would have rather stayed and explored her burgeoning feelings for Aaron. But then those feelings had burgeoned even when she'd been away from him.

He expelled a ragged sigh. "That was why you left? It wasn't because she was excited to get a dress for her wedding?"

Charlotte chuckled again—this time with real mirth over Whit's ignorance. "Gabby had no intention of marrying either man her father promised her to."

"That's why you put her in your unofficial relocation program," Whit said with sudden understanding.

"I wanted her safe and happy." And now she wasn't sure she was either anymore.

"So are you going to track her down and make certain she's all right?" Whit asked with an eagerness that revealed his true feelings for the princess.

"No," she said.

He jerked with surprise. "I thought you cared about her?"

"I do," Charlotte insisted. "But I'm not going to track her down, because you are."

He nodded. "Of course, in your condition, you shouldn't be doing a lot of traveling."

She could have pointed out that her condition was a lot healthier than his at the moment. But she skipped it. "I'll tell you where I sent her, and you'll find her and make sure she's all right."

"I'm probably the last person she wants to see," Whit admitted with a heavy sigh of regret.

Charlotte wasn't so sure about that. "Just find her and keep her safe." She pressed a paper into his hand with Gabriella's last itinerary.

Whit clutched the piece of a paper in a tight fist. "If I hadn't already told Aaron he was a lucky man, I'd tell him again."

"Why is Aaron lucky?" she asked.

"Because he has you," Whit said. Without waiting to talk to his employer or friend again, the man turned and headed out the front door.

Before Charlotte had a chance to point out that in order for Aaron to be lucky, he'd actually have to want her. And he'd already said that he couldn't be with someone he couldn't trust.

The door to the den opened, but only one man stepped out. Her father. She braced herself for his anger. For his demands.

She hadn't braced herself for a physical confrontation, for the man throwing his arms around her and pulling her close.

"I thought you were dead," he murmured, his voice cracking with emotion.

Tears stung her eyes at his seemingly genuine and heartfelt relief that she was alive. "I'm fine."

"And I will be forever grateful for that," her father said. "I never should have let you become Gabriella's bodyguard."

She flinched. Here was the rejection she'd expected. The firing she'd anticipated.

"I shouldn't have allowed you to put yourself at risk," he said. "I should have had protection for you, too. But I have remedied that situation. You now have your own bodyguard."

"Who?"

"Me," Aaron said, as he joined them in the hall.

She laughed. "I don't need a bodyguard."

"Then consider him a bodyguard for my heir," the king said.

Charlotte clasped her hands to her belly, as if to protect the child. "You haven't claimed me. How can you claim my baby?"

"That's something else I'm going to remedy," he promised. "I'm claiming you as my daughter. As my firstborn."

She nodded with sudden understanding and soul-stealing disappointment. "Of course. Having me as your legal heir will take Gabriella out of danger."

The king groaned with frustration. "This isn't about her. This is about you—about my finally doing right by you."

"Then don't lie to me," she said. "Don't claim feelings you don't have."

"I've always had the feelings," he said. "I just denied them—for the sake of my wife while she was alive and then for the sake of my honor and my kingdom. But I realized, when I thought you were dead, that none of that mattered anymore."

His wife had been dead for years. But for him to say his honor or kingdom didn't matter...

Could he be telling the truth? Could he actually care about Charlotte?

"Maybe you shouldn't publicly claim her," Aaron said. "As her bodyguard, I think we can keep her safer if no one else knows she's related to you."

The king turned to Charlotte. "I don't want to wait another day to declare you as mine. But I don't want you in danger, either."

"Or is it your heir you're worried about?" she asked. "I think she's a girl. You still won't have that boy you want."

The king shook his head and turned back to Aaron. "I can't get through to her. She's too stubborn." His voice cracked with more of that emotion that seemed to overwhelm him. "I wish you luck with her."

"What did my father mean by that?" Charlotte asked once she and Aaron were alone again in the room they'd shared. "Is he talking about you being my bodyguard? Because that's ridiculous. I don't need a bodyguard."

She needed Aaron though. She needed him for her lover, her friend—her soul mate. But if she couldn't have him as those things, she wouldn't settle for less.

"No, you don't need a bodyguard," Aaron agreed with a slight chuckle. "You need a husband."

"Why? Because I'm pregnant?" She snorted derisively. "That's archaic—kind of like a man arranging a marriage for his daughter." She groaned with sudden realization of the conversation that must have taken place in that den. "He arranged for you to marry me, didn't he?"

"He gave his blessing," Aaron admitted.

And now Charlotte fully understood Gabby's horror at being auctioned off, like a side of beef, for money and power. Aaron could give the king neither of those for her hand, though. But then she had never been the daughter that mattered. He must have been bluffing about claiming her. Maybe he had prearranged with Aaron to reject that idea under the ruse of keeping her safe.

They could keep her safe from danger. But not from pain…

"What did you promise him in exchange for his blessing?" she wondered aloud. Because the king was too shrewd and too mercenary to give up something without receiving something in return—just like her mother had been. No wonder Bonita had been his mistress for so many years—after they'd met at a charity ball at which her missionary parents had been guest speakers.

"I did make him a promise," Aaron admitted, "that I would love you and cherish you the rest of our lives."

Her heart shifted, kicking inside her chest like the baby kicking inside her womb. Her legs trembled and she dropped onto the edge of the bed. "Why would you make a promise you can't keep?"

Why would he give her foolish heart such hope when he couldn't possibly really want to marry her?

AARON DROPPED TO his knees in front of Charlotte and took her hand in both of his. "I don't make promises I can't keep," he said. "You know that. You know me. If you accept my proposal, I will spend the rest of my life loving you. Will you marry me, Charlotte Green?"

"No."

He felt as though she'd kicked him. But as her father

had warned, she was stubborn—and totally convinced that she was unlovable.

"Why not?"

"Because it's not the nineteenth century," she said. "And we don't need to get married just because I'm pregnant."

"I don't want to marry you because you're pregnant," he said. "I want to marry you because I love you."

She still refused to believe him, to believe in herself. "No, you don't."

"Have I ever lied to you?" he asked.

She stilled and shook her head. "No, but…I've lied to you. And you said you wouldn't be with someone you can't trust."

"You lied or kept secrets to protect people." And maybe to protect herself if Whit was right and she actually loved him, too. "Except when you told Trigger where to find Josie. Why did you do that?"

"I told you that I couldn't risk your life."

"Why not?"

She groaned as if in pain, as if she were being tortured for information. And then she made the admission in the same way—begrudgingly, resentfully. "Because I love you."

He fought the grin that tugged at his mouth. He wanted to rejoice in her love. But he couldn't accept it until she could accept his—his love and his proposal. "You can love me but I can't love you?"

"You love Josie Jessup," she said.

"As a friend." He'd already told her this. But it was easier for her to believe that he loved Josie than that he loved her.

"You mourned her like a lover."

"I mourned her because I felt guilty," he admitted.

Then, with sudden realization, he repeated, "I mourned her. But I didn't mourn *you*."

She flinched with pain, and he realized that this had been her problem all along, why she had fought to hide or probably even admit to her feelings for him. She had believed him in love with another woman. She'd felt second best again, like she had to her sister.

"I didn't mourn you because I knew you weren't dead," he explained. "Everyone else tried to convince me that you were. Whit—"

"My dad?"

He nodded.

"You have more respect for my skills," she said.

He shook his head. "You're amazing, but that wasn't the reason. I knew that I would have felt it if you had died. Because there's this connection between us—this bond that I've never had with anyone else—not Josie. Not Whit."

He entwined his fingers with hers. "I knew you were alive because I could feel your heart beating. Thousands of miles separated us, but I could feel your heart beating in my heart. We are that connected."

Her breath caught, and her beautiful eyes shimmered with tears. "Aaron..."

"Do you feel it, too?" he asked. "Do you feel this connection between us? Between our souls?"

She nodded. "You are my soul mate."

"So I am going to ask you again," he warned her. "Will you marry me? Will you make me the happiest man in the world for the rest of our lives?"

"Yes, I will," she said with a smile of pure joy.

She wound her arms around his neck and pulled him close. And just as he'd said, her heart pounded against his—inside his, as if they were one. He felt her happiness, too, as it filled him with the warmth of joy and love and relief that she had finally accepted his proposal. But more important, he knew that she had accepted his love.

Her mouth pressed quick kisses to his lips and his cheek and the side of his nose. "I will marry you," she clarified, as if he could have mistaken her intentions. "And I will spend the rest of my life making you happy."

"You already have," he said. "By giving me your love and our child."

"Our child…" Those tears shimmered even more brightly in her eyes. "*You* gave me our child," she said. "You gave me the family I never had. You have already made me the happiest woman in the world."

A thought occurred to him and Aaron chuckled with sudden amusement.

"What?" she asked, her smile still full and bright. She looked more like her sister now—younger and more carefree and optimistic.

"It's a good thing Whit didn't hear any of this," he shared his thought. "He would tease us mercilessly for being hopeless romantics."

She chuckled, too, but then she said, "We might not be the only ones."

"Whit? A hopeless romantic?" He snorted at the ridiculous notion. He had never met a more cynical person—until he'd met Charlotte. If she could let herself fall in love…

Maybe it was possible that Whitaker Howell could find happiness, too.

"Since I will no longer keep any secrets from you," she vowed, "I need to tell you that I sent him to find Gabriella."

Aaron tensed with concern for his fiancée's sister. "Do you think she's in danger?"

"As the king's daughter, she's always in danger," she reminded him.

It was why Aaron preferred that the king not acknowledge her now or maybe ever. He hated the thought of people coming after her because of her father. But then Trigger had already come after her because of who she was. Charlotte could take care of herself though. Despite what she had taught her sister, he wasn't so sure that Princess Gabriella could protect herself.

In that interest of full disclosure to which she now endearingly subscribed, she warned him, "Going to her may put Whit in danger, too."

"He can handle himself." Even after a bullet had ripped through his shoulder, the man had saved their lives.

"He can handle armed gunmen and thugs," she agreed. "I'm not sure he can handle Gabby. She might hurt him. I don't know that she can go against her father's wishes to marry another man."

It hadn't occurred to him that Whit might have been so concerned about Gabby because he'd developed feelings for her. For so long he had believed his friend hadn't possessed any feelings. "Well, I don't know if Whit can protect himself from a broken heart."

Aaron hadn't been able to protect himself from that pain—when he'd thought Charlotte could never trust him and therefore never love him.

As if she'd felt that pain, sadness momentarily dimmed her eyes. "I'm sorry I hurt you," she said, "with all my secrets."

"You had your reasons."

"Not anymore," she said and repeated her earlier vow. "There will be no more secrets between us."

There would be nothing between them anymore but love.

* * * * *

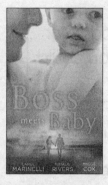

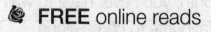

The World of Mills & Boon®

There's a Mills & Boon® series that's perfect for you. We publish ten series and, with new titles every month, you never have to wait long for your favourite to come along.

Blaze®
Scorching hot, sexy reads
4 new stories every month

By Request
Relive the romance with the best of the best
9 new stories every month

Cherish™
Romance to melt the heart every time
12 new stories every month

Desire™
Passionate and dramatic love stories
8 new stories every month